"I recommend this book to anyone who enjoys a good yarn set in a historical context. It is an epic tale of Roman Britain, family conflict, politics and fighting between the occupying forces and rebellious indigenous Celts. Backed up by careful research. I couldn't put it down. A great debut book. I hope we may look forward to another."— **S. Brown**

"Well-written, good historical background, interesting characters. I found the story enthralling and couldn't put it down. Definitely recommend." — **J. Carter**

"…I was hooked. I couldn't put it down, so exciting and so accurate. I thought the characters were well-drawn, events were believable, and I liked the divisions into sections with different happenings as the story progressed. Great achievement". — **D. G.**

BROTHERS

M. E. TAYLOR

authorHOUSE®

AuthorHouse™ UK
1663 Liberty Drive
Bloomington, IN 47403 USA
www.authorhouse.co.uk
Phone: UK TFN: 0800 0148641 (Toll Free inside the UK)
     UK Local: 02036 956322 (+44 20 3695 6322 from outside the UK)

Published by AuthorHouse 03/02/2021

ISBN: 978-1-6655-8528-6 (sc)
ISBN: 978-1-6655-8529-3 (hc)
ISBN: 978-1-6655-8530-9 (e)

Library of Congress Control Number: 2021903676

Print information available on the last page.

ACKNOWLEDGEMENTS

I am greatly indebted to Derek Gore of Exeter University, to the Devon Archaeological Society and to the Association for Roman Archaeology for the valuable insight into life in Roman Britain without which this story could not have been written.

To Derek & Anne.

Many Thanks and best wishes

Margaret - M. E. Taylor.

INTRODUCTION

In the ancient world of the Romans, slavery was legal and considered normal. The conquered were taken into captivity and made to work for their captors; some slaves were bred for the purpose. Slaves were bought and sold in open markets and used by all levels of society. Many were highly skilled. Freedoms were regularly granted to those considered worthy or too useless to continue to feed and clothe. A freed slave over the age of thirty could become a Roman citizen. Many freedmen gained great wealth. In the case of a woman, she would be expected to have produced three children and be thirty to gain her freedom.

BOOK I

A PRESENT FOR GAIUS

1

The boy was taller than he had expected. He must be – what, twelve? At the very least twelve, a good four years older than Gaius. And sullen too, scowling and defiant – not at all the slave for his precious child. Quite unsuitable. Dangerous, most probably. What had possessed his son to choose this creature?

Lucius sighed and groaned aloud; he wrapped his face in his hands. How the gods mocked him. Had they not tormented him enough? He saw now that they had not. The contrast between this rough and brutish young Briton and his own weak and fading child was further cruelty. Gaius, his own dear and most precious son – seven years old last May, sweet natured, tender, and loving, adored by his parents and sisters – his darling Gaius was lying pallid and enfeebled on his bed, stalked by Death himself, and this young ox, this rag-clad, ill-bred, unschooled barbarian, radiant in health and strength, with sun-gilded limbs and a dense ochre mane, was now placed before him as if he were the remedy.

Yet again he sensed the doubt within himself; this was wrong. He was wrong to yield to a child's coercive tactics. It should be otherwise; Gaius should obey his father and accept his decision – not so stubbornly, so determinedly, oppose him. Was he master of his household or not? Apparently not, and now that he faced the cause of all this madness, he could see that he had been right; the culprit was by far a worse choice than even he had imagined. The contrast between the two boys was more than cruel; it was grotesque – an obscenity.

Lucius was hot and tired and sweaty and thinking how greatly he was in need of his bath. Yet dutiful as ever to the needs of those who depended upon him, had he not postponed his own comfort to attend to this matter and, in doing so, hopefully to restore his son more speedily to health as a good father should? Had he not come straight home from the anniversary parade, the parade held to commemorate that day, the ninth before the calends of October and the birthday of the divine Augustus? Had he not dutifully so absented himself from the traditional banquet? What else could he, as a good father, have done?

The parade had been a rare occasion to don his military attire once again, but now, within his study, he had done no more than cast aside his helmet, cuirass, and sword and slump into his favourite chair before having the boy, his newest acquisition, placed before him for approval. He frowned and scowled also at the absence of his wife, who had not yet greeted his return. It seemed to him that even the pleasure of Aelia's welcoming embrace was to be denied him until he had complied with his family's demands. Of course, she must be with their son and not yet aware of his return.

It was the twenty-third day of September in the tenth year of the reign of the emperor Domitian. He, Lucius Marcius Phillipianus, sometimes known to his chagrin as Mollis, or 'Softy', son of Consul Quintus Marcius Phillipianus, had recently arrived in the province of Britannia. With him had come his wife, Aelia Paula; their surviving children – ten-year-old Marcia, seven-year-old Gaius, and five-year-old Marcilla-Gaia; and their essential personal slaves. For that much he knew he should count himself fortunate; senators who displeased their emperor were seldom given the option of keeping all of their wealth and their family with them when posted into what, it might as well be acknowledged, was virtual exile. His crime was that he had been at the side of his dying son Lucius when he should have been supporting Domitian in the Senate. Perhaps the death of little Lucius had touched Domitian's heart, and for that reason alone the family had been spared a worse fate. More than one of his friends had pointed out the advantages of being in the young province of

Britannia and the opportunities which awaited him to acquire much land and wealth.

Had he travelled alone, different accommodation would have sufficed for Lucius' needs, but Aelia had insisted that he would not leave without her and their children; and so he had selected a place for them in the territory of the friendly Dobunni tribe. It was a small and rude but well-situated farm complex. And small it was – much smaller than any of their properties in Italy. To bring Aelia to such a place was for him a matter of great shame. But she was resolute: they would be together wherever Domitian placed him; a good Roman wife could bear any hardship to be beside her husband. And as the vendor had pointed out, the small house had much potential and was ripe for development. And Lucius had great plans for its development.

The farm, the Roman House as it was becoming known, was sited in a prime position tucked into a fold in the wooded hillside beneath the site where the now-deserted hill fort had stood for many decades. There was a fine view across fertile fields and the new settlement and, on a clear day, well beyond the silver coiling bands of the river Sabrina – as far as the territory of the Silures, a less tractable tribe than the Dobunni.

The local name for the place, he had concluded, was unpronounceable but sounded like Daruentum and referred to the nearby oak-covered hillsides. It lay to the south-east of the fortress at Glevum, within an easy walk and a quicker ride. The proximity of the garrison afforded them a degree of security should it be required, and at first it had seemed that Fortuna was again smiling upon them. How mistaken he had been!

His study was a small and ill-lit cubicle into which the exquisite furnishings he had brought from Rome were crammed and badly positioned. There was little room for more than the finely carved and painted chair into which he had slumped, its matching partner, a rather large table inlaid with ivory, a tall lamp holder, and a strong storage chest. Shelves had hastily been assembled to hold his books, ledgers, and drawings and to hide the awfulness of the smoke-stained walls, discoloured from the leaking flue tiles, and the unfinished and

3

poorly worked wall paintings. It left a lot to be desired, but he had plans, and even at that moment a new and much larger house of a more suitable design was already under construction.

His mind had wandered. He drew himself together and looked again at the boy. Was this really what Gaius had set his heart on? What a debacle! In any other circumstances he would have rejected him, saying simply, 'No, not suitable,' and waving a hand and be rid of the creature immediately, or he would have found a use for him more suited to his age and ability, and that would be the end of the matter. But that he could not do; he dared not risk it.

Unless, of course, he mused, Palatus had fetched the wrong one. That could be it; the fool steward had bought the wrong one.

Lucius frowned again and scowled impatiently. 'Place him forward, man, so that I may see him properly.' At the same time, he rose and with an open palm of welcome attempted to make a friendly approach.

The boy glowered across the space between them. His squared chin rose a little, and his lips whitened as they sealed themselves even more tightly against any leakage of sound, as if even one syllable might seem to express acquiescence. His face made it plain: purchasing him was one thing; taming him would prove another.

'It must be daunting, I have no doubt, for such as him suddenly to be confronted by this,' he said, indicating the scarlet tunic and shining cuirass and sword cast aside. Then, to the boy, he said, 'Do not be afraid; I shall not harm you.' Lucius always made it his business to master native tongues; he found it paid in the long run.

Verluccus understood the words well enough despite the thick foreign accent, but they were lies. How could any man who had caused him so much pain make such a promise? He fought off the dreadful trembling which had taken control of his legs and watched wide-eyed as the sour-faced speaker, a swarthy, thickset soldier, drew back his lips in a sham of friendliness and took yet another step towards him, and he felt again the shove from the bony hands at his back.

It was the man who was pushing him forward who had hurt him

but only in obedience to the orders of this one, the master. The pain again shot through his body, and his head swam as he fought the desire to weep or to allow his legs to crumple under him and to kneel, to beg for mercy. He gulped and swallowed hard. What he had done to anger this man and the gods he did not know, but he did know for certain that yet more torture was intended for him.

His fierce resistance and brief bid for freedom had proved futile and had been punished severely. He had realized what his captors were about when they had cornered him in the smithy. Their fear of this brutal man had left them unmoved by his pleadings. They had made him watch the brightening of it heating in the furnace so that he would know what was to come, and so, despite his resolve, he had been unable to stifle the scream that had escaped his clenched lips when the hot metal seared into his shoulder, and he had fallen senseless at their feet until they revived him. Now, his knees knocking so loudly that surely all must hear them, he waited their next move, and his eyes wandered from the soldier and came to rest on the discarded sword belt.

'Great beneficent Jupiter!' muttered Lucius as he followed the direction taken by the boy's eyes to the discarded sword. 'What does he think I'm going to do to him?' This he had said in Latin, but now, gently, so that the boy could understand, going even so far as to bend his own knees to give the clearly needed encouragement, he asked, 'What is your name? Shall I choose a name for you?'

There was no answer. Lucius' first impression that the boy was totally unsuitable appeared to be confirmed.

'Calm yourself; I shall not harm you,' he felt compelled to murmur as his hand descended into the ochre hair, trusting not to find it 'full of life' as the saying went. The boy shook again and curled back his lips in threat as if he were some wild animal. The teeth were strong and even and surprisingly clean. Lucius looked into the boy's eyes and saw that they were a most deep and brilliant blue, really quite dark, like lapis, wide and glittering and gazing with courageous defiance into his own. Such a boy, once disciplined and instructed, made presentable, might be put to good use, Lucius reflected, and perhaps his mere presence within the house would be enough to appease the gods and restore Gaius to health.

But there was clearly something wrong. Lucius straightened up and spoke to the steward, who had strategically placed himself between the boy and the door. 'He looks strong and healthy enough, Palatus, but what is wrong with his arm? He holds that shoulder most awkwardly.' Surely Gaius had not settled on a cripple?

Palatus hesitated; it was a hesitation which did not go unnoticed by his master. Thick black eyebrows rose in question, and Lucius' fingers probed along the boy's neck and across his left shoulder. It was too much; his victim could bear no more. He screamed in agony and would have struck out at his tormentor, but more quickly than he could do so, release came as if it were he who had inflicted hurt on the other. Too soon the cruel hands were again upon him, causing yet more pain as his tunic was stripped from his back. The room began to revolve, and as he fell to the ground, the words he heard were angry, foreign, and unintelligible to him.

'What is this? On whose authority was this done?' Lucius looked from the steward to the inflamed and weeping wound and back again. 'Explain yourself. I demand an answer. Speak, by Hercules, speak!'

Now it was Palatus who trembled. He was unused to being the target of anger and discovered that it was an exceedingly unpleasant thing to experience. Beads of perspiration oiled his high forehead, and his slightly protruding eyes bulged as he fought to quell his protest at the injustice of it. But he too was a recent purchase into the household of Lucius Marcius, and he did not dare. Palatus, a man who habitually carried himself splendidly erect to distinguish his rank from lesser members of the staff, made a rare, deep bow.

'Master, the boy is wild; he tried to run away. He needs discipline –'

'Discipline? You call this discipline? He is what? Twelve? You put a hot iron on a twelve year old and call it discipline? Not in my house. *Not in my house!*' Lucius' voice was raised as he shook with rage.

Palatus bowed again. It was safest not to speak.

The master hissed through his teeth, outraged at the man's behaviour. 'Take the boy away. Take him to the slave rooms and see to it that Victor has that wound attended to. I want him treated kindly. Kindly! Do you hear? You may inform my wife that I am at home. And return yourself. I shall learn more of this!'

Raising the boy to his feet and half-dragging him from the room, Palatus withdrew. Lucius returned, stumbling to his chair, and into his outstretched hand a cup of dark wine was suddenly placed.

Another man had been present in the room, occupying the second chair. Until this moment, his part had been that of a silent onlooker. He was Cordatus, Lucius' freedman, an older man than Lucius with a stooping, angular frame and hair meagre and grey half-encircling a growing pate. Now he spoke. 'Drink, Lucius; you are quite shaken. I think you should compose yourself before Aelia arrives.'

'That such a thing should be done in my house! Be done in my name! And done to a child. Where did my wife find that man? What kind of a creature has she introduced into my household?'

'You should not distress yourself so, Lucius. The boy will recover quickly; he is a strong and sturdy lad. Gaius has made a wise choice. Would you like me to talk to him?'

Lucius shook his head. They both knew why Cordatus offered; he was the only man within that household to bear a slave brand, although in his case it was the letter M, small and discreetly placed upon his right thigh. 'When my father did that to you, you were twenty-five, mature. You could comprehend. But I vowed then that never, never, never, would such a thing be done to a slave within my household; yet now it has. It has been done, and I am helpless: it has been accomplished, and it cannot be undone. It never occurred to me that Palatus would presume so much.'

Both of their minds had returned to the days of Lucius' childhood in Rome where, when Lucius was ten years old, his favourite uncle, Lucius Marcius the elder, had given him his best Greek slave, the highly educated and cultured youth Cordatus, whose hair was as black as a raven and whose mind was as wise as a crow. Young Lucius had seen then the savage endorsement which his father Quintus Marcius had inflicted upon his tutor. Such had been Quintus Marcius' custom, and he had allowed no exception. That laws limited such actions to the marking of criminals disturbed him not. 'Every slave is a criminal,' he would have it. 'He would not be a slave otherwise.'

But Lucius had freed Cordatus. When he himself was twenty, he had married the young Aelia Paula, and the ex-slave had become his friend and secretary, invaluable and indispensable, loved as much by Aelia and the children as by himself. It was high time he relinquished him to undertake the tutelage of Gaius – he knew that. There was no other to whom he would entrust the boy. *If he survives, of course.* He checked himself. *No, he must live. Now he must live.*

A handle turned, and the study door opened quietly. Both men roused themselves, but it was only Melissa with a taper come to light the ready lamps. The windows were narrow, and though the heavy shutters had not been closed, they let in little light; so in addition to those on the stand, numerous little lamps needed to be lit. The girl glided silently around them, a young and graceful presence ignored by Lucius, silently approved by Cordatus. 'No,' Lucius tersely answered her brief query; he did not want the shutters closed. 'Let them remain open and give in some air.'

The girl genuflected respectfully and withdrew, closing the heavy door firmly behind her; she had sensed the tension and knew that something was seriously wrong. This was a time, perhaps, for wise slaves to keep their heads down.

From the far end of the passageway came the voice of the mistress shouting for Irene, the freedwoman, to hurry to her, and Melissa quickened her footsteps lest lamps not lighted in the remaining rooms give cause for the mistress's displeasure.

'I should discuss this first with Aelia. Alone, I think,' Lucius said to Cordatus. 'Keep that creature of hers from me until I have spoken to her.'

In the nick of time, Cordatus reached the door and swung it open. The soft, quick tread of sandals, Aelia's approaching footsteps on the paved floor, had forewarned them of her imminent arrival. The air filled with the fragrance of roses as she entered, acknowledging Cordatus' immaculate timing with a dazzling beam of intimacy as their smiling eyes met and he matched her laugh with a huge and stupid grin. Even if her husband was on this rare occasion displeased with her, Cordatus would never find fault in Aelia.

Steering her to face Lucius' concerns and questions about Palatus, Cordatus left the room to be confronted again by the steward, who was close at his mistress's heels.

'The master does not require you immediately, Palatus.' He nodded towards the adjacent triclinium. 'Be sure you wait in the dining room until he calls for you.'

Palatus took himself into the room, expecting the other to remain and talk to him – to advise him, he hoped, on how matters might be resolved to his advantage. But something more pressing now diverted Cordatus, and he immediately hurried away to his own bedchamber, signalling that the girl with the taper should follow him.

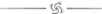

Aelia's face was alive with love and excitement, and Lucius' heart had leapt as it always would at the sight of his dearly cherished wife. She was as beautiful as ever, and even to her husband, it seemed impossible that she could be the mother of four children – four because he counted poor dead Lucius. She was wearing the fine gown, pale green wool trimmed with threads of gold, as if especially to please him and some of the many rings and bracelets and beads which he had showered upon her, a curvaceous and vivacious, sparkling armful of humanity to whom he was fortunate enough to be the husband.

She could barely contain herself. Her voice was breathy with excitement. 'Lucius, darling husband, the boy is here. You will see him quickly? I beg you not to delay. Palatus fetched him, and Gaius is so much better already, so eager to receive him – you would hardly believe it; the improvement is remarkable. He is eating again and speaks of rising from his bed! Is that not wonderful? Oh, I do give such thanks to the gods!'

'I have seen him.' He lifted her arms from around his neck and held her hands gravely between his. A moment later he was lost and yielded to his passion for her, taking her into his arms and indulging himself on her lips.

She laughed as he put her onto her feet again. 'For a moment I thought I was in disgrace – you spoke so dryly, looked so solemn. Well? What do you think? Shall we take him to Gaius at once?'

The scowl returned. 'I think you cannot have seen him. He is as wild and filthy a brat as I feared, but I still harbour a hope that Palatus has fetched the wrong one. He is much older than Gaius, and a lot of work is required to produce the kind of slave you and I are accustomed to have around us. That is one matter. That steward of yours, Palatus, however – the manner in which he carried out my orders – Aelia, do you know what he has done?'

The suggestion of a frown puckered her broad, pale brow. 'Done? Why, nothing to displease you, I am certain; he has saved our son's life. Is that not something to celebrate? We knew the boy would be uneducated, and no doubt you have paid more than he is worth, but did you not hear me? Gaius is so much recovered and that merely from knowing the boy has been brought here.'

'Palatus has burnt the boy – branded him.'

'Oh! Oh, no!' Her shock was genuine. 'Oh, Lucius, no! I know your views on that.'

'Burned! A wound deep into his skin.'

'Does it show? Does it disfigure him?' She saw his outraged expression and realized her mistake. Her voice became coaxing, reassuring; her fingers teased him. 'Lucius, it is for the best that we have him. We have him for Gaius' sake. The haruspex showed you that. We mortals act only as the gods indicate. And so too did Palatus. He too saw how poorly Gaius had become. If he has acted in a manner of which we may disapprove, it can only have been from his devotion to our family.'

'The gods are fickle friends at times. I have no need of a steward who can act in such a wilful and cruel manner. This has not been well done – not well done at all. I fear this transaction was not straightforward; I dread what more may unfold. Before I deal with

Palatus, you must tell me what instructions you gave him before he set out on this sorry errand.'

'I gave him the purse of money which you provided and said he should purchase the boy from whoever had possession of him.'

'And? No more than that? The boy tried to run away.'

'I did say that he must brook no refusal,' she admitted when she saw she must. 'But I only meant he must impress upon the owner or parent how important he was to us and that we would pay any amount for him. That was all.'

'I fear Palatus has exceeded his commission. I would send the boy back at once were it not for the branding. He is clearly unsuitable, coarse and uneducated. Well, we feared that much, but he is much too old for Gaius; I do not know what the child has been thinking of. But now, were Gaius to change his mind, as I am sure he will when he sees what an unsuitable slave he has chosen, how can I return him to his family with such an obscenity on his back? Here he must remain. As you may imagine, he is in some distress.' His voice hardened. 'I hope my son is pleased with his work. I have to say that I find this sudden recovery highly suspicious.'

'You surely do not doubt his illness? The physicians could do nothing for him. We had no hope before the priests advised you.' Even now, when his recovery seemed assured, she wrung her hands as she remembered how close to death he had been.

'No, I know his condition was real enough, although I felt at the start of it, and I still do feel, concerned that for a whim our son should prove so stubborn, so obdurate, to force his father to give in to him by starving himself until he is too weak to stand and so engineer his own illness. I know, I know – he misses the company of Lucius. Do we not all? But this ill-kempt brat cannot replace Lucius; never will he be a suitable playmate for my son. Why, the age between them is greater even than that between Gaius and his poor brother. I tell you, wife, I rue the day you ventured away from the garden and took the children to walk beside the stream. It all stems from that time. That was where our son set eyes on him, and now he has coerced me into yielding to this whim.'

11

They were both remembering then that hot August day when, quite uncharacteristically, Aelia had allowed the children to lead her (escorted by Palatus, Melissa, and Delia, of course) on an expedition into parts of their new territory. All the land they trod upon was their own, though they did not cover it all; and the native settlement remained some safe distance from them, though the native people were considered harmless – friendly, even, should anyone desire friendship from such. When conquest of their forebears had been completed and peace established, they had been encouraged to move down from their hilltop fortifications and settle in the fertile valley. Now, more than two generations later, they posed no threat to the authorities and were responding well to civilization, producing abundant crops and paying their dues, not entirely without complaint but with no more than one might expect. With the whole of Britain from which to choose his home, Lucius had considered this site in Dobunni territory the most agreeable.

Aelia and the children had walked along the path above the rushing stream, and then, in a rare moment of silence, they had caught the first glimpse of the boy. Stilled as if carved from marble, they had watched in fascination until the trespasser had completed his task and the last slippery fish had been scooped deftly from the water and secured with its glistening companions. Then, whether because he had taken enough or because he had become aware of their presence, as silently as those who observed him, he had slipped into the undergrowth and had been lost to sight.

For all the following days and through most of the following nights, Gaius and his little sister, Marcilla, who insisted on doing everything her brother did even to the point of being called Gaia (she would answer to nothing else), had talked of nothing but the boy. Gaius' desire that he might be allowed to go to the stream and catch fish alongside the urchin had been dismissed as ludicrous. Even more absurd was the notion that he might instead go to the other's home to play with him there. 'Nonsense,' he had been told. 'He is a dirty, filthy creature. You will catch something nasty.'

There were tears, tantrums, and finally, when the next appeal was refused – that the boy might instead be brought to the house to play there with him – sickness. The malady grew so serious that his very life had hung in the balance.

Lucius adored his little son; he had witnessed a lively, sweet, and bright child become weak and fractious, pale and listless, thin as a skeleton. The unspoken reproach in Aelia's eyes had pained him as much as the agonising possibility of seeing a second son die not from some foul infection but because, as father of the household, he had supposed himself master of his family and was becoming, like his own father before him, unbending and autocratic. He had wrestled with his conscience and doubts and the conflict in his mind, and after much heart searching and many offerings, he had yielded to the priests' advice. It was a comfort to learn that Gaius had shown such a rapid improvement, but he could not help feeling as he did about it, no matter how happy the outcome might prove.

He felt Aelia's caressing hand soothing his cheek cajolingly. 'Lucius, I could not stand by and watch Gaius die knowing that it was within my means to save his life. What mother could? I have one son; you have one son. If this boy should prove freeborn, I cannot believe his mother is similarly placed; these women always seem to have hordes of children around them. And if he was some other man's property, then consider the advantages he will enjoy from living with us: good food, fine clothes, education, and a really kind master. He would not receive a proper education otherwise, I'll warrant. If he will be good and obedient, he will have a fine position. His people will be proud to see what becomes of him. Nor will they be out of pocket; your purse did not return with Palatus.'

'So it may prove.' He nodded his agreement with her argument. 'I shall have Palatus in now, and I mean to get to the truth of this.'

'I am sure Palatus will be truthful; he is most loyal. He is a most excellent steward. If he has been over zealous on this occasion, it will have been only out of his devotion to us and to our children,' Aelia answered, filled with concern for her steward. Lucius was entitled to beat the truth out of Palatus whether or not he thought the slave would prevaricate.

'Loyal? I expect no less. I know he is loyal to you and grateful. It is necessary, however, for him to learn more of what the master of this house demands.'

He opened the door, a signal for the steward to enter.

It was not only concern for the precarious situation he now suspected he was in that caused Palatus to bow with extra care to both master and mistress as he entered. Palatus was scrupulously correct in all his conduct towards his betters, but towards this mistress he already had reason to be especially grateful. He was now a mature twenty-eight years old and a highly competent steward who had been well bred and trained for his position, and he knew that his boy, his own son Felix, had it within him too. Until very recently, he had been entrusted with the stewardship of a far greater mansion than that in which he now found himself. Just a few weeks previously, however, his world had fallen apart: debts had persuaded his previous owner to slit his wrists. That man's heir had selected such goods as he could find use for, which included Felix's mother and other women, and had returned to Gaul, instructing that the residue of the estate be turned into cash. Palatus had been confident of his own worth – such servants as he were greatly valued – but how it was that Aelia had realized his connection with one particular small and skinny boy among the cheap drudges, he had no idea. He just knew that he would be eternally grateful to her for reuniting them. He had not witnessed the manner in which a pair of grave hazel eyes in a thin and anxious face had fixed themselves unflinchingly upon him. Aelia, escorted by Cordatus, had gone to the other side of Corinium to secure this high-quality slave; she had told the freedman to bid for the boy also. For that act of compassion, he would do anything for Aelia and those whom she loved.

He bowed again as his mistress addressed him.

'Palatus, the master will question you. Be sure that you answer him truthfully.'

'Indeed I shall question you,' cut in Lucius. He had taken down a bundle of rods which spent their life as a decorative item on walls and placed them within reach on the table, hoping that the sight of them would concentrate the slave's mind. 'Be in no doubt. I charge you to speak truthfully, or I may do to you what you did to that boy and more. No, not may – I swear if you do not tell me the whole of it now, I shall do so to you.'

Again the steward bowed. 'Master, as you directed, I took the purse and four men.'

'I gave no order about any men save you. Who were they? Were they armed?'

'Master, I took three of Victor's menials and one of the porters. They carried staves; I and the porter went on horseback. We did have swords.'

Swords? Horses? To travel less than two miles to buy a child? It was worse even than he had feared, Lucius thought with increasing alarm. With difficulty, he controlled his anger. 'Did you encounter obstruction? Was there trouble? Did you employ all this force? It is important that I know it all. The very security of our home may depend on it.'

'When we reached the settlement, we attracted some attention, and children crowded around us. The boy himself was with them; I recognized him without difficulty – that shock of hair! He led us to his home willingly enough, a poor sort of hovel' – he paused for effect and allowed his eyes to drift meaningfully around the study – 'compared with this fine house.'

'Yes, yes. Get on with it.'

'I left the men outside and went in alone.'

Only Lucius' obvious impatience deterred him from elaborating further on the impoverished state of the round house.

'The mother was there. There was no sign of the father.' He paused as if considering how best to put his case. 'Master, I thought it prudent, if you will forgive me, seeing as how he was not a slave but freeborn, to tell them that you had seen the boy yourself and desired to adopt him. I know I did not tell the truth and most humbly beg your pardon for this, but from my immediate impression of the mother's attitude towards him, I did not think his family would agree to sell him to be a slave. I offered to compensate her, of course, with the purse, but she would have none of it; she kept fondling the boy and saying that he was her own dear baby, though you have seen for yourself a baby he is not – almost a man, in fact. She asked me to thank you for your kindness. I offered her more money, but it was to no avail; she would not have it. Gracious lord, pardon my presumption, but I could not come back to the young master empty-handed.'

'So you took him by force!' Lucius' worst fears were realized.

'Master, it was the only way. And I am not unscathed. He fought like the savage that he is. I had to use the men to guard us while I got him away. He struggled and fought the whole way. I could not have achieved it had I not taken the men with me. See here where he has bitten me on the arm and hand.'

It was true enough; blood had been drawn.

'And so for that you burned him? Marked him? What instrument of mine did you put to that use?' He felt disgusted and tainted. And now he was hearing worse – Palatus' wounds raised more doubts. How could he entrust his son to the company of such ferocity?

'I could not hold him; he freed himself from me and escaped into the courtyard. It was in the smithy that we caught up with him.' Palatus again hesitated, but as Lucius stared impassively at him, waiting for the explanation, he found he had to continue. 'There was some resistance from him; he fought wildly, seizing whatever came to hand. Some work was scattered, damaged. A bridle ornament, the bronze triskele that you had ordered be repaired, fell into the hot embers. I could see then that such a mark would make him yours … Should he run away, you would have your mark on him.' He hesitated again and was spared.

'Leave me. Get out of my sight.' There was no need to hear more; the rest of it he could imagine.

Palatus bowed, withdrew, and carefully closed the door behind him.

Whatever business had drawn Cordatus away had now released the freedman, who was again in the triclinium, discussing the need for more lamps with Melissa, who immediately left the room.

Somewhat nervously, Palatus approached him. 'Is there something you desire, sir? The master will be engaged for some time I think.'

'I have no need of anything.' Cordatus was conscious of an unreasonable irritation because of the foolish man's attention to him. 'How is the boy? Has he recovered?'

'Sir, he is quite recovered. A very tough creature, that one. I have placed him in Victor's care.' Palatus was never totally sure where he stood with the freedman who enjoyed a status in this household far superior to anything he had come across before. Why, the man even addressed the mistress with easy familiarity and was never reprimanded for it. He recognized the value of cultivating a relationship with such a being. At this particular moment, there was a real danger that he would be sold out of the household, and he hoped that Cordatus might be persuaded to speak on his behalf. Cordatus, however, was not interested. He had turned his attention back to the scroll he had become engrossed in studying. Palatus cleared his throat. 'Sir, I appear to have acted in a manner which does not find approval in this household. I trust I have not caused you any offence?'

Cordatus shrugged. 'In what way can your actions have offended me? The offence was done to the boy – and to your master. Beg their pardons, perhaps. That boy is nothing to me.'

'I am so sorry, sir. I thought – that is, I – ' He broke off in embarrassment. 'Perhaps you will understand, sir, that being new to this household, I am not yet fully acquainted with its rules of conduct. I assure you of my utmost devotion to my mistress and all her family. I hope my master will come to understand this.'

'He will, no doubt, if you assure him of it,' Cordatus replied briskly, wishing rid of him.

'Quite so; then, sir, if you have need of nothing, I shall be about my business.' Palatus bowed respectfully and departed. Cordatus watched his retreat. He disliked few people, and the man was indeed an excellent steward. No, it had to be acknowledged that the fault lay within himself, and he could see no remedy for it.

He glanced again at the study door; it remained closed.

Beyond the door, Lucius was pacing about in a high state of

agitation. 'That slave is a disgrace. He will have to go. I cannot keep such a creature in my house.'

'Oh, Lucius, please don't say that. He was sent to fetch the boy for us, and he did that. He did not know of your abhorrence of the branding iron. His actions surely demonstrate his great devotion to us and to our poor child. Consider his other excellent qualities, I beg you. We have the most superior steward. Do you want him serve in a lesser household?'

He sighed. She was right, of course. But at the very least, the man deserved a flogging.

'I shall punish him if that is your wish. I shall see to it that he is punished and that he knows why. Will you leave it to me?'

He nodded his assent. 'Were it not for the fact that you value him so highly, I would insist you get rid of him for this. I trust you will see to it that a fitting punishment is meted out to him?'

'Of course, if that is your wish, but I cannot see what he has done that is so very wrong.'

In disbelief, he stared at her. 'You cannot mean that, Aelia. Quite aside from the injury that has been done to the boy, surely you can see that I have no right to take a child from his home in such a manner? That was not my desire. Palatus should have respected the mother's refusal and reported back to us. Another approach might have won her over. Were I of lesser standing, the fact that it is unlawful would be bad enough, but my position demands, in my opinion, integrity and respect for the laws of Rome. Our emperor himself requires me to demonstrate as much to our provincials, not to cast fuel upon any smouldering embers of discontent! You know that I bought this place to provide a family home, a safe haven for you and the children when business sends me abroad. I chose the territory of the Dobunnian people for our home because of their character, their willingness to live in peace. Now, from now on, when I have to leave you, I shall be wracked with anxiety every moment. That is what Palatus has brought about. And for that he must be punished.'

'Lucius, darling!' She reached out to stroke his face and comfort him. 'Surely you are not suggesting his mother is another Boudicca who will rise in anger to bring hordes of savages upon us?' She tried to keep the levity from her voice, for he looked serious.

Being advised not to over react was extremely irritating in the circumstances. 'No, of course not; of course not. That would be absurd.' So he hoped. 'Even so, I should be prudent.' He freed himself from her caress and crossed to the door. 'Cordatus, my good friend, I need your help. Please come in.'

Cordatus would put him right. Aelia smiled conspiratorially at the freedman as if to say, 'Humour my poor Lucius; he is deranged.'

Does she understand now? wondered Lucius when he had finished recounting the story. Perhaps she did; her face had grown more serious.

'In what manner can I be of service?'

Lucius noted he did not offer advice, a sign, surely, of Cordatus' disapproval.

'Firstly, I want you to write out my letter to the tribune Lepidus Aemilius Virens. He is frequently suggesting that we could put to use that odd piece of land across the way for training exercises; he complains that lack of action dulls the men. I suggest that he bring that laggard century he spoke to me of; he says it is most in need of rousing. Let's have them here at dawn tomorrow. Put that in – a training exercise. You understand?'

Cordatus nodded. 'I am with you.'

'I think not!' Lucius spoke ruefully. 'Your silence hints of disapproval. There is something else. I would not normally require this of you, but I need someone I can trust, someone who understands the delicacy and urgency of the situation.'

'You wish me to deliver the letter to Virens for you and explain the reason for it?'

'Lucius, really!'

Aelia's interruption was silenced by a dismissive gesture from her husband. 'Exactly. Speak privately to him and let him know sufficient to achieve my purpose. You may tell him what has transpired and that I hope that the sounds of Mars and the sight of a few blades and armour will deter any thought of protest.'

'Lucius!' She would be heard. 'Cordatus is as tired as you are; you are forgetful of his age. Any one of the slaves can deliver a letter for you.'

'No, my dear Aelia.' Cordatus turned to reassure her. 'With respect, Lucius is right. It is better done this way. I am fully acquainted with all the circumstances as no slave can be. It is a task better done by a freedman than by a slave. Virens knows that I have the confidence of you both. I do appreciate your concern for my health, but please allow me to do this service for you.'

She went to him and squeezed his arm affectionately. 'Dearest Cordatus, if there is nothing to prevent Virens from complying with my husband's proposal, do not hasten back; rest overnight in the *praetorium*. You are too old to be despatched on such errands.'

'You are, as always, kindness itself. Do not be concerned for me; the sun has yet to set, and the sky is still clear and a full moon due. In any event, darkness will barely be here before I am back again.' He positioned himself at the table and took up a tablet.

Lucius said, 'Cordatus, I am conscious that you do not offer advice. That is because I do the best thing?'

'The best thing, Lucius? You know what the best thing is, and it is not this. You do not need me to tell you that. If you sought my advice, I should say this: have his parents brought here and explain it to them. You are not to be blamed. Explain about Gaius, perhaps let them see how poorly he has become, how much their child means to him, and tell them how well he would be cared for.' He could not bring himself to say, 'Tell them of poor little Lucius.'

'I cannot do it. I cannot. Not now that he is branded. And if my case were to be rejected and they demanded him back? What then? How do I send him back to his home now? With a message? "Here is your son. I find he is not suitable after all. Sorry about the damage"? Never have you given bad advice, and it is a rare event when I reject your counsel. But I do now; I must. Is this an omen? Should I send for the augur? Oh, Cordatus! What will be the outcome of this? It is an ill-omened thing. It was my lucky piece he used. It had been damaged, and I sent it to the smithy for repair. Now it must be spoilt beyond recovery, and Fortuna will desert me.' The triskele was an ornamental circular device with a peculiarly Celtic symbol of three legs or horns moving like liquid within a ring. Lucius' grandfather had secured four of them from a captured chariot as a trophy of the invasion and given them to his son Quintus and his three grandsons, Quintus, Marcus, and Lucius.

'Calm yourself. I will fetch the piece and take it to a bronze smith myself. And be more gentle with yourself; the boy is in good hands. He could want for no kinder master. You will have him schooled with Gaius?' He received no answer from the distraught man and so continued, 'If the local people choose to create trouble about this, then your action in inviting Aemilius Virens to bring some arms here is not unwise. As to the augur, I could call upon him also if you wish.'

'I would that you had the time, but I would prefer that you return here safely for tonight. I acted as I believed the gods thought fit and hope that my actions now are under their guidance. Let that be enough for now.' Lucius sealed the tablet, and immediately Cordatus departed. The swiftest horse at his disposal was Ravus, the iron-grey charger belonging to Lucius. Lucius now turned again to his wife.

'I don't know what the end of this will be. You think I am over reacting? I know you do, but these are only measures to deter. The sight of drilling ranks should be enough, I trust.'

'I know that you have acted for the best', she replied, 'as I did for Gaius' sake. Now may he be given the boy? Shall we have him fetched in? It will do him so much good to see that he really is here.'

Lucius nodded grimly. 'Gaius may see him, but he is not yet trained. You may bring the children into the triclinium, and I shall have the boy brought there.'

She left him at once. Irene was waiting outside to tell her Gaius was getting anxious, wondering what was happening. Like Cordatus, she had been with her mistress since Aelia's childhood, and like him, on Aelia's marriage, she had been given her freedom. 'He must be fretting at this delay.' Aelia fumed. 'I promised him that he would see the boy as soon as his father returned home.'

His sisters had joined him in his bedchamber, fearful lest they miss some development. Delia was with them, of course; she rose to bow respectfully as her mistress entered.

Gaius now felt well enough to sit up. He stretched out feeble arms to greet her. 'Mother, when may I see him? Is he to be brought to me here?' It was a weak, excited voice quite unlike his own. Aelia kissed his head and smoothed his brow with her cool fingers.

'Yes, you shall see him; we shall have him brought into the dining room. Your father has been busy with Cordatus.' She glanced around the tiny room, and her voice sharpened. 'I told that boy Felix to keep you company. Where is he?'

'Marcia sent him to carry my dishes back to the kitchen. He has only just left and will return very soon. I ate up every scrap, Mother. Are you pleased with me?' His elder sister nodded in confirmation, and his mother kissed him in reward.

'When am I to have my own maid, Mother?' Marcia whined. 'I am older than Gaius by three years, and now he is bought this new boy while I still have to share Delia with Marcilla.' As she often did, Marcia ignored her little sister's mouthed correction, 'Gaia.'

'Gaius is a boy, my sweet, and your father's only son. It is right that he should have his own cup boy. After all, you do have Gaia for company.'

The child of whom she spoke had wriggled free of her nurse and claimed her place on her mother's knee. She was given the cuddles and kisses she sought and consented to be handed back to Delia without making a greater fuss. Marcia was not to be so easily pacified.

'Gaius already has Felix. He is quite obedient, and he's just a little older than Gaius. I don't see why Gaius needs two slaves, and I may not have one for myself. It isn't fair!'

'That is quite enough.' It was not like Marcia to be difficult; Marcilla-Gaia was the wilful child, a lively and mischievous little girl. In her younger daughter, a passionate but charming little being, Aelia fancied she saw something of herself; it was more usually Marcia who exhibited her father's easy-going good nature, was biddable and quietly serene. 'Irene, go and tell Palatus to come and carry Gaius to the triclinium.' She lowered her voice to an excited whisper which she knew the children loved. 'It won't be long now!'

'My name is Victor. You call me Overseer.'

The one who had brought him to this place had gone now. They had spoken briefly about him in the Roman language, which he could not understand, and now he was sitting on a low cot, reluctant to rise. He wondered if he was expected to stand up. At home, that would have been expected – standing up when a stranger addressed you was good manners. But he did not feel like being good mannered to anybody in this place. Instead he looked upwards, his face still grimacing with pain and resentment.

This man was not like the other. He was a much larger, stronger man wearing a simple brown tunic. His hair was dark and cropped very short, and he had a beard, though it was neat and tight on his chin. He was no friendlier, however.

'Take off your tunic.'

The man spoke in a thick foreign accent, and the boy made no response but tightened his body as if he would fight anyone who touched him.

'Placidus,' the man called to another young slave who had been concealed by the dimness of the room, 'remove his tunic.'

The whelp would, of course, be exaggerating the pain and injury in order to gain the sympathy of the master; too many slaves knew that Lucius was an easy touch. Well, Victor would make certain there was none of that.

The boy Placidus, a little taller than the newcomer, dragged the shirt from his back, and again the boy winced and stifled a gasp.

Victor examined the wound. He knew something of wounds, having inflicted many on others and experienced some himself. Now he could see that the pained hesitation of the boy was no sham. He turned to Placidus. 'Go to Irene and fetch a remedy for this. Bring a clean tunic for him also. This one won't do.'

Victor's mastery of the British tongue was limited, but he had learned fundamental phrases so that those over whom he was placed should not get the better of him. He spoke again to the newcomer in a mild enough tone, asking carefully, 'What is your name?' Palatus would need the details for his records. There came no answer.

I am not going to cry, his victim vowed privately, biting his lip and studying the ground. He felt the rough hand raise his chin and stared into searching brown eyes.

'What do they call you?' From what he had seen, Victor judged it unnecessary to press the issue now, for this reaction was more distress than defiance. The former could be tolerated for a short period, the latter not at all; and even he, who had seen and caused so many wounds in his time, recognized the reality of this agony.

Placidus returned with a phial, but it was the big man himself who smoothed the cooling lotion over the wound. 'Today you will remain with him. I place him in your charge. Today you may speak to him in your own language to explain matters to him. If there is any trouble with him, you may secure him and report to me. Do not allow him the chance to run away. And tidy him up. Trim that mane and clean his face at least.'

'Drink this wine,' said Placidus when they were alone. 'Normally it is not allowed, but I explained to Irene what the ointment was for and she told me to give it to you. It is sweetened with honey.'

Perhaps it would help. He gulped it down; the taste was foreign to him, but its warmth comforted.

Placidus had more to say. 'You must be a bad boy, I think. Is it true you bit Palatus?'

There was a nod in reply.

'You're lucky to be a slave in this household. Everyone here'll tell you that. Lucius Marcius is a good master. Some call him Softy, but he don't like that, so not to his face or to anyone who'd tell 'im, got it? We all eat well here, and Victor is fair; there ain't many overseers you could say that about. He used to be a gladiator for the master, but he had to retire because of his wounds. Lady Aelia – that's the mistress. She gets a bit mad when things get broken or she finds summat's not been cleaned properly, but apart from that, she's no trouble. The only thing is do not cross the children – not ever. If the children like you, you can't go wrong with her. You let 'em do as they please, especially that Marcia. Ten she is, the eldest, and she likes to show that she can give orders. Gaius is seven. He's all right; not as bad as Marcia anyway. We haven't seen much of him since he was taken ill, but I think he must be over the worst, for the physician left today. When he was really poorly, the physician stayed all the time; everyone thought he would die which would not have been good for us! Lastly there is the little one, Gaia. She is very fond of her brother. Little as she is, she stayed by his side when he was at his worst, and she is not yet six years of age. A proper little tyrant she is.' He paused and chuckled as if recollecting some escapade of hers to which he was privy and which for her sake would remain a secret. 'She leads poor Delia a merry dance, I can tell you, but she would not do a spiteful thing; she is full of fun. Are you feeling better now?'

The boy nodded again. The wine had helped; at home he was not allowed wine – only the weakest beer. Tanodonus said wine made you ill. This must be a different sort of wine.

For the first time, he took in his surroundings. They were in a long wooden building; gaps in the wall were covered with wicker screens through which light entered. Above his head were thick beams under a bowing thatched roof badly in need of repair. Besides the cot he was on, there were a number of identical sleeping pallets side by side. At the furthest end were some partitions. Behind the partitions were more beds, affording a degree of privacy to those who claimed a higher status. In such matters he was not interested and remained in ignorance. Bed straw had been strewn liberally on the floor as if some of the occupants cared about the conditions they were kept in and had made a bold attempt to make its pungency less unpleasant. It was a horrible place to be in, and it looked as if he was intended to remain there.

'This is the slaves' house,' Placidus said helpfully. 'You will sleep in here; that's my cot next. Victor'll tell you what your duties are. He's the overseer.'

'I am not a slave.'

He had spoken at last.

'Of course you are. Why else are you here?'

'I don't know, but I shan't stay.'

Placidus frowned. 'If you run away, it's me as'll get a beating. Victor's put you in my charge. I'll tell him what you said; he'll make sure you don't go. They'll put shackles on you.'

'Why don't you come with me? We could go together. My mother would take you in.'

'You are a stupid boy. D'you think no one'll look for you? I know where I'm well off! You listen to the others when they return, and you'll learn from them what a good place this is.'

Placidus allowed the boy to rest but, conscious of his threat to run away, remained at his side, wishing that Victor would soon return to relieve him of his responsibility. That was the only thing; the master expected disobedience to be punished, and he would regard failing to prevent an escape as disobedience. And he got rid of troublesome slaves too. This boy would not last long unless he changed his attitude.

Palatus and Victor arrived together. The boy was required by the master.

As he trotted beside his escort, the boy became more aware of the relative grandeur of his new surroundings – of the smooth level floors beneath his feet, some earthen, some paved, some even made of neatly fitting tiles arranged in fancy patterns; of the covered walkway along which he was hurried from one block of buildings to another and then, inside, past decorations and furnishings he might well have thought palatial had he had knowledge of palaces.

To Lucius Marcius, however, it was a poor place, rough and unfinished, a mere foundation from which would rise the kind of home in which he might have pride. The new bath suite had already been commenced. Macrinius, the most skilled builder available to him, a veteran with great experience in fortress building and responsible for many fine commanders' houses, was doing an excellent job. Next he would build a new house and consign the present one to his estate workers. He knew the conditions they lived in were far from satisfactory, but then those endured by Aelia were by no means what she was accustomed to. He would improve the heating arrangements and possibly add an upper floor. Timber would yield to stone; walls would be vibrant with colour and floors with pattern. If an admiring world beat a track to his door, he would not be displeased. His house would fulfil the role of educating the native businessmen with whom he must have dealings and impressing those who came seeking advantage by his favour with his wealth and taste. But primarily it was to be his family home, its luxury his gift to his beautiful Aelia, a reward for her love and devotion and for the beautiful children which she had given to him.

But the boy now being guided swiftly along the mystifying lengths of corridor had no such imagination; Lucius' grandiose ideas were far beyond his capacity to dream. He had been to Glevum, but never had he set foot inside the fortress and yes, to Corinium also but not within any of the splendid public buildings erected there.

He was brought to a different room now, and it seemed to be filled with them, a whole family of them: all sizes. Some were standing, some were sitting, all were staring – staring at him. For a while he stared back, scowling. There was a boy there, younger than he, pale and sickly looking, thin as a scraggy dog. He tried to remember what Placidus had told him about these children but could not and so gave up the attempt. The thin boy smiled at him and held out a limp hand; he obstinately looked away and, from the corner of his eye, saw the hand drop back at his rejection.

Now the painted walls caught his attention for the first time. They were smooth and white in the upper part, dark red-brown below, and there were figures of people painted upon them. He looked down to inspect the floor, allowing his eye to follow the lines of black and white tessellation the like of which he had never seen before.

They were watching him; he could feel the curiosity in the eyes studying him and became aware that he was looking downwards as if submissively. He jerked up his head and stared in defiance at the man.

An involuntary smile played around Lucius' mouth as he fancied he read the boy's mind, and when the blue eyes squared with his own, he asked, 'What is your name?'

There was no answer. Lucius had spoken gently, encouragingly. It was relief to see the boy could stand erect, and, thank goodness, that awful trembling had ceased.

'Bring him forward, Palatus. Place him before Gaius.'

'Go to your master.' An encouraging hand pushed from behind.

'That's not him. He's not the one.'

'What is this? What is Gaius saying?' Startled, Lucius' eyes interrogated both his wife and the steward in turn.

'Master, this is certainly the boy. He looks different now, because I have had his hair trimmed and he has been cleaned up.'

Gaius pouted. They always spoiled things. The boy he had wanted to play with had been unkempt and natural, a tribal lad. Gaius had imagined a new friend, a boy he could run through the woods in freedom with who knew where all the animals dwelt and which were the best trees to climb, someone to play with other than his sisters – not this caricature of a Roman.

'Go to your master.' Again came the prod.

He rounded on his tormentor. 'I have no master. I am not a slave. I have done no wrong. You cannot do this to me.' It was a plea and a protest both. Lucius swallowed hard.

'What does he say? What does he say? Make him speak Latin.' Gaius had suddenly regained strength and was almost jumping out of his seat.

'Young master, this boy knows no Latin, and until he does, he cannot understand you. We shall see that he learns.' *Oh yes, we shall see to that,* affirmed Palatus privately. His hand impelled the boy forward again.

'Well, what is his name? You ask him that.'

The boy uttered a name too difficult to catch and too unpronounceable to repeat. This he followed by a jet of spittle directly towards Gaius. If it was intended to hit the child, it failed and landed on the floor a short way from him.

'Ugh, he is disgusting.' It was Marcia's squealed opinion, but her mother shared it.

Suddenly the boy seemed to be a lot bigger than he had at first appeared; Gaius was still not wholly convinced that this was the right boy, no matter what Palatus might say. He felt his eyelids droop. Sleep was struggling to take possession of him, and now that his objective had been achieved, he was content to yield.

It was only in Gaia that the excitement remained. She took advantage of a momentary lapse of attention by Delia to spring from the woman's arms – not to leap onto her father so that he could swing her high into the air as she had done when she first entered the dining room but to examine this newcomer more closely. She was halfway across the floor before her nurse recaptured her and bore the protesting little girl to a safe distance.

'Remove him, Palatus,' Aelia commanded. 'Have him taught some manners – how to behave amongst decent, civilized people. Have him learn Latin as soon as possible.'

The children watched his departure as avidly as they had watched his arrival.

Gaia was enthralled. He had spat right there on the tiles of the triclinium floor. Imagine a slave daring to do that! He would be whipped for it, of course, Marcia reminded her, but still her eyes danced with excitement at his daring. Already another boy had been directed to clean it up. Reluctantly she allowed Delia to lead her away.

Lucius lifted his son from the couch to carry him back to his room. The child was exhausted now, almost asleep. He smiled weakly at his father and raised his arms to embrace him. 'I thank you, Father. I sincerely thank you for getting him for me. He will be good – you will see. He will be my special friend.'

He fastened his arms around his father's neck and was conveyed tenderly to his bed. Lucius smoothed his sheets and adjusted his coverings. Relief that the boy was so much improved was tempered by a nagging suspicion that he had been deceived.

'My son, the boy is a slave, and you must treat him as such. He is yours now, wild and uneducated though he is at present. There is much improvement to be attained before he can be considered trustworthy and safe for you. Palatus must be responsible for that.' Lucius was forced to raise his hand to quell protest. 'Do not argue with your father. You have what you wanted, though I do not much care for the manner by which it was achieved, either by you or by Palatus. However, be that as it may, he is in our house now, and here he must remain.'

'May I not have him with me? Have him here now?'

The answer was no. And though the temptation was strong, Gaius recognized that there was no sense in further contention, not now that the boy was within the household. His knowledge of his father was sufficient to warn him not to press for even greater concessions. 'He will be brought to me tomorrow?' Of course he would, Lucius reassured him.

Nearby Felix hovered, bright and lively, dutifully anxious and attentive. Lucius turned to him. He beckoned to him to approach and put an encouraging arm around him to present him to his son.

'Felix will stay with you again tonight. Fetch your mat, Felix, and sleep beside your master.' Lucius rose to go. 'I ache for my bath, young man. You have made me postpone it for too long.'

'You are angry with me, Father?' Gaius could sense that something was wrong. 'Father, why did you have him trimmed and dressed like a Roman? He doesn't like that.'

'Your mother will have no savage in this house, and neither will I. You have the boy you craved for, though he has cost your father a great deal – much, much more than you can imagine. As yet, his character is unknown to us, and he is somewhat older than I would have selected for you. I hope I do not have to dispose of him, but should he prove unsuitable, then I shall do so. Now go to sleep.'

Lucius kissed him and left him. Delia would be here shortly, but already Felix had returned and was curling up beside the cot.

Cordatus rejoined him before he had finished his bath.

'My poor Cordatus! What have I done to you? You must have sped faster than Mercury himself. Yes, in both directions! You look all in. Crispus,' he addressed the slave who had been massaging him, 'pass me the *strigil* and prepare some oils for Cordatus. We ought to have heeded Aelia; I am too unkind to you. Well? Is your early return bad news? Is Virens not to come?'

'Do not mistake my early return for bad tidings,' replied the freedman. 'The Tribune Aemilius Virens has begun to prepare already. He will be here as you asked. You have a good friend in him.'

'But not as good as you. No friend as good as my Cordatus.' He hugged the man, selfishly glad to see him returned. They completed their bathing together, and he felt the depressive mood lift from him as the steamy heat soothed. Yes, when the new bathhouse was built, they would have great bathing parties here. For the moment though, to enjoy this and the dinner to follow would suffice.

Within the house, Aelia was confronting Palatus. 'My husband insists that you be punished for what you did.'

Exactly what that was remained not totally clear. It seemed illogical to her that a slave should be punished for accomplishing his master's requirements, and indeed, how was Palatus to know of Lucius' abhorrence of branding? Some punishment had to be meted out, however; Lucius did not forget such matters, and he would be sure to ask what her sentence had been. She had been surprised that he had left the detail to her.

'Firstly, in order that you may see how leniently I deal with you, I shall tell you of things I considered doing. If my husband were meting out the punishment, you would be flogged – no question about that – but he is content for me to deal with you; and I know that your actions were not reckless or evil and that you did not know of my husband's policy in respect of branding. I have considered also that we might sell that boy of yours, Felix, but he is a good boy and will serve us well in time. My decision is that you must sell Melissa. When my husband goes next to Glevum, he can take her with him and get rid of her. See that she is ready.'

'Mistress – lady, please. I beg you.' Palatus was stunned. Such a penalty had not entered his mind. It raced to think up some means of averting this misfortune. 'I had it in mind that she might one day make a suitable maid for your eldest daughter. She is learning very quickly.'

'That is my final word, Palatus. Do not provoke me. Would you prefer one of the alternatives I mentioned? No, I thought not.'

There was not a thing he could say or do. Aelia stood grimly before him, and he conceded her right to dispose of his own slave woman as she wished.

She dismissed him, and he went to find the girl and break the bad news to her. He was envied for his possession of Melissa. Of course that was it. One of the other members of the house, and he had a good idea who, was jealous of him and had put Aelia up to this. He was lucky to own Melissa; he knew that. She was just seventeen and a real jewel; her hair and eyes were the colour of amber and her skin as soft and pale as milk. She was compliant and responsive to his demands and already had shown herself quick to learn. Fortune had doubly smiled on him – first when he had won her in a game of dice and second when his new owners had agreed that she might remain in their house provided she was useful to them. Palatus smarted at the injustice of his impending loss and drew comfort from the fact that it would be Aelia's loss as much as his own.

He found her easily enough. She was in his room, where he liked to find her, working on some fabric, turning it into a gown for Marcia. She rose when he entered, putting the fabric aside dutifully to embrace her master.

She was wearing blue, a cast-off of Aelia's. The mistress herself had observed how much more flattering the colour was to the slave girl's fair skin than to her own. Palatus then had been pleased to point out the generous nature of their mistress. But now this fine gown must be returned to the pool for one of the other girls to wear. His mind strayed briefly to selecting a suitably becoming dress to increase her price when she was put up for sale.

Omitting such facts as cast him in a poor light, he outlined her fate.

Her reaction to his news was flatteringly passionate and surprising; she had never demonstrated such devotion to him before. She wept aloud and implored him to rescind, to forgive whatever she had done to displease him, but he would hear no appeal. His decision was made; she must go.

Until that moment, however, her duty was still to him and his needs. She was at his knees still weeping as he was unfastening the pins that secured her gown and requiring her to remove it and bend to his will.

It was clear she harboured no hope of reprieve. Despite her protestations and tears, she came no closer to him; he could do much better. After a suitable delay he would venture into the marketplace and find a replacement for her, someone who would better satisfy both his own needs and his mistress's requirements.

Elsewhere within the household, two boys were passing very different evenings.

The cause of all the unhappiness was sleeping soundly in blissful contentment, a smile of dreams realized still hovering on his lips. When the next day came, he would rise, and soon, certainly in a day or so, be strong enough to go with the boy fishing by the stream where he first had seen him. He must think of a good name for the boy, one he would like to be known by. How pleasant life would be; now all would be perfection.

For the object of these dreams, however, life was not and did not promise to be nearly so enjoyable. In the first place, it was time for painful and hungry reflection. The hunger was entirely Verluccus' own fault; he had sulkily refused to eat the food offered to him, and that, he could now see, had been a mistake. It had also been a mistake to suggest to Placidus that he too might escape. That had achieved no more than a plank being dropped into its lugs to secure the door, a thing reputedly unheard of before. It won him no friends. During the night panic ensued when oil spilled and a fire broke out, though it was easily and safely quenched and no one was harmed. Placidus hated him. He had even asked for him to be put in the charge of another – to no avail.

Spitting had worked; he had seen it in their faces when he had done it. If he did something else they did not like, perhaps they would send him home. Why had his people allowed this to happen? Surely someone would come soon and rescue him. He wondered what his own family was doing to help him.

2

Carantua, distraught and alone, had followed the men to the Roman house and had beaten upon the solid outer gate with her fists until they bled. Even when she collapsed and lay tearing at her hair and sobbing, screaming for her child to be restored to her, her cries went unheeded by the porters, men unmoved by such histrionics. Had that been the gate through which Lucius and Cordatus entered their home, the outcome might have been different; but for convenience they used the workaday farm access on the other side of the house, and so master and mistress remained in ignorance of the mother's anguished appeal.

When the day ended, when he had brought down the sheep and found his mother absent, Colymmon went in search of her. He scooped her up into his strong arms as though she were the child and he the parent and bore her home to sit and nurse her until Tanodonus returned from Glevum market.

It was Tanodonus, tired, hungry, and toil-stained though he was, who took it upon himself to appeal to their neighbours for assistance. There were few of them; the transfer of the community from the fortified hilltop had fragmented it, and most families had chosen not to settle there but to surrender the land to the newcomers, the previous occupants of Lucius Marcius' house, and move further down the valley, electing to distance themselves with dignity from the encroachment of Rome. What might have been a thriving community had dwindled to a few farmsteads, and the standing of the foreigners, their rank and their immediacy, was not lost on any of these neighbours. This was the community of Daruentum. Within it was the small but viable farm of Cunobarrus' widow Carantua and her sons; nearby was the rough scatter of ill-maintained huts that was home to Belanius and his wife Brutha, who lived with an enlarging brood in seemingly happy penury; and further away from the Roman house but occupying a site of its own distinction was the rather larger and more prosperous farmstead of Bodellus and his family.

It was from Bodellus that they most needed support, and Tanodonus was confident that he would get it and that it would be effective. In his self-assumed role as elder of the community, Bodellus, Tanodonus reasoned, must frequently engage in business with the Roman administrators – directly with the newcomer himself perhaps. Bodellus was certainly the best man to speak up about the outrage that this man's actions had caused to the native people, was he not?

Word of the event had preceded him to both households via the excited children. Belanius, warm-hearted and generous as ever, was ready enough to accompany him to the Roman house at once, though the voice of Bodellus, Belanius was the first to admit, would carry more weight with the Romans. He guessed what Tanodonus must be thinking as he stood in his great round living hut eyeing the swarm of giggling children: Why Verluccus? Why that boy when there were so many more mouths to be filled in this ragged hovel? Belanius made a poor joke of it: the Roman would have been welcome to take one of his own brood to adopt, he ventured. But Tanodonus did not laugh. It was an easy enough remark to make when it did not apply to you.

Belanius walked with him, bringing his own two eldest sons, their ages bracketing Tanodonus' seventeen years, and Bodellus welcomed them to his hearth with the greatest courtesy. This was a wealthy household by any standards; the formidable oaken gateway and the equally formidable number of neatly thatched circular buildings that housed his family and farm stock bore testimony to that. Bodellus' family was summoned, and Tanodonus was granted the hearing he desired.

He sensed even as he spoke that these were unsympathetic ears – they seemed not to share his view that the changed course of his young brother's life was a misfortune. What had been a feeble joke on the part of Belanius was a real assumption of Bodellus and his wife. Any outrage they felt – and they contained their feelings well – was at the thought that another family should be favoured above their own. Their own younger children had been present when Palatus visited, and they had faithfully reported all that they had heard and seen. It was clear that they envied Verluccus and his family their good fortune.

Bodellus quite reasonably pointed to the advantages. 'I know only good of the man. Lucius Marcius Phillipianus is his name. Mollis – Softy – is what some call him; he is famed for the mildness of his character. He sought to adopt the boy. Tanodonus himself has confirmed this. Our children heard it said, and Carantua has told him that herself. I would we were as fortunate as Carantua to have a child so favoured. Remember it was the steward, not the master, who so forcibly dragged the boy away. Be assured in that house he will be well off indeed.'

'Carantua should have been more reasonable,' added his wife. 'Instead of shrieking and fighting as she did, she ought to have let the man put his case. She might then have been more pleased with the outcome and seen the benefit of this not only to her but to her neighbours also. If she does not see her son again, it will be her doing. I have no doubt that he will soon compare what he has been taken from to the better life awaiting him.'

A son of the household said, 'I think Tanodonus will be short-handed now, but he has harvested his grain, and we all helped with that. There are many hands among us; we can pull together. And what of the cash? The man gave compensation, did he not?'

'You think my mother kept that money?' Tanodonus was furious. 'It has been thrown back at them. We do not think of my brother as a pair of hands. He is strong and keen to work, but he is the light of our lives. My mother dotes on him. Can you not see?' he pleaded. 'This man has done wrong to all of us – not just to my family but to us all. If my father was alive, he would be speaking to you, but he is not here now. Since he passed on, I have done my best to take his place and to protect my family. No neighbour can say we have been a burden to them, but now I come to you and beg for your help. Verluccus has been stolen into slavery – I know it. For what purpose I fear to think. He has done no wrong. Let any among you say he has committed a crime. It is this Roman who has committed the crime, a crime against us all. His wrongdoing threatens you too. If he can take any boy of his desire like this, for no reason and with no protest, what rights do any of you have? Look to protect your own children! Guard them now by making a protest with me against this evil, and help me to recover my brother. If we go to him as a body – if we are prepared to take this to Glevum, even to Corinium – justice will bear out my case, and he will have to return my brother. Please give me your support and help and come with me.'

They argued on. He found it impossible to believe that they could not see it his way. In his anger, he spoke bitterly and disparagingly towards Bodellus. The man refuted his allegations and retorted that he never would have recommended a boy from the family of such a hothead to be so privileged. It was with considerable restraint and greatly to his credit that Bodellus absorbed the insults and allowed Tanodonus to vent his feelings in words and gestures. He would allow neither himself nor his grown sons to physically strike the rash and angry youth.

Finally, when the night was well advanced, wearied by the accusations and encouraged perhaps by the possibility, suggested slyly by his wife, that one of their own children would be a more suitable adoptee, the elder conceded defeat. The following morning, he would accompany Tanodonus to the Roman house and seek an audience with Lucius Marcius. If that failed to secure Verluccus' release or to reassure Tanodonus as to the man's good intentions, then they would take the matter to Glevum and seek a remedy in law. It was less than Tanodonus had hoped for, but at least it was better than nothing.

But even as they dispersed, that plan was being foiled.

3

In Glevum a young and enthusiastic tribune was already active. Decimus Lepidus Aemilius Virens was only twenty years old and embarking upon what was generally agreed must become an illustrious career; he would almost certainly rise to command a legion and, after a senatorial career, probably be entrusted to govern a province. Afterwards, who knew? Such had been the course to the greatest position of all. Such things were not said directly to him, but they had been voiced to his father; and the elder Aemilius had seen the wisdom of the young man departing from the proximity of Rome to begin his career. He had arrived with letters of introduction not only to the commander of the Second Augusta, now at Isca Silurum in the west, but also to an old friend of his father, Lucius Marcius. His disappointment at being posted to the supply garrison which remained at Glevum was alleviated by the discovery that the old friend of his father was not so old and had a very attractive wife and three enchanting children.

Virens had been greatly entertained by Cordatus' account of the day's events at Daruentum, though he did not doubt the necessity of his friend's concern. You never should trust these natives, no matter how much you did for them. And who had done more than Lucius Marcius even in the short time since his arrival? No matter what generosity and goodwill the Romans showed, every village, every settlement, would have its core troublemakers, agitators out to take advantage of any situation, out to inflame the least of grievances or imagined provocations, to magnify the slightest offences beyond all substance. Oh yes, Virens was certain Lucius had every reason to be concerned. Even sleepy Daruentum would have its share of malcontents.

And yet there was that temptation to delay, to give them that little longer to assemble, to rabble-rouse – to give these idle soldiers some real work to do rather than merely to make a show of strength. No, he must not delay. Cordatus had been most insistent, and with the gorgeous Aelia and their children at risk of the merest suggestion of danger, who could blame Lucius for his concern?

Perhaps he should have sent men at once to accompany Cordatus? Was even this interval now subjecting the lovely Aelia to unnecessary peril? Were they in fact already besieged by angry natives? He must move at once; he had delayed too long. Ah, what joy for him to render real service to her delightfulness! He gave the order to rouse the men.

Night had not fully departed when they arrived, and a heavy mist still veiled the hill, giving it an eerie light; it was doubtful that the full impact of their arrival would be appreciated. But if the gleam and rattle of breastplates and weapons was less impressive than intended, Virens made certain that as the column of men breached the forest and set about the business of making camp, even the dead in the village would be aware of his presence.

Tanodonus stood by the door of his hut, hearing the dread sounds of the trumpets and shouts of command and catching an occasional glimpse of gleaming metal. He understood exactly what this meant, why they had come. He felt sick. He knew that Bodellus would do nothing now; that one would know where his best interests lay, and they would not be in interfering with so powerful a man as Lucius Marcius, a man who overnight could command such resources. He laughed bitterly at his foolishness for expecting his neighbours to help; there would be no help forthcoming. He and his mother and brother were on their own. It would fall to him to do what must be done.

'Escaped? What do you mean, escaped? Explain yourself, Victor! Are you saying the boy has run away?' Lucius glowered with disbelief at his overseer, the slave breathless and sweating profusely from the exertion of his run. Lucius had made an early visit to his friend Virens.

It appeared to be the case. The boy had run away – was gone.

'Well?' Lucius barked. 'What else? What has been done to find him? Has a proper search been carried out? Surely it is not beyond your ability to contain one juvenile slave for half a day?' From the distance came the sound of baying hounds. 'Go back! Get those cursed dogs locked up! If the soldiers are to search the countryside, and now it seems they must, I don't want them torn to pieces by those savage brutes.' Nor did he want the boy torn to pieces; the gods alone knew what state Aelia must be in to resort to such measures. He found himself thinking that Palatus would have had a large part in such a decision. He spoke again with a steadier directive. 'Go back to the house and organize a proper search; inform my wife that with Virens' help I shall do what may be done from here and then return to her with no undue delay.'

Victor departed, and Lucius turned to Virens. 'It seems your men are to have a more practical lesson than we had intended for them. I must ask you to send men to search the boy's home and have his father brought here to be questioned.'

Virens smiled at the older man's naivety. 'Oh, no! Forgive me, my dear Lucius, but that won't do. That won't do at all. Allow me to advise on this.' He turned to issue his orders. 'Every hut, every building is to be searched. Search thoroughly and miss nothing. Ignore no animal stall, no grain pit, no basket, no jar, no chest. And look above the cross beams too. If necessary, make use of fire; if it is necessary when you think you have found his hiding place, smoke him out of it.' The man saluted and departed. Virens turned to Lucius. 'You would be surprised, my dear friend, how small a place a fugitive can hide within. The men know what to do; leave it to them. We shall have your runaway back in no time. And we shall have the whole family brought here also, not merely the father.'

'Not the mother. Not the mother. The others, yes. But not his mother. And not fire. Not to burn down their homes!' Lucius was horrified at such a prospect. 'I cannot face his mother,' he admitted privately to his friend.

Virens sighed heavily at this. 'Very well, if you insist, for now, not the mother.' He had the centurion fetched back. 'Leave the mother at home, but question her properly. And just smoke, mark you, not fire. This is not a punitive exercise. Bring the others here – all of them unless they are babes in arms.' He looked quizzically at Lucius for his approval of this before adding, 'Someone from Lucius Marcius' farm will direct you to the right house.' The man left again. Virens' spirits were high. Here was the prospect of a hunt. 'One good thing,' he joked, 'there will be no doubt which one he is, eh?'

Tanodonus had been to the Roman house as he had vowed – alone. Home again, he was given little time to wallow in the misery of failure and the discovery of what an abject coward he really was.

At the gate he had been brave enough, demanding, not requesting, to speak to the owner. 'My business is with Lucius Marcius,' he had declared, and the porter had grinned knowingly and pointed to the encampment of soldiers.

Tanodonus had stood for a long, long time, debating inside himself what to do. He knew the man to be callous and ruthless and cruel. He had already deprived Carantua of one of her sons. How would she and Colymmon fare if he also was taken from them? The price was too high. After much heart searching, he had turned away and gone home to weep at his cowardice and beg his mother's forgiveness – which she readily had given. Carantua sought to console him, to reassure him, to praise him for his prudence. But her words gave him no comfort. He prayed to the gods to make him a wiser and braver son and brother; and into the sparkling waters of the rushing stream he tossed his father's golden ring, for he was now not fit to wear it.

And it seemed as if the gods had heard his prayer. When the

soldiers burst in upon them and they learned the reason their home was being ransacked and threatened with a torching, they were strangely comforted. But it was a short-lived comfort.

Carantua threw herself screaming upon them, pleaded with them, wept, and tore at her hair. But they took Tanodonus all the same. One of them stood guard over her when they had done with their questioning. 'Orders', he said brusquely, 'from the tribune.' The tribune did not wish to see her – would not see her. She was to remain where she was or not expect to have this one returned.

'What is this?' asked Lucius in disbelief. A single youth had been marched into the command tent and placed before them. 'One only?' So much for Aelia's ideas about the fecundity of the native families. 'Where is your father?'

'There was only him and the mother there, Tribune.' It was the centurion who spoke, addressing Virens. 'You said not to bring her.' The youth had been released to stand freely. He was a tall and good-looking blue-eyed lad. His fair skin and reddish-yellow hair had caught the sun, and every inch of him declared him to be a farmer. That he was impressed by the uniforms and his surroundings was pleasingly evident.

A scribe was set to record the details. Virens spoke first, but Lucius translated for them.

'State you name, status, and age.'

'I am Tanodonus, a farmer, son of Cunobarrus and Carantua. I am in my eighteenth year.'

'Your father? Where is he? And where is the rest of your family?'

'My father has been dead more than two years. I have two older brothers who left home some years ago, and we have no news of them. I do not know where they are now.' He frowned, trying to establish which of the two men was Lucius Marcius. He supposed it must be the elder of the two, the one in civilian dress whose hair was black and sleek and whose dark eyes were hard and piercing. The other, some years his junior, was taller and more lightly built. His hair was lighter in colour, mid-brown and wavy. They both looked equally unpleasant, haughty, hostile, and arrogant; theirs were the faces of men who took for granted their possession of all things and all places. These were not the friendly faces of the soldiers and traders with whom he was familiar. He had been on good terms with such soldiers, very cordial terms, had drunk with them, gamed with them. His father had welcomed them into their home when he was alive, and Tanodonus had done the same since then. But no more, not ever again, not after this experience – should he survive it. One thing he saw with clarity now: those brothers, Barr and Cadrus, had been right; Romans were not to be trusted. They had been absolutely right and he and his father most horribly wrong.

'Who comes between you and the young one?' Lucius refused to accept that this was the extent of the family.

'Verluccus is next after me; he is the boy you have stolen from us. Others were born between us, but they did not live. Our mother is an old woman now.'

'You are lying!' It was a stab in the dark from Virens, but it found its mark, for the youth's unguarded eyes betrayed him. The centurion stepped forward and spoke to the tribune quietly.

'You keep sheep!' barked the same tribune again. 'Who watches them?'

'He can be of no assistance to you, my lord.' The voice trembled in defeat.

'I shall be the judge of that. I asked you who he is. Answer me!'

Tanodonus knew further prevarication was hopeless. 'He too is my brother. He is older than me by two years.'

'I advise you not to be clever with me!' snapped Lucius as the young man glanced involuntarily towards the close-cropped hilltop rising above his own home; the cloud was lifting, and the scattered remnants of abandoned and derelict buildings could be seen.

'Fetch him here and search those shacks.' Virens spoke in Latin to the centurion, but Tanodonus guessed his instruction.

'No, no, please. Please, my lord, don't. He cannot help you.'

'So that is where he hides!' Lucius scented victory. The concerned expression convinced him his hunt was over. He bade the soldier wait; the youth had more to say.

'Sir, my lord, I honestly do not know where my young brother is, but I do not expect him to be there. It is an obvious place for your men to look, among the ruins of our forebears' huts. He is not such a fool as to go there. I am sure he is not.' Some insight directed him to appeal to Lucius. 'I am sorry I lied to you, my lord. I truly do not know where Verluccus is; it is Colymmon I seek to protect. If you send your men for him, he will not come, and they will take him by force and injure him, perhaps kill him. Colymmon will only abandon his sheep if I tell him to. Allow me to go for him; there will be no trickery.'

'So there is another tiger in your family?' Lucius knew he was smirking and disliked himself for it.

'Fetch him!' Virens snarled, impatient at all the delay, but he was forced to detain his men as, with a courage he thought he did not possess, Tanodonus recklessly stepped between them and their exit from the tent. He was unceremoniously dumped onto the floor. From there, with Virens' permission, he clambered to his feet and appealed again.

'My lord, Colymmon is no tiger.' Tanodonus was unsure what a tiger was but guessed it to be something wild and angry. 'He is a gentle, quiet man. But he is simple-minded. Though he is a grown man, his mind is that of a child. He will be of no use to you. If you want him here, let me go with your men and he will come passively.'

'So be it.' Virens could tell from his friend's expression it was what Lucius wished. 'On your return, we shall question you. Your concern for this Colymmon may encourage you to think more lucidly.'

It took almost an hour for the party to return with the shepherd, during which time Lucius received no good news and grew increasingly anxious. The search was spreading over a wider area. It was ludicrous that one child could evade so many trained men; he must be receiving help from some quarter. How Gaius would cope with this he dared not think. How fortunate he was that he could rely on Cordatus to take care of the family during his absence. Yes, better to remain here and see this business through.

In the intervening period, Virens had taken the opportunity

to advise his friend on how they should approach the interview. Lucius was now seated behind the writing table; Virens lounged as if carelessly on a bench in the corner of the tent.

The youth had not exaggerated; the shepherd was indeed a simpleton. The round, happy, boyish face ill befitted the manly body. A child he was, quite unconscious of the gravity of his predicament. Yes, he might well have refused to come without his brother's encouragement. A few simple questions confirmed what they had been told, and – again with much reassurance from Tanodonus – he was persuaded to wait outside.

Lucius began the interrogation badly, and he knew it.

'Your brother, this Verluccus – he belongs to me now. If you know where he is or assist his escape, you put yourself beyond the law. I charge you now to tell me exactly where he is, if you know, or where you think he may be, in order that I may recover him.'

'So,' replied Tanodonus, hearing himself speak in a voice more controlled than he would have supposed possible, 'your "adopted son" is no more than your slave! I guessed as much. What law permits you to steal a child not yet eleven years who has offended no one? I see no reason for me to assist in his recapture.' The older man had confirmed his identity as Lucius Marcius.

Ten, not twelve as he had supposed – the same age as poor dead Lucius. He was a tall lad indeed, well grown for his years. Lucius did no more than commit the fact to his memory. He leaned forward and stared into the youth's face. 'Do not suppose I would hesitate to use that simpleton to persuade you to become more helpful. There are men here who would soon have him squealing! But consider instead the boy's plight. He is foolish to run away from me. He would be well cared for in my household, raised and educated at my expense, a companion for my little son. A better life, I think, than he might otherwise expect.'

He saw at once half of the anxiety on the young face before him dissolve and yield to profound relief. The greatest fear which had tormented Tanodonus was that his brother had been taken for some vile, unspeakable purpose. Lucius saw the change but, unlike Virens, had no immediate inkling of what it signified.

'I cannot help you, my lord.' He almost wished now that he could, though he could not hide his bitterness. 'I do not think he will return to his home. It has not proved a safe place for him in the past.'

'You must know many places where he might hide. Places in which you amused yourself as a child.' Lucius supposed a British childhood to be a wild and unschooled experience.

'Indeed, yes. Here is one such place.' Tanodonus swept his hand in a gesture to indicate the place of the encampment. 'This was my haunt.' He laughed bitterly. 'I used to play at soldiers here. But for Verluccus, it has always been the stream and the trees below your farm. He has perhaps caused some offence to the spirits of that place to have this calamity heaped upon him; but I tell you now, if he should die of it, I pray to those same spirits that you never again have a restful night and in your waking hours you are forever haunted by this evil work which you have done.'

Lucius considered him for a while. 'You speak boldly. You do not appear to be afraid of me, but I advise you not to let that tongue of yours run away with you. Your mother would be in poor straits with only that one left.' He jerked his thumb to indicate the excluded Colymmon. 'I could easily find some excuse for your dying.'

'That would indeed be a noble victory for you!' cried the boy, making a further discovery about his courage. 'No, I am not afraid of you, despite your contempt for the laws you claim to uphold. I am a farmer; I grow my quota of corn and wool, and I pay my dues. Rome has more to gain by my being alive than from my death at the hands of a tyrant.' He stopped in dismay, appalled at his own temerity. Surely he had gone too far now?

'Tyrant?' It was a novel experience for a man accustomed to being named Softy to hear himself called a tyrant; even his most disappointed petitioner confined himself to the sarcastic misuse of the name Mollis as an insult.

'Were I that tyrant, those would be the last word you uttered. To speak to me so boldly in this situation takes courage; I commend courage. You have the makings of a good Roman, I think.' He nodded approvingly.

Tanodonus could only stare at him in disbelief. He supposed
the man intended this as a compliment rather than the affront that it
was, but wisely he held his tongue. He looked towards the tribune,
who had remained silent during this interrogation; he now was
convulsed in barely stifled laughter. Supposing himself to be the
object of some ridicule, Tanodonus felt his face redden with anger
and embarrassment.

'You may go now,' Lucius informed him. 'And take that poor fool
with you. I shall have you here again if my men suspect you have
been deceiving me.'

He watched the brothers embrace and walk out of the camp,
comforted each by the arms of the other. They made at once for their
home. It was a perfectly understandable course; neither Lucius nor
Virens was farmer enough to wonder about the shepherd who did not
immediately return to his flock.

Even before the tent flap had closed upon them, Virens surrendered
to the hysteria he had fought so long to contain.

'Oh, Lucius, you are priceless! Did you see his face when you
told him he would make a good Roman? I thought then he was going
to strike you! And did you note the change that came about when
you said the boy was intended as a companion for Gaius? You know
what he had supposed, don't you? You, of all people!' and his laughter
continued unabated.

'Yes,' said the other sadly. 'It came to me; I could not put my
finger on it immediately. I could cheerfully kill Palatus for putting me
in this position. It never occurred to me he would make such a mess
of things. I honestly wish I could say to that young man, "When we
find your brother, he may go home." But that can never be – not with
that vile mark upon him.'

'And if we do not regain him? What of Gaius? What of him?'

'If we do not find the boy alive, I pray Gaius will cope with it.'
The alternative could not be contemplated. Neither he nor Aelia had
yet come to terms with the loss of their firstborn son, who was buried
far away in Rome; to lose another would surely cost them both their
sanity. 'I must go home now and make offerings for Gaius' health

and the speedy discovery of this Verluccus boy. I shall expect you later to bathe and dine?'

It was an invitation gladly accepted. But Virens needed a matter to be settled. He walked towards the tree line with his friend, scanning the countryside around them for tell-tale movement, with no reward.

'Lucius …' he began with a diffidence he was not noted for. 'I need to know what action to take if you – if you find you no longer have need of this brat?'

'If I am to have no son,' said Lucius dismally, 'then I have no wish ever to see that boy again.'

'Then you need say no more; I understand exactly. But take heart. Go home now, and may the gods give you better tidings.' Virens raised a hand in farewell; he returned to his camp to receive only blank reports and to encourage his men to renewed effort.

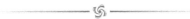

Tanodonus and Colymmon went together to fetch the sheep. They were followed, of course, by one of Virens' men, and while Colymmon continued upwards to recover his charges from the guarding dogs, Tanodonus stepped aside to enter a narrow limestone crevice, a cleft in the hillside known to the family as Colymmon's cave because the shepherd used it as a shelter. On the ledge he concealed a cake of corn bread, and he almost collided with the soldier as he turned away to scramble up the bank and join Colymmon on the hilltop.

'An offering to Earth Mother for my brother's safe return,' Tanodonus said by way of explanation.

The soldier grinned knowingly. He settled himself for a patient vigil. In a few hours, he would be rewarded; it would fall to him to bear the runaway triumphantly before his tribune.

The sheep were safely driven home and enfolded for the night. It was a sad little family that settled around their fire, wondering where Verluccus might now be and whether they would ever see him again.

49

Belanius and Brutha with their tribe of children had come to meet the brothers. The man was ashamed that he had not been more supportive of Tanodonus in his argument with Bodellus and had been soundly berated for it by his wife. The arrival of the soldiers had confirmed Tanodonus' warning. They walked together to Carantua and helped her to straighten her home. But Bodellus did not come; nor did any member of his family. On the contrary, he had promised the centurion, that he, as elder of the community, would personally have the boy taken to Lucius Marcius as soon as he came to light. On this he could rely. The soldier, despite this avowal of loyalty, was unimpressed; he spat on the floor and left that farm in no better condition than he had its neighbours.

4

There was a far more cheerful party at the Roman house that night, for Lucius had found on his return that he was now even more deeply indebted to the loyal Cordatus. There had, of course, been tears, the freedman told him; all of the children had sobbed their little eyes out, 'but Gaius bravely dried his tears, and I carried him to the shrine, well wrapped up because of his poor disposition; he seemed to draw strength from the visit. There he offered prayers and sacrifices, first to Fortuna the Home Bringer (a pigeon seemed appropriate) and then to Fortuna who Protects (again a pigeon) to invoke the goddess's aid in recovering that which was lost or, if that is not to be, then to take care of him and protect him. He stood there so forlorn as the smoke curled upwards that my heart grieved for him. I went to comfort him, but he waved me away and stood in silent contemplation, quite absorbed, watching the smoke curling upwards. When he withdrew, he was so much changed, so much reassured, and then he calmly announced to me that the slave was safe and one day would be restored to him. I was astonished by the transformation.'

'Does this mean he knows where the boy is?' Lucius was baffled – and angry.

'I don't see how he can. It was weird – quite uncanny.' Cordatus frowned, still puzzled by the event. 'It is impossible that he could know the whereabouts of the boy. Victor had reasoned that a taste of hard labour under the builder would make the lad more appreciative of Gaius, easier to train and grateful for the relief, so he had put him to work under Macrinius. He disappeared from the building site well

51

before Gaius was ready to receive him. They could not possibly have met.'

'Who has been punished?' Someone undoubtedly must be for this disaster.

'Only Placidus, and not for that. The boy was under Macrinius' supervision when he made off.' There was no question of punishing the builder; both of them knew how hard it was to find a reliable man. 'You may feel that Victor is to blame – he certainly blames himself – but to flog him would be harsh; he awaits your ruling and has sworn to beat himself severely if that is your wish. No, Placidus got a beating from Aelia for attacking her garden. He had some idea that the boy was hiding among the vegetation and set about the plants with a stave. You may imagine your wife's reaction to that, especially since Rufus had been working there for the whole of the morning and could confirm that the boy had not entered it. Aelia wants rid of Placidus. She is very angry with him. In fact,' Cordatus added, knowing that it was Lucius' intention that this particular young slave should be trained up to serve him personally, 'she insists upon it.'

'You may tell Victor that I do not hold him responsible. I know he is not careless with my property. And tell him also that Placidus is to be employed on the farm for the time being; keep him out of the house. When I learn of a suitable place, I shall sell him, unless Aelia has a change of heart. And Palatus? What of Palatus? Has he been dealt with?'

'Aelia has not advised me of her decision,' Cordatus told him.

Lucius' briefing had taken place apart from the others. The welfare of Gaius and Aelia had been his chief concern, and now that his biggest fear was allayed, he happily welcomed their guest.

The arrival of Virens at Glevum had brought a new and amusing addition to their small circle of friends. His gallant and open adoration of Aelia had quickly made him her favourite too. Lucius regarded this with detached amusement; it did not threaten his marriage or his fondness for the young man, and he treated the exaggerated courtship of his wife with the greatest tolerance and good humour.

The tribune was commonly considered a handsome young man;

his face was lean and well boned and his physique finely athletic. If he had a flaw, one might say it was in his strangely green eyes, dark as olives. From this feature he had derived the surname Virens. He was witty, well informed, and a good raconteur – unfailingly the perfect guest. He was, of course, aware of his good looks. How could he not be when they were so openly admired? But he managed to shoulder that burden with a commendable lack of vanity, and he devoted himself to pleasure and service to his emperor in equal measure. The companionship of Lucius' family he regarded as a privilege, and from the first of many visits, he had become as one of the family. For the opportunity to share their table, he would gladly have excused himself from many less engaging commitments.

Secure in the knowledge that Gaius had suffered no relapse, the two men relaxed in the sweating heat of Lucius' bathing rooms.

'It is not so surprising to me,' Virens said, feeling sure he understood the situation exactly. 'I have a young half-brother. Glaucus is his name, for unlike me, his eyes are blue – from his mother, my father's second wife. He is a charming little man and greatly doted on by all who meet him. The result of this is that he is refused nothing he craves. But it is often the case with him that no sooner is his desire satisfied and he is pacified with the thing demanded than he has no further interest in it and looks again for something new. He is a child, and it is a childish trait. You did right to appease Gaius, but now his health is on the mend, that craving no longer exists.'

Lucius shook his head, still bewildered. 'But Gaius is not like that. This reaction is most unlike him. My son is a stubborn little fellow. When he sets his mind on something, he will not be turned, and he guards his treasures closely. I do not understand this change of mind.'

'Then do not resist but be grateful to the gods for it.' Virens paused, strigil in hand. He looked his friend directly in the eye. 'Take guidance from your son: you are well rid of that boy. A nod from you to me, and he will trouble you no more.'

—————— ৩ ——————

Gaius was allowed to wait up until his father came to the triclinium. He was very tired and did not protest about his removal after he had received kisses from both the men. On this occasion, both Marcia and Gaia remained, reclining in quite grown-up style.

That was the nicest thing about Lepidus Aemilius Virens, Gaia decided, for when other guests dined, the children were banished elsewhere. But if Virens alone was present, he insisted that he wished to be part of the family, and he would tell stories which children could understand and patiently play board games with them. Now he was even allowing her to snuggle up next to him on the dining couch, which Marcia said was shocking behaviour. Marcia had taken advantage of Gaius' absence to recline on the couch next to Cordatus.

Gaia liked the smell of Virens; he had used her father's bath oils and smelled sweet and clean – of rosemary. She pressed herself close to his body, and he tolerantly eased himself beside her. She turned her melting eyes to the exciting visitor and gazed full into his face, fluttering long, black eyelashes and pouting her lips to invite a kiss. He cuddled her with amused pleasure and fed her choice titbits. She whispered to him, 'Are you married, Lepidus Aemilius Virens?'

He had to admit that he was not.

'Nor am I married.' She grinned impishly.

He gravely acknowledged that he knew this to be the case and fed her a spoonful of honeyed custard. Aelia was ready to reprimand her, scandalized that her own young daughter could behave so badly, but Lucius just laughed and allowed the interesting exchange to continue.

'Will you wait for me to marry you when I am bigger?'

Aelia half rose to her feet and would have taken hold of the girl, but Lucius signalled her not to intervene.

Virens grinned and tickled her and kissed her gleaming dark curls. 'When you are old enough to be married, you will look at me and say to yourself, "Why does Father make me marry such an ugly old man?" and there will be a much nicer young man whom you will have in mind when that time comes.'

'No, I shall not,' she said. 'I want to marry you.'

'But what of your elder sister? Marcia might wish to marry me,' he teased. 'Perhaps I ought to offer myself first to her?' He smiled at the solemn girl and winked.

Virens was teasing them; Marcia knew it. Even so, it was with much trepidation that she looked at her father. He would not really do that to her, would he? What should she say if her father thought this was a good idea? He was looking from her to her mother in a worryingly thoughtful way.

Aelia, knowing more than Lucius in this respect, knew she must speak up. She cleared her throat. 'Dearest, I have been meaning to speak to you concerning Marcia. I had not expected to have to do so quite so soon. Our elder daughter lacks none of the resourcefulness of her sister. She too has determined whom she will marry.'

Lucius made a rueful sign of abject surrender. He warned his friend, 'You see how it is in my household, Virens? I am ruled by these women. Take heed and be advised by my plight.' He turned to his wife, growling in mock severity, 'And to whom do you propose to marry our eldest girl, who is all of nine years old?'

'You will recall young Publius Julius Calvus who has moved to Corinium with his parents. His mother assured me that her husband would speak to you. It seems that a strong affection has grown between the children – and there has been correspondence.'

The truth of this remark was written in Marcia's blushes.

Lucius considered the idea and was content. He had not been approached by the lad's father but could not take such a match amiss. 'If his father should speak to me on the subject, I would not be displeased.' He nodded to Aelia and then turned to Virens. 'You are freed from the one; now extricate yourself from the other,' he challenged.

Virens laughed. 'I might not wish to,' he announced, kissing his adorer full on the lips, and laughed again as she scrubbed them with the palm of her hand. 'Indeed, Lucius, since Aelia is spoken for, I would be honoured to be the husband of her daughter.'

'I would be as glad to have you as a son-in-law as any man,' announced Lucius and looked at Aelia. Would she agree to this?

She studied Gaia and Virens. 'They could be betrothed,' she said finally. 'If Virens would agree to wait until she is of marriageable age. I would be delighted to have such a connection. I just hope that Gaia will not regret this whim when she is older.'

'I give you my word,' the young man answered, 'that I will not force her to marry me against her will. When she is of age, I shall seek her out, but I will not hold her to any promise made in her tender years. I only know that if she grows up to be in any manner like her mother, no man could desire a better wife.'

Delia came at Aelia's bidding and lifted the child to take her and Marcia to their bed.

'See how unimpressed she is,' observed Virens ruefully. 'Already I bore her and have driven her to sleep.' He rose and stretched his limbs. 'I too should go. If you have no objection, I shall look in on Gaius, though he also may be sleeping now.'

'By all means,' said Lucius, 'but mind your feet. Felix is asleep on the floor; take care you do not stumble over him.'

There was a bundle on the floor in the small cubicle; Virens trod carefully around it and stroked Gaius' pale forehead. He bent and kissed him goodnight and silently stepped outside.

Lucius was waiting for him. 'That is the most restful sleep he has had for well over a month. Did you see how pale and thin he has become? About that other business: I think there would be no harm done if the boy did not return here. If you would deal with that, I should be greatly in your debt.'

'Be assured,' said Virens. 'Concern yourself no more. Do not give the matter another thought. What needs to be done shall be done. Now I must return to my men. Bid goodnight to Aelia for me.' Aelia was tucking her daughters into their bed.

Cordatus, close at hand, caught his breath, but he did not say anything. He was at heart a good man, but he had a favour of his own to beg of Lucius and would not help himself by challenging what he knew must be a most painful decision. He was forever afterwards ashamed of himself for his silence.

5

—— ⟋⟍ ——

'Do you have business in Glevum today, my darling? When do you go there next?' his wife asked Lucius the following morning.

'I am in no great hurry, unless you wish me away,' he answered dryly, giving a knowing glance in the direction of Virens' encampment. 'Do you have some design in ridding yourself of my presence?'

She made a face, amused by his response, but spoke in a more serious tone. 'My only design is that you wished me to punish Palatus, and the penalty I have settled on is that he must sell Melissa. I thought you could take her up with you. It is no great matter except that your own maxim is that any punishment should be executed without undue delay.'

'It seems a curious punishment,' he said, genuinely failing to comprehend her reasoning. 'Has the girl given offence in some way, committed some misdemeanour I have not noticed? I had it in mind that Palatus should be whipped for his actions.'

'And who would do it?' his wife demanded. 'And what respect would Palatus command in the household afterwards? No. He values this girl. It is true that he won her playing dice, but he does value her. He will consider himself quite deprived by her departure. He at least considers himself cruelly used by me. He will not gain from the sale either, for you shall have whatever price she fetches.'

'I had not intended to return there quite so soon, but a punishment should be carried out promptly.' He turned again to his freedman. 'Cordatus,' he said, 'it seems that you must again make that journey but this time to Glevum market.'

If Lucius was surprised by his wife's idea of a fitting punishment

57

for her steward, an illuminating conversation with Cordatus, who had drawn him aside, positively staggered him. As a result, he was obliged to address Aelia again on the same subject.

'My dear, this Melissa girl – do you have any personal objection to her being here, or are you merely sending her away to deprive Palatus of her?'

'Lucius, it was you who insisted I punish the fellow. I certainly do not find her presence objectionable; she is clean and capable but nothing more, a common chit. Palatus had the sauce to suggest she might make a maid for Marcia. But she has the appearance which pleases men, and she will make a good return; he will certainly suffer loss of both her and her value. Cordatus will see to it that he does not get a penny.' She smiled and nodded at the freedman.

'Then you have no objection to her remaining in the household but belonging to another?'

'Belonging to whom? What are you suggesting? I have told you she is not fit to be Marcia's maid. I really don't understand you, Lucius. I punish Palatus to please you, and now you seek to undermine me. If she remains in the house, Palatus will exercise his authority and have her in his bed again in no time. She has to go.'

'It is Cordatus who has asked me to intercede. He has, I think, more authority than Palatus,' Lucius said mildly, entertained by the image evoked.

'Cordatus?' Aelia laughed at the idea, but it was a laugh of pleasure, not of mockery, for she was genuinely fond of the freedman. 'But Melissa?' Sheer disbelief entered her voice. 'Would she be faithful to him? He is so old. Why, he must be forty-four at the very least.'

'More faithful to him than she has been to Palatus from what I hear.' Lucius grinned.

In huge delight, Aelia looked across at the freedman, who, most oddly, had been hovering in a self-conscious manner near the window. He blushed deeply, which delighted her still more. 'Why, Cordatus, you old rogue! For how long has this been going on?'

'A little while,' he admitted. 'I am truly fond of the girl, my lady, and she is, I believe, equally fond of me.' He used formality as a shield against his embarrassment. 'As far as I am aware, Palatus does not suspect her. I think she would have suffered had he done so.' He hesitated before continuing. 'I should like very much to give her freedom and marry her, if that were possible.'

'No, Cordatus, I do not think that is a good idea.' She said it as kindly as she was able to, finding it hard to credit that Melissa would return his feelings and remain faithful to him. 'But buy her? Why not? I agree. You may purchase her and keep her. Lucius must estimate a fair price.'

'You had better have Palatus bring the girl here now,' said Lucius. 'Aelia is right; it is too soon to think of freeing her.' To his wife he said, 'Do not let that man get his hands on her when I needs must take Cordatus out with me. Your close supervision of her would be a kindness to him.'

'I shall do my best, but if the girl finds she prefers the former master to the latter, we may face difficulties. But I think Palatus will accept it; after all, were he truly in love with her, he would have taken a flogging rather than suffer her loss.' She blushed as she realized she had admitted to her husband that some negotiation had taken place as to the steward's punishment, and he nodded grimly but let it pass.

'Palatus is right about one thing though,' she told him, changing the subject. 'I must do something about a maid for Marcia. Delia really has far too much to do with three children to attend to. I shall write to Mother and ask her to send us a suitable girl – a Greek, I think; these local girls are really quite useless.'

He was left no time to dwell upon the expense this would incur as Cordatus returned with Palatus and Melissa. She was dressed ready to travel, with a cloak over the green gown which Palatus had decreed she must wear. It would show her off to advantage to a prospective purchaser and enhance her price; he retained a hope that the cash would find its way back to him.

'I have consented that Cordatus shall buy the girl,' Lucius announced. 'Her price is agreed between us, and now you must hand her over to him.'

On entering the room, Melissa had genuflected to the master

and mistress, her eyes cast down but her face composed so that she betrayed no emotion. Now she gasped convulsively and swayed as if she might faint. Aelia was fearful that hysteria would follow, but the girl composed herself and bowed her head even lower.

Concealing his own feelings rather better, Palatus bowed and left the room. The girl looked up at her new master. Now her face was radiant; her cheeks were wet with emotion. Cordatus took her into his arms and kissed her passionately, and there was no doubting the sincerity of her response. This was a very different girl from the silently efficient creature they were accustomed to; now she was alive with unconcealed happiness. The transformation shook both Lucius and his wife. Each was thinking, *I never realised how beautiful she is.*

'I think, Cordatus, we should know how this was accomplished,' Lucius chided him mildly.

'Gladly I will tell you. When I first set eyes upon Melissa, the very day Palatus brought her here, I knew I was hopelessly lost, but I kept my thoughts and desires private; my age was such that so lovely a young girl could not possibly have come willingly to me. And so it might have continued – ' He was not permitted to finish the sentence.

'Were it not for that vase. I broke a vase,' the girl confessed.

The slave had clearly cast caution to the winds, noted Aelia. Cordatus would have to remind her of her status. 'What vase?' The only recent damage to a vase had been done by Cordatus in a clumsy moment. He had readily been forgiven.

'Palatus had a large ceramic urn,' said the girl.

'A Greek urn from Alexandria,' the freedman corrected her. 'But you tell it.'

'Palatus owned – I thought it was his – this large urn, and when I accidentally knocked it over and it smashed into a thousand pieces, I knew I was in for a whipping. There was no remedy that I could see – no way that I could repair it. I could only dread his return.'

She looked to Cordatus for assistance, and he happily took up the story. 'Palatus was on an errand for you in Glevum. I heard this poor girl sobbing and went into his room. It was plain to see what had happened, but it was some little while before she would hear how I could help her.'

Aelia saw it at once. 'So you put its good twin from your quarters into the room of Palatus and placed the broken pieces in your own! That, I think, Cordatus, must be the naughtiest deception you have ever practised.'

'No, lady, I fear it is not!' Lucius was enjoying this. 'Continue – we will hear more.'

'I was very grateful.' The girl was blushing profusely.

'Melissa offered me the only thing she could, that which she had no right to give and I had no right to take, but when I kissed her … then we both knew my first instinct was right; we were intended for each other. I do regret my deception of Palatus, but I saw no likelihood of his accommodating me and selling her to me.'

'And now he has been forced to do so.' It was Melissa who spoke, but she voiced the thoughts of all. Aelia felt moved to reassure the freedman.

'He will get over that. He did not love Melissa as you do; she was a prize he had won at gaming, nothing more. Do not fret over that.'

'You may use the *bigarum* and take Melissa to our rooms in Glevum if you wish. I shall be along in a few days.' The loan of the small two-horse chariot was a generous offer from Lucius, and he added drolly, 'But, by Hercules, do not spend the whole time mooning around like some young lover. I still depend on you to do my work!' They were released to make preparations for their journey.

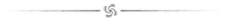

'What has happened in this place?' Lucius asked his wife as they waved them away. 'Have we been trifled with by the gods? Why have we been subjected to all this commotion? Was all of this turmoil – our second son rendered near to death, that boy tortured, his unhappy family destroyed – merely for Cupid's amusement? Did I promise my eldest girl to a boy of fourteen and my youngest, a child barely six, to a man of twenty? Was all of that necessary simply for my celibate Cordatus to take a honeymoon?'

'Perhaps it was,' she answered, smiling. 'Be happy for Cordatus.'

They returned to the house. From a room within, they could hear the children laughing and chattering together. She felt a deep sense of relief and gratitude. Only one thing could mar it. She turned to her husband.

'I don't want that boy back here, Lucius. Gaius has taken the loss far better than we could have dreamed. I fear that his return would cause only greater distress to our darling child. Can you not do something to prevent it?'

He held her closely to him, sickened by the words he heard himself say. 'You need have no fear of that; you won't see him again. Virens will attend to what is necessary.' And he comforted himself by the thought, *He is in the hands of Fortuna now; if this was done by her, or by Cupid, or by any of them, let them take care of him.*

BOOK II

NINE YEARS LATER, DEEP IN THE MOUNTAINS OF WESTERN BRITAIN

1

'No prisoners' had been the order of the day. 'There will be no prisoners, and none are to go free. Your task is to destroy them all – to leave none alive. Your purpose here is to rid this land of these murderous parasites, to cleanse and purify this ground with their blood. And do not fear that they have any god-given power when they resist; we are brought here by our gods to send them to their other world and to make this one the better for their leaving it. Nor will you hesitate for the sake of age or sex. Remember instead the innocent, those whom they have slaughtered. Remember the crimes which they have committed, and remember those who cry to you for vengeance. They hide in this place like vermin. They have thought themselves secure, but here they are trapped and here they are to die. Your endeavours this day will be fairly rewarded; have no fear of that. They await their fate. Go now, and in the name of our beloved emperor Trajan, deliver it to them.'

Then came one exception: 'But', he said, 'Cunobarrus – the man who finds Cunobarrus alive, to any degree alive, may bring him to me. If dead, his head alone will suffice. His only. Bring me no other.'

So he sent them off. He had made no promise, offered no reward, but those who knew him also knew him to be a man of his word, generous both with stick and with carrot. There might be no slaves to sell, but other booty, goods and livestock, would be apportioned all the same.

The wise did not grumble.

They carried out his orders with their customary enthusiasm, efficiency, and thoroughness. It was true there were some among them who hesitated at what they had to do and needed some encouragements – threats, even: the tactful reminder from a centurion's cudgel of who they were, why they were there, and what their oath required of them. It was a good lesson in battle craft for the youngsters. It became, as he had anticipated, a testimony to their dedication and attention to detail, and underfoot the ground became sodden, a swamp of mud and blood; and the enemy corpses quickly had outnumbered their own.

The assignment was completed. He received the report with mixed feelings. Now all that remained was to recover the wounded and commend the dead, not neglecting to heap generous praise on those to whom it was due. Their own wounded to be recovered, their own dead to be mourned, of course; the others were to rot where they had fallen, a cardinal lesson to any who might seek to emulate their filthy crimes. Not that there were any to view this scene. Here was a place to which no legitimate tribe laid claim – the Ordovices, the Cornovii, the Demetae, and even the Silures had never considered it worth fighting over. It was too remote, too desolate, too unearthly in its savage beauty, a place where only the outcasts of civilization – robbers, runaway slaves, and the scum of the earth, those rejected by their own kinsmen – would elect to dwell and where no innocent settler or peaceful native would wish to live.

He had ignored the beauty of its wildness with its sweeping mountain backdrop not only because of his single-minded purpose but also because shafting rain pelted them relentlessly as if even the gods of that place presumed to defy the rule of the Olympians. And now it was over, only the strange and terrible beauty of heroism and death was to be seen. Twisted bodies barely clad were strewn everywhere, some not yet dead, and strange unhuman wails and pitiful cries mingled with the shouts of his own men going about their business, delivering aid and succour to their own wounded and passage to the next world to the criminals not yet departed from this. He heard the cries impassively; he had long since inured himself to such sounds, though for many of the younger men it would be a new and terrible experience.

He turned to the tribune at his side. 'The cohorts performed well,' he commented as the successes were reported to him. He had known that they would, of course, but it was a satisfaction to him nonetheless. Spanish they were, ideal in this hilly, mountainous terrain. The enemy had fought hard but hopelessly; the outcome could not have been otherwise. 'They may drill for days on end; they may practise interminably with weapons, wooden or real; they may even experience easy kills when there are prisoners to be disposed of; but when it comes down to it, there is nothing like the taste of a real battle to test a man's resolve. To be confronted by one who intends to kill you if you do not first kill him – there is the true test. That is the trouble with too much peace; it softens men up. Where would our empire be if men lost the craft of soldiering?'

He deferred with good humour when the tribune offered the opinion that to glorify this encounter as a battle was an exaggeration; it was merely an eradication. He laughed heartily with the others at the fine joke.

'Eradication – yes, I like that. An eradication.'

He watched and waited, expressing none of the amazement he felt as he saw the heap of trinkets, gold, silver, and bronze grow ever larger in the corner of his headquarters tent, telling his companions that he had anticipated no less; they were, after all, dealing with a den of thieves. But the news he really wanted to hear – that the robber chief had been found, dead or living, did not come. When his patience was exhausted, he went himself to look, stamping through the ruined stronghold, gazing in disgust at the naked and semi-naked warrior corpses, irked by the lack of certainty, though how it could have been otherwise he did not know. 'Some fool has surely stripped him of his jewellery, and now his carcass is indistinguishable from those of his followers. If only my singing birds had not been allowed to die, I would have marched them around and around until they showed him to me.'

He returned to the pile of spoils to pick it over and lament aloud that one too many of the scum had fled to his other world too soon.

'I'm thinking it's a pity they no vultures in this land,' one wag observed as he helped drag yet another of the enemy dead aside in the search. 'Think of the trouble they could save us.' He had a thick Iberian accent, difficult to understand.

'Who needs vultures?' His companion nodded towards the waiting raven and cheerfully stripped another corpse of its baubles before kicking it out of his path. Suddenly he caught sight of the one he was searching for. 'Centurion! 'Ere! We 'ave 'im! Over 'ere!'

The centurion saw at once that it was true. They had found him, and he was dead.

They had feared it must be so. A mad and reckless act it had been to plunge so far ahead, so eager, so unwise. He had encouraged his men by example, but it had not been his place to charge his reluctant cohort into the thick of it. That brave and handsome face which had teased and laughed and stolen so many female hearts was stilled and sober, his ready smile a firm line of determination set in a pallid mould. The green eyes, glazed and lifeless, stared into eternity, and the soldier bent down and closed them respectfully. The despatching sword was still within him, as it had been abandoned, pinning him to the ground. What malevolent spirit had allowed this parting of his cuirass? What powerful arm had breached it? The arm, no doubt, of the corpse lying beside him, for even as he died Virens or another for him had wreaked revenge, and they had had to shove the brute aside before they could recover their own. The auxiliary viciously kicked at the huge frame, and it rolled over, betraying a fearsome skull wound.

Yet amazingly, a groan escaped the savage's lips, and the blood poured afresh from the gaping fissure. The soldier raised his sword and would have smashed it into the brute with the greatest satisfaction had not he been peremptorily thrust aside as the centurion stooped to examine the dying one more closely.

'What's goin' on?' the first comer protested. 'You want 'im for yourself?' He shrugged and stepped back.

'Look,' said the centurion, 'look at this mark. Here, on his shoulder. D'ye see what it is? Now tell me, where've you seen that before?'

The soldier peered through the body paint, a blur of blue scrolls and twirls and triskeles, to see the underlying scar, which only the centurion's hawk-like eye had spotted. He shook his head, baffled. It took a little while, and then he came up with a solution. 'There's that thing on the commander's 'orse,' he wondered aloud, doubtfully.

'Well done!'

He considered the implication, sheathing his sword. 'You think him a spy? Him a spy?' It was common knowledge that the robbers' fort had been betrayed from within, but it was also known that the informers were now dead themselves – Marcus' 'singing birds'. Marcus had said nothing about having a spy within.

Another piped up. 'He said no prisoners.'

'You think he's Cunobarrus?' asked a stretcher bearer who had come at the centurion's signal to convey reverently away the body of the tribune Decimus Lepidus Aemilius Virens.

'As far as you or anybody else is concerned, that is so. As for Marcus Marcius? Well, this may be the end of a very promising career for me.' He pretended to give the matter further consideration. 'But again, on the other hand, I may gain rapid promotion for my enterprise in recovering a valuable property for him.'

The others laughed at the joke, for the centurion had been so long in service he was overdue for discharge. Instead of fighting on a battlefield, he had every right to seek a cushy number and ease himself into his retirement. 'Rather you than me, mate,' said a bold one. 'Rather you than me.'

There had always been the faint hope that Virens might be found alive. News of his confirmed death spread rapidly, and Marcus knew that the arrival of tribunes at the *principia* was not merely to deliver their reports. A vacancy now existed, and for the lucky ones, consequential promotion was assured. He cursed Virens for his reckless action. Why had it not been Annius Festus? But of course

Festus would not have been nearly so impetuous. The decision was made, and he announced it without delay.

'Annius Festus is to take command of the auxiliaries at least until I have orders to the contrary. I shall send dispatches of these matters to governor Neratius, of course; he may have someone else in mind for the command. You know how these things are ordered.' They all knew that there was no other equestrian officer eligible for that position. The best man for the job would have been Gnaeus Vitellius Drusus, Marcus' deputy, left in charge at the fortress, but his rank was senatorial, and that would not do. He addressed Annius Festus directly. 'The work here is all but completed, so there is no more to it than seeing the men returned to the fort. Do you have any questions?'

Festus saluted formally and assured him he was more than up to the task. He had no questions.

'Good.' Marcus nodded. 'On your return, the first thing for you to do is to get the gold moving as quickly as possible. Now we have disposed of the robbers, the muleteers should experience no hindrance, but keep a proper guard all the same.'

The new commandant of the auxiliaries reiterated that his commander could have complete faith in him; the task presented to him was straightforward enough.

The arrival of a centurion with a report to make interrupted them.

'You believe you have him? Bring him in. Where is he?' Marcus looked beyond the man as he listened to his claim.

'You have put him in the infirmary? I want him here now. On whose authority was he put there?'

'None but mine, Legate.' Confident enough of the rightness of his actions, the centurion spoke up boldly. 'He's alive but only just – unconscious right now; won't be able to tell you anything.'

'I don't intend to have a conversation with him,' snarled Marcus. 'I just want to know for certain that I have him. What makes you so sure this man is Cunobarrus? Did he claim as much?'

The centurion shook his head. 'No, Legate. Fact is I dunno know for certain who he is, but he'll be of interest to you and he'll have a tale to tell if he comes round. I reckon you'll be very interested to look at his left shoulder. There's a mark there which exactly matches that fancy piece of bronze work on your horse's bridle.'

'What do you mean, a mark? A tattoo? What's so odd about that? These beggars are covered in 'em. Where d'you think my own bridle piece came from?'

'No, a burn mark, a brand, as if a thief or a valuable property. He was wearing this stuff.' He laid on a table a neck ring of twisted gold; chased bronze armbands; and a necklet of beads strung on a wire, a jewel more fitted for a woman than a warrior.

'I'd say he had some rank; he could be Cunobarrus. Or perhaps a spy on your behalf?'

Marcus was shaking his head. Again he knew it was a mistake to have let his informants kill themselves. 'I had no spy in there. I can't place any runaway, and I certainly know nothing of any such branding. In what circumstances was he taken?'

The centurion told him. 'I'd say he was the owner of this, the sword that cut down Aemilius Virens. If you want him dead, there's more than my hand ready to finish him.' He had brought a long-bladed British sword, and it joined the pile of booty.

'No, leave him be for now.' Marcus nodded thoughtfully. 'My curiosity is aroused. We shall leave it to the gods and to the skill of our surgeon. Pass the word he is not to be molested. That is all. Carry on.'

Marcus turned again to the tribunes. 'Now be seated and consider this. Tertius, pour the good wine.' He summoned his personal slave, and the man appeared from the shadows and served them all before withdrawing. 'Here is a conundrum. I have lost no slave so marked. None of my household has run off. It is a mystery. The triskele is, as you know, my lucky piece, though the design is common enough among the natives, but I know of no one outside of my family who flaunts it.'

The piece was familiar to all who had dodged Tempestus' vicious teeth.

'Perhaps it is intended as some personal decoration, some rite of passage? Some proof of fearlessness? Do you think he is Cunobarrus?'

Marcus shook his head. 'Maybe, maybe. I am not convinced. No, if Cunobarrus had such a distinguishing mark, I would most certainly have been told of it by that pair who sold him to us.'

'Is the centurion to be rewarded for bringing him in?' Sestius Gallus, the most junior of the tribunes, wanted to know.

'Rewarded?' Marcus looked at him with pity. 'That man has wilfully disobeyed me and thinks he has got away with it. You, Gallus, may deal with him. See that his pay is stopped one month and defer his retirement – unless, of course, I discover that this slave really is Cunobarrus. Then you may reward him.' They all laughed at his good humour.

'We should not forget that this prisoner is the man who killed our friend Virens,' said Festus. 'There will be no shortage of volunteers when you want him dead.'

'Then you must see to it that the men know he is not to be killed except I so order it. I shall examine him for myself. If he is not Cunobarrus and will name his true master, then to him he shall go.'

'I'll have him brought from the infirmary.' Festus rose, anxious to demonstrate his new authority.

'Don't be ridiculous, man. Apart from the fact that he is supposedly half dead, I will not have this made much of. No, let him remain where he lies. After I have visited our own wounded, I shall take a look at him. Gallus, you are responsible for arranging the funerals. Report to me when all is ready; I have much to praise.'

The young tribune looked horrified. He had never before undertaken such a task. A friendly voice whispered in his ear, 'There's nothing for you to do. Just instruct your centurion it is to be done, and he will report to you when all is ready. Then you tell Marcus.'

Gallus excused himself and left the tent.

Marcus loathed the infirmary whether in encampment or in fortress. He loathed the smell of it, of sickness, and the sights and sounds of slow and wasting deaths. Better to be killed outright on the field – the fate of mad, impulsive Aemilius Virens – than be brought to this. In his eulogy, he had praised the man well enough, for he knew he deserved it and those who had served under him expected it; privately, he deplored the stupidity of his charging into the thick of the melee when he had no need. There were times when such leadership was necessary and times when it was not, and it had not been necessary in this place. A man with ambitions should act in a more disciplined manner, take control and command, and not display such foolhardiness.

He composed his face into what he hoped was pride and confidence and, taking a deep breath, crossed the threshold into the crowded tent. If those who lay around him had any inkling of how pained he was to see brave men reduced to crying out in agony as their lives ebbed inexorably from them, they might lose their only hope: the will to live. That could not be. He assumed a cheerful approach and halted by the side of one whom he hoped had a good prognosis.

'Why is that one here, Legate?' A man swathed in bandages boldly spoke for his companions.

In his mildest voice and with a pleasant expression, he answered, 'Because I so choose.' To have such low life imposed on them was not popular, but Marcus had never concerned himself greatly about being popular.

Encouraged by the mildness, the man went further. 'Are we not in need of all attention? Why do you squander our surgeons' time and skills on scum like that?'

Another said, 'I agree! Is it true that he killed Tribune Decimus Aemilius Virens? Even if he is Cunobarrus, why should he live when Virens is dead?'

For a long time, Marcus stared at him. This was no time to remonstrate with the soldier. Gallus, at his shoulder, mistook the delay for amnesia and supplied a name.

'Decius Rufus of the fourth cohort.'

'Thank you. I am aware. What injury do you have, Decius Rufus?'

'A blow to the head, and my leg – my leg is speared. They say these savages tip their spears with poison. Is that true? Am I to lose it?' He was sweating profusely but whether from pain or fear of its consequences was impossible to tell. Marcus glanced at the surgeon, who shook his head. He held out no hope.

The patient knew he had erred. 'My cursed leg – it makes me speak out of turn. I beg your pardon, Legate.'

Marcus spoke loudly for all to hear. 'The poison business is a lie. I am surprised it reached your ears. In this infirmary, you will receive the best care and medicine available. Nowhere, not even in the court of Trajan himself, are there better surgeons to be found. And none of you will go short of proper treatment on behalf of any barbarian.'

A weak but brave cheer arose from all around, and he made his careful progress throughout the tent, taking care to miss none of them and forcing himself to leave the one who most consumed his curiosity until the last.

There was a deep and vicious wound parting the man's skull; Peritus, the surgeon, had carefully peeled away the dressing so that the face might be better seen. He need not have bothered. Both eyelids and the skin surrounding them were swollen and livid, and the eyes were firmly closed. His head had been shaved not only to treat the injury but also as a precaution against infestation. *He won't like that,* thought Marcus, *if he lives long enough to know where he is and what has become of him.* He was familiar enough with the dressing and liming of hair that Cunobarrus and his followers had adopted, imitating the fashion of warriors from the past.

'Turn him over. Show me this mark.'

'It may finish him; he is very weak,' Peritus gloomily warned. He did not like to lose patients even when they were the enemy.

'If the mark is not what was reported, I shall finish him here and now myself, and then none of our men need complain that his presence deprives them of your attentions.' His hand patted his dagger hilt. 'Turn him over.'

He peered closely at the shoulder and traced with his fingers until he could make out the detail of the damaged skin. Then he straightened thoughtfully. He had indeed recognized it and if he had not known better would have thought the same as the centurion. 'So it is true.'

He demanded to see the captive's face again, and reluctantly the surgeon had the body turned back. It was no help. Without the disfigurement and with his hair grown, it might have been possible to recognize him, but as it was … Marcus shook his head. He did not know him at all.

'If he regains consciousness, see that I am informed. I shall question him personally.'

He felt dirty, in need of oiling and scraping by the competent hands of Tertius and then a good meal with good company. For the first time, he thought how greatly he was going to mourn the loss of Virens.

During the night the gale rose as if to avenge the dead with even greater ferocity. It shrieked down the mountains into the valleys, ballooning the leather tents, struggling to wrench them from the guys. In the infirmary, it speeded the death of the doomed and terrified those who had hope of survival. It brought inside the acrid smell of the ebbing pyres, and the more fanciful among them feared they were already attending their own funerals.

The unconscious remained untroubled. They did not hear the screaming wind or the wailing men. Nor did they smell the blood and the smoke. Among that fortunate group was the prisoner. He drifted close to the brink of departure but was not yet destined to make that journey.

Slowly awareness returned to the captive one. Something was covering his eyes; later he learned it was the dressing wrapped around his wounded head, but as he struggled to comprehend his situation he supposed it was to obstruct his sight. Sounds he could hear, and though some were familiar, such as the rattle of falling dice and glad shouts of success, the voices accompanying them were not speaking his own language. He lay still, gathering his wits. This was not the other world. These were not spirits, and neither was he.

He was lying on a pallet on the ground in some makeshift shelter. He had the most unimaginable pain in his head, and he was surrounded by foreign tongues. So, he reasoned, he had been captured. He and how many others? The battle must have gone badly for them, but even if there were a mere handful of survivors, they might still achieve something. Later, when he was stronger, he must find the means to escape.

Not yet; not yet. He had neither the strength nor the will to rise. He tried to ask for water, but he had no voice.

'Keep still.' Moisture from a sponge dripped onto his lips. As if from far away, voices spoke in Latin – of him, not to him.

He slept for a while, and the next time he woke, he felt stronger. He took broth from a slave in a blood-encrusted tunic, the one who had provided the water. He stood, with much assistance, to relieve himself. He discovered his ornaments were gone – stolen, he had no doubt. Why suppose otherwise? They had shaved his head too, even taken off his lip hair, a petty but typical act of tyranny. The growth of stubble told him he had lain there more than a day.

Footsteps with a heavy tread approached. Instinctively he feigned unconsciousness.

'What is your name?'

The abrupt accent jarred in his ear and took him by surprise so that he opened his eyes unwittingly. The speaker was a Roman officer. He saw thick iron-grey hair, a high and broad forehead, a hawkish nose, an unsmiling mouth. As rapidly, he closed his eyes again.

In that instant, Marcus had seen eyes as deep blue as violets. A rare colour indeed. A slave of some value, his wife would think. 'I think if I had once owned him I should remember it.' He spoke his thoughts aloud. 'Speak, curse you!' he snapped peevishly, reverting to what little of the British tongue he knew. 'What is your name? Who is your master? To whom do you belong?'

The eyes opened again, framed in yellowing, bruised skin. Still he uttered no sound. Marcus rounded on the surgeon. 'You said he could speak,' he accused.

'So he can; he is shamming.' Peritus did not care to be made a fool of.

'British, you say? In the British tongue?' He could be German with those eyes. That could explain it; his brother Quintus had spent much time in Germany.

The slave who had been tending him said he was definitely a Briton of the Dobunni tribe. He had gleaned as much from the woad markings with which he had painted himself.

'See that he stands before me tomorrow,' Marcus hissed and stalked away. Peritus, trotting beside him, assured him that he would.

The prisoner had by now become more aware of the activities and persons surrounding him. None of his compatriots were present, and his ankles had been shackled as if they suspected he was strong enough to run away. His hands remained free which, he ruefully observed to himself, meant that they supposed he could do them no harm; how little they knew.

Enquiries as to the location of other prisoners were met with a blunt rebuff which indicated exactly where the Celtic slave's allegiances lay. 'I am not here to answer your questions', he was told, 'but you to answer ours.'

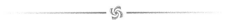

The short distance from his pallet to the command tent, the *principium,* even with the support of two slaves, proved more than taxing, and once there he was forced to depend heavily on one of the support posts even to remain upright. He was unaware how, despite his plight, his stature impressed his small audience.

The man who had questioned him before was there. There was something about him; he struggled in vain to identify what it was and gave up that effort to instead focus his mind on resisting whatever they would seek to learn from him. On the table before him were the jewels they had taken from him. He had supposed them to have been stolen; now he saw they, like himself, had merely been delivered to this man, their commanding officer.

He glanced with a heavy sigh at the two other men who sat in judgement on him, and six eyes stared with curiosity towards him.

'You are not a pretty sight,' observed the chief man. 'Do you know who I am?'

The prisoner frowned and listened intently. Marcus' and the captive's words were to be relayed through an interpreter.

Be careful; let him tell you. A cautious voice within gave warning. He moved his sore head delicately from side to side. 'No.'

'"No, my lord." Say "my lord" when you address me,' Marcus drawled. 'My name is Marcus Marcius Phillipianus. What is your name?' He waited; there was no response.

'You are Cunobarrus!' It was the younger of the man's companions who spoke.

Not so, Marcus thought as he saw the astonishment on the face of the prisoner. It was positively comic. He pondered again on the pity that the robber chief's body had not been identified.

In the silence that followed, the slave spoke. 'Where are the other prisoners?'

For some reason this was a funny question. Instead of reprimanding him for the omission of "my lord", the man let out a hearty chortle.

'They are where you ought to be.' He nodded genially.

'Then I beg to be with them.'

More laughter, now raucous. All the men about him including his escort joined the laughter with gusto.

The prisoner was bewildered.

'Later', said Marcus, 'to grant such a petition will be my pleasure. I have not finished with you yet.' He watched intently for comprehension to dawn, but the savage was too dull-witted to appreciate the joke. He spelled it out more clearly. 'There are no prisoners but you. The rest are dead – all dead. Every one of them is dead, deceased, departed.'

Still the slave stared dumbly at him, and he had to have his interpreter repeat it. 'They are all dead, gone to the other world. My men have had good sport, unchecked. I took no prisoner bar you.' It was a most satisfying experience, one he always enjoyed, to observe that little moment when a minor triumph was accomplished and defeat acknowledged. He saw it again as the dumb stare changed to puzzlement and then doubt and finally to horror as the slave came to understand what had taken place. Now he should fall to his knees and beg mercy. Marcus waited.

There was no pleading for mercy. Hatred and rage replaced the expression of horror. He lunged across the space between them, hurling a torrent of abuse, and fought against the guards who leapt upon him.

When calm was restored, Marcus asked, 'Who is your master? Whose brand is that on your shoulder?'

That came as a shock. The slave reacted as if struck by a physical blow. Now he understood. Now he saw why he alone lived while a whole community was slaughtered – because somewhere someone could lay claim to own him. He swayed where he stood, and but for his custodians, he would have slipped to the ground.

Marcus spoke again. 'I am Marcus Marcius Phillipianus. Sometimes I am called Adamantis, the hard man.' This failed to make an impression, so he continued, 'My father is Quintus Marcius, and so is my brother.' Still no response; he was mystified. He would have put money on the runaway having once belonged to Quintus. How greatly he would have enjoyed sending him back to him with a memorandum on carelessness. Of course, there was always the remote possibility, he thought, remembering what Peritus' slave had said about the markings, that they were of the Dobunni tribe. He ventured, 'I have another brother. It may be that you belong to him. Lucius Marcius? He lives near Glevum.'

Unbelievably he had hit spot on the target. The prisoner had not replied; the stiffening of his posture, the rapid breathing and the clenching of his fists had betrayed him.

A slave branded by his pious brother Lucius, Marcius Mollis? It could scarcely be believed. 'I have never known my brother Lucius to brand a slave. You must indeed be a dangerous criminal. More than a common thief, I think. What name do you go by?'

'I am no slave!' The reply was more hurled than shouted. 'You are the thief, I think!' and reckless as to the pain, he tossed his head contemptuously towards the table with his ornaments displayed upon it. Marcus' eyes followed.

'The spoils of battle, mine by right – as are you.' He picked out the delicate necklet of amber and blue glass beads threaded on a wire of twisted copper, playing it through his fingers before tossing it towards the slave's naked chest. 'Put that on; let us see how pretty you can be!'

He was unconcerned at their mockery of his having a woman's trinket. To have Bodyn's relic restored to him, he could bear that and more. He wound it into its accustomed place on his arm and stared defiantly into the steely grey eyes before him. Now he could see the mockery had given way to something which might, in a more worthy enemy, have been respect.

'Maybe there is something else you would care for?' Marcus indicated the pile of loot. 'Look through it, by all means,' he urged. 'Let us see what takes your fancy.'

Heedless of his audience he knelt and scrabbled around until he found them. He had prayed they might not be there, but they were. He held them to his breast and wept openly, nodding when the question was put, 'Cunobarrus?'

He held not only the ornaments of Cunobarrus but also those of Cadrus, but to the Romans they were all one and served to reinforce their belief about the renegade and his greed for their gold.

'Excellent! That is all I require of you – confirmation that he is dead. Replace that. It is not yours; it belongs to Rome now.'

The prisoner rose again to his feet. 'Yes, they are dead. You have won the day. One thing – just grant me one thing. Give me Belacon and Belcadon. There is nothing here for them now that you have destroyed our people. You surely have no further need of them.'

'What a joy it is to meet you,' answered a delighted Marcus. 'I am truly grieved to have to tell you that you are robbed of your revenge, for I should have delighted in seeing you fight. Alas, they too are dead; they killed themselves when they saw what I did to your obdurate companions when they rejected my terms. That, you may agree with me, was possibly the only decent thing they ever did during their worthless lives. However, do not be downhearted; I have other sport in mind for you. I intend to spare you for now, and later you shall repay this mercy by providing us with entertainment.' He spoke to the custodians. 'Remove him and keep him secure. Make sure he does not defeat my purpose by taking the same course as that other pair. And those beads – he keeps them.'

The tent flap dropped into place behind the departing prisoner.

'He appears to be the property of my brother Lucius. I wonder that he has never mentioned this runaway to me. You do not know my brother Lucius Marcius; he has a heart too soft for his own good. The puzzle is how it came about that he inflicted such a scar on this man. He did so wisely; his action was justified by virtue of the slave's absconding and has led to his recovery. There is surely a story here, which my curiosity compels me to discover. Afterwards I shall make a gladiator of him, and those who mourn Virens may attain the revenge they think I now deny them. Now we must break camp and return to Isca.'

With the robber band disposed of, there was no reason he should not take some well-earned furlough and pay Lucius a visit. Vitellius could continue to be entrusted with the fortress for a little while longer; he was an excellent deputy and would relish the position.

The tribunes saluted and went to do his bidding.

Much of what the man had said the prisoner had not understood. He knew that Cunobarrus and Cadrus were dead along with all of their comrades, but he knew that their betrayers too were dead. All of those things he could comprehend, because he had lived a hard and brutal life and had brought death to others many times. What he could not understand was how, from the scar he bore on his shoulder, the Roman had so quickly known from where he had come. He had tried to disguise it by having the woad patterns worked into it, but that had been to no avail. Cadrus had shown him what it was, drawing it on a slate, and he knew it was just a triskele and not by any means unique. But he knew the Romans used writing to convey information; he had to accept that perhaps there was more written within it than Cadrus had been able to show.

They had not returned him to the infirmary; instead he was in a smaller tent guarded by custodians who could not speak his language or chose not to. He was still very weak and not yet fit to attempt to make the escape he planned; for that he must act with cunning and choose his moment with care.

He cursed their gods. What kind of gods favoured such monsters as Marcus and his kind, he wondered. Now he had a third hateful name to add to those, which at every sunrise he swore vengeance on, first there was Lucius Marcius, second there was the man he only knew as Drusus, and now there was this man Marcus, another by the name of Marcius – some kinsman perhaps.

He felt no disgrace at being alive while all of his people were dead. He had fought hard as he always did, and he could account for many Roman dead. He had certainly avenged the death of Cadrus. He had seen Cadrus die and had run his sword through the man responsible for that. At first he had not remembered it, but as he had lain recovering his wits, he had seen the battle over and over again. Killing that man was the last thing he could recall before finding himself taken. If the gods had any thought for him at all, he prayed, let that one have been Drusus. If he had killed Drusus, then his life as a warrior had been worthwhile. Cadrus had taught him and had taught him well. At killing he was as good as any man and better than most – at killing.

He knew that he could do appalling things. Often he had wondered at himself; often after a raid, he had nightmares. The terror in the eyes of those he had butchered haunted his dreams. Often he had wanted to run away, to abandon that life and revert to the farmer who was still somewhere within him. He had never really understood

Cunobarrus, though he had served him loyally. Now he understood. How wrong he had been and how right had been Cunobarrus; the Romans were evil, evil men.

He could hear the sound of wood being sawn and hammered. Some intuition told him that it concerned him and that it was sinister, some elaborate device of execution, a painful and degrading death they were preparing for him. The half-formed plan in his mind had to be acted upon quickly, and as soon as his guards' attention was distracted by a noise sufficient for them to go outside to see what it was about, he took his chance. The only thing available to him were the trews he still was wearing. He ripped them from his legs and tied them around his neck and the tent pole so that by winding his head round and around he created a kind of garrotte. It was useless; the men returned too soon and prevented his suicide. The only thing he achieved by it was to be deprived of the trews so that he could not attempt such a thing again.

The hammering ceased, and his custodians responded to the call. He was led outside, dreading the style of execution he was to face. There was no scaffold that he could recognize but a cage-like structure mounted on a wagon into which he was driven. Whether by accident or design, the cage had been made as if to contain a beast, not a man. He was driven inside as if he were a bear and compelled to sit or to crouch upon all fours like an animal, for it was too small for him to stretch to full length. He snarled at them ferociously and cursed them so that they jeered at him, hugely entertained until they heard from far across the encampment a voice bellowing like a bull; it silenced them and him. Leathers were suddenly thrown across the cage, and darkness fell. He had not seen who had shouted at the men, but he had a strange feeling that it was Marcus himself and found he was angry for finding himself grateful to such a monster. The wagon moved, and the cage tilted, and he felt himself being conveyed downhill.

2

⟨◎⟩

Marcus did not accompany them; he returned to his fortress at Isca Silurum with the soldiers to update his senior tribune, Vitellius, with his intentions and assure himself that all was as it should be there. The man received the news of Virens' death with regret, having known him well and liked him. He received the word of his replacement, temporary though it may be, with something approaching derision. But though he was an ambitious man, he knew the command of an auxiliary unit was not for him and he must wait for a legion to be assigned to him. Being given command of the Second Augusta in the absence of Marcus was a good opportunity for him – he knew that – and Marcus knew he left his fortress in safe hands.

Marcus rode Tempestus quickly along the route to Glevum with his slave Tertius and a small escort of men, some of whom were retiring as veterans from the army; at Glevum they would be granted land, and those who could not already claim it, citizenship. They travelled a good road and a safe one and made better time than those conveying his prize, arriving only two days after those he had sent ahead.

The prisoner in the oxen cart had endured a tediously slow and painful journey. His route had been along poor native tracks and through almost continuously lashing rain which reduced the ground to thick mud and fords to swollen rivers. When the escorting auxiliaries could provide insufficient manpower to shift the cart from where it had slipped, a not infrequent event, locals were enlisted to assist, and from their curiosity about its contents a lucrative scheme evolved. A small sum of cash granted a brief viewing enhanced by a lurid story of the captive's exploits, much of which came closer to the truth than the narrators suspected.

By the time they reached the crossroads where Marcus had said they should meet, it was obvious to anyone downwind of the wagon that their charge was a very sick man. They dragged him from it and brought him close to their campfire and pressed their own food upon him. He could not or would not eat and took only the thin wine issued to them and that only when they forced it between his lips. Concern for their own welfare caused them to send a man into Glevum for a physician. The man prescribed native beer and soporific herbs.

When Marcus arrived and peered into the crate, he found a far less sick captive though one far from restored to full fitness. 'Greetings to you, thief,' he said. 'Still alive then? Good; brother should not call upon brother empty-handed. It would be a pity to have come so far and not completed your journey.'

He dispensed with the crate. 'Just chain him securely in the wagon and keep it covered,' he ordered the men. 'When we enter the town, you will reveal the contents of this wagon to no one. You may talk in the taverns of the taking of Belconia' – for such was the name he had assigned to a nameless place. 'I would not deprive you of that, but if you are asked about what I keep in the wagon, then be silent.'

By now the rain had ceased falling, but the river Sabrina was high and underfoot was sodden as they crossed the bridge and entered the gates of the Colonia Glevum Nervensis. Streets were awash, and townspeople were loudly complaining about the paucity of drainage. The town was developing but not quickly enough for anybody, and the rain had delayed the work yet again; there was no reason now why it should not continue – and yet the builders delayed.

If the harangues were intended for him, they fell on deaf ears. Marcus ignored them all and forced his way through the throng into what remained of the old fortress, where he demanded the presence of whoever was in charge.

Tribune Cloelius Draco, now in command of the Batavians, an auxiliary contingent based in the new fort, welcomed his unannounced visitor cordially, bidding him welcome and offering refreshment. Marcus took the wine and waved the cupbearer away.

'This is a private visit,' he announced. 'I'm here to see my brother, Lucius Marcius. Is he in town?'

'Ah,' said a relieved Draco. 'Lucius Marcius is not here but at Daruentum. We do not expect him to return before the ides.' He referred to the thirteenth of November, three days ahead.

'Then I'll accept your hospitality for tonight and travel there tomorrow,' Marcus told him. 'I have some men with me who need to be given their allotment of land. Perhaps the man responsible for that will join us? I trust my brother has left some accommodation intact for the likes of us?'

Draco answered that for the foreseeable future the old praetorium, though no longer the commander's house, served as a *mansio* for visiting officials and housed brother officers. 'Calpurnius is responsible for allocating the veterans' properties. He lives with his family, but I will send for him and inform him he has work to do.' He indicated a tribune who had entered. 'This is Antonius Secundus, who assists your brother. Perhaps he will join us at dinner?'

Marcus was happy with this arrangement. 'There is another matter. I have a captive; he is in the wagon drawn up by the infirmary. He is in a pretty poor state after his journey, but I want him fit to travel to my brother's home tomorrow. He is a surprise for my brother, and I do not want a word of this whispered abroad – not mentioned to anyone.'

'A captive?' Surprise was evident. So word of the massacre had preceded him. Marcus experienced a warming glow of satisfaction. He had Cloelius accompany him to the vehicle. One glance inside was enough for the tribune.

'Legate, you're not thinking of taking that down to the farm? The lady Aelia won't like that.'

Marcus grinned. 'You don't think so? I intend to have some fun with this one. You'll regret not being there to witness it.'

Cloelius knew there was nothing he would regret less.

'He will need at least two days yet,' he said. Besides being so ill, the creature was deplorably filthy. 'You will want him cleaned up and attired in fresh clothing, of course. What should I do? Send him down in the wagon?'

'No! No! Put him up on a mule or something; you will have to unshackle his legs, but I advise you to manacle him,' answered Marcus carelessly. 'I shall go down in the morning tomorrow. Dispatch him immediately after me. I do not wish him to be cleaned up or have his rags changed. This is what I want delivered – as it is. And watch him carefully; he is very crafty. I doubt he is as ill as he pretends. There is also a box which I wish to be delivered with him. Two men should be enough to escort him. Use your own men. Now that mine have arrived in the town, they may as well enjoy themselves.'

Not at all happy with the situation, Cloelius accompanied Marcus to the bath suite and by a more subtle flattery induced the man to relax and yarn with him. They were in a good-humoured state of mind when a young man rushed towards them.

'Uncle Marcus?' he ventured. 'Marcus Marcius?'

The speaker was a youth of about sixteen years, slim of build with dark curly hair and a wide grin across his face.

'The same,' Marcus drawled. 'Why the "uncle"? Are you my nephew Gaius, Lucius' son?'

'Indeed I am,' cried the young man, delighted to have tracked down his quarry. 'News of you is all over the town. They say you have killed every one of a band of robbers. It is true? Is that true?'

Marcus conceded that it was true. It was gratifying to learn that his service was valued so far afield.

'The word is that you have brought their loot with you and you have it in that wagon; that is why you bar all from approaching it. May I see it?'

'No, young man, you may not. But what is in that wagon is for your father. If you wish to see it, you must accompany me to your home.'

'You are a very silent young man.' During their dinner, Marcus had regaled them with his recent activities, receiving from Cloelius and Antonius a more enthusiastic endorsement than from his nephew. 'Am I to understand your silence as a rebuke? Do you disapprove of my actions? Do you have an opinion on what took place? Come, you need not fear offending me. I am not easily offended though sometimes irritated. Speak.'

Gaius had listened in rapt awe at his uncle's account of the events at Belconia. He blushed to be thought of as girlish, but the account had been so graphic he had felt his stomach churn on more than one occasion. He sought words with which to impress the man, words which might indicate his admiration for the action.

'On the contrary, Uncle Marcus Marcius, I think you did right. As you say, they were a band of evil renegades and caused harm to many innocents. And you gave them the opportunity to surrender which they scorned. No, they undoubtedly brought their destruction upon themselves.'

'I have to admit that without the assistance afforded me by Belcon's sons, I might yet be there searching even now. They were a treacherous pair, but they served their purpose. They did no harm by hanging themselves. To have given pardon to two such unworthy dogs would have been shameful to us. Here is a piece of advice for you: do not put your trust in the words or deeds of men who so readily betray those to whom they have sworn allegiance.'

Gaius was puzzled. 'But', he wondered, 'was not allegiance was owed to them by their people? By those very same people who spurned them and allied themselves with this Cunobarrus, the man who had killed their father and usurped his authority? You say they were the sons of the old chief?'

'Indeed they were. So far as a criminal may be credited with such a title as chief, Belcon had been their chief. And so anxious were they to regain their domain that they asked me to kill all who opposed them. And so I did.' He allowed himself the small white lie; it would not be a lie for much longer. 'Allegiance', he continued, 'is like Janus: facing two ways. As well as being the recipients of allegiance, those who govern have a duty of loyalty to their inferiors. You may well ponder on what possessed all those people to reject my offer of clemency and elect to die beside their father's murderer rather than have that pair restored as their chieftains. Does it instruct us on the nature of the mob or on the personality of Cunobarrus? I think I should have liked to meet this Cunobarrus. If only briefly!' he added drolly, to which his companions politely chuckled.

'If those people had given him up as you demanded, you would have spared them?' Gaius was of a more serious vein.

'That question is impertinent, boy! It implies I am not a man of my word. They would have lived; I promised them only that. And we would have been richer in slaves. Remember we were not dealing with honest subjects but with thieves and robbers and murderers who had plundered our gold trains and terrorized the civil population. I scarcely describe them as men; these creatures have plagued honest settlers and native farmers with their terrifying attacks for far too long. They were responsible for crimes such as a boy like you can have no conception of. They were no better than vermin and deserved to be treated as such.'

'I think I understand what you mean about allegiance and loyalty,' said his nephew thoughtfully. 'It means that if you have authority over others, then you have a duty to treat them honestly and decently, does it not? It is Father's maxim on how we treat our slaves. Perhaps those brothers you spoke of were not wholly honest about the events which led to their expulsion from that community.'

Marcus was nodding. 'I believe you have it exactly. Whatever lay behind the quarrel was not nearly as simple as they would have had me believe, and of course I did not believe them. My doubts were confirmed when my offer to restore Belacon and Belcadon to their rightful place in exchange for Cunobarrus was so scornfully disdained. Criminal though he may have been, that man commanded their loyalty, even to death.'

He changed the subject. 'Now, young man, tell me what career you propose to follow. Are you to be a soldier like me, your grandfather, and your uncle Quintus Marcius, or a lawyer and builder of towns like your father?'

It was an unfair way to put the question. Lucius had served as a military tribune and had acquitted himself honourably. Even Cloelius winced.

'Oh, I shall serve some time in the army, of course, but as yet I have to decide in which legion. And I do find Father's business most interesting. I have often accompanied him on his travels to inspect other towns and report to the governor on the work in progress. Here in Glevum we have a youth corps. Tribune Antonius Secundus organizes it, and I have some position in charge of the younger boys. In fact, we are going to camp shortly down near to Daruentum if the weather holds.'

'If the weather holds?' sneered Marcus. He reflected on the torrential rain which had lashed his recent camp. 'What kind of a soldier is Rome to depend on that dares venture out only when the sun is shining?' He had to down several gulps of wine before he could speak again. Feeling the need to defend himself, Antonius pointed out that some of the boys concerned were much younger than Gaius and that their mothers gave him much grief when they damaged themselves. Marcus felt he had no words to respond to this.

'What subjects do you study at this school of yours?' Marcus asked abruptly, thinking himself tactful in changing the subject.

'Greek and rhetoric, of course. I have learned the British tongue too from our steward. Otherwise the usual subjects – philosophy, mathematics, law, history, geography. Father wishes me to improve my rhetoric, but I shall need another tutor for that. Anicetus is not a master of it. Father wishes me to take after him, but I fear I am not so clever.'

'You think that to be a soldier like me does not require so much cleverness?' He spared the boy having to answer this. 'Who will teach you rhetoric?'

'Father says we shall return to Rome in the spring,' he answered with a grimace. 'I am to study there or in Greece.'

'You do not sound very enthusiastic about returning to Rome. Why is that?'

He knew better than to give the true reason. Marcus would be sure to tell his father, and he had no wish to experience again the ridicule or wrath which would follow such a disclosure. Instead he said somewhat feebly, knowing the man would not be deceived, 'I feel as if I have lived here the whole of my life. To me Rome is foreign; this is my country. But Mother suffers greatly from the cold. Her limbs are stiff and pain her a lot. Father has promised this will be our last winter in Britain. He would go immediately, while travel is still possible, but he has not yet been granted leave.'

Marcus studied him shrewdly. He knew when he was being lied to, and Gaius was a poor liar. He guessed that there was some girl the youth was reluctant to be parted from. Instead he picked up on another point. 'Your mother's health? I think it would be better that she remain unaware you told me of this unless your father or she mentions it. Tomorrow you are to come with me when I visit them. Be off to your bed now, and be ready to make an early start. I leave at break of day, so be ready to travel with me.'

The abrupt dismissal combined with the directive that he was to disobey his father's strict injunction to attend his lessons shook Gaius. He was unused to such peremptory treatment, though he was keen enough to obey. He hoped also that by the next day the contents of the mysterious covered wagon would be revealed to him. That had caught not only his attention but the interest of his school friends also. He was very conscious of the envy his having such a famous relative as Marcus Marcius engendered among his contemporaries.

It was a disappointment, therefore, that when the morning came only he and his uncle were to set off for Daruentum. Whoever or whatever was in the wagon – and rumour fluctuated between it being a wild bear, a deformed monster, or a cache of treasure – it was not to be taken to his home. He dutifully waited at some little distance, trying unsuccessfully to quiet his fidgety colt until his uncle completed whatever business he had at the mysterious vehicle.

3

Verluccus had guessed that he was in Glevum. He knew that had been his destination, and now the sounds of activity surrounding him told him that it had been reached. Someone had entered the wagon and forced something herbal between his stubborn teeth, after which he had slept. The sleep had cleared his head, still painful from the throbbing wound, and a fresh dressing had been placed over it. When food was brought the next time, he found he had an appetite and ate it.

He had been thinking about his circumstances. He was being returned to Lucius, that much was clear, but as to what next would be done to him, he could only guess. The very least that would happen would be some form of punishment for running away; the worst would be to kill him. But he had one hope. He had the hope of revenge. In a very short time, he would be within reach not only of the monster responsible for this current miserable plight but the vile Lucius also – thus the workings of the gods. He must make certain he would be strong enough to act when the opportunity arose and destroy them both. The will to survive and fight back had replaced the almost overwhelming desire to die.

His plans were disturbed by a visit from Marcus.

The Roman grinned at the sullen, tight-lipped face which turned at his greeting. 'Awake then? And not nearly as ill as you look, I'll be bound.'

But he had stepped closer than was wise. A hand, large, grimy, and fast, shot for his throat until the chain checked it. Marcus laughed, appreciating the gesture. 'That's the spirit! That's what I want to see! But save your strength. Now is not the time, here is not the place, and this is not your audience. I have a larger arena than this in mind for you!' He spoke in Latin, uncaring that Verluccus could comprehend not a word of it.

He took up the reins of the rested Tempestus to swing into the saddle with the agility of a lad, bidding his slave Tertius, 'Follow us and do not be idle.' Then, calling to his nephew, he was gone.

He and Gaius rode for a little way barely speaking, for the horses were fresh and demanded a great deal of attention to restrain them from racing each other. This difficulty was exacerbated by the road to Daruentum being barely more than a track and very muddy, though the rain had eased somewhat.

A tombstone had been erected by the side of the road. Marcus halted beside it.

'That was not there the last time I visited. Surely I would have been told …?' He perused the bright red lettering. 'Cordatus has died?'

Gaius too was a little surprised that it had not been reported to his uncle. 'He died during last winter. Father erected the stone to honour him. On a clear day, there is a fine view down the valley from here, and it was a favoured halting place of them both. The school which he founded in the *colonia* also has a memorial tablet dedicated to him by many parents.'

'No,' said his uncle sadly, 'I did not know that he had died. Cordatus was a good man; I always envied my brother his possession of him. That is truly sad news.'

He spent a little while reflecting on his memories of the freedman. 'What else is new? What of your sisters? I seem to remember the elder to be a married woman. She is a mother?'

'Marcia is married to Publius Julius Calvus, and they live at Corinium. They have one small child, and she expects another.' Gaius was clearly not very bothered about that sister, and his tone was dismissive, though in reality he counted Publius Julius a good friend and made use of his hospitality whenever he wished to attend the entertainment to be had in Corinium. Of his other sister, however, he spoke more warmly. 'Gaia is at home. She would come with me to school if she could, but mother will not allow it; she says it will not do. She is to be married to Decimus Lepidus Aemilius Virens. I believe he is with you? Mother hopes that since we wish to return to Rome, he will not delay in claiming her. She is old enough now.' Gaia was fourteen. His younger brother Quintus, he also added, was now four.

'I regret to say your sister will never be married to Aemilius Virens,' Marcus told him. 'He acted rashly in this last skirmish and paid the penalty of folly. Your sister is a widow before becoming a bride.'

Gaius was shocked. He grieved for his sister and knew she would take the news badly, for now that Marcia was a wife and mother, she envied her openly and longed for her own wedding. Marcus had not made Virens' death sound like that of a hero. He hoped the man would be gentler when he broke the news at home; it was not information he wished to be the bearer of.

The road forked, and they turned to the left. Between the denuded trees, smoke could be seen curling, and there was a teasing glimpse of a red-tiled roof which Gaius happily pointed out to his uncle.

As they came to the gate, Gaius could see that they were not the first visitors to call on their father that morning. Already neighbouring farmers had paid their morning call and were leaving. He knew them and greeted them as they met – Belanius and Bodellus; they farmed the adjoining land. They were on good terms with their neighbours, Gaius told his uncle, who seemed surprised that Lucius was not the sole owner of the extensive land around his home.

Marcus was greeted warmly, Gaius less so and scolded for absenting himself from his school. He was told that he must return there the following morning without argument.

'Your son tells me you have at last been granted permission to return to Rome,' Marcus said, pleased for his brother. 'Your reprieve has been a long time coming – a great injustice, many think.'

'We have made a good life here, but yes, I shall be glad to depart. My work is now considered complete.' More than nine years had passed since Lucius had offended the emperor Domitian, but then that emperor had relented and given him the responsibility of overseeing the colonization of Glevum by veteran soldiers, after which he could be confident of his return. Then Domitian had died, and his successor, Nerva, had asked Lucius to remain in Britain and continue the work. After two years, Nerva too had died, and now the emperor was Trajan. His only demand was that Lucius should await the approval of his provincial governor, Neratius Marcellus, who was newly appointed and would before long be visiting the colony towns. Aelia was going to have to endure yet another winter, but she made no complaint. Her husband and children were with her. If she had not accompanied Lucius to Britain, what an awful punishment she would have borne, she often told him, and there would not have been darling little Quintus either. Lucius never even considered that had his wife chosen to remain in Rome she might have exerted pressure for him to return sooner. In Britain he had provided her with an excellent house as fine as any praetorium, certainly the best for many, many miles. There was within it every obtainable luxury, under-floor heating for Aelia's comfort, and smart black and white mosaic floors in sharp patterns. In all but the humblest of rooms, the smoothly plastered walls were brightly painted with a variety of schemes, from architectural pilasters and friezes with delicate scrolls of birds and flowers; to human figures engaged in wrestling, as in Lucius' study; to hunting scenes in the triclinium. In Lucius and Aelia's bedroom there were small wall panels of Venus and Cupid.

Aelia's treasured garden had been remodelled and lay within the courtyard. There were beds of flowers and herbs surrounded by low box hedges, and a pool lay at the centre with a fountain supplied by one of the many hillside springs. A shrine dedicated to Mercury, considered by Lucius to be his most propitious god, had not been forgotten, and this was conveniently positioned to confront visitors and so that it could be attended simply by crossing the paved area outside the main house door. Beyond this pleasant garden, separated by a neatly sculpted hedge of holly and laurel, was an area where a small supply of fruits and vegetables could be cultivated for the table. A solid door in the lower wall gave the occupants access to open pasture, below which lay the woods and the stream.

The original house, its outbuildings, barns, and workshops had been strengthened and improved and now provided a home for a number of slaves headed by Agricola, Lucius' farm manager, and Victor. One disastrous harvest in what was generally reckoned a good year had convinced Lucius that neither he nor Victor knew what they were about. A considerable outlay had secured Agricola; he and the overseer made a very good team. Victor had been given Penelope as a companion, and Agricola, Grata. Both women had successfully borne children, one of each sex. In respect of the fruitfulness of the estate, Lucius had every right to feel satisfaction.

It was obvious to Gaius that Cloelius, with consideration for his mother's feelings, had sent word ahead of them to forewarn Lucius that his brother was about to pay him a surprise visit, so there were warm and dry togas awaiting them both, and Aelia had seen to it that her table would not let her down; game was plentiful, and venison and hare supplemented by a variety of small birds were to be served to the unexpected guest. The kitchen and furnaces were bustling with activity.

The sudden visit by his brother delighted Lucius enormously, though later, when it took the inevitable direction of its predecessors, he had cause to wonder yet again at his gullibility.

Aelia was less than pleased even from the outset. At first she concealed her feelings well and allowed his dutiful embrace without betraying the pain his iron arms caused to her, for he had forgotten what Gaius had told him of this – she looked so fit and comely.

But her opinion of him had undergone no change. To begin with, she looked and acted the part of the gracious hostess and managed to ignore his sneer to Lucius when he asked his brother why he was still playing the provincial politician when true power lay with the army and with Rome. His family status and wealth could give him all the power any man might desire; he need only conduct himself in the manner appropriate to one of his birth. It was not long before she and Marcus discarded the false veneer of politeness and spoke their minds.

The visit started reasonably well. Marcus met his pretty young niece and, in a manner which flattered and charmed her without offending her mother, behaved most gallantly towards her so that she positively glowed. He even allowed young Quintus to clamber onto his neck to be paraded loftily around the room. Then, to entertain them, he gave a most graphic account of the despatching of Cunobarrus and his followers, noting with much satisfaction the distaste which manifested itself in the eyes of his audience.

'Was that really necessary? You could have achieved as much and had slaves to show for it,' Lucius objected. 'It is no wonder we have a reputation for bloodthirsty brutality.'

'Do we have that? Do we really have such a reputation?' Marcus feigned amazement. 'And that despite your efforts at seducing the natives with your fancy towns and buildings? Do you not have slaves enough? What do you do with them? Do you immure them in your buildings to placate the spirits, or have you wasted them all in the arena? No, Brother, you are wrong; the continued existence of that renegade and his followers did more to damage our cause than anything you or I might. Now that we are rid of them, the land is safe for farmers and settlers. He and his kind are best destroyed.' Not time yet to tell them of the death of Virens. He had cautioned Gaius not to speak of it before him. He turned his attention to his sister-in-law. 'You have not enquired into the purpose of my visit. There is one – something which will be revealed later today. I confess it is something of a mystery even to me, but I am confident that Lucius will soon resolve it.'

'You are always welcome here, Marcus Marcius. You need no purpose to visit us,' Aelia lied, her voice heavy with sarcasm. 'You know how well we like to hear of your valiant deeds.'

'That does not become you, Aelia.' He was delighted with her insincerity. 'You and I should always be honest with each other.'

She excused herself on the grounds that their meal required her supervision and left the room. Because their guest was Marcus, she had decreed that the light repast she had in mind be served with some formality in the triclinium, and until it was ready she did not intend to return.

Melissa, who since the death of Cordatus had been granted her freedom, had long since proved herself to be far more than the 'common chit' of whom Aelia had spoken so disparagingly. Now she had become a dear friend and a valued companion of her patroness.

Accustomed to eating with the family, she took her usual place beside Aelia. The women were seated on upright chairs of wicker facing the reclining men, so that with Aelia opposite her husband and Gaia opposite Gaius, Melissa had to be placed to sit facing Marcus, who was reclining beside his brother. The years had not in any way diminished her beauty, and Marcus, now setting eyes upon her for the first time – for Cordatus had kept her well concealed on his previous visits – was entranced.

'Who is this beauty?' he demanded to be told, staring hard at her.

The woman blushed, embarrassed by his bluntness.

'Melissa is a freedwoman,' Lucius provided, sensing danger. 'She belonged to Cordatus, and out of respect for his wishes, after his death I freed her. She assists Aelia in many ways.' He felt compelled to make something clear. 'And she is not available to you.'

Marcus sneered. 'I wondered what Cordatus had died of! A freedwoman, you say? Then she is free to choose, is she not?'

'Marcus!' Aelia angrily interposed. 'Really, Lucius, this is too bad. I won't have Melissa treated in this way.' Such conduct at her table was unforgivable.

Unperturbed, Marcus had already risen and stepped around to where Melissa was seated in order that he might scrutinize his target more closely. He took her by the hand and raised her so that she stood and had her turn in a circle before him while he silently appraised her figure. 'As you say,' he said to whoever cared to listen, 'Melissa is a freedwoman; she is free to come to my bed if she chooses. Is that not so, Melissa?'

She could not speak and only shook her head in reply, her face by now quite scarlet.

'What does that mean? "No, you are not free?" or, "No, you will not come?" I cannot believe you are rejecting me, Marcus Marcius, such a splendid person? A man of such repute, of such wealth? I shall expect you in my bed tonight.'

By now Aelia was on her feet. *Nobody,* she thought, *nobody has worse behaved kinsmen than my husband! Marcus has dragged Gaius away from his schooling merely to disport himself in this disgusting barrack-room manner, and what sort of an impression Gaia must be forming I cannot imagine. A fine example to set the young people!* Leaving Lucius' brother in Italy had been the only attractive aspect of settling in this inhospitable province. And then Marcus had to get himself posted here also. She was sure he had done it for no purpose other than to annoy her.

'Melissa, please do not heed the general. He is not serious; there is no compulsion on you whatsoever. My brother-in-law's sense of humour is quite objectionable, I fear.' At Aelia's appeal, the freedwoman resumed her place at the table.

'Ah, Aelia,' he rejoined, reclining again. 'You are so unkind to one who is so far from the comforts of a wife and home. My sickly Claudia will not forsake the pleasures of Rome to join me here – I did not choose so well as Lucius in that respect. What else have you for my entertainment and comfort? And who am I to do if not Melissa?'

'Lucius!' Annoyance had become outrage. She appealed to her husband, 'Stop him at once. He is intolerable – to come here uninvited and be so offensive. Your brother would do better to seek his comforts in the baths at Glevum.'

Acknowledging that perhaps he had gone too far, Marcus made a brief if insincere apology to his hostess, promising to make amends shortly when his surprise was delivered. This did nothing to improve her humour; they had all seen something before of Marcus' surprises. He had once brought a bear "to amuse the children" which had broken free and rampaged around their lovely garden, thus allowing him to display his prowess with a spear in destroying it. And on his first visit to them, he had arrived with friends who had behaved as abominably as he. Lucius had resolved that problem by organizing boar hunts which had taken them into the forest for the best part of each day. From her husband Aelia now exacted a promise that the next morning he would return to the colonia and take his obnoxious brother with him. The master of the household accepted the banishment cheerfully; he would enjoy Marcus' company in Glevum; they would relive youthful days again. At Aelia's insult his brother merely laughed.

Already Marcus' little surprise was making its reluctant and uncomfortable journey towards them. He had been pushed onto the back of an indifferent mount by an exceedingly doubtful Draco – a man fervently hoping that Lucius would not hold him responsible for this outrage – and it took all of Verluccus' enfeebled concentration to maintain his balance. Again he had abandoned all idea of taking vengeance, realizing it was quite beyond his present capacity. He tried to visualize Lucius but could only see the arrogant face of Marcus. He tried to imagine what his reception would be like but knew only that it must be brutal. As a child he had been treated savagely. What would they do to him now as a man?

But it was not those thoughts which caused hot tears to sting his eyes and pour unchecked down his cheeks. The clouds had dispersed, and the air had cleared. The sun, for so many days concealed, now streamed brilliantly from the sky, the still damp vegetation sparkled and steamed, and the bright colours of autumn lit the shrubs beside the path. A flood of emotions surged through him as he recognized the familiar shapes of hills and the ancient track. At a break in the trees they paused, and one of them read the legend carved on the tombstone to his companion. While they did so, he gazed at the smoke rising far in the distance – perhaps from his own home, he thought, and sobbed unashamedly.

The escorting men sniggered and nudged each other, entertained by the spectacle. He despised them the more for it; they knew nothing.

Word of his arrival was delivered promptly to Marcus, who excused himself, begging his host and family to remain at their places.

The condition of the slave was perfect, exactly as he wished it to be. He noted the tear-stained face with added satisfaction. 'You have the box?' They had. They removed the small chest from the saddle pack and would have given it to Tertius.

'No, he is to carry it.'

'Carry that and follow me,' he ordered, remembering his rehearsed British phrase. Unable to summon up the strength or the will to think or to do otherwise, Verluccus obeyed, shuffling in the direction of the house. At the touch of the prodding stick, he paused and might have turned on his tormentor, but there were many hands beside him ready to prevent any worthwhile action.

Within the house the family had heard the drag of metal from the approaching chains and had almost prepared themselves for something terrible to appear – but not for what did.

The sight and the stench of the filthy, stumbling, and haggard creature which Marcus now paraded in triumph into her dining room appalled Aelia exactly as he had intended it to.

How could he? How could he do this? Has he not already done enough? He has been here for a matter of hours, and now this! A dirty, stinking prisoner fit only for the mines brought here into my home – unspeakable. 'Lucius, do something,' she muttered, her hand clasped across her nose. From somewhere Melissa produced a phial of lavender oil and pressed it upon her.

Lucius spoke in fury. 'What is the meaning of this?'

'What?' His brother affected pained surprise. 'Are you not pleased? You thought I should have taken captives, and so I have – one at least. Especially saved for you. Out of all those who were slain, this one I kept alive just for you. Truly, Brother, you ought to show me more gratitude.'

'Why have you brought me this? Why here? What mischief are

you about?' Lucius had risen to his feet and advanced to confront his brother. The household slaves stood aghast, unsure of what they ought to do.

Gaius, from his place near to his sister, cautiously sat upright, wondering what was to happen. His heart was pounding, and his breath was short. He did not dare to crystallize the sensations in his brain. Gaia's hand had locked his wrist in a steely grip; she too was sensing what he sensed.

'I am returning that which you lost,' Marcus was saying. 'Good of me, is it not?'

'It might be had I lost him! But I do not know this creature.'

'Give the casket to the lady.' Out of the unintelligible Latin, the words in Celtic shook Verluccus into action, and he relieved himself of his burden dropping it clumsily onto the low table in front of Aelia so that there was a resounding crash. Slaves scurried forward to retrieve the spinning dishes. She opened it wonderingly and took from it his own precious pieces and held them to the light, admiring the softly gleaming coils of the golden torc and the polished silver and bronze brooches with their finely tooled decorative swirls and the enamelled armlets; he wished he had thrown it at her.

It must be him. Could it be any other? Gaius grasped Gaia tightly by the arm in his excitement. His throat was dry. He thought his heart had stopped beating. He no longer noticed the stench. He had stopped breathing, waiting, waiting for confirmation. The years raced through his head, the years of patiently waiting, of believing, of struggling to master the language, of dreading the day they must embark for Rome without him, of knowing, knowing beyond a shadow of doubt that he must return.

The waiting was over. Verluccus was home – home where he belonged. Gaius looked at his sister and saw in her eyes that same intensity of excitement. Neither dared to speak. They watched the drama in silence, fearful to make a sound.

'Turn round. Turn him around,' Marcus wearily instructed, gesticulating as, fuming with anger and impotency, the slave stood rooted to the spot, ignoring his command. Marcus ripped apart the sodden tunic to reveal the scar, and Lucius could deny the fact no longer.

'Verluccus? It is Verluccus? Truly, Marcus, I did not know him. Aelia? Did you know him, Aelia?'

Aelia could not have identified him as the child whose enslavement she had sanctioned had he come to the door of his own accord and abjectly begged for their mercy and forgiveness for running away – which he had not. He stood smouldering in mutinous hatred before them while they crowed triumphantly at his recapture. Marcus explained to Aelia that the gold he had given to her had been found on the slave. He prodded Verluccus' arm with his ebony rod.

'Remove that piece.'

The slave did not speak but shook his head, his mouth clenched even more tightly and his hand closed over the necklet. There was a struggle before the escort could loose it, and the wire was torn asunder so that the beads scattered as they fell to the floor and a small slave boy dived hastily to retrieve them. They were presented to Gaia by Marcus himself since the slave had robbed him of the final spectacle he had in mind.

The girl received the fragmented necklet in wonderment and for the first time looked into the slave's tragic eyes, seeing now the tear stains on his sweaty face, the faint remains of bruising around the still-livid wound. She suddenly saw her idolized uncle in a new light. He had become sullied, tarnished, befouled. She did not like this; it was wrong.

Aelia had already retrieved the beads and sent them away with instructions to Delia that the jewel must thoroughly be cleaned and repaired before it was returned to her mistress. Now, belatedly, Lucius intervened.

'Palatus, remove him. Instruct Victor to find a suitable place where he may be held securely; he will require chains.' He turned to Marcus. 'Your men may be relieved now.' He had had enough of this; all of his slaves were treated with the respect due to their station. He had not raised his children to deal with their inferiors in this manner, and he could see how distressed Gaia had become.

Marcus at last seemed chastened and silenced. He acceded to Lucius' requests, and the escort was discharged. He wondered when he would receive the explanation which he considered he was due. There was certainly consternation here – not at all what he had anticipated. He had seen the sheer terror in the steward's eyes when Lucius had instructed him to conduct the slave from the room. Palatus had summoned Victor to achieve that task, and it was not solely because the man considered the role beneath him, he was certain. Nevertheless, he waited with considerable patience and even allowed Lucius to conduct him around the estate first, trying to make amends for his impossible conduct by admiring the many improvements made to the house and outbuildings since his last visit. To do so was not difficult, for he could agree with his brother's implicit belief that the place was as close to perfection as any house of its size in the province.

At length they found themselves in the stables comparing Tempestus with Cervus.

'This is a fine animal your son has; I hope he treats him well. A beast like this is too good to be wasted on a boy. And you still have old Ravus, I see.' Marcus' attention to the colt was interrupted by the jealous nose of Lucius' ancient iron-grey gelding.

Lucius fed the grey an apple. 'Ah, yes, my old friend. I would not insult him by pensioning him off yet. He bears me very kindly. Young Cervus here is a fine animal, the best to be had. I bought him for Gaius' fifteenth birthday to celebrate his coming of age. Did you race?'

Marcus laughed. 'No, much to Tempestus' disgust, we did not. He thinks the colt an upstart. We talked a lot. The boy has turned out well, I think, but he is a bit serious. Do the young of today have the fun we used to when we were children?'

Lucius grinned. 'Ah, yes, I have no doubt about who dragged him away from his lessons. It is too reminiscent of our own schooldays. But he is not averse to enjoying himself when he so chooses; there is plenty of time for wildness yet, but speaking as a father, I shall not encourage it. Shall we ride awhile?' He was itching to try out Tempestus.

'I would rather not. Tell me about this slave. What's to be done with him? You have no use for him here, I think?'

'No, I do not make it a practice to keep runaways. It is not good a good example to set the others, and they can never be trusted. This one has been absent for nine years, and he was with us less than two whole days.' He dropped his voice and agonized. 'I did not do it, Marcus. It was done in my name and I accept the responsibility for it, but it was not sanctioned by me.' He related the story of why and how he had come by the slave and how he had escaped. 'For all this time I have supposed him dead. To discover that Virens did not kill him after all goes some way to lifting a heavy burden from me. We never spoke of it, and I lacked the stomach to enquire.'

'How ironic, then, that it should be he who killed Virens,' said Marcus casually. 'Now I understand the terror on your steward's face. A full-grown man exuding hatred is a different proposition from a small and frightened child.'

Lucius was still reeling from the shock. 'Virens is dead? Killed? Up there? My poor friend. My poor daughter.' He groaned and clutched at his head. 'You should have told me sooner. I counted him the best of my friends. Why did you not tell me at once? And that one killed him? How do you know that?'

Marcus recounted how they had been discovered. 'You may be sure that damage to his head was done either by Virens or on his behalf. The girl will be upset?'

'Upset! We all are upset!' A patriarchal Lucius spoke angrily. 'Gaia lives only for the day she will be married. Forgive me, but I must go to her and break this bitter news.' He departed hastily.

He took the precaution of warning Aelia first, and when she had composed herself they went in search of Gaia. They found her deep in wondering conversation with her brother, making plans about Verluccus' future and speculating on his past. She was gently drawn away and taken into her father's study, where the sad facts were related to her.

Her mind struggled to deny what she was hearing. At first she screamed aloud and refused to believe it. Then in her mother's soft embrace she gave herself up to broken-hearted sobbing. She ran from them to her room and would allow no-one to enter. She would not speak to Gaius, did not want to know any more about the returned Verluccus. They had added to her heartache by telling her that it was he who had killed her betrothed, and she hated him.

Gaius joined his father and uncle in the bathing suite.

'I suppose you will sell this slave?' Marcus speculated. 'I had thought he would make an arena fighter. You have not had one since you retired Victor; that is a long time. I think that he should die. If it is not done soon, he will be wondering at the delay. Dedicated to the memory of Decimus Aemilius Virens, his death should be a comfort to your daughter, and the spirited battle to which he should treat us will make an entertaining spectacle.'

Lucius, ignoring the ironic tone, was minded to agree with him. 'To witness that end of him would give satisfaction and be a comfort to us all. Virens was a beloved friend to all my family. I was proud to look forward to our connection through marriage. His death is a devastating blow of which I do not think you have any conception – you spoke of it so casually.'

There was an immediate protest from Gaius. 'Father, remember you gave Verluccus to me. Surely it is for me to decide what is to be done with him. I have my manly toga now.'

'My apologies, son. You are right. Pronounce what is to be done with him.' Lucius accepted the rebuke with a fond grin.

'I shall keep him.'

'Good man!' It was Marcus who spoke. 'I believe you will get good sport with him in the arena when he is fit again.'

'Oh no!' The youth was quite decided. 'Verluccus is to be my body slave instead of Felix.'

'Impossible!' His elders spoke in unison.

'That is out of the question, my son,' added Lucius. 'Even if he were suitable for such labour, and surely even you can see how unsuitable he is, the fact that he has killed Virens requires that he pay the penalty of his own life. Decimus Aemilius Virens is dead, and that brute is his butcher. Your sister is inconsolable. Do you seriously intend that she should suffer the pain of seeing him alive, flourishing? Seeing him round the house, about you, every day knowing what he has done?'

It was as if the death of the fine young tribune meant nothing to the boy.

'Father,' he said, 'I have known Verluccus would come back to me; for all these years I have known it. Why do you suppose I have learned to speak the British tongue? Only so that I could talk properly to him. I know it is intended that he be with me. It would have been all right then had I been allowed to have my own way.'

'I seem to remember you did have your own way then!' replied Lucius with some heat. 'You do your case no good by reminding me how badly you can behave! No, in this I agree with your uncle. He must die, but he may do so fighting. We will get him fit and send him to the gladiator training school at Corinium. In hope of living, he will give a better show, and it will be something for you to take your school friends to see. I think none of them own their own gladiator?'

He agreed; none did. But he was more determined than his father suspected, though he had grown wise enough not to make an issue of it there and then. Instead he suggested that they might look at him again, perhaps have him brought before them after the evening meal, cleaned up and rested.

Equally certain that the boy would see how ill he compared with Felix, Lucius agreed. He reminded his son that he still had to return to Glevum early in the morning and then firmly had the subject of the slave put aside.

They passed what remained of the afternoon pleasantly enough, amusing themselves with shocking stories while their attendants got on with the business of cleansing them; Tertius had brought Marcus' favourite oils and perfumes freshly replenished from the town, and he shared them with generous liberality. To be included with his father in men's talk of the kind in which they now indulged was a rare experience for Gaius and a very enjoyable one. Too often Lucius forgot his son legally was a man.

—————— ᎒ ——————

Verluccus too had received a bathing of sorts. When they had exchanged Marcus' chains for those spared by Agricola, they had swilled the muck from his skin and replaced the rags with a cast-off tunic supplied by Victor, the only slave in the household large enough to provide a garment for him. Victor also had poured some foul-tasting medicine down his throat and advised him to sleep. He was secured again now, lodged in a substantial wooden outhouse and overseen by a huge one-eyed mastiff so dark a brindle in colour it was almost black, whose kennel the place appeared rightly to be. The half-opened door allowed the dog to come and go at will, but since the slave was chained to a ring cemented into the wall intended once to secure a bull, there was no danger of his escape.

The captive eyed his guard warily. He had the distinct impression that the opportunity to hound him on a long chase would be very welcome to the monster, whose cold nose inspected him very closely each time it entered the shed as if he were a favoured bone, or as if fixing the scent of him for some future pursuit.

Woken from fitful sleep yet again by the hound's thorough and somewhat menacing examination, Verluccus sat with his chin cupped in his hands and considered his situation. That briefly nurtured hope had died; there was to be no possibility of revenge. As yet their intentions towards him remained, so far as he was concerned, a mystery. But that they were not to be favourable towards him he had no doubt. He was gaining his strength, however. Whatever the overseer had dosed him with appeared to have done much good. Now he might have eaten, but the food which had been left for him had obviously not been allowed to go to waste; he trusted the black hound might view him more favourably for its meal.

He risked talking to the dog, speaking friendly words and praying that it had not been trained to rip to pieces any man not able to speak to it in Latin, and tentatively dragged its bucket of water towards himself. The dog's ears pricked, and its eyes followed the movement, but it made no objection as its charge scooped handfuls of water from within and drank. He sighed and spoke to it more boldly, hoping that it was fed regularly.

The Romans had a plan for him, he was certain of that, and that it would involve his death required little imagination. But if he was to die, he preferred it to be by his hand or, since that possibility seemed to have been denied him, by forcing their hand to be swift. He must do something which would force them to kill him instantly. If he should get into that room again or if the chance came in some other way, he should attack their women. They would not allow such an action to pass unpunished, would they? He was not destined to die the heroic death granted to his brothers, but he could make it swift and certain, and more importantly, it would be very, very welcome.

Satisfied that, in a manner of speaking, he was again master of his own destiny, he allowed healing sleep again to overwhelm him. The mastiff sighed heavily, consumed the remaining water, and shook its loose jowls so that saliva splattered them both. Then it lay down with its head across his chest, and the man drew warmth from the sleeping dog.

They were stuffing their faces again. It was the splendid meal over which the cook had laboured for most of the day. They were in the same situation as before, and it crossed Verluccus' mind that they might well have been eating continuously since he had last been placed before them. They lounged gesticulating to one another, and he knew they were discussing him. Women were present again, but he looked in vain for the girl who had been given Bodyn's necklet. He had that determined she would be the first one to die, and he would snatch the beads from her throat as he strangled her.

But Gaia would not come to the table or touch the delicacies placed before her in her bedchamber. She lay weeping as she had never wept before, and had Verluccus known that and the reason why, it would have cheered his heart.

He considered the others, calculated which of them it would be the easiest to reach. He could certainly kill one of them if he acted swiftly. He had been placed immediately before the young man – Gaius, he presumed, recalling the name from long ago, though he would not have recognized him. The sickly pallor of vague recollection was gone. Tight dark curls framed a lean, sallow, somewhat earnest face, and large dark eyes scrutinized him thoroughly. A small, full mouth smiled at him as if the man were about to speak or as if he were concerned for his predicament. He scorned such fake concern. He was no fool; he would have no truck with such artifice. Unconsciously he drew himself up, scowling arrogantly at the diners as if he, rather than being their prisoner, saw them prostrating themselves before him.

'He is an arrogant bastard,' Marcus commented, looking up for a moment. 'Such a pity you let him escape you. Properly trained, he might have proved really useful.'

Marcus had placed himself very close to Melissa. In order to obtain this position and be permitted to retain it, he had allowed Aelia to extract a pledge from him that he would behave properly, and he was endeavouring to do so, putting his hand out to the food before them as she did and confining his offensive remarks to whispering, 'Tonight, my beauty; do not delay.' Apart from that, his conversation with her was general and bland, or so he supposed.

Lucius nodded in unsmiling agreement. 'I recollect he was an extremely badly behaved youngster. I think training him would even then have been a full-time job for someone. Now he is beyond such service. There are suitable places for such as he but not in my home. I am confident that Gaius will come to reason and we shall send him to the gladiator school at Corinium.'

Verluccus was looking at the woman seated before Marcus. His woman, he supposed – a suitable victim. He considered the other woman, the one to whom his jewellery had been given, Lucius' wife. How careless they seemed of their proximity to him and the danger they were in. When they were distracted, when something drew their attention away, then he would act. He needed only a fragment of time; he would dive and grab both their throats and choke the life out of their jewelled necks.

He turned his attention again to the youth, the Gaius. There was no woman seated before him; to attack him would be as good as taking the women and less shameful.

A slender boy, a slave a few years younger and considerably smaller than Verluccus and bearing a large dish of oysters, approached the youth. He knelt and offered the dish to his master in an exaggerated show of subservience, an ostentatious gesture but at the same time a display of easy familiarity, as if the slave as much as the young master was enjoying the charade. Gaius had not, so far as Verluccus could see, demanded the oysters, but he smiled with pleasure at his slave, choosing carefully the best in the dish and rolling his head back so that the choice morsel easily slipped into his throat.

This callous indifference to his plight was too much; rage coursed through Verluccus' blood, and he seized the moment. He wrenched his chains from the grip of the one holding them, and in one bound he launched himself across the small serving tables to take Gaius by that exposed and tempting throat. Cups, plates, flasks, and Aelia's carefully selected delicacies scattered and spilled, and the slave crashed heavily onto the surprised youth. The momentum carried them both off the couch to land in a heap on the floor beyond.

In the brief stunned silence that immediately followed they lay quite still, each contemplating the other. But he had loosened his grip on Gaius even before Marcus and Lucius were there, hauling him to his feet.

No words could be heard above Aelia's hysterical screams.

When they were certain the poor lad was neither dead nor scathed, Marcus turned to the men who had now once more got a grip of the troublemaker. 'Punish him,' he ordered. 'But do not break any limbs or do serious damage. I have other plans for that one.'

Aelia, almost composed again, could scarcely believe her ears. He must be destroyed instantly. Nothing else would suffice.

'What do you say, Gaius?' demanded his uncle. 'You have a little brine on your face and a few wine stains on your toga, but I see no other damage. You are not harmed, are you?'

Marcus was right; it was the speed and surprise of the attack from one they had presumed to be half-dead that had been most alarming. Gaius remembered how their eyes had met, how he had placed his own hands on the threatening wrists in what should have been a hopeless attempt to fight for his life, and how the grip on him – which so easily could have taken the breath from him forever – had immediately loosened. *And that was before the others intervened.* He grinned at his uncle. 'Not even a bruise.'

'What are the other slaves to think?' Lucius demanded. 'I dare not allow him to live after doing such a thing. You of all people, Marcus, should appreciate the necessity of good discipline.'

'Who said he was going to live? The slave is condemned. I merely suggest you postpone his demise. He did that in order to be killed; you may be sure of that. I, however, do not have my actions dictated by slaves.'

'You are all forgetting once again that Verluccus belongs to me.' Gaius still managed to surprise them. 'This makes no difference. As you can see, I am without a scratch. I shall go to him. I shall learn why he did this, whether it is me he hates or life itself.'

He did not linger for permission but left immediately.

Polyphemus, who necessarily had to be restrained while the punishment was meted out for fear of his enthusiastic assistance, now bestowed his affectionate energy in a noisy greeting of Gaius and happily accepted the friendly reproof. He watched the youth carefully and now discovered that his kennel mate was once again to be regarded as a friend.

The offender was very firmly secured, no longer linked to the ring on the wall but flat on his back on the mud floor, his wrists and ankles extended and fastened to stakes driven into the ground so that he had no hope of levering them free. His face was barely recognizable. Blood was streaming from the head wound again and now from the nose and mouth also. By morning his eyes would be black and his face swollen beyond recognition. Chaining him in such a fashion seemed superfluous; a man in such a condition could barely move unaided. He was choking on the blood, spluttering and gasping for breath. Gaius knelt to clear the airway himself.

'Bastard!' was all the thanks he received. At least that meant the man could breathe properly, since he could speak. There were signs of bruising on his chest, and Gaius wondered if ribs were broken. Soon that area too could be black and blue. Now surely was the time to practice his studiously acquired Celtic.

'Do you know me, Verluccus? I am your master, Gaius, Gaius Marcius Phillipianus.'

'Piss off!'

The sound was distorted due to the damaged mouth. He could not have heard correctly.

'What did you say? Try to speak more clearly.'

'Piss off!' the slave hissed. 'Go away, bastard. Go and torture someone else, you repellent bastard.' There followed a torrent of Celtic obscenities which Palatus most certainly would not have taught to Aelia's children and probably did not know in any case. Their meaning, however, was quite explicit and the venom with which they were delivered quite shocking. No one had ever spoken to Gaius in such a manner; no slave would have dared to. He hastily ordered Felix and the men to leave them. At the very least such disrespect merited a flogging, and that was the last thing he wanted to do right now.

He deliberated on the problem. 'I know why you did that, why you attacked me. It will avail you nothing. It is my intention that you are to live. Here as my slave you will be treated well and have a good life. Surely that is preferable to being sold to work the mines or death in the arena?'

There was a long pause as if the slave was evaluating the options.

Finally he opened his eyes again and, seeing his tormentor still awaiting a response, spoke quite slowly and almost distinctly so that there could be no doubt of his meaning.

'Preferable? What I prefer is to be rid of you. Now piss off!'

'I am not going to allow you to die. It will be all right. You will see.' Gaius wished he felt as confident as he hoped he sounded.

'You will get nowhere like that.'

The voice that interrupted belonged to Marcus. Gaius had not heard him approach. He must have heard those last abusive words even if he had not heard those uttered earlier. The young man rose and turned to face him.

'If you are so bent on keeping him, hand him over to me,' Marcus continued easily. 'I will soon get him into shape. I am perfectly willing to undertake his training for you, but your father is right; he can never replace that little shadow Felix. It is too late for anything like that.'

Gaius replied firmly, 'I thank you, Uncle, but no. He would then be your man, not mine.'

Marcus laughed. 'That's true.' He drew his nephew aside. 'Leave him as he is for a while to think over what you have said. He will be of a different frame of mind in a day or two.'

In the interval afforded by Marcus' abrupt departure, Lucius found the opportunity he had been looking for. Since the return of Verluccus he had discovered his guilt had not been assuaged but rekindled. Even the failed attack on his son had not altered those feelings. He remembered the brother whom he had once questioned and how greatly that young man had impressed him.

At the sound of her mother's screams, Gaia had come running into the dining room. She turned to her father, her face stricken. 'You know why he did that, don't you? It was because of what Uncle Marcus did to him. He thought he was going to be tormented again.

Did you see his face when he was first brought in? He had been crying. Was that because he had been fetched back to us?'

'Had he?' Lucius had not noticed. He held her close and comforted her, saying, 'Perhaps it was because he was returning to his old home. I may well shed tears myself when I see Rome again.' He turned to his wife. 'If, when Gaius returns, he is still of the same mind about Verluccus, I am considering giving the boy a chance. Can you moderate your objection to his being here? If he will submit to our authority, perhaps I could find work for him around the farm or sell him into a reasonable situation. Fit and obedient, he could be really useful to Agricola.'

His wife was horrified. 'Lucius, are you mad? Clearly he did that to accomplish his death. If this plan has failed, what more will he do? Attack Gaia? Attack young Quintus?'

'I can make sure he does not get the chance until I am satisfied he is safe. It occurs to me that this would afford an excellent opportunity to give Gaius some real responsibility.'

She could not believe he was serious. 'Lucius, he is beyond everything. How he hates us! Did you not tell me yourself he killed Virens, our own dear friend who would have been your son-in-law? Is Gaia to bear the pain of seeing the criminal who murdered her betrothed strutting before her eyes every day? To know that he is living here on this very site, thriving? Imagine the effect his presence will have on the other slaves! No, Lucius, I beg you, no. Marcus should not have brought him here. He could have easily have handed him over to you in Glevum, but that is not his way! He did this to mortify us because this creature is so awful.'

'I know, I know.' He raised his hands defensively. 'Verluccus is quite appalling, but I feel in part responsible for what he has become. He was a child when we obtained him, and if we had not interfered in his life, in all probability he would have grown into a decent young man like his brother. That brother has never, to the best of my knowledge, transgressed any law.'

'That may be so,' she answered. 'He was foolish to run away. Had he remained with us, he might have become an excellent servant and companion, but he did not and he is not. He has had these past nine years to brood on what happened to him here and to cultivate his hatred of us. And who would undertake his training? Agricola and Victor have enough to do; you cannot expect Palatus to accomplish it.'

'Gaius seems to think he can do it. I could give him a fixed period of time, but he must show me that he is in earnest. It may be that already he has discovered the futility of his enterprise, and if that is the case then so be it. But, my darling, don't you see? This is the best way to silence Gaius. When he has tried and failed to bring this fellow to submission, he will concede defeat and defer to my wisdom.'

She would not see it his way. 'Lucius, he is far too dangerous for Gaius. Why, even Marcus kept him in chains. Give him a chance if you must, but not here – send him somewhere else. And please, please, my lord, don't give Gaius the idea that he may keep him.'

He all but resigned the argument. 'I am sorry you see it that way. He will have to remain here for a while – at least until he is fit to be moved. He can stay in the outhouse until he has recovered from his punishment. Are you so fixed against him? What if I told Gaius he might have him until after the kalends of December, say for twenty days? What if we gave him that small amount of time? If he agrees to that and fails his purpose, he shall not pester me again. In the meantime Verluccus will remain strictly confined and quite unable to harm you.'

'Oh, Lucius,' she wailed, 'why must Marcus be so awful? Every time he comes here he does something quite outrageous, but on this occasion he has excelled even himself.'

This he could smile at. 'I shall return to Glevum tomorrow and take him with me. He enjoys teasing you because you rise so beautifully to his baiting as you did when he was toying with Melissa. You should call his bluff sometime. You would see him turn tail. Remember, my darling girl, he is only my brother.'

It was as though Aelia caught a drift of mind he had not intended. She looked suddenly inspired. 'Why, how right you are. I have it!' she exclaimed after a moment's consideration. 'I shall let this Verluccus creature stay here and pretend I am glad of it at least until Marcus has returned to his barracks. That will fox him!'

He hugged her. 'You never cease to surprise and delight me. I shall allow you to inform Marcus of our decision.' He bent his head to hers to enjoy the taste of her lips, Gaia quite forgotten.

After a few moments, the girl interrupted them. 'Father, Mother, what of me? Am I to endure this? Am I to be forced to see him as you say, strutting daily before me, while the man I was intended to wed lies dead by his hand? I was glad for Gaius when Marcus brought him back to us, for I know how much he longed to have him restored to him, but now that I know that he killed Virens I want only to see him dead. If Marcus wants him put to death by the sword in tribute to Virens, then that is what I want also.'

Her passionate stance shook Lucius; he had not expected opposition from this quarter, because she was such a staunch supporter of her brother and the betrothal to Virens had been arranged at such an early age. He had not supposed she could harbour real love for him, not of the kind he and Aelia had for each other. He knew himself properly defeated. Gaius must be persuaded to part with the slave and quickly too. He drew an arm around her to comfort her. 'Do not be sad, my sweet. I do not think Verluccus could have known whom he killed. In the heat of battle men are killed; that is the way of it. Virens was brave if unwise, but you can be proud that he chose you to be his wife.' He remembered ruefully that the choosing had been done by his daughter, but that did not need to be said.

She was stubborn, her dark eyes flashing as dangerously as could those of her mother, her face still reddened by her tears. Her breast was heaving with emotion as she drew herself up, and he saw that she was indeed a woman now, no longer his little girl. 'Virens was a tribune, not a common soldier,' she said angrily. 'Of course Verluccus knew whom he was killing! Is he to be rewarded for that by the licence which Felix has? Or will you do your duty to our dearest friend and have him executed for his crime?'

He had no answer. He was tortured by her argument and torn in two by his children.

Footsteps heralded the return of Gaius and Marcus, and Melissa took advantage of the warning to make a discreet departure. She was clear of the room before he entered it, and he looked at the place she had vacated and turned to his hostess with a quizzical eyebrow. The lady could not totally suppress a smile for her small triumph as he inclined his head towards her in acknowledgement of the fact. Marcus and Aelia understood each other well. The intimacy was lost on her son.

'Father,' Gaius began, innocent of the fresh dilemma, 'please overlook this misdemeanour and allow me to keep Verluccus. I know I can get through to him; already he has spoken to me.'

'Really?' Lucius sounded impressed. 'That is progress. What conversation took place? He has apologized to you? Begged you to forgive him? Prostrated himself at your feet and invoked your mercy? He has responded quickly to your uncle's government, I think. Perhaps that should give you some guidance on the best way to deal with troublesome slaves!'

'Well, not exactly.' He was horribly aware of his uncle's amused interest. 'It was not exactly a conversation.'

'But he spoke? What did he say? We are all ears – are we not, Aelia?'

'Indeed we are.'

'He was rather rude, Father. I admit that. I cannot repeat the things he said. But it was a response, and that is progress, is it not? He had not spoken at all before.'

'And insults convince you that he will make a loyal and devoted servant? I am amazed. What kind of an education are you receiving at that school I waste so much of my money on?'

'I know, Father, that you expect me now to make some fine speech eulogising those virtues which I claim to see in him but others do not. But truthfully I cannot, for there are none. Verluccus is to me every bit as savage and dirty and coarse as he is to you. His manners are probably as bad as they ever were, and he has, thanks to Uncle Marcus, no reason to do other than to hate us. I am sorry, Marcus Marcius, but he cannot like what you did to his people. You may well say that he has not returned to me of his own accord, that he had no choice, but I truly believe it was no accident that he alone out of that massacre was delivered alive into Marcus' hands. Nine years ago it was the gods who spirited him away from us. Can there be any other explanation for his so complete disappearance? And now those protectors have restored him, and you should hesitate to scorn their wishes. When you sent Palatus to fetch him for me you acted as the augurs indicated. Have them advise you now, and you will see if I am not right. I know there is a bond between us. More than that I cannot explain, but I know in my heart it will be all right. It is meant to be so.'

What on earth had made him say that? His father would think him deranged. Crimson faced, he waited anxiously for Lucius to respond.

'You seem suddenly well acquainted with the deities,' sneered Lucius. 'I had not realized you had aspirations to a priesthood! The family shrine has not seen more of you than custom demands, I think! So this creature is a visitation on us from the gods, is he? I must confess I had not looked upon him in that light. Are we to learn more of what is intended? Do we do wrong not to house him in a temple, I wonder?'

Gaius flushed again. 'I have no aspirations to become a priest, Father. I simply expressed my feelings. I see now that I should have chosen my words with more care, given the matter more thought and come to you with some tale that he had apologized for his conduct and begged our forgiveness – had sworn to serve me faithfully. That, perhaps, you would accept? I beg you to allow me to try to tame him. What do you lose by it? Give me until we come with Antonius to camp. If by then I have achieved nothing, I shall hand him over to you and make no further complaint of it. Whatever decision you then make about his future I swear I shall accept unreservedly.'

'And what', Lucius demanded, 'can you say to ease the pain of your sister? What can make his continued existence tolerable for her?

Why should Gaia have to endure his presence here, whether as your body slave or otherwise, in the knowledge that he killed her betrothed and our dear friend, Virens?'

Gaius had anticipated support from his sister, not opposition. He went across to her and took her hands in his. 'Gaia, do not be pained by this. Do you really want him to be put to death?' He looked into her eyes and saw bewilderment; she did not know what she wanted now. 'Gaia, if you demand it, he must die. I give way to you as I love you and cannot deny you your right to vengeance. But think! Marcus told you how it was. Could Verluccus know Virens? Know that he was your betrothed? Think you for only that reason he killed him? No! Consider, I beg you! Marcus' men killed every man, woman, and child of his community. Could Verluccus see his own wife and children die and do nothing? Thieves and criminals they most surely were, I will not deny it, but they too died, many perhaps killed by Virens' own hand. Cannot so many deaths atone for your bereavement?'

She wrapped her arms around him and wept. 'Oh, Gaius, I did want you to have him. I was glad to see him restored to you, but what shall I feel when I see him living and think of Virens dead?'

He held her close. 'Gaia, I promise you sincerely, if Father will allow me to keep him and I tame him, and even if he becomes my body servant and as close to me as Felix, if you are still unhappy about it, I swear now before these witnesses that I shall bow to your wishes in all things. Is that a comfort to you?' He sensed a change come upon her. 'Will you now withdraw your opposition to my keeping him?'

She dipped her head, and he turned again to hear his father's decision. It seemed Lucius had relented.

'If you are correct about the wishes of the gods, the time you ask for should be ample. What do you say to that, Aelia?'

'Gaius,' she said, taking the hint, 'your father and I have been discussing this, and we are minded to let you try with him.'

Whatever Marcus' initial reaction to this may have been it was impossible for her to see, for her manly son forgot his dignity enough to fling his arms around her and hug her tightly. 'Oh, Mother, thank you, thank you, Mother. It is true, Father? You do really mean it?'

Aelia smiled and nodded, unable to conceal the enormous satisfaction she felt in defeating the purpose of Marcus twice in such a short space of time, for now she could see the genuine bewilderment on her brother-in-law's face.

'Yes, my son.' Lucius decided it was incumbent upon him to set out a few conditions. 'You may try to do something with him, but I shall allow you only the time you requested. Your encampment here is due to commence on the day following the kalends of December. If by that date he has not shown any sign of submitting to you, you will hand him over to me, and there will be no argument. Do you consent?'

'What do you require of him?' It was Marcus who asked the question, curious to discover what his brother had in mind.

'For Gaius to keep him, he must openly acknowledge Gaius to be his master and that he will serve him and obey him in all things. That acknowledgement will be made before the household so that there is no doubt about it. Otherwise he is to be mine, and I shall determine his future.'

Marcus scoffed at the idea. 'Then you may as well bring him with us tomorrow, for he will never reach such a condition, no matter how long you allow.'

'No, Father, I agree,' Gaius hastily interrupted his uncle. 'I agree to that stipulation – to anything. I shall do whatever you say.'

'In that case, Gaius,' Marcus said, quite intending to be helpful, 'you should accept my help. You are given little more than half a month, for the ides are almost upon us. It will be a complete waste of your time. Resign him to me now; let me train him for you.'

'Furthermore,' Lucius interposed, 'until I am satisfied that he is safe, he is to remain confined securely. I mean he is not to be admitted into the house at all. He must not appear before your mother or Gaia or Quintus or behave in any manner calculated to disrupt the management of this household. From now on he is solely your responsibility. I shall have no more said on the matter.' He raised his hand in warning; the subject was closed.

———————— ⑤ ————————

'You are crazy, Lucius. Whatever possessed Aelia to change her mind?' Aelia had retired to her room with her daughter, and the men relaxed taking a last cup of wine together. 'That slave is good for one thing only; send him to Corinium without further delay.'

'My wife has a whim; you know what women are.' Lucius shrugged to indicate the matter should be put aside. 'I consider this creature has taken up more of our time and breath than he justifies. I do not want another word on the subject either from you or from Gaius, and Gaius, tomorrow morning, first thing, you return to your lessons.'

His son wisely held his tongue.

The little that remained of their evening passed pleasantly enough. The brothers brought each other up to date on their careers, and Gaius found he was fascinated by his father's enthusiasm for the work he had undertaken, proud even of his achievements in administering and more fully Romanizing the native people not only in the Dobunni tribal lands but beyond. Gaius had always harboured a secret shame that while his uncle and his uncle's exploits were known to everyone of his acquaintance, his father was unlikely to be known of beyond the limits of his estates or the towns he had cause to visit on official business, and he always had considered the life of his father exceedingly dull compared with that of a military man.

Lucius had enjoyed a career in the army, of course, up to a point – not to commanding a legion himself. He had served in the Senate too, and had he not offended Domitian, no doubt the family would have continued to live in Rome. Gaius discovered he was scowling at the thought of that. Had they done so, he never would have encountered Verluccus. He stopped himself from that line of thinking and concentrated instead on trying to recall what had caused his uncle and father to laugh so heartily.

Marcus had noticed his absent-mindedness. If he knew to where his nephew's thoughts had strayed, he kept his thoughts to himself and instead regaled them again with a series of stories which would surely have turned Aelia to stone from shock had she been present.

'How can you two be brothers?' Gaius wondered aloud, noting that all of the entertainment was being provided by Marcus. 'You are so unalike. Gaia and I might be taken for twins we are so similar.'

'That, young man, is not at all the sort of thing you should say.' Marcus laughed. 'You cannot lay the blame for that at my door, Lucius! Truly, Gaius, we are certainly brothers, and should you meet up with your uncle Quintus and your grandfather, Senator Quintus Marcius, then you will realize how very mild-mannered and gentle this particular uncle is! That is not what you are thinking at the moment, is it?'

Gaius was spared having to answer this by Lucius. 'Yes, Marcus, despite your merciless teasing of my poor Aelia, I consider us very close, and I enjoy your visits immensely. Do not take it badly that we return to Glevum tomorrow; you will find much there to divert you, I am sure. The public baths are no disgrace, and we have a comic theatre too. Had you brought captives, we might have had reason to go to Corinium, but as things stand there are but a few poor wretches awaiting execution there, not worthy of the interest of a cultivated man.'

'Maybe by December?'

'No, Marcus.' Lucius frowned. 'I will not have that subject raised again. In any case, we shall then be approaching the Saturnalia; I see no merit in giving our slaves such ideas!'

They laughed at his joke and retired in good humour.

4

―――――――――― ⟡ ――――――――――

Gaius rose early. He had barely slept from excitement and making plans, relieved and happy that Verluccus had been restored to him. He had a duty first to the Home Bringer, to give thanks and make good his promises of the past. So many things he had promised that he could barely recall them, and yet an altar would have been among them, so he must see to having one installed without delay. He poured a dutiful libation to Mercury and then, with firebrand in hand, he went to where Verluccus awaited his master.

Already Victor had called to Polyphemus, and the dog could be heard at the slaves' quarters volubly rousing the menials to their tasks. Despite this, Verluccus still slept soundly.

Gaius had to be careful with the flame for fear of setting the place ablaze, but he could see even in the difficult light that someone had cleaned the blood away from Verluccus' face, though it did not improve his appearance, for the bruises had swollen and darkened overnight.

In what he believed to be a commanding but not threatening voice, Gaius called him by name. He was ignored, yet he was certain his presence was known; the steady rise and fall of the slave's chest and the rhythm of his breathing convinced Gaius of that. Even when he kicked Verluccus in the ribs – quite mildly due to the injuries – there was no response. He waited for some time until finally, knowing that he should not delay his departure any longer, he cursed him and told him that if it was his wish to do so then for all he cared he could lie there and rot.

He hurried to the stable, where Cervus whinnied in delight to see him, and with Felix beside him he made a speedy departure across the still-benighted countryside.

Marcus too rose early, and shortly after Gaius' departure, he was groping his way into a tunic held for him by Tertius, who was wondering what had become of the leisurely morning and idle day he had anticipated.

A girl whom Marcus had rejected now crawled out of his slave's blanket, her appearance in the room rewarding Tertius with a slapping from his master. It was not a friendly gesture and signified that Marcus was in a filthy mood. Exactly what had brought it on, Tertius had no idea, but he supposed it to be due to something he had eaten. He remembered then that Marcus was to return to Glevum; that must be what his bad humour was for. Tertius had been with Marcus long enough to know how best to behave in these circumstances; he must keep his head down and anticipate his master's every whim.

'Remain here,' Marcus told him, leaving no instructions. Tertius began to pack his master's belongings.

The house was not particularly large, but there were a number of small rooms and in not one of them did Marcus locate what he was looking for. He even entered the kitchen, much to the amazement of the slaves working there. It was to no avail. Finally, as early light pierced the sky, he went to the shrine which his nephew had not so long since attended and made a somewhat perfunctory offering.

She was in the garden, of course; he saw her as soon as he turned from the shrine, and the anger which he had determined to convert into punishment for her vanished immediately. She had been gathering bay and rosemary to sweeten the rooms, and now she was simply standing on the terrace steps in the dawn light, marvelling at the wonder of the awakening day.

For some minutes he made no approach but simply admired her in silence. She had not yet dressed her hair, and it fell below the neckline of her amber gown in burnished waves as the rising sun caressed it.

He thought he had never seen a more beautiful sight and felt no desire to do more than gaze in awestruck silence.

She sensed his presence and turned, embarrassed to be seen in such a state of undress and nervous of his intentions. There was no point in remaining in the garden longer – she had picked sufficient for her needs – so she had to walk towards him, making a polite genuflection of acknowledgement and asking permission to pass by.

He blocked the path and demanded bluntly, 'Why did you not come to me last night?'

She was shocked and frightened. Surely Aelia had made her position clear enough to this man. As a freedwoman she had privileges above the slaves. She had sent Vera to him. The girl had expressed eagerness for the task, yet she must have disobeyed her. She thought of how angry he must be. She feared his anger and what might be its outcome for poor Vera. She began to apologize.

'My lord, I sent a girl. Did she not come?'

He cut her short. 'Yes, she did as you ordered. My slave had pleasure of her! It was you I wanted; I told you that. I lay awake all night waiting for you. Look at my eyes. See how bloodshot they are? I cannot afford to be without my sleep, you know; it was most inconsiderate of you.'

She gaped at him. 'My lord, I truly thought you were making fun of me. Please do not mock me. My patroness is not present now to suffer from your provocation.'

'My eyes may be bloodshot, but I am not blind!' He stopped abruptly. He was not saying the things he had intended to say. He searched for the right words. He could speak to men well enough of women, of those who attracted him and those who did not. But he could not say such things to this woman; such things said now would be too coarse, too vulgar. What was worse was that, rather than speak to her, he had an almost overwhelming desire to rip her gown from her and take her where she stood. He wished he knew what she was thinking. She was standing before him waiting for him to speak, and precious moments were passing; within the house lamps had been lit, and voices could be heard.

'My lord, may I pass?'

Oh you are smart! he conceded silently. *"May I pass?" not, "Is there some service I can render you, my lord?" She knows too well what my answer would be to that!* Aloud he said, 'No, you may not pass – not until I am done with you. Tell me, what service do you render my brother?'

'I render service to Aelia Paula and to your brother but mostly to your sister-in-law as a companion in spinning and weaving and reading.'

'Ah, yes, of course.' He paused to digest this and then demanded, 'Tell me, do you too weep that Decimus Aemilius Virens is dead?'

'I am sorry he is dead. He was greatly loved by the family.'

'And by you? Do you grieve?'

'I did not know him.'

'He came here. He would not be uninterested in you.'

'I saw him once. It was a long time ago. It was before I belonged to Cordatus. He was not interested in me.'

'Did you love Cordatus?'

'Very much.'

'I think Cordatus kept you close. Virens would surely have wanted you.' *Why am I only able to talk of Virens and Cordatus?* he wondered. *What she thinks of me is what I want to know.*

'He did not have such an opportunity,' she admitted. Cordatus had seen to that. Then she asked him with more audacity than was perhaps prudent, 'Does your estimation of a woman depend only upon the opinion of other men?'

His admiration for her leapt. *Oh, lady, I like you more and more.* But still he could not say what he wanted to. He scowled. She had spurned him the night before. She had described his passion for her as a mockery of Aelia. He was at a loss to know what to say to her. This was a new experience for Marcus, and he was most uncomfortable with it. He wanted to detain her, to experience more of her company, to hear her speak again. He had her tell him how she came into Cordatus' possession.

'And he taught you to read? Read to me. Fetch a volume now and read to me.'

'Here? Here in the garden? What should I fetch?'

She had every reason to be baffled, he conceded later, but at the time it seemed the most logical thing to do in order to keep her with him. He would have done anything to detain her. 'Anything you choose. Get rid of those twigs and hasten back to me.'

He allowed her to pass, and the sweet aroma of the herbs only enhanced his desire for her.

'He wishes me to read to him,' she confided to Aelia, who had been observing them from within the house.

'Read to him? Marcus would have you read to him?' Further speech failed Aelia. She peered through a window at the solitary figure before following Melissa into the study. 'What will you take? Horace? No, I don't think so. And not Ovid – definitely not Ovid!'

'Perhaps Vergil? Aeneas and Dido?'

Aelia doubted the wisdom of that but allowed her to search out the scroll. Melissa returned to the garden only to find that Marcus had gone. She felt foolish and knew he had played a trick on her. But he had not. He returned immediately after her bearing in his own hands a cushion for her to sit on and a shawl to wrap around her.

He listened in silence to her reading, hardly paying attention to the story, with which he was quite familiar. Instead he listened to the sound of her voice and wished he had asked her to sing for him. He was sure she would be able to sing sweetly.

Her eyes moistened as they always did at the lovers' parting and the death of Dido, and he rose and with his fingers carefully wiped the tear away. He gently took the scroll from her and helped her to her feet. She felt certain he intended to kiss her, but he did not do so. She allowed him to return her to the custody of Aelia in silence. He was deep in thoughts which could not be disturbed.

Lucius, being driven from his home, was making a hurried visit to the farm, completing essential business with Victor and Agricola. This was generally an enjoyable time, and he would happily have lingered over it. He approved the tasks for the coming days, not knowing how long Marcus intended his visit to last.

'And your son's new slave?' asked Victor. 'What of him?'

'My son's slave is my son's slave,' replied Lucius tersely. 'You must take your instructions only from Gaius; this is his testing time. I have promised not to interfere.'

Victor frowned and would have spoken, but he was told again that Lucius would be playing no part in Verluccus' training. Victor must only act as instructed by Gaius in that regard and do nothing else. There was a curious expression on Victor's face, but he quickly controlled it and continued with his report and recommendations. Lucius was proud to own two such good men as his overseer and the farm manager; they were hard-working and trustworthy, and he intended to reward their loyalty and application when he returned his family to Rome by giving these two, among other deserving ones, their freedom.

Within the house, in the guest room, Tertius had packed his master's belongings.

He was verbally savaged. 'You don't need to be in such a hurry!'

The slave halted in his tracks, observed the few items they had brought with them, and wondered how he was to prevent the rapidity of their being put away. He solved the problem by tipping them all over the bed. This decision did not please his master either.

'Get on with it. No, stay. Go and find that woman Melissa. I wish to speak to her. No, finish the packing; I shall go and find her.' *And I shall say it.*

'I want to speak to you.' He had arrested her progress along a corridor. She looked startled. 'I only want to speak to you; come into my brother's study where we will not be disturbed.'

He bundled her inside before she had time to object and attract the attention of Aelia. He wasted no further time.

'My departure is imminent. I have no time for fancy speeches. I see before me the woman I want to be mine – I mean to share my life. Come with me now. What must I do to tempt you? Offer you riches? Gold? Wealth? Slaves? I have an abundance of all. Will that do? Are you mine for such things?'

She did not know how to answer him and stood stupefied and open mouthed.

'Is there any need for you to be told how beautiful you are and how you have smitten me? You must know that. That you are beautiful must have been told to you a thousand times.' He gazed at her, gesticulating as he spoke. 'I see this hair, these eyes, such teeth, breasts, limbs, fingers, toes – perfection, all perfection: incomparable.' It was with great difficulty that he resisted the temptation to touch as he itemized each virtue. 'Does your heart match your beauty, Melissa? How brave are you? Can you throw aside this sanctuary, this peace and security, and come away with me today? Come with me now to Glevum and afterwards to my fortress at Isca Silurum?'

She found a voice and, standing, feeling too uncomfortable to be seated in his presence and in Lucius' study, though Marcus had invited her to do so by a gesture, she answered, 'My lord, your reputation is not a secret. I do not think you would keep me with you for long. I am no girl but a mature woman, seven and twenty years old. Can you not see this?'

'Your doubt is only that I would be constant? Then you do not find me repulsive? Do you find me repulsive? Is that why you hesitate?' Self-doubt was a new experience for Marcus, and he had never before been considered less than well featured.

'No,' she conceded weakly, 'you were kind to speak of my beauty, and I can honestly say you are a handsome man.' Her eyes searched his for the honesty of his intentions.

'Do not look at me like that, Melissa; it melts me. I know those eyes of yours can laugh. I see mischief within them even when they are so grave as now.' He risked taking her hand in his. 'Allow me to be the one to make them laugh again.'

'My lord,' she said gently, 'do not take this amiss, but I do not think you and I would laugh together. Your sense of humour is most odd to me.'

He became contrite. 'I see now where my fault lies. It is the sport I make of my brother's wife. I find Aelia an irresistible figure of fun – there, I admit I do wrong to her. But you will find there is more to me than that. My time is short, Melissa. I am to be sent away for my sins like some naughty schoolboy. Never let my men know how I have been chastised by that woman, I beg you. They must continue in awe of me to respect and obey me. I am the emperor's man, stern and adamant, a man to be feared and obeyed, one who will tolerate no indiscipline. See how I put myself into your power! One word from you, and I shall be undone.'

'I have not said I will go with you,' she protested weakly.

'But you will? You will, won't you? Say you will.'

She nodded, her mind suddenly decided, and he embraced her in victorious joy. 'Wait until Aelia learns of this!' he crowed, and she pushed him angrily from her, his purpose made plain.

'What a fool you must take me for. To be taken in so easily.' She was hurt and offended, and he heartily wished he could cut out his tongue.

'Please forgive me,' he said helplessly. 'The truth is your beauty is such a delight to me I desire only to make you happy. I am sincere. Did I not say I lay awake all night thinking only of you? I wanted you beside me there and with me forever afterwards. Be patient with me; my sister-in-law has been the butt of my jokes for so long it is hard to break the habit. Go now and tell her you are leaving today. I shall not ask or trouble you again.' Before she reached the door, he detained her. 'You cannot ride a horse? I shall have the bigarum prepared for us. Go quickly now and pack your things.'

She left the room without a backward glance.

He felt like a boy again, a youth suffering the agonies of a first and unrequited love; it was many years since a woman had left him in doubt as to her feelings towards him. And now Aelia would bring all her influence to bear against him. That ill-judged shout of triumph had cost him dear.

He told Lucius he needed a chariot for his return journey but not why. Lucius made a joke about not realizing Tempestus was a draught horse and received only a sour scowl for his pains. Assuming, not unreasonably, that he too would be riding in the chariot, Lucius pointed out that Tertius would have his hands full leading both Tempestus and Ravus. But had he been privy to the conversation then taking place between his wife and the freedwoman, the reasons for the chariot would have been clearer to him than his brother managed to make them.

'Have you lost your mind? I always thought there was a brain behind that pretty face of yours! It was no accident that Cordatus always took care to keep you from my brother-in-law's sight. Surely his conduct towards you at the dining table showed you his character? He is doing this purely to vex me because I scored a small victory over him in the business of that wretched slave. Oh, I would rather Marcus had taken him as he wished than let him make a fool of you. I shall tell Lucius I have changed my mind and the slave is to go. Let Marcus have him. You will see a change of heart towards you then!'

'Dear Aelia, you have been most kind to me and generous too; I know the freedom you granted me was purely to honour the memory of Cordatus and carries no legal weight, for I am under age. If you forbid me, then I cannot go. I shall remain here with you, for I am greatly obliged to you for your protection. He has said that he wants me, and I do believe I can please him. He will not ask me again; I must be ready when he goes or stay here forever.'

'My dear girl, I hope that to live with us is not such a hardship! I know you must miss Cordatus, but you will not find his like in Marcus. And do not suppose that because he is my dear Lucius' brother he will prove to be the kind and considerate husband that I have. I shall not prevent you from going, but you must do so with your eyes open. You do know you can never be more than his concubine? Marcus Marcius Phillipianus would never take a freedwoman for a wife – not even if he were divorced from Claudia.' She bristled as her temper took hold. 'He really is impossible. Every time he comes here, he does something outrageous, but never before has he equalled this performance.'

'Madam, you are fortunate indeed to have a man who cares for you and loves you as Lucius Marcius does. I too have need of a man who will care for me, and yes, I do believe Marcus Marcius will do so. I know that he has a wife, and he has not implied he will marry me. It may be that I am making the greatest mistake of my life, and if it should prove so, I shall make no claim on you. I shall not come running back and beg you to take me in; I shall accept my lot.'

'Melissa, do not say such a thing. There will always be a home for you under my roof. Promise me that if he mistreats you, you will return to me? I could not let you go otherwise. Promise that you will write to me often and let me know how you go on? I have grown so fond of you and could not bear you to suffer hardship because of foolish pride.'

Impulsively Melissa kissed her and then, fearing that she had abused her liberty, began to apologize profusely. Her words were brushed aside. 'Wait here,' said Aelia as she swept from the room.

She was alone and fearful that Aelia had detained her merely so that Marcus would leave without her, but quickly the mistress returned carrying a bundle which she placed on the table before her.

'Take these with you. I want you to have them. That wretched creature from whom they were taken would surely prefer they were yours rather than mine. You may never need them, but they will always provide you with the means to leave him should you wish to do so.'

They were the jewels which Marcus had given to her. She wrapped them up again in the length of fine wool and pressed it upon Melissa. 'I do not think it a good idea for Marcus to know you have them.'

Melissa was deeply touched. 'You are too kind, Aelia. There is no need. I assure you there is no need.'

'I shall not allow you to go if you will not take them. It would be cruel of you to deny me this peace of mind. Say no more. You should go and pack what you wish to take for your new life. Return and say farewell. Oh, Melissa, how I shall miss your friendship and good advice.' Tearfully she took the ex-slave into her arms and held her close.

Melissa realized that now she had committed herself. She refused to allow any more doubt to enter her mind. In her room she began to draw together items of clothing – and she had, thanks to Cordatus' generosity, acquired a respectable collection of gowns and sandals – a good thick cloak, and her toiletries. She looked at the few possessions which she had kept in memory of him; Lucius and Aelia had allowed her to keep them although strictly they might have laid claim to all. She took a few moments to select items she thought would be especially welcomed by individual members of the family. For Lucius, his books; for Gaius, an ornamental inkwell; for Quintus, a puzzle; and for the two girls, a pair of vases, one each. Aelia proved most difficult, but in the end she took a last precious leaf of writing board and wrote a letter of loving affection and gratitude, expressing her admiration for the lady and all her family, promising to think only kindly of them all. It was time for a last look around the room which for so long she had shared with her dear Cordatus and in which she had developed from the despised 'common, ignorant girl' into the accomplished and beautiful woman who had captivated Marcus Marcius.

He was waiting impatiently. Aelia had detained him craftily so that Melissa had plenty of time to pack, but he was unaware of this and was torn by a desire for the woman to come to him and the fear that she would not, in which case he was best away quickly. Aelia had confided in Lucius with the understanding that Marcus was to remain in ignorance until Melissa appeared.

She had said her goodbyes to Quintus and the household. Gaia came to the gate with her, weeping at their parting.

When Marcus saw her, his heart leapt in a way he had never believed it could, and treating her as though she were glass, he carefully helped her into the chariot. They moved off, and Lucius, lingering to give his wife a kiss, followed behind in the company of Tertius, taking the opportunity to ride the fiery Tempestus, Hardalius, his own slave, having been sent ahead of them.

5

The striping Gaius received on his hand was both for his absence the previous day and for neglecting to prepare himself for the discourse he was supposed to have on the subject of the actions of Marcus Antonius at Actium. He took the punishment with gritted teeth and knew that it would be of no use to complain to his father; Lucius and Anicetus seemed to have strikingly similar views on his education. Gaius had begun to complain that to continue in the school was a waste of both time and money, but his father would have none of that.

Worse for him than the physical blows was learning that he must make up the lost time of the previous day, and when he and his fellow students were finally released, he was promptly placed on fatigues by the tribune Antonius for omitting to obtain permission to absent himself from duty and being absent from sword drill. To return to Daruentum that day or the next was out of the question. It was a terrible blow, but he was allowed no avenue of appeal; he did what was demanded with a good grace.

He was burning to tell his best friend, Titus, about the recapture of the runaway, but not until the end of the following day when it was too late and too dark to travel the homeward road was he pardoned and released.

It was the ides of November, the thirteenth day, and a holiday. Cervus took joyful wing beneath him as they sped home, Felix left far behind. At the gate he applied to one of the porters to deal with Cervus and was greatly taken aback by the servile and deferential attitude of the man. To be treated with such respect was a new and not at all unpleasant sensation for Gaius; even so, he was somewhat puzzled as to the reason for it.

But that kind of subservience did not cease at the gate. All the slaves he encountered took care to speak respectfully to him. *I might be Marcus, not Gaius,* he thought, *so formal they are with me today.* How his uncle's presence had influenced them to the good. It was a principle to follow in his own household when the time came.

All thought of filial duty to greet his mother and his sister discarded, he went directly to Polyphemus' kennel, not running as he desired to do but striding along in his most authoritative manner, encouraged in this masterfulness by the respectful slaves who hovered around him. He was anxious that Verluccus had now passed two whole days with no opportunity to accept him as his master. It was important that he should understand he belonged to Gaius now and not his father.

He pushed wide the door.

The smell hit him first – the stench of an uncleansed latrine. His eyes had not yet adjusted to the dimness after the brightness of the sunshine, and he stumbled first into the fussing dog. On the floor his victim lay insensible, stiff as death, exactly as he had left him two days before except that the iron rings on his feet and ankles had cut into his flesh from his vain struggles to free himself. Gaius knelt and, in fearful disbelief, touched the slave's face. The eyes opened and the lips moved, begging soundlessly for water.

Gaius rushed to the door and screamed for someone to come – Victor, Agricola, anyone. He turned back. Polyphemus had water. Gaius took it to the man and squeezed it drop by drop, using his tunic as a rag, into the parched lips. Verluccus then did speak. 'Water …
give me water.'

Someone arrived, and Gaius shouted that he wanted the chains loosed. How had this happened? Who was responsible? He saw Agricola's man lever the iron spikes out of the floor, and he himself eased the prisoner into a sitting position, holding him around the chest, willing him to live. Where was Felix? He cursed his slave for being too slow to arrive, fearing that only he could be trusted to give the care

Verluccus so obviously needed. 'Fetch someone to clean him up,' he ordered, knowing he should not demand such a task of Felix in any case.

When he was satisfied, he went angrily in search of Palatus. The steward would have to account for Verluccus' condition.

But Palatus was stiff with indignation. 'Master, you gave me no instructions. The slave has not been accepted into the household; he is not my responsibility. The outdoor slaves are the responsibility of Victor and Agricola, not me. My duties include the management of the household and the domestic slaves. That one is not a domestic slave.'

'Then send Victor to me.'

Curiously Victor's explanation was much the same. 'Master, you gave me no orders.' The man looked baffled at the anger confronting him. 'Had you given me orders contrary to what I understood your intentions to be, you may be sure they would have been carried out.'

'And what gave you to understand my intentions were to leave him to die?' As he formed the words, he saw the truth of it in the overseer's eyes. 'That is it, isn't it? That is why all the slaves are suddenly so deferential, so respectful to me. The porters, Agricola's boys, even Palatus himself. Because Verluccus leapt at me, they – you, all of you – think I would abandon him to lie there and die of neglect.' He was appalled. 'Victor, you have known me all my life. My first memories are of being lifted up to receive a kiss to give you luck in the arena. How could you believe such cruelty of me?'

The ex-gladiator could only look embarrassed. Gaius answered for him. 'It is Uncle Marcus, isn't it? You believe he would do such a thing and I would take instruction from him. Well, you are wrong! Wrong on both counts.'

'Please believe me, master, I know I was wrong. I wanted to act differently every time I passed the shed and heard him call out. I gave Polyphemus food and water, but I fed him outside. I could not bear to enter. I wanted to do so – to put him out of his pain – but I heard what you said to him on the morning you left, and so I forbade any to attend to him. The fault is entirely mine. Instruct me how I should be punished for it.'

'No, Victor, the fault is mine, and you have just pointed it out to me. I never appreciated before how careful I must be in the things I say and do. I wish the physician to be sent for. Would you tell Palatus for me? I shall return to Verluccus. Will he forgive me for this, do you think?'

Felix arrived and was unfairly berated for his tardiness. Verluccus had been cleaned and provided with a fresh garment. A young slave was trying to spoon broth into his mouth, and Gaius took the spoon from him and fed him himself.

'Do you feel able to stand now?' he asked. 'Are you able to walk outside?' He had the last link freed from the floor and led him into fresh air and light, where he examined his injuries. Victor brought a basin of salt water, but Gaius insisted on bathing the wounds himself.

The fragrance of roses and lavender wafted over them, and Verluccus turned his head to catch sight of a woman's gown and daintily slippered feet. He heard a girl's voice, but Gaia spoke only to her brother and in Latin.

'Delia told me he was dying, so I have come to watch.'

'Gaia!' He was shocked. 'How can you be so heartless?'

She did not speak again, but Verluccus knew she was still beside them. Her words had angered the young man though; that much he could tell.

Gaius spoke to her again in Latin. 'He is not going to die; Agricola has said so. He knows these things. Go away; there is nothing for your amusement here. Mother will be angry if she knows you have come.'

'Mother is angrier with you for neglecting her than she could be with me!'

Verluccus looked up and saw a face which might have been pretty looking only stormy and angry. The girl scowled at him and turned on her heel, and the fragrance went away with her.

Polyphemus joined them and sat with his head close to Verluccus' shoulder, salivating. Gaius thought this was no bad thing. The man, still in chains but not fixed to anything, might be deterred from precipitate action by the dog's presence. To his dismay, however, the slave began to stroke him, noting the scars concealed by his gleaming coat. Verluccus had endured a nightmarish memory of the huge animal standing over him as he lay helpless, terrified that it was a prelude to being devoured alive as the animal licked the blood from his face. But when the hound had completed cleaning him, it had thrown its body across him and, ignoring his protests that it was too heavy and he was suffocating under its weight, it had slept. Only after he had realized that despite appearances the dog was possibly the only friend he was likely to have in that place had he remembered something once told to him of the healing power of a dog's tongue.

'The hound likes you,' Gaius said rather pompously. 'His name is Polyphemus now – like the man-eating Cyclops. Father so named him when he lost his eye in his last fight. He was Victor's best fighting dog. He won many prizes.' It did not occur to Gaius that Verluccus would not have the faintest idea who or what a Cyclops might be. He continued hopefully, 'When he was fighting, his name was Torvus. It means "savage". I might name you Torvus instead of Verluccus.'

The response to this suggestion – for Gaius had intended it as one – was merely a tightening of the jaw and closer attention to the dog.

'Victor uses him to supervise the field hands, and yes, he has tasted the blood of man. A slave ran away from him once, but he didn't go very far. Victor says he is worth a thousand links of chain.' He looked at the chains still hanging from the man's limbs. It didn't occur to him what a weapon he had left the slave in possession of, but he offered, 'May I take those off you now?' He hoped his casually dropped information as to the ferocity of Polyphemus would be edifying.

Verluccus glared at him. 'Yes, if you dare. Take them off, you little shit. Take them off and see what happens next!'

'You must accept me as your master and promise to obey me – not to try to escape.'

'You? Master of me?' The voice was scornful. 'You will never be my master.' The haggard face defiantly met his. 'If you think that to leave me without food and water confined here to lie in my own muck for days on end while my limbs are torn from their sockets is going to make me submit and call you master, then you are a pitiable fool.'

'It was not days on end,' Gaius protested. 'It was barely

more than two days, and it was not intended. It was a mistake, a misunderstanding. I never intended this, and I promise you will not be treated so again. I have no wish even to keep you in shackles. As soon as you submit to my authority, they will be removed. Give me your word now that you will be obedient and will not try to escape.'

'My word! My word to you is that I intend to escape from you at the earliest opportunity. Is that clear enough for you? You are a pathetic fool to suppose otherwise. You dare to approach me so closely? I suppose you think me too weak to be a danger to you?'

'I could have let you die for trying to kill me,' Gaius pointed out. 'Just now you begged me for water, and it was I who fed it to you.'

'My thirst drove me mad. But I did not submit to you and call you my master, did I? If I did, then those words I retract. If ever again I beg you for water, practice a Roman mercy on me and slit my throat instead!'

How could such venom come from the mouth of a man so weak? Gaius allowed a fit of coughing to pass. 'There will not be a next time. I told you this was not intended. It was a misunderstanding. You will be properly cared for here; none of our slaves is mistreated.'

'I am not your slave. You have no rights over me.'

'Why do you argue so when it is clear you are and I do?'

Verluccus felt too ill to pursue the point. To make his escape, he would need to regain his strength; in his present condition, he would get nowhere. He clambered to his feet in silence and shuffled back inside the building. Gaius followed, still earnestly addressing him.

'You will be provided with a pallet and a bucket. I shall have a slave attend to you in my absence. It seems you must remain in chains, but they will not be so restrictive.' He secured him again to the ring in the wall.

Verluccus was coughing again. 'Am I supposed to be grateful for that? What wrong have I done you that I must suffer like this? If it is my gratitude you seek, then grant me my death as that other bastard delivered death to my comrades.'

Ignoring this insult of his uncle, Gaius reluctantly left Verluccus and went in search of Palatus only to be told that his mother had vetoed the idea of a physician being sent for; he must rely on such remedies as Agricola and Victor might have. He went belatedly to Aelia, and she scolded him sharply for his neglect. She was more interested in hearing news of Melissa and of how Marcus was treating the freedwoman than in her son's slave. Gaius had nothing to say of interest to her – his time had been fully taken up apart from his uncle and Melissa – so she busied herself in supervising the kitchen slaves preparing the day's meals.

Gaius was free to tackle Gaia.

'You know how I feel,' she answered him. 'I have said I will not demand his execution, but I won't be at all sorry if he dies. Why should I? He took my betrothed from me, and I feel as if I have been widowed. You are more concerned about him than about my feelings. I pray to the gods that he does die.'

He could see there would be no reasoning with her. He had hoped to have in his sister an accomplice in Verluccus' management, but now he could see she was more likely to be an opponent. He did not speak to her on that subject again during his visit, confiding his plans and intentions to Victor and Agricola, both of whom seemed less than convinced that he would achieve anything approaching his aims. Gaia, hurt and disappointed at his neglect of her, abused him for it and sought the company of Quintus, who thus became the only member of the family to feel any pleasure from the current situation.

Gaius returned to Glevum sooner than he needed to, but by now he had made arrangements for Victor to ensure that Verluccus was properly taken care of. Leaving him at his home, however, was unsatisfactory, and he had it in mind to find alternative accommodation for him.

His quest took him to Cloelius Draco, who listened to what he said in bemused disbelief.

'What does your father have to say about this?' he asked, certain that Lucius could not approve it.

'He is only anxious that I keep him secure,' Gaius could truthfully reply, and before the morning had passed, Cloelius had confirmed the truth of that and so agreed to help.

It was small and dark but dry and secure, a wedge-shaped cellar with a substantial door to seal it. It was underneath the fort praetorium, the result of levelling the floor when it was built, and being next to a hypocaust, it was not unduly chilly. The door had a lock too, but the key seemed to have been mislaid. However, it could be – and now was – secured by a bar which dropped into place and could be further fastened by a locking chain.

The floor within was several feet below the pavement level, but there were three large stone blocks which a previous user had placed there as steps. There was not much room within, and the floor slanted upwards quite steeply; but it was the best which he could achieve, and he hoped it would be needed only for a brief period. Draco was cooperative enough to agree that he could store elsewhere most of the jars it contained and make space for what Gaius considered to be the basic necessities of a prison, and with some bribery and coercion Felix was persuaded to carry out tasks which they both knew would have met with parental disapproval had he consulted his father on the subject. Draco did see fit to acquaint Lucius with the details of Gaius' activities, but he shrugged and said he must take care of the business as best he could, warning only that the prisoner must die if he tried to escape and that he should discreetly post guards.

When he next returned to his home, Gaius enjoyed again the casual familiarity which was his normal experience of their other slaves. Verluccus, whom he went to immediately, was much improved, considerably stronger but no more cooperative than before. His expression of disbelief when it was revealed to him that he was to be conveyed to Glevum guarded by no more than Gaius and Felix was almost comic, but Gaius was far too anxious to appreciate the humour of it, and Felix was almost numb with fear. Aelia, however, would not allow it and insisted that Victor take the wagon and Polyphemus to ensure safe delivery. She craftily suggested that Penelope could go also and provided the girl with a shopping list which included calling on Melissa so that she should receive a faithful report of how things stood with her and Marcus; she anticipated bad news.

It was late in the day when the slow wagon rumbled up to the fortress gate. Gaius guided them through the town to install his captive in his new quarters. Victor enlisted the services of a couple of soldiers to supervise his transfer across the pavement, and the chains dragged noisily on the stone, attracting the attention of a group of lads of Gaius' own age.

One young friend asked him, 'What do you have here, Gaius?'

'It is a warrior my uncle captured, Titus. He has given him to me. I am entrusted to undertake his training; he is considered too dangerous to be kept at home.'

His bragging impressed his friends; if it was not quite the truth, it did not matter. They were fresh and sweet-smelling young men who had exercised and bathed and were now to prowl the town looking for unguarded girls. He grinned and waved them off, promising to seek them out later.

Victor pulled open the heavy door and indicated that Verluccus must enter. The slave made no move.

'Get yourself inside. These are your new quarters. Get inside.' Gaius surprised himself with the roughness of his tone, but he had to be firm. He was conscious of the proximity of the soldiers.

But the men were already assisting. The captive lost his footing and tumbled down the steps into the cellar. Gaius slammed the door rapidly upon him and instantly regretted it.

In the pitch blackness, the fall seemed much further than the three stone blocks. He lay for several minutes, lost for breath and sightless. Even as he fell, he heard the thud of the bar dropping into place hard upon the slamming of the door. He hauled himself to his feet and straightened only to be felled again by a blow on the head as if by some unseen assailant, but it was the low ceiling and he quickly discovered that only in a restricted area was it possible to stand upright without colliding with the roof. Thus he was immediately made painfully aware of the limitations of his quarters. He crouched on the floor, trying to comprehend what ghastly fate now awaited him and shocked at the treatment which Gaius, who had professed himself so concerned with his welfare, had now meted out to him.

He had been entombed alive. He had actually believed the boy when he claimed a mistake had been made when he had been left chained and starved at Daruentum. What a fool! This, then, was to be his fate: incarceration in the walls of the fortress itself in some strange Roman ritual, a sacrifice to their gods of the underworld. Nothing had prepared him for this – nothing. He had been totally deluded by Gaius, had begun to think him different from Marcus and Lucius, had even begun to feel he might trust him, might even be able to beguile him into releasing him. He had been amused by the patient concern shown for him and the boy's initial and erroneous assumption that he could actually bring him to Glevum without the aid of the overseer. What a fool he had been not to make a bid for freedom during the journey; if he had killed the hound first, he might well have succeeded in getting away.

He moved cautiously to where the faintest hint of light outlined the base of the door. He might have been put in there to die, but his passing would not be silent. The world would know what had been done to him and by whom. He began to beat upon the door with his fists, yelling at the top of his voice, 'Cowards! Filthy child stealers! Murderers! Thieves! Marcus Marcius, Lucius Marcius, Gaius Marcius.' For good measure, he added the name of an old enemy: 'And you too, Drusus, whoever you are! All foul and stinking Romans! May the gods condemn you all, may your animals be plagued with sickness and your horses drop dead under you, may your crops rot in the ground and your wells be fouled. May worms and maggots infest your food and all manner of diseases infest your bodies and your children's bodies. You people, Dubonni, Romans! Listen to me! You have among you the most wicked of men. May the gods condemn him. Let him face me if he dare and let him deny the wrong he has done me. Lucius Marcius, you are that wicked man, and so too is Marcus Marcius and your son Gaius Marcius. May the whole stinking tribe of you be cursed. May you all rot as I rot here; may you never have a quiet night again. May the sky fall upon you and the sea overwhelm you if you do not release me from this tomb!' The tirade continued, punctuated by the pounding of his fists upon the door.

In the immediate silence which followed the closing of the door, Victor had departed, taking Penelope to where they expected Melissa to be. He did not hear the tirade, or if he did, he closed his ears to it and certainly did not expect Gaius to open the door again so soon. Few apart from Gaius and the bemused soldiers standing close by heard his shouts; the door was too solid for that. Gaius had anticipated a protest and wondered at its delay, and when it came it was muffled; but for all that the venom was there, and its meaning was explicit enough. He ignored Felix's agitation and ordered him to open the door.

'What is it you want?' he demanded. 'There is a bed, a bucket, a pitcher of water. You shall have a meal shortly. Be silent.'

'I want my freedom!' he hissed into the face, but the boy had said enough to indicate it was not to be his tomb. He wanted to say, 'Stay, remain here with me, don't abandon me in here where there is not even a rat for company,' but instead he shouted, 'You have no right to do this to me. I demand to be set free. If I am accused of a crime, I demand to be tried by the law.' Brilliant – why had he not thought of that before?

'I have every right to do as I please with you, and the sooner you realize that, the better it will be for you – and the sooner you will be out of here.' He half expected the verbal onslaught to become physical, but Verluccus must have seen the interest he had aroused in the soldiers, who had ranged themselves close by with swords in hand, and realized the futility of such an action.

'So I am to be kept alive? In here? Treated worse than a dog? For what purpose?' He was speaking more quietly, more rationally, as if he really was wanting to know.

'You must accept my authority over you – that I am your master.

I have no wish for this to continue; it is you who makes it necessary. Say what is required, and I will take the chains off you and you will have as much liberty as Felix.'

Incredulity crossed Verluccus' face. He scoffed openly. 'You call that liberty? That is not liberty! I demand my true freedom.' Since this made no impression on Gaius, he added, 'I could give you the words you want to hear; I could say anything.' What a fool he would be if he believed them. 'What makes you so certain I would not say what you wish to hear and then make off as soon as you rid me of these?' He shook his wrists in Gaius' face.

'You have made no secret of your desire to escape, but you have not used a lie to gain advantage. I do not believe you would demean yourself by dishonesty. It is my belief that when you give me your word you will not break it.'

Can he really have so little idea of my past? Has Marcus told him nothing? Would he not call dishonest the things that I have done? He found himself silenced, amazed at the naivety. Finally he said, 'I see; you have stolen all but my word from me, and now you would take even that. Never! Fasten me up again.' He turned away and paused. 'This I give you freely.' He spat deliberately onto the step in between them.

Gaius dropped the beam into position and tried to think that it was not such a bad thing; he might have spat in his face. He turned to the quivering Felix. 'You must not let him see your fear, Felix; he will take advantage of it. You are in far less danger of him than I, and I do not fear him. But I shall ask a soldier to stand nearby when you take his food to him.' It would cost him more cash, but it would be worth it.

Felix was suitably grateful. 'Thank you, master. I would feel more confident with him for that.' He hoped he would find the courage to ask Gaius to employ a different gaoler.

'So he has been installed in new quarters?' commented Marcus when Gaius found his father and uncle in the praetorium. 'I trust he finds them satisfactory? Let me know when I might visit him and pay my respects.'

'Yes, I shall do so.' He grinned at his uncle's amused interest. 'And you, Father?'

'I shall view him as and when I see fit. You may rely on that,' Lucius answered crisply.

'Yes, Father.' He sighed and hoped it did not mean what he feared it might. A sympathetic wink from Marcus, however, cheered him somewhat.

'And your plan? What is it?'

Marcus' interest was embarrassingly intrusive. As yet, Gaius' plan was unformed. He improvised rapidly. 'I think that if I can get his trust, talk to him every day, and let him see the life Felix leads – that he will be treated well and need have no fear of injustice – he will realize how much better his life could be, a life better than he has ever known before. At the moment he is angry and frightened; I need to gain his confidence.'

'Angry?' Marcus chuckled. 'Yes, he will be angry, and for that reason dangerous. But frightened? I don't think so. He did not strike me as being afraid of anything. He certainly was not afraid of me! And you doubt he has lived well before? Don't forget those trinkets which I gave to your mother and sister. They were gold, silver, bronze, amber, blue glass. He may have obtained them by perpetrating wicked crimes, dwelt with fellow thieves and murderers, but he will have lived like a king; be certain of that. You, however, are the expert, and you have been given the chance to prove your point. I think you will be disappointed with the outcome, but at least you will be feeding him and he will be the fitter when he commences his gladiatorial training.'

Lucius frowned, irritated. 'I will not have this slave the sole topic of your conversation, Gaius. I have given my consent to this trial, but I will not hear of it each and every day. Be careful you do not drive me to change my mind.'

It was threat enough; Gaius desisted, and Marcus took the hint. He in any case considered that he had been absent from Melissa for long enough and went in search of her. She had acquired a considerable number of lengths of fine wool cloth which she assured him was ample to provide her with the wardrobe he wished her to have and to which she could ply the needle herself. She still lacked a maid for a female companion, but a local trader had undertaken to assemble a selection of well-trained girls for her approval and they were expected to be delivered within days. He urged her to name whatever she wanted and he would see that she had it; and she, for her part, assured him that in him she already had more than she had ever dreamed of possessing.

He recognized Penelope as soon as he saw her. 'Aelia has sent a spy, has she? You may tell your mistress that Melissa will not be returning with you; she is content enough with me.' He placed a possessive arm around her, and she responded with a fond kiss. 'Tell Aelia,' he added, 'I wake her every morning with a sound beating and invite all of Draco's men to watch me when I take her; then I share her with them.'

Melissa laughed at Penelope's horrified reaction. 'Surely you don't believe such nonsense? You may tell Aelia that I am perfectly content and most thoughtfully provided for.'

'Now I am hurt,' Marcus protested. 'I did not hear a word there that said you love me. When will you tell me that?'

'I shall tell you that', said Melissa, 'when I do not think it is obvious to you.'

Gaius decided that his first words to Verluccus every day must be, 'Do you now acknowledge me to be your master?' In that way, if he had thought overnight about the matter and come to terms with his lot, then he could be released the more rapidly. Felix always did the first duty of the day – after he had serviced his master's own needs, of course.

The response on the first morning was predictable. 'Are you mad, or is it that you think to drive me mad? Perhaps you think I am mad already, kept like some mole that lives underground, buried as I am? Acknowledge you to be my master? It would be funny if it were not so pathetic! In what manner can such a boy as you claim mastery over me? Can you outride me? Can you throw a spear further than me? Have you ever brought down a flying bird with a sling stone? Have you ever killed bear? Dare you put a sword in your hand and raise it against one in mine? My master? You? Never!'

There was no answer to that. He closed the door. If he was late for school, Anicetus would be sure to tell his father which would not help his cause.

He was not able to visit again until the evening, as Antonius deemed his duties in the junior cohort as important as Anicetus deemed his studies. He kept his curious friends and others at some distance with many excuses. It would not do for them to hear the things Verluccus was likely to say; they did not need to understand Celtic to guess their meaning. From one or two there came ribald comments and unsolicited advice as to how he should deal with a recalcitrant slave. None of it he took, and most of it was obscene or cruel or both.

'How are you?' It seemed an inadequate question to put to a man confined in such a tiny, dark, and solitary place. 'I see you have eaten. Did you enjoy your meal?'

'Why? Does it matter?' He was looking up from the foot of the steps. 'Am I some beast you fatten without exercise? How much longer am I to endure this?'

'That is up to you. I don't want to keep you in here; you give me no choice.'

'I intend to give you nothing!'

'Now why take that attitude?' he began, motioning Felix to stand close by but remaining at the doorway. 'I intend you no harm. You will be treated well as my slave. Look how well Felix is dressed. You may ask him whether he is happy or not. You reject the opportunity of a good life for what? For nothing but to sit here in discomfort and solitude. I would have put you in a better place, but without your cooperation I could not risk less security. I cannot afford someone to guard you day and night.'

'What?' he sneered. 'Are your means limited then? Are you no longer able to do anything you like? You are a rich and arrogant brat, the spoiled brat of a vile and wicked brute and the nephew of one indescribably worse.'

'My father is not vile and wicked. He is a good man, a just and kind man who is allowing me to try to save you despite yourself.' Now that he knew what Verluccus' idea of mastery was, he dared not risk telling him of the alternative end; he would probably welcome the chance to fight in the arena.

'I know what your father is and what he did to me. Do you think such an act is so easily forgotten? Forgiven? I did nothing, nothing. Do you hear? Vile and wicked he is! No, those words are too mild. There are no words fit to describe him. And you are his son! I spit upon you.' And he did so. 'Crawl away like the toad you are! No, I do wrong to toads! To call you so degrades a decent creature. You are a vile and filthy beast of a nature all your own, the son of another, and the nephew of a monster more foul than the foulest shit heap.' The torrent ceased, and he civilly awaited Gaius' reaction to being so abused. In its absence, he continued in a quieter, more controlled voice. 'When I found myself alive in the hands of my enemies, I knew that my future could only be slavery, however long or short my life might be. I expected it – no less. It is the rule, is it not? Then I learned that the man who had captured me had slaughtered every other man, woman, and child and living thing, but me he had saved because his revolting brother had burned his mark onto me. Enslavement by any other man I would accept as my misfortune but my lot, but to belong to you – that I cannot stomach.'

It wasn't fear, Gaius told himself, that made him choke and tremble before such hatred. He found his voice. 'I shall visit you again tomorrow. You are wrong about my father. He is not the man you describe, and were you not so blindly obstinate, you would see it for yourself. As for the legate, yes, he did the things you say, but only after his offer to accept surrender was refused by Cunobarrus. Why did you all turn against the chief's sons and support the man who had murdered him? Why did you all spurn Marcus' offer?'

The shadowed eyes stared hard at him. 'You know nothing! You know only his lies. Go away! Just go away.'

It was total failure. Now he could see the futility of his enterprise. Verluccus would be the gladiator his father wanted. The only thing he could do now was delay the inevitable.

That night he spoke privately to his father. Not even Felix was present. 'Tell me, Father, what happened to Verluccus when you bought him for me? Why does he so hate you for the actions of Palatus?'

'I am Palatus' master. In Verluccus' mind, Palatus merely carried out my orders when he inflicted that mark on him. I hope you have not enlightened him?'

Gaius shook his head, and Lucius continued.

'Good. I forbid you to do so. It is fortunate that he blames me. We have to consider that he if he knew the truth he might harbour great resentment against Palatus, and while he may hesitate to attack you or me, should you succeed in your objective, he may not think twice about killing a fellow slave or in some way terrorizing him. Palatus is nervous enough about him as it is now that Verluccus is a grown man. Even if you are successful in taming him, son, unless he comes to terms with what has happened in the past, I cannot admit him into the household. You must understand that, Gaius.'

'It is so unfair; he thinks you the cruel one, and because of that he hates you. How can I show him that he is wrong if you do not allow me to tell him the truth?'

'That is a problem for you to solve. Do not disobey me in this. Wilful as you are, I trust you will not place Palatus' life in jeopardy from some misguided notion of truth and justice on my behalf?'

He promised his father that he would not disobey and hoped that the question would never be directly put to him. He would face Verluccus every day and take the abuse and pour a libation to the goddess Concordia as often.

In the silent darkness, Verluccus sat on his bed and contemplated his loneliness. He took it hard that he was left alone for so long. He had no idea of the regime under which Gaius toiled at his lessons and afterwards to maintain face in society. He had spent his ill temper on the boy and felt no sense of satisfaction from it. He was sure that from now on he would see only the brief face of Felix as he reluctantly dropped food and water close to the door. He decided then that if Gaius were to return, he would listen to what he wanted to say. He would not give in to him, but he would encourage further contact by him and would not try to frighten him again. Having thought of all this, he again considered himself and was quite appalled to discover how weakened his resolve had become. His attitude changed again. He would not give in; let the boy try as he may.

He considered Felix. Felix he despised. To suggest that to live such a life as his would be an incentive to him was ludicrous. He considered trying to escape. Getting out of the cell would be easy enough, but he had a thick leather collar around his neck and chains still attached to his wrists and ankles. No one seemed to have considered what a weapon he had in them. It would be easy to throttle Felix. But there was always a soldier or two lurking nearby when the door was opened, and it would be harder to get past them. He thought about his family at Daruentum. How he longed to see them again. If he should escape, of course they would pay the penalty. He wondered if they were still alive, whether they already had paid with their lives when he had run away before. He wondered if he might find out about them from Gaius but decided on reflection that to bring them into the young man's mind might place them in a danger which might otherwise not exist. Sometimes he simply wept in lonely despair.

Gaius did return, and so grateful for it was Verluccus that he listened patiently to all he that had to say.

Discovering a more quiet and contrite audience than he had known in Verluccus before, Gaius decided it would be a good idea to enlighten him about his family, who they were, and about the household slaves, so that he might comprehend better what lay in store for him. This list not only included his parents; his sister Gaia; little Quintus, now four years old; his sister Marcia; her husband,

Publius Julius; and their baby son but also a freedwoman named Irene; all the slaves, Palatus, Felix, Hardalius, Florus, Argus, Delia, Chloe, Penelope, Grata, Vera, Lepida, Victor, Agricola, little Rufus, the porters, and a host of others without whom it appeared neither the household nor the farm could function.

Having endured all this in silence, Verluccus finally said, 'I can't think why you need me, having so many already. Who would notice if I were to be let go? You could take these hindrances off and send me on my way. I would be gone in no time, and I would never tell anyone how it was accomplished.'

Later, when he had returned to the praetorium, Gaius thought about that remark and how he might have turned it to advantage instead of responding in the somewhat surly manner that he had. For surely it was a gesture, a joke? A real joke offered, and for the first time. He ought to have been prepared for it.

He sighed and regretted again that he had been so clumsy. For once Verluccus had listened to him and had spoken without rancour, and he had failed him. He must be more alert in the future.

It was the following day when the bad news came. It arrived on a steaming horse in the hands of a grimy and sweating courier, and by the time the day was finished and Gaius learned of it, Marcus was long gone.

Melissa was numb. She wanted to weep, to cling to him and beg him not to abandon her. She loved him so much, and instead of telling him so she had teased and played a stupid game with him, let him beg her to say the words she denied him. How she regretted that folly now; it made it so easy for him to leave her.

She had witnessed the incredulity with which he had received the news and his rage both with himself and with the man to whom he had entrusted the gold shipments: Cunobarrus was not dead but alive, and he had raided the mule train with its precious cargo in order to proclaim that fact. Marcus had tried to tell himself it was some imposter, but imposter or not, he had made a serious error of judgement and had to rectify it speedily; he could not be slowed down by a woman. He made his arrangements in haste and avoided her. He would not come near her or look at her, and when she overheard him telling Tertius that he must await the arrival of Mango, the slave dealer, and then make for Isca Silurum with the greatest swiftness, she knew that he intended to sell her and be rid of her.

She could appeal to Lucius, of course; he had freed her. Marcus had no power to sell a freedwoman. But she knew that she had no legal freedom, that she was with Marcus as a gift from his brother, whatever Aelia might choose to think. She remembered then the golden pieces hidden among her garments and thought perhaps with them she might buy her freedom from Marcus. After all, if he was prepared to sell her to Mango, then he could not care greatly what became of her.

It seemed no time at all before Tertius announced that Tempestus was awaiting his master. Still Marcus would not look at her, would not come near, not even to give her a farewell embrace. She followed him to the door in silence and then, as he prepared to mount, she could bear it no longer and cried out, 'Marcus!'

He stopped in his tracks and turned, and their eyes met as she silently mouthed his name again. He strode towards her, holding her gaze. 'By the gods, it's tearing me apart to leave you.' He held her in a close embrace so that she could barely breathe and kissed her fiercely. Then he said, 'I have to go now; I have to go. That fool Annius Festus and my madness for you have ruined me.'

He turned quickly, mounted Tempestus, and with the small hand-picked escort rattled out of the fortress. Melissa gave herself up to her grief.

With Marcus gone the reality of her status was quickly confirmed to Melissa. It was as she had feared; her future lay in the hands of Mango. The room she had been so happy to remain in alone awaiting the frequent attentions of Marcus had now become her prison. Tertius, despite her angry protests, locked her within and simply said in response that these were his master's orders – to keep her secure.

She wallowed in misery, imagining the possible horrors that could be in store for her as a cast-off woman, sold for expediency to whoever would bid the highest and to the gods alone knew what end, the protection of Lucius and Aelia denied her.

Then the waiting was over. Tertius advised her she had best array herself decently and tie up her dishevelled hair, and she knew there was to be no escape. And then he was asking her if Mango might be admitted to her presence, and she fearfully nodded her assent, and so her understanding of her situation changed. The man had brought women for her to inspect and to choose who might best serve her, and it was all she could do not to weep again but now in relief.

Finally impatient, Tertius said, 'Oh, Marcus will not care if you have two maids. Take both of those you cannot choose between.' And so the transaction was completed, and now she was not the property of another but herself an owner of two.

It was several days' journey to Isca Silurum and Marcus. As they drew nearer to the fortress, she again knew fear of rejection. At every shrine she had stopped to make an offering and pray for safe deliverance and a kindly welcome – much to Tertius' annoyance as he made clear he considered the journey slow enough without her delaying them even longer. There was no delay at the gate, however; their arrival had been long looked for, and all of the terrors that had invaded her mind were quickly swept away. Marcus came out of the praetorium to meet her and almost dragged her from the carriage, feasting hungrily on her lips to the obvious entertainment of some impudent young soldiers passing nearby.

'Why have you taken so long to join me?' was all he wished to know. He told her that he had returned to the fort expressly to welcome her when her approach had been signalled to him; they had one night only before he must depart and resume his hunt for Cunobarrus.

6

When Marcus had so hastily departed, Lucius had broken the news to Gaius. Neither of them had any thought of Melissa.

'Verluccus must not know, Father.' A pale-faced and shocked Gaius contemplated the slave's reaction if he learned of it.

'I agree, most emphatically, and I am glad you can see it. In fact I wonder if you might now wish to reconsider? I have business to attend to in Corinium, and I could take him to the *lanista* for training as a gladiator when I depart tomorrow. There would be less chance there of his learning that the leader who inspired him is still alive, despite our best endeavours, and of his making a bid to join him.'

Gaius shook his head.

'Very well, but do not do anything foolish while I am absent. Refer to Tribune Antonius or Cloelius Draco if you need advice. Here, Son, take this as a token. Take it; you need not say anything. When I find it lying on my desk, I will regard it as the key to that place in which you house him. I will have a speedy end made of him.' He put into Gaius' hand a bone amphitheatre ticket and placed a consoling hand on his son's shoulder. 'You may take comfort from the fact that you tried. He will bring his fate upon himself, and you have no reason to feel any guilt that you failed to save him from it.'

He nodded his thanks to his father, too depressed to talk.

'Have you no idea what it is like in here?' was the astonishing response he received in answer to his customary morning enquiry. 'When you come, the door is opened and you can see within. But when you are gone, I do not know whether it is night or day, so black it is. Dare you join me inside with the door closed?'

This was a staggering change of attitude. Felix thought so too.

'Don't do it, master; he will overpower you.'

He admonished Felix and told him to close the door upon him. Thankfully the boy had addressed him in Latin, but Verluccus probably understood what he had said.

It was terrible. Utter blackness. He stumbled forward, and strong hands gripped him and covered his head so that he should not knock himself out, and then those arms were supporting him and he was being manhandled over the narrow, uneven floor. For a terrible moment he thought that Felix' fear was well-founded and that he was now the captive, but when they reached the mattress he was pressed to sit on it and the hands freed him. He was horrified by what he had done. Day after day while he had enjoyed the fresh air and daylight, Verluccus had been locked up in this dreadful place. And he had thought he had been treating him humanely. He had experienced better conditions in the guardianship of Polyphemus.

'I will get you a lamp, an oil lamp. You should have told me sooner,' he said into the blackness.

'Ah, I see – it is my fault. I should have realized it would be my doing.'

'Forgive me. I did not think – I had not realized it was like this. Tell me what else would add to your comfort. What else do you want?'

'I want to get out of here.'

'You know the conditions for that.'

'You ask too much. You take my freedom from me and lock me in this tomb, and then you offer me an oil lamp. An oil lamp! I want the sun.'

'It is not possible.' Gaius clambered to his feet and began to grope his way back to the crack of light which marked the door and knocked for Felix to let him out.

'Those soldiers. They would not let me slip past them.'

He was being very cunning, thought Gaius, but he could see that it was a possibility. 'I would have to keep you chained up. People would stare at you.'

Apparently that prospect did not bother him at all. If Gaius had known he was hoping that one of those people might have been from Daruentum and would recognize him, he might have been less willing to allow the experiment.

The soldiers agreed – for a price.

The next day Verluccus was allowed to breathe again the sharp November air, and he breathed deeply of it. His ankles were hobbled together and tethered by a chain to the wall, but his hands were left free. To Gaius' utter amazement, he and the soldiers quickly became on friendly terms. He did not abuse them; between them they achieved a kind of dialogue, and soon he was actually throwing dice with them. It was too much after all the abuse and obstruction to which he had been subjected to see Verluccus so perfectly at ease with these rough men.

'What have you got that you can wager on dice?' he demanded.

'I clean their boots for them when I lose.'

'And when you win?'

'They give him money,' Felix answered. 'I have seen them.'

Felix found the coins hidden in the pallet. A few worthless pennies. 'I think they have robbed you,' Gaius told Verluccus. 'These are practically worthless. What did you hope to achieve? Did you think to bribe them to let you go?'

He had of course. The expression on his face gave him away.

'You little shit,' he hissed at Felix who made the mistake of showing his fear and dodging behind his master, an action which only served to enrage him more, and the boy was hastily ordered to move away.

'Why do you keep that creature?' demanded Verluccus. 'He is useless to you.'

He ought to have defended Felix; his father would have expected no less. Instead he heard himself saying, 'I know. That is why I want you.'

'The only danger you can possibly be in is from me, and yet you are not afraid of me. Don't you have any idea what I am capable of?'

'I know that you killed the Tribune Decimus Aemilius Virens, a brave and honourable man, the dear friend of my father and mother, and so deprived my sister of her husband.'

'Did I?' He positively preened. 'Well, that is something! Your father's friend? I did not know that.' The pleasure on his gloating face vividly reminded Gaius of his uncle. 'And made your sister a widow?'

'Gaia was betrothed to Decimus Aemilius Virens; they were not yet married.'

Verluccus shrugged. 'I expect he would have killed me. He was about that business.'

'He was administering the law,' Gaius pointed out calmly. 'You were breaking it.'

'Roman law! Law to benefit the oppressors and impoverish those who resist their subjugation,' he sneered. 'You even think to make a slave of me and have me feed you oysters from a fancy red dish.' He grinned suddenly. 'I would have stuffed them all down your throat.'

'I thought you were trying to get yourself killed.'

His prisoner snorted derisively. 'I did not think to be executed for that. But you are partly right. I did have a plan in mind: to do something which your father could not possibly overlook.'

'Oh? And what was that?' It was an idle question; surely he would keep such a scheme to himself.

'Since your bringing me here has deprived me of the opportunity to carry it out, I shall tell you: I was going to attack your women. I was going to strangle your mother and rape your sister. Your father would not let that pass, would he?'

He did not know what he had expected to feel on making such an assertion. Pleasure, he might have supposed; triumph perhaps. Instead it was shame and disgust with himself as he saw misgiving and revulsion in the pale face of Gaius as the boy for the first time shrank from him. Then he heard what must have been his own voice yelling loudly for the benefit of the world at large, 'Romans! Men, women, children, death to all of you. Do you want me to tell you

159

of how much blood Verluccus has spilled? Of rape and killing and burning? He has reduced the numbers of Romans – that's what he has done – and he will do so again once he is rid of you! And you desire to turn him into a thing like that!' This last was directed at Felix again, who ran off in search of assistance.

Gaius dropped the bar into place. He leaned on the outside of the door, reeling from genuine shock. This was utter failure. Never again could he risk Verluccus being outside. He had forfeited all concessions; there was no way he could risk taking him into his home now. If he did not act at once as his father had advised, he was an utter fool.

'What is wrong? Did he attack you?' Antonius, alerted by Felix, had arrived in some haste.

Gaius shook his head. 'He is locked up again; no harm is done.'

7

Gaius yelped at the clout across his head.

'What answer should you give to that?' Anicetus was standing before him with the dreaded stick in his hand looking for the opportunity to lower it again across a recalcitrant student's head.

Gaius struggled to think what the question might have been. He looked at Titus, but his friend could do nothing other than offer a sympathetic grin.

'Could you repeat the question?'

'It would be pointless to do so.' The schoolmaster turned away. 'Remain at the end of the day. You and I have matters to discuss.' Another more attentive student supplied the argument which they had been preparing for the rhetoric session.

Later, when the school had been dismissed, Anicetus sat scrutinizing him.

'Lucius Marcius pays me to educate you. I wonder that he does not ask for his money to be refunded. It is a disgrace. It isn't as if you are stupid. Things have gone downhill rapidly since the ides. And there is no secret about the reason for that, is there?'

'I truly am sorry, doctor.' Gaius agonized over what best to say.

Anicetus had come to the conclusion long since that he was required more to confine the older boys to class to keep them from getting into mischief than in hope of completing their education. He shook his head in despair; this was not a good situation for him. The school had been founded by Lucius' freedman Cordatus. Since the freedman's death, Anicetus had been in charge of it, but it was largely subsidised by Lucius Marcius. If Gaius were to withdraw, would Lucius then remove his patronage?

'It will not do, Gaius Marcius. This is not the standard which your father and I expect of you. You are capable of much better work. I am surprised that he has not confronted me already about your recent mediocrity! No doubt he will on his return from Corinium.'

'Felix takes notes and rehearses me,' he admitted ashamedly.

'So your father is deceived?' Anicetus let the words sink into the miserable boy before continuing. 'Some men, through age and infirmity, are forced to rely heavily upon their slaves. You have your eyes, your wits, and your health. The gods, through your parents, have bestowed all these things on you and position and wealth too. Think, Gaius Marcius! Do not mock the gods and throw these gifts away. You must harden your heart and rid yourself of the barbarian.'

Gaius felt sick. 'I know that is the thing to do, Anicetus. He has said such things to me that I should not let him live. But even now I cannot bring myself to abandon him. I just feel that he is not half as bad as he pretends to be and I could prevail over him given time. You will ridicule me if I tell you I sense the gods intend him for me. I offer prayers, yet they do not assist me. To whom ought I to pray? Father puts his trust in Mercury and Fortuna, and I have sacrificed also to Concordia to no avail. Would you speak to him? He may listen to your wisdom. Time is against me; I know that Father will return from Corinium in time for the kalends, and I must honour the agreement.'

'What is your father's wish?' the cautious Anicetus asked.

'He will put him to death if he shows no sign of submission. But I am sure that he would rather see me succeed than fail. He need not have granted me this time of trial.'

'I doubt your prisoner would listen to me!' Anicetus pondered for a moment and then said, 'But in one thing you are correct; it is the native way to listen to the counsel of older, wiser men – a dictum some Roman youths might do well to follow! There is a man, a friend of mine; Coridumnus is his name. He is a healer, a wise man, and a teacher, a respected elder of the Dobunni tribe. From him you may learn how to solve your problem. Go to him and seek his guidance.'

'May I? May I absent myself for that?'

'You are more absent in mind than present these days. If leave of absence will more speedily return your mental faculties, a brief suspension of your attendance will be worth the sacrifice,' said Anicetus dryly. 'I will write a letter of introduction for you.'

BOOK III

VERLUCCUS THE BLOODSPILLER

1

The directions given to him by Anicetus were clear enough: to take the road as if to Corinium but would not go so far. He would quickly meet up with fellow travellers heading for the same destination. The way to the home of Coridumnus, he would find, was a path well-travelled by supplicants making their way to the shrine of the Healer in the woods. Gaius shrank from imagining what his father would say should he learn of his having business with such a person.

The school day ended with the morning, and so, leaving simple instructions with Felix, he left without further delay.

Better equipped pilgrims than he had brought torches and provisions and were a noisy crowd convivial among themselves. But he on Cervus had no need of such company; his time was precious, and he could not pass it idly even if they were all heading for the same destination.

The throng became thicker and seemed to have come to a halt. There was a solid wall ahead and a closed gate. People were camping now, prepared to wait out the night for first attention in the morning.

But Gaius had a letter of introduction and had no intention of sleeping on the ground without a tent. He drove forwards, using his horse's weight to force people aside, and hammered on the solid door, imperiously demanding to see Coridumnus.

'Open the gate to me. I am Gaius Marcius, the son of Lucius Marcius, and have come from Glevum to see Coridumnus.'

He was ignored by the porters and abused by the crowd. 'Queue jumper!' 'Get back, we were here first.' 'Arrogant jackanapes.' 'Just because you are a Roman you think you own the world.'

He struck out with his whip, something he had never needed to use on Cervus and which he carried only for show. 'How dare you? My father is Lucius Marcius! Get away from me,' he said and to the porters, 'I demand to be let in.'

'My master will see no more tonight,' responded the slave courteously. He was obviously impressed by Gaius' credentials enough to say, 'If you wait until tomorrow, you may make an appointment to see him at his convenience.'

'Who does your master think he is? He's just some jumped-up quasi Druid. I insist that he see me now.' He thrust Anicetus' letter into the man's hand. 'Take that to him. At once!' he barked as the man hesitated. He was confident that it would be enough to obtain his audience.

In a little while the man returned. It seemed the word of Anicetus carried more weight than the name of Marcius. 'Coridumnus can't see you tonight, but you're to stay in one of the guest rooms. Come this way.'

The room was one of a suite and adequate for a traveller's needs. He was directed to where he could bathe and was provided with a meal, but it was made perfectly clear to him that to see Coridumnus he would have to wait until the following day; no exception was to be made for him. There were other privileged travellers in the guest suite comparing their ills with each other. He did not speak of his; he doubted that any of them had a problem comparable to his.

He was roused from his bed earlier than he anticipated and, without the services of Felix, was forced to scramble into his clothes himself.

It was suggested to him that an offering at the shrine was the usual practice, and he was led across a neatly laid out garden with box and lavender hedging to where water gushed under a small stone canopy.

'The god of this place is Nodens,' he was told. His guide accepted his coin and left him with his prayers in the darkness.

He wondered how long he ought to stand there as if in prayer. He had not come all this way for ritual but for counsel and advice – real, practical help. Even so, he had no wish to cause offence and risk disaster. He sprinkled small coins into the waters.

He lost himself for a while in thoughtful silence, and when he turned he saw that his guide had been observing him; the man beckoned for him to follow.

He was led into a building beyond the guest quarters, and now he grew concerned. He had taken occupancy of his quarters without a thought, but now he could take in his surroundings he could see how Roman this place was. The buildings were rectangular, not round, and they were made of wood on stone foundations. Even worse there were smooth stone floors, some tiled, and the walls were richly decorated. It was all very familiar to him, but this was not what he had expected to find. The man who lived here would be no native sage but a rich man like his father. Gaius had not envisaged such a situation. Coridumnus should live a mean and austere life, denying himself all luxuries; clearly he did not. It did not augur well; Verluccus would have scant respect for such a defector.

Eventually he was delivered to a spacious and airy room within which a number of benches were ranged and on which students, whoever they were, presumably sat and listened to profound and worthy declamations from the revered master. To his dismay this room too was decorated with plastered walls painted with pillars and garlands and a tessellated floor, warm beneath his boots.

'Do not be so surprised, young man,' said a voice in impeccable Latin. 'Should I disdain to accept gifts from people who feel that I have helped them in some way? I could live as easily the life you suppose I ought, but I am blessed with the ability to help others and for that they thank me in the manner they suppose adds to my comfort.'

'How did you know what I was thinking?' He turned to look at the speaker, a tall man, quite aged judging by the sparse white hair on his head and his long, silky beard. His dress was simple enough, just a homespun robe of undyed wool, though the fastening brooches, Gaius noted, were of very high quality enamel. Dark and bright eyes glinted with amusement, and a smile hovered on his lips; Gaius was certain he did not take himself very seriously.

'I fear I shock a good many people by living as I do. They expect to find me a solitary, but how can I be solitary when so many people seek me out? You brought me a letter from Anicetus. Is he as well as he claims to be? Come and join me at breakfast. My day starts early and finishes early also. Late arrivals should not be impatient and demanding.'

Gaius apologized and told him that yes, Anicetus was very well.

'And you knew Cordatus? I met him once. It was I who recommended he take Anicetus from here to help him when he started your school. A very wise man, Cordatus.'

Gaius sat and shared the man's bread. He wondered how much of his problem Anicetus had written on the wax tablet but decided that it was best to tell all. If he did not do so, then the advice he received might be flawed. He poured it out.

'Well? What do you think? Can you help me? Will you talk to him? My time is short, and if you cannot help me, he is doomed. In ten days he will be sent to the gladiator school.'

'And you have little faith in his ability to become a successful gladiator? Your father and uncle are of a different mind. They are more experienced in these things than you. The slave may well make a famous gladiator.'

'They do not intend that. For the crimes he has committed, and I do not deny he must have committed many crimes in the time he has been absent from us, they condemn him to death. You are right, of course. Were Verluccus to learn he might become a gladiator, he would probably do his utmost to achieve it, thinking himself an able contender. But he would enter the arena under a delusion; he would not depart from it alive. But I know that if he would yield just a little, my father would find him employment. I know now that he won't accept me, and I dare not return him to Daruentum, but we have other estates where he could be sent to work.' It was not what he wanted, but he had come to terms with the inevitability of compromise. 'I would pay you anything you asked. Name another ornament for your home, and I shall provide it.'

'I am sure you are a rich young man, but I cannot do the impossible. It is your father you should be talking to, not me.'

'I am not so rich. I have an allowance from my father, most of which I pay to the soldiers who watch him for me. But I have jewellery which I can sell, and if you will allow it I can pay you so much every month until the debt is settled. With interest, of course.'

'Your opinion that I am mercenary is unjust.' Gaius was reproved. 'I will talk to this slave of yours, but do not expect me to succeed where you have failed.'

'Then you will return to Glevum with me now?' A delighted Gaius rose in expectation.

'Indeed I shall not. I do not go to Glevum. You must bring him here to me.'

'I cannot do that. Haven't you heard what I said?' Gaius despaired. He imagined Coridumnus talking to Verluccus within his prison, glad to visit his friend Anicetus; he had supposed an invitation to do so had been in the letter.

'I am not able to help you.' Coridumnus indicated the interview was concluded.

'What if I manage it – to bring him here? There are some restrictions on what you may speak to him of. Will you agree to those?'

'Tell me what they are. If I find they hinder me, I shall tell you so.'

'First I have promised my father that I will not let Verluccus know it was Palatus acting on his own account who branded him. Verluccus believes it was done on my father's orders, and he is not to be informed differently. It is for Palatus' protection – no other reason.'

'And what else?'

'He must not learn of the time limit my father imposed on me; he would simply become more obstinate if he knew of it, more set on defiance. And finally he must not know that Cunobarrus is thought to be alive. It may be that even as we speak Marcus Marcius has dealt with him, but word has not come of that, and until it does he must remain in ignorance or he surely will do something desperate.'

'I see. You may bring him. As I told you, should these things prove obstacles too great, I shall not proceed. However, you must understand that while I will not betray your confidence to him, neither shall I reveal to you what he wishes me to keep secret from you.'

This came as a shock to Gaius. After a long and thoughtful pause during which he wondered just how dangerous such secrets might be, he nodded and gave the man his hand. 'I agree.'

There was the anticipated abuse when he returned. Felix had not risked letting Verluccus outside, and so Verluccus had been confined during his master's absence and made his feelings clear.

'You will certainly be outside tomorrow,' he was told. 'I am taking you to for a chariot ride.'

He delivered a letter to Anicetus which secured his further absence from the school. To Antonius he did not actually lie, but he certainly allowed the tribune to believe he was taking Verluccus to Corinium. Antonius, supposing it to be at Lucius' instruction, raised no query.

Early the following morning, Antonius helped to secure the slave on a suitable chariot by means of the chains and watched doubtfully as he negotiated the narrow streets with the cumbersome vehicle. Gaius was not used to driving more than two horses, and for this large wagon four were necessary. Felix, a better horseman than his master, was granted a rare treat and allowed to ride on Cervus, and this went a long way to ameliorating the hurt of having been left behind the previous day.

'Let me come with you,' begged his best friend, Titus, the son of Justinius Severus, a veteran centurion. 'It is too much for you to handle the *quadriga* and him as well.' Like Antonius, Titus supposed Verluccus was being taken to Lucius and the arena at Corinium.

'We should only anger both our fathers,' Gaius dissuaded him, 'yours and mine, for interfering with your education.'

'Then take this.' Titus surreptitiously handed him a dagger. 'And do not hesitate to use it if you must.' They both had received training in arms from Antonius, but Titus excelled in the use of all weapons. He demonstrated how Gaius should use it to best effect. He was only a little older than Gaius but had a clear aptitude for the army. His father was immensely proud of him and delighted in his friendship with Lucius Marcius' son which would surely enhance his career prospects.

The horses tolerated him until they had left the city behind and a flat road stretched before them. He had scarcely been paying attention to them, more concerned with what thoughts might be going through the mind of the man trussed up securely beside him and what his reactions would be to the man he was being taken to meet.

Suddenly he was wrenched from his daydream by the reins being yanked out of his careless grip as the four horses sensed freedom and broke away, the chariot dragged rather than driven behind them. Gaius struggled to reach for the reins, but they were quickly beyond his reach, slapping on the rumps of the horses and seemingly goading them on. He could only grip the rail in terror, as there seemed no means of stopping their mad dash, and the chariot bounced and shook as if it might fall apart. From his side Verluccus lost his footing and, unable to rescue himself, fell into the well of the vehicle where he could only brace himself against being catapulted backwards onto the track behind them.

Felix, who had been until then riding quietly a little to the rear, suddenly drew alongside, urging the enthusiastic colt onwards until Cervus was breasting and then heading the chariot. He grasped at the lead horse's bridle and succeeded in drawing the vehicle to a halt.

Gaius could not speak. He clambered down and took himself some distance away to sit, shaking and sobbing from the fright he had experienced. Felix tied up the horses and went to comfort him, but he could take no comfort. It was his own fault, he acknowledged.

There was no one else to blame for this; he should have been paying proper attention.

'It is not your fault,' Felix declared stoutly. 'It is his fault. You would not be trying to drive that thing if not for him. Give up this mad idea and return to Glevum now. Or at least turn aside and go to Corinium and let your father have him.'

'You saved us from disaster, Felix,' Gaius answered, 'but don't presume. We are going to Coridumnus. I shan't have any more trouble now they have had the gallop they needed. Antonius should not have sent them out so fresh. And in any case they have a high bank to climb; that will sober them up. We shall continue.'

'Are you all right?' he asked of his captive when he remounted the chariot.

'No thanks to you.' He had taken a severe shaking and was well bruised but thankful, he discovered, to find himself still alive. In other circumstances he would have relished driving such a team of horses, but not even their presence could persuade him to surrender to this arrogant and self-serving brat. He stubbornly said no more.

'I cannot talk with a man in chains,' Coridumnus protested, horrified with what he was presented. Gaius had successfully negotiated the remainder of the journey without mishap and had driven with some force through the throng of hopeful supplicants to be admitted through the gate of the old man's homestead. Coridumnus had emerged to greet them.

'They must remain on him. He is dangerous.' Gaius had supposed Coridumnus understood the situation. It seemed that he did not.

'Then there is nothing I can do.' The elder raised his hands in resignation.

'Look, old man,' said Gaius angrily. 'I told you what the situation was. If I were able to take off his chains in the knowledge that he would not run away, I would not have needed to seek your help in the first place!'

Coridumnus was unmoved by the show of ill temper. 'I suggest you take food before your return journey,' he said calmly, indicating the route to the mess.

'Can your men guard him adequately? Is there a secure room in which to lodge him?' Gaius begged in despair. To have brought Verluccus here only to be rejected – it was so futile. He wished the man would speak Latin; Verluccus could understand every word they uttered. How he must be smirking.

'Do not be misled by our mild habits, young man,' Coridumnus reassured him. 'The porters here are very capable.' Seeing no further protest from Gaius, he ordered the irons removed.

'Go now, Gaius Marcius. Go. Leave us together. Your slave and I will talk. You have ample time to visit Corinium while we are engaged.'

'I am not going anywhere,' said Gaius, 'not away from here.'

'If your slave wishes to confide in me, he can scarcely do so in your presence,' Coridumnus pointed out reasonably. 'Since you are not prepared to go to Corinium, perhaps you might profitably spend some moments at the shrine of Nodens, and there is a pleasant garden also where you can lose yourself in meditation. I commend them both to you. When we are done, I shall send for you.'

Verluccus had said nothing up to this point, and indeed it was arguable whether he did wish to confide in Coridumnus. As soon as the chains were struck from him, he asserted his viewpoint, easing his wrists and smiling sardonically. 'You are mistaken, old fool: I am not his slave. His prisoner I may have been, but no longer.' He pointedly ignored Gaius and eyed the doors and windows.

'You see how obdurate he is?' Gaius could only hope that the porters were as capable as Coridumnus claimed. Incredibly the old man either had not heard or chose to ignore the slave's utterance and behaviour.

'Go,' he said again, urging Gaius to take himself and Felix away. 'Leave us alone. We shall talk.'

Gaius went only as far as the other side of the door and would have stayed there had it not been for the capable porters, who posted themselves where he intended to remain and made it clear by their presence that his was neither wanted nor required. He then took Coridumnus' advice and headed for the shrine.

'What makes you think there is anything I have to say to you?' sneered Verluccus. 'Look at this place. Look at you! You have betrayed your tribe and sold yourself to Rome.'

'I am a Briton just as you are. But unlike you I am a citizen and not a slave.'

'I told you,' he hissed. 'I am not his slave. I reject him.'

'That is an interesting notion.' Coridumnus nodded thoughtfully. 'I wonder how long the empire of Rome would survive if all slaves took that attitude – that they are not slaves unless they willingly submit to being so? There are few, I think, who would run to embrace servitude in the mines and quarries.'

Whatever Verluccus had expected to hear, it clearly was not this. After some careful thought he answered, 'Appealing to me on the grounds that I can assist the Roman Empire is the last method you should employ. I don't give a shit for any Romans, and if I thought that there were some means of doing what you have suggested, of persuading all slaves to revolt against their masters, then I would leap at so inviting an opportunity. But I am not the fool you think me. I know that some must be masters and some slaves; I too have owned slaves. It is being his slave that I object to. I say, "I will not call *him* my master."'

'You are very bitter towards him,' responded Coridumnus equably. 'Perhaps you have reason. He seemed to me to be singularly concerned with your welfare. You must grant that this is an unusual circumstance – to bring you here for counselling rather than to simply flog you into submission as I expect he has been advised to do? I beg you to sit down. I am uncomfortable standing still for long periods, and sitting in my company you will be at no disadvantage from me. As you can see, I am not so agile.'

Verluccus sat and acknowledged that he had never encountered the like of Gaius before. 'But do not be misled by his mild expression! You will know of his father and his uncle? He too practices their cruelties. Until today I have been confined in a cell no larger than' – he rose and paced out a description of the tiny space – 'than this, yes, in those chains, with no light and no companionship. I have been kept so for days on end as if I were entombed.' The contact he had had with the soldiers and the daily attention of Gaius and Felix conveniently had slipped his mind.

Coridumnus agreed that such treatment did seem excessive.

'And yet', he answered, 'I know his father; at least I know of him. I do not mix in his social circle, but I know he is well respected and not only in Glevum and Corinium. They call him Mollis, and such a name is not given to many. I have heard it said many despise him for being a soft touch.'

'Soft touch? Mollis? Do you know what he did to me? Look!' He displayed his damaged shoulder. 'I was a child, a boy of ten years! I had done no wrong to anyone, committed no crime, and yet this man whom you esteem so highly seized me and did that to me. He did that and then gave me to that brat of his, this Gaius.'

'The brat who goes to such lengths on your behalf?' Gaius had told Coridumnus of the scar. He dutifully examined it and agreed that when inflicted it must have been very painful.

'On his own behalf, not on mine. If he were concerned for me, he would let me go free.' He rose to his feet and challenged the man to detain him. 'I have had enough of this; I am off.'

'You have thought about where you will go then?' Coridumnus made no move to rise.

Verluccus was defeated. 'There is nowhere, is there? Nowhere for me to go. I talk a lot, but I know that if my family are alive they will be hostage for my recapture. Cunobarrus is dead and the whole of his followers destroyed. This brat has everything, and I have nothing.' He kicked his foot against the wall in futile anger.

'You escaped when you were a child. Surely you have more ability to do so now?'

He eyed the old man suspiciously. 'Are you not supposed to prevent my escaping?'

'I am a counsellor, not a gaoler, but if you leave it will be my responsibility. Who knows what punishment may be visited upon me by this young brute? I may be made to serve as a slave in your place. But unlike you, I believe I would have a considerate master.'

'I have told you – he is not my master.'

Unperturbed, Coridumnus invited him to sit again. 'Tell me about yourself. You may have confidence that whatever you say will be private unless you wish otherwise.'

'I was born at Daruentum. Do you know of it?'

'Until I met Cordatus, no. And I should then have been hard put to place it. It lies near Glevum?'

'Some distance beyond as I remember. I lived with my father and mother and four brothers until my eldest brother quarrelled with my father and he and the second eldest left home. And that was about the Romans. You see, my father thought that the Romans brought us prosperity, and he welcomed them into our home. When I was very small, I sat on the knees of soldiers as they talked with my father around our fire. Cunobarrus did not like that, and he and Cadrus, as I say, quarrelled with him over it and left home.'

'Your brother? Cunobarrus was your brother?' Coridumnus was startled. This he had not expected. 'That same Cunobarrus in whose company you were when you were captured?' He was certain Gaius did not know it, or else he would have told him. He wondered whether this was the point at which he should call the discourse to a halt.

'The very same. He bore the same name as our father. It was he. It was a great good fortune for me that I met up with him again. But that was many years later. Our father died when Cunobarrus and Cadrus had been gone for only a year or so; he had a wound from a rusty nail turn poisonous. Only Tanodonus and I were left then to help Mother. I discount Colymmon, because although he was older than Tan, he was not quick-witted. He was a good shepherd though, and from him I learned skills which I made use of later.

'Then one day, completely without warning and for no reason that I knew of then or know of now, men sent by him – the Roman I mean – appeared at our house. The one who is his steward was arguing with my mother over me. Suddenly he snatched me from her

178

and took me back to his master, Lucius Marcius. That man branded me to mark me as his property and made a gift of me to his son, the brat Gaius. He had no right to do that; I had committed no crime. My family owed him nothing.'

'Can you be sure of that?'

'Of course I can. My mother would not have us in debt to anyone, and if it had been so, why would his steward have offered her money?'

Coridumnus could not argue with that.

'I got away from them the following day. I saw the opportunity to escape when they put me to work labouring for a builder. It was easy. I climbed an ivy vine while no one was looking and found myself in a garden. As it was late summer, all the plants were thickly grown and so I stayed put. There was a real danger of being discovered when one of the slaves started to search the garden, beating at the plants with a stick, and I was certain he would find me. I was on the point of revealing myself when he was called off and given a good beating. That convinced me not to give myself up.'

He stopped suddenly and scrutinized Coridumnus. 'I shall tell you more. There was a man who helped me. If I tell you his name you must swear that you will not reveal it to these Romans. Swear or, from the next world, if my trust in you is misplaced, I swear that I shall never rest but haunt and trouble you forever.'

'I have already given you my word. Everything you tell me in this room is a confidence between us. If you choose to let Gaius Marcius know of what has passed between us, that is your privilege.'

The porters brought food, a mountain of bread and fruits and a variety of meat dishes. Coridumnus' angular frame was clearly not due to a lack of appetite. Verluccus began to eat, speaking between mouthfuls.

2

'I stayed hidden in the garden until nightfall. I heard men coming and going, and I knew they had sent for the army to search for me. I heard their trumpeters and their voices. I was very frightened, but when it was completely dark I cautiously made my way onto the hill where Colymmon took our sheep in the hope that there might be a cache of food he had left behind. The hill once had been the dwelling of my grandfathers, but the Romans overpowered them and shifted them to the valley. There were heaps of stones, and rubble and I knew the whereabouts of Colymmon's favourite caches.'

'And did you find any food?'

'Even more than food, I found a knife and a purse of coins too which had obviously been left there for me. I cried then, for I knew it meant my family dared not see me again and I had to make my own way in life.

'I made my way to the road. I recognized that road as we came along it today, but then, foolishly, because I did not want to travel the same route as the soldiers, when I saw a troop of them coming along it, I hid and then went in the direction they had come from.

'Before long I caught up with an ox cart, and thinking the driver had not seen me, I followed it for a little way. After some time he stopped and offered me a lift. It was from him I learned that I was about to enter Glevum, almost the last place I wished to be.'

'And this was the man who helped you?'

He laughed bitterly. 'I told him my name was Magnus and that I had been sent to Glevum to purchase a horse for my master. It was a stupid and obvious lie, but I was only a child and thought it would explain why I was on foot alone and had a purse of money.

'When we reached the town he drove straight to the barracks storehouse and ordered me to guard the oxen for him. His load was mostly jars of oil, and they took some time to be unloaded. I stood there quite terrified, convinced when he was done his last task would be to take me into the office. But he went in alone and came out looking pleased with himself. He took me to a tavern and bought me food to eat and ale to drink.'

Coridumnus wondered about the man; Verluccus had not revealed his name.

'I was unused to such strong ale. The next thing I remember is waking up and finding myself bound and gagged inside a moving vehicle, another cart. I started to struggle, and the vehicle stopped. The covers thrown over me were removed, and that was when I came face to face with Bodenius.'

This was a startling revelation. Bodenius, a travelling vendor of many items, was a name not unknown to Coridumnus, and it was rumoured he was not averse to delivering slaves to the mines along his route. Mothers of fractious babes were wont to warn them that if they did not behave they would be taken by Bodenius.

'I see from your face you know of him. Remember what I said. I have reason to be thankful to that man and good remembrances of my journey with him, though at the time of our parting I was angry and disappointed with him.

'I pretended indignation, of course – insisted that I was Magnus and that I was on an errand and that he would be in serious trouble for stealing me. But when he took out some salve and spread it on my wound and treated me kindly, I told him the truth.

'He said he had guessed in any case and that I was too young and green to fool anyone. That I should trust him and stay with him and if I worked for him I could earn a few pennies. My purse had disappeared, taken by the oil carrier, I was sure.

'Bodenius was a trader. The wagon in which I had been smuggled out of Glevum was hauled by a pair of large and aged oxen named

Patience and Haste, and as I bragged that I knew all about animals, as I had been raised on a farm, the care of them was made my responsibility.

'Bodenius told me that he travelled from Corinium to the marketplaces as far as the Silures tribe and then back to Corinium. He would buy and sell all along the way. He sold everything imaginable, anything anybody was prepared to buy, and he bought things for resale to others – pots, dishes, ironware, earthenware, tools, trinkets, ornaments, lengths of fabric, some very fine wool, and even silk when he could get it for his better customers. I remember at some stage making a joke that there seemed to be nothing he would not sell, and he laughed and agreed with me.

'He did not press me for more about myself than I felt able to tell him, but as we journeyed I gave away more and more about who I was and where I came from.

'He told me things too; we travelled alongside the Sabrina for a good distance as the road took us in and out to farms and habitations. He told me a fine tale about the great sea god coming up to claim his river every autumn and spring, how he could be seen riding his sea chariot and turning back the flow of the current. I wanted to linger so that we might see him, but he would have none of it and hurried me along to our destination. He also told me of a prince named Caratacus who had defied the Romans for many years; he seemed surprised that I had never been taught these things. I think Cunobarrus knew of them, for I had heard the name spoken in our home though not what it meant.

'Bodenius protected me well, even when we met soldiers, even though he made me lift things down to display to them, beads and brooches and suchlike. He used to say that the soldiers had to see what they expected to see, and if he scolded and cuffed me in front of them it was better than hiding me. Occasionally one of the soldiers might express interest in me, but he would always say that he had promised me to another and I was not available.

'On another occasion a Roman woman came to me. She had slaves and seemed to be very rich like the family I had recently escaped from, and I was very frightened. She too had small children who were curious about me. When Bodenius told her the tale about my destination, she smiled and sent me to the kitchen in her house where I might obtain some honeycomb, which I did, and it was good. Her children pestered her that she might buy me, but Bodenius would have none of it. Later he left me to prepare our meal while he visited the nearby solitary at the shrine of Mars Nodens to obtain ointments. The children came out to stare at me; our languages were different, and I did not much care to have them nearby but did not dare to chase them off.

'A man suddenly strode up to me and demanded to know where Bodenius was. I told him I did not know, for I did not like the look of the man, whom I supposed had been sent by this woman to buy me for her. But he was not from the farm; he grabbed hold of me and began to march me quickly up the road in the direction we had come from, and I knew for certain I had been pursued from Glevum and was now being taken back.

'We had gone some distance when there was shouting behind us, and Bodenius with some other men – these really were from the farm – came running after us. The man did not flee but stopped and stood his ground, and when Bodenius, puffing and out of breath from his running, caught up with us, the man threw some coins down on the ground. There was a lot of shouting and arguing about my being too young and in any case already promised to another before I was released. Bodenius told me the man was the overseer of a local mine, and sometimes he brought slaves out to him to work in them. I was very relieved to be saved from such a fate, and Bodenius told me I owed it to the children who had run to their mother. She had sent a man to find him and tell him what had happened, and so they had all run after my kidnapper. I was sent to say my thanks to the woman. She was a kind woman; she asked me if I would like to live with her family, and I had to tell her that there was another person who was expecting me. She actually bent down and kissed me, and then she let me go.

'I often thought about that woman afterwards when I met up with

Cunobarrus and I did the things which I did. But the area in which she lived was not in our territory, and so she and her family were safe from me; and I am glad of that.

'Soon after this Bodenius began to ask me if I had given any thought to what I should do when we reached the end of our journey. This was a surprise, because I had grown so used to travelling with him I had assumed I would go on doing so. But he pointed out that it would be much too dangerous for me to return to Glevum. I must find work for myself elsewhere and give up all thought of returning home. I was very sad and spent a lot of time apart from him, talking instead to Patience.

'One night while were eating our meal, he said to me, "I know of an old woman who would give you a home." I did not like the sound of this. "She lives alone far away in the distant hills and is in need of help," he said. "You would be of great help to her." I did not want to live far away in a distant hill farm; I considered myself far too worldly after the experience I had gained in selling things for Bodenius. He said that it was just an idea and a pity that I did not wish to make myself useful, and then no more was said about it.

'We arrived at the market of the Silures to find it full and bustling, and I had to take Patience and Haste away to hobble them for grazing while Bodenius set out his stall. There were already a number of people crowding around it as I made my way back, and suddenly they all turned round and were looking at me. One of them was an old woman. She came over to me and grabbed me and pulled me towards Bodenius, complaining in a shrill and scathing voice that I was too young for her needs and not nearly big enough to be of any use to her.

'I heard Bodenius telling her that I was fourteen and though small for that age I was a very good worker and very strong and fit. Better still, I knew about sheep, for my previous master had kept sheep, among other animals.

'If she had not kept a hold of me and if her companions had not then crowded around me, I would immediately have run away. As it was, I fought to free myself from her and shouted at Bodenius as the sickening realization came to me. I had trusted him as if he were my grandfather, and he had betrayed me. I shouted, "I trusted you, I told you about myself, and now you sell me just like you sell your pots." Just like he sold everything.

'He sought to placate me and took me to one side. "Now don't take on so. It is true she will pay me for you but not so much as I might have got elsewhere or if I chose to sell you in the marketplace. Look at it this way: here is an old woman who needs you, and here is you who needs a home. I just brought the two of you together."

'"If you want money for bringing me here, take the money you paid me for work." I begged him, "Don't sell me to her; she is horrible and she stinks of sheep," and he shook his head firmly.

'"And what would become of you then? You, alone in a strange town, with no money and no home?"

'I told him I would not remain with her as a slave – that I would run away. "Then you would be a bigger fool than I took you for," he told me. "For a start there is that brand, which sooner or later someone here will recognize. This town is only a few miles from Isca Silurum where the Second Legion is based, the same legion whose veterans are at Glevum; soldiers are constantly travelling to and fro. And just look at her! Look how ancient she is. She has no one to inherit her estate – her farm or her sheep. For the want of a few years' patience, you would be throwing away the chance to become your own man, to marry, to have children, to be a farmer. You take my advice and go gladly, and don't be troublesome. She will work you hard, yes, but in the end the reward will be yours."

'He hugged me and gave me a bundle of things, clothes which he said would be useful to me, and he let me keep the money, though I could not see that I should ever have the chance to spend it if her farm was so remote. But it would be useful for when I ran away.

'My new mistress could see she had a bad bargain, but she took me all the same, demanding a chain from Bodenius, which he provided, and loading me with her purchases so that I was encumbered. I would not look at Bodenius. It hurt me that a man I had so trusted had proved so treacherous. You may recall that I described him as my benefactor? Later, when I was more rational about the situation, and even today, I realize how indebted I am to him for what he did for me. It must be obvious to you that to sell me had been his purpose from the start. But you are a wise man, and I was neither wise nor a man, and for a long time I hated him.'

Verluccus had come to a pause. He looked at Coridumnus to see what answer he might make. The old man rose unsteadily to his feet, stiff from his patient listening. 'I am in need of exercise. Give me your arm and assist me; we will walk in the garden for a while.'

They were out of sight of the gathering of people at the gate but within the sight of a shocked Gaius, who saw Verluccus walking freely and with no apparent hindrance to his escape. He would have darted forward, angry at the carelessness, but a hand descended onto his shoulder and one of Coridumnus' faithful followers bid him to hush and let well alone; the master was in no danger. Gaius subsided, intensely watchful but unwilling to be the cause of trouble. He wondered what his father would say should he ever have to be told of this and silently prayed that he never would know.

The garden was low and formal and well provided with benches, but Coridumnus had sat for too long and walked silently along the neatly tended footpaths.

'What is it that you are thinking?' Verluccus asked him. 'Are you expecting me to escape? Have you brought me out here so that I may do so? Do not fear that; I have no will to cause harm to you, though you are an imitation Roman.'

'On the contrary, I was merely wondering why you make such a pretence of having a violent disposition. It is a pretence, is it not? The boy you have described to me could not have grown into the evil barbarian you present yourself as being.'

Verluccus laughed bitterly. 'With the Romans as instructors, the mildest of boys can become the most vicious of men. I have done my share of evil things; there is no pretence. I have killed many pitilessly, citizens and soldiers alike. I have stolen goods and cattle, burned property, farmsteads, people's homes, even raped. Do not suppose me to be better than I know I am. But what I do not understand is this: why do I have no will to kill or even harm that Roman boy, Gaius?

My bare hands are as good as any weapon, and yet even with so many chances given to me, I hesitate. I cannot understand the reason why. It cannot be from fear of the consequences. I have faced death too often to fear that. I do not consider him to be a cause worth dying for – it is true there would be no glory in causing the death of one so insignificant – but I do not think that a satisfactory explanation. Wise and good old man, can you explain it?'

'It cannot be explained unless you will accept that you are not as evil as you pretend to be. Perhaps you are enjoying the attention you are receiving at the moment and enjoying his discomfiture as he struggles to make you submit to him.'

'Are you mad? Enjoying it? To be kept caged like a beast? I have no pleasure in that! And I do want to live – but to live in freedom.'

'That you have no right to hope for,' Coridumnus pointed out equably. 'You are most fortunate to have not only your life but a good master too. You boast of many crimes, and for those you must pay the penalty with loss of your freedom if not your life. No matter what the circumstances were which led you to join them, you affirm that you lived and fought with thieves and murderers and rebels against the empire. You boast of many crimes. Should you live long enough to be granted legal manumission, it will be remarkable, I think, perhaps for good service to your master – certainly not for abusing him.'

They had stepped inside the building again and now into a fresh suite of rooms where braziers and lamps had been lit. Seeing them enter, Gaius sighed with relief. He was highly impatient but could see that the man was getting through to Verluccus, though it was taking longer than he wished.

Having satisfied himself that he had the only exit from that room under surveillance, he took a post to watch the door.

Within the room more food was laid out. A banquet of oysters, apples, loaves, and fowl awaited them, though there was neither wine nor beer to drink but only water drawn from the spring. Other men were already present and at their meal, but Coridumnus said, 'It is not my custom to eat at this time but to read. However, I have neglected my other duties both to the people who have called on me and to my students, so I shall leave you now and we shall continue our discourse later. My brothers will take their meal, and they will not harass you, so feel comfortable to take the food you require but do not leave the room until I return; they know you may not.'

The other men ate and cleared away the remains, and finally he was left alone. He wondered where Gaius was and what he was doing and how long it would be until the old man returned. That he made no attempt to leave the room surprised him, but he told himself that there was sure to be a guard beyond the door awaiting the opportunity to spear him, and for that reason – and in order to annoy Gaius – he stayed put.

It was not until darkness had fallen that Coridumnus returned. Apologetic for his long absence, he explained that many people had called upon him that day. He was drained and tired, though he did not say as much.

'My good brethren insist I rest tonight. You will be comfortable in here? Tomorrow, if you will grant me such a privilege, I will hear more of your story. I don't expect a young man like yourself will sleep so soon as this. Would you like Gaius Marcius to join you? You may wish to talk to him.'

Verluccus shook his head. 'For your sake I shall remain here,' he answered. 'You need have no fear; you will find me waiting for your ears in the morning.'

'You may find a little work on some wood amusing.' Coridumnus produced a block of wood and a sharp knife. 'Is such a skill of yours?'

'No.' Verluccus shook his head and grinned. 'My skill is in forging metal and using arms. But I shall see what can be done.'

Coridumnus bade him goodnight, and for a long time he sat in the light of the flickering lamps and contemplated the knife in his hand, wondering if some better use might be made of it.

3

The morning sun woke him, and he realized that he had finally slept and slept long. Some raised voices could be heard beyond the door, and he felt a sense of satisfaction that Gaius' patience had finally been exhausted. The door was flung open, accompanied by the words, 'I will see for myself. I thank you.'

The blade in Verluccus' hand gleamed in the light, for he had taken up the wood to carve more. He saw the expression on Gaius' face change from relief at seeing him still within to horror at the weapon he now possessed and which was pointing towards him.

As the two stood in silent contemplation of what next might happen, Coridumnus entered, saying, 'Do you insist on taking him away? We had to break off last night only due to my age. If you wish me to assist in this matter, we have much ground to cover today. Do we not, my friend?'

Verluccus nodded. He held up the piece of wood, hacked about in a crude fashion. 'As you can see, my skill lies elsewhere. I had thought to carve a pony from it, but I doubt it can be seen yet. More time is surely needed.'

'You gave him a knife? A weapon? What are we to do now?' Gaius demanded in Latin, backing towards the doorway.

Coridumnus ignored him but held out his hand to receive the wood. 'I think I see the possibility that this could become a pony. You have the basic shape but the detail is rough. It is a good effort since you say it is a skill not known to you.' He turned to Gaius. 'Can you see the horse?'

'Get the knife,' Gaius hissed. 'Don't you know how dangerous he is?'

Coridumnus said, smiling, 'I feel sure we are in no danger.' He held out his hand again, and the knife was gently placed in it by a smug Verluccus, who grinned evilly at Gaius.

Gaius spoke rapidly and quietly to the counsellor. 'That was a foolish risk to take. How did he persuade you to let him have a knife? It was a risk you ought not to have taken. Now we must leave; my father does not know that I have brought Verluccus away from Glevum, and if I delay longer, he may well return there before I do and discover this absence. I must return today without fail.'

'I would prefer you not to appear underhanded. Speak only openly. Verluccus will think you are being dishonest with him. If you are concerned about your time absent from Glevum, take him now, by all means, but I do not advise it. I am not a magician; would that I were. Such business as we have cannot be hurried. Go and be patient a little longer. Should I find I can assist no further, I shall send for you.'

'Mayn't I speak with you apart?' How stupid the man could be. He could not talk in front of Verluccus about his fears – not while his chains were removed. Surely he could see that?

Coridumnus put an arm around him and led him from the room. 'I know, I know. Do not worry so; he remained here overnight without any restraint other than concern for my welfare. Has not his conduct reassured you? I did not give him the knife as a test but to provide an occupation during his time alone, but you are right; he had ample opportunity to attack us both but did not do so. Allow me a little longer. But first we each have duties owing to the gods; go now and make your offering, and consider perhaps what reward a provident god may deserve. We shall allow Verluccus time also to his gods. Be as patient as you can. I do believe that my services will not be necessary after today.'

It was impossible that they could be, Gaius thought. Whatever the outcome of Coridumnus' efforts today, they must return to Glevum. Fear of discovery by his father brought a sweat upon him. So he took the old man's advice and performed the rites, promising that he would give an altar to Nodens if only he would make Verluccus surrender himself to him, and quickly too. Then he returned to his nail-biting vigil.

Coridumnus indicated that he was now free to hear more of Verluccus' story.

'As I told you, I was fastened with a chain around my middle, and loaded with my own bundle and her purchases too, I was led as if I were a pack animal. There were about ten of them altogether – mostly men, some boys, and this old hag. I had no choice but to go where they led at that time, but I knew in my heart I would not remain with them for long. We travelled for three days, camping at night around a fire. The boys took it in turns to be torch bearers and carried the fire before us all of the way, and at night the men took turns to keep watch.

'When one of the boys, who was, I learned, named Bodecus, the son of the elder Bodlan, was not carrying the fire, he made a point of walking close behind me, knowing that I could do nothing about it, because Merriol – that was the old woman's name – was determinedly holding the tether and walking ahead of us. Suddenly I tripped. He claimed it was over a root, but I knew better – it was his foot that did it. I and all the things I was carrying were strewn on the ground. The breakages included a crock of salt which poured wastefully onto the woodland floor. Now the old woman was really angry. She beat me around the head with her fists and screamed that I was useless to her. I was a further curse inflicted on her, and she was a woman wronged by the gods and her fellow men. Only when one of the men intervened did she desist, and I was reloaded and set to move on. I could not catch what he said to her, but I heard the old woman say that she did not want Trenn to help me; I must manage for myself. But this man, whose name was Rignis, was quietly insistent that his son should help, and I felt that perhaps this was someone who would protect me from her.

'That first night when we made camp and I was tied up where the watchman could see me, Rignis came and brought me my meal. He said that if I was ever in need of help for myself or Merriol, my mistress, I should go to him for it. He asked me what my name was, and unsure what name to give, I offered, "Magnus."

'He frowned and said, "That is a Roman name; you are not Roman, so why call yourself that?" To discover that at least one of these people had no love for my enemies was welcome news. I told him my real name and admitted that I had run away.

'"That was not wise," he said. "Do not run away from us. Where we live the country is very wild. Even here there are wolves, but where we live there are wolves and bears also – many wild beasts. You will be safe if you stay with Merriol and do as she bids you. My son and I shall give what help we can."

'That gave me cause to ponder, for I had been planning how to escape; but I was afraid of the wild beasts and did not doubt the truth of his words, for at night I heard the wolves and other strange noises. I said nothing, but I felt the eyes of Rignis often on me.

'When Trenn took the watch I was almost asleep, but I asked him if it were true that there were wild animals where they lived and if they were dangerous. He said that they were but that robbers were more dangerous. I need not fear the robbers, however, for they had soldiers to protect them. It was clear from the way Trenn spoke that unlike his father, he admired the soldiers. I remembered then how I too had felt just a short time before and, though Trenn was older than I, how much better than he I knew the Romans and their soldiers.

'The following day it seemed to have been agreed that when he was not carrying the fire, this boy Bodecus could lead me. Now the path was steep and more difficult, and we were emerging from the forest onto wild and bleak windswept hills.

'Almost immediately he began to tug on the chain and tried to make me walk more quickly. When I could not, for without free hands it was most difficult, he took a stick and began to lash me across the backs of my shins. I kicked out at him, and at first he merely laughed; but when we came to a more difficult place, he tried it again. I put my bundle down very carefully. He was not expecting me to hit him and so was taken completely by surprise. I grabbed hold of his tunic and set about him before he realized what I intended. I do not know what I might have done to him if the men had not stopped me, but when they hauled me off him his nose was bloody enough to satisfy me, and though Merriol took a stick and gave me a good beating about the legs I felt it was worthwhile. She made me carry everything again after that, though Rignis told Trenn to walk close and help me if I needed it but to be watchful, as I had a "nasty temper." Rignis himself led me from then on, and Bodecus kept his distance. The boy was not punished at all; his father was most indulgent towards him and merely said it would be better for him to carry the torch instead of leading me. I strode indignantly towards my destination, smarting at the injustice of their judgement.

'Merriol's home was a good distance beyond the others, and she and I reached there alone. Someone had kept her fire burning and put a pot of soup on so that hot food was awaiting us. Someone also had attended to her animals, sheep, ducks, and geese which lived around the place and the lively dogs which guarded them. I remembered that Bodenius had said she lived alone and wondered who had done this.

'She said I was to look after the sheep and leave her to attend to the rest of her chores and then she might get her wool spun. We decided that I was to be called Verluccus and I was to address her as Merriol or mistress – mistress if there were any soldiers around. I told her then my age. "Not yet eleven!" she shrieked. "Ten! That thieving rogue told me you were fourteen. I knew it; I knew it. He robbed me. That Bodenius robbed me. Not yet eleven!" She stopped shrieking at the absent Bodenius long enough only to shriek at the dogs who had joined in with her; perhaps they thought I was attacking her. Then she paused and considered me. "You are big for ten. Are you strong?" I told her I was very strong and that, while I was big for ten, I would be very small for fourteen and so she was getting the best of the bargain. Surprisingly, perhaps because she thought she was getting the better of Bodenius, this seemed to placate her, and we ate our soup in comparative silence.

'When it was time to sleep she led me around the holding and showed me how to secure the animals. If the dogs started to bark during the night, it would mean there were wolves about, in which case I was to take a brand from the fire and go outside and drive them off. She was perfectly serious about this. I dared not tell her that the only wolf I had ever seen was a dead one and the only bear had been a performing one brought to entertain the crowds in Glevum. She handed me a sling, telling me I must learn to use it; and at my request, she restored my knife to me which had been transferred as part of the deal with Bodenius. She warned me against fighting, stating that "that Bodecus is a bad lot" and I must have nothing more to do with him.

'I had to share her bed with her or sleep on a skin on the floor. I chose the floor and stripped off my tunic without thinking as I wrapped myself in the fleeces; soon I was to stink of sheep as much as she did. Her sharp eyes missed nothing. "What is that?" She pounced on me and turned my back towards the flame. I told her what it was – not all of my story, just what it was and that I had run away. I could, even after so short an acquaintance, predict her reaction.

'"That thieving Bodenius knew of this, didn't he?" She took hold of me and shook me violently. I admitted it. What else could I do? "He can have you back. If you survive the winter, I shall take you back to him." The joy I felt on hearing this was unabated even when she added, "He can find some other fool to take you. They don't ask questions in the iron quarries." I was confident that Bodenius would not allow such a thing to happen to me.

'The following day I commenced a routine which was to vary little for the whole of my life with Merriol. She counted herself fortunate that she kept a scraggy cow, and I let her show me how to milk it though I knew how already. Its calf she had taken to market, and I supposed I had been bought with her profit from it. She showed me how to control the dogs and demonstrated what I must do with the sling, advising me to practise hard. Then she turned me out onto the hillside with the sheep and some small bread and told me to return when the sun set. In the daylight I could see what a dilapidated state her outbuildings had got into. There were a number of small huts with no roofs at all, and the one covering her own dwelling was in such a state that in many places the thatch was absent too. Weeds had grown up within the unroofed buildings, and the whole place seemed desolate and unkempt. It was clear that Merriol needed help, but I doubted that I was the one she needed. I noticed too that she paid no heed to the gods, offered no corn bread, and spared none of her milk for them as my mother would have done. It was small wonder they took no care of her.

'It was a meagre flock of sheep – never did it reach above fifty – but there was a ram among them whose duty it was to provide the ewes with lambs. She made me count them in and out and if she came near me during the day always asked when I had last counted them. I once made a feeble joke that there would be no increase until lambing time, for which I was cuffed about the head and sharply reminded that my duty was to ensure there was no decrease.

'I saw nothing of her neighbours, though I heard them and saw the guardian fires lit at the time of the dead and later in midwinter when they held a festival which we could clearly hear, distant from them and their celebrations though we were. I once risked suggesting we might go to it, but she would have nothing to do with them.

'I continued to take the sheep out even when the first snow fell, for I thought that this would save the fodder she had put aside for them. It was then I first met Enemno.

'My sheep had run into his flock, a larger flock than Merriol's, and by the time I had reached them the two were inextricably intermingled. Because this could only be to his gain, the stranger paid no heed while I, terrified of Merriol and her anger, in panic at seeing her sole means of support being stolen, ran hither and thither trying to drive them apart. Eventually, when I was all but exhausted and close to tears, I marched up to him and demanded to know why he was stealing my sheep. "I have not stolen any sheep," he pointed out quite reasonably. "There they all are. But who are you?"

'"I am Merriol's shepherd," I told him with dignity, "and I know exactly which of them are hers," which was not true. I threatened him that Merriol would be coming soon, not expecting her at all; but she did come, striding towards us across the hill.

'The fact that her sheep and those of this stranger were inextricably intermixed gave her no more concern than it did him, and I heard the cackle of her laughter as he described my antics to her. "This is Enemno," she told me. "It is a good job he is not a thief if that is the best you can do." After that experience I made it my business to learn the faces of every one of my sheep. It was the first lesson I had from Enemno, the first of many.

'It was shortly after this that I encountered Bodecus again. Merriol told me to keep the flock nearer to the farm, and I was happy to do that, because for some days I had suspected that a wolf had been watching. I had not seen it; it was just that feeling you have when you know eyes are upon you – you turn round, and there is nothing to be seen, and yet you fancy there was a shadow moving. As the dogs were content, I settled down in the lee of an outcrop and thought no more about it. Suddenly, without any warning, the boy launched himself from above. It was not a wolf that had been spying on me but him. Although he started with the advantage, I got the better of him, and by the time Merriol reached us, attracted by the dogs' excited barking, we were sitting together counting the score. It was I who had won, for whereas he had two black eyes and a bloody nose, I had only one bruised eye.

'"You wicked, wicked boy. Look what you have done." She did not speak of the injury I had inflicted on Bodecus or of his injury to me but of her flock. Distressed by the barking of the dogs, it had scattered far afield.

'She sent me across to the stream to cut a bundle of twigs from the alders growing there, and when I returned with an armful of good springy ones – I did not know what they were for – she had restored order as far as she could, though one of the ewes had fallen into the stream and broken a leg. Bodecus had been sent on his way. I saw him pause and turn in his tracks as her first blow descended.

I started to beg for mercy but knew none would be forthcoming. By the time she had finished with me I too could scarcely walk, and she had exhausted herself.

'Surprisingly, given the circumstances, she did not deny me my meal, and it was while I was supping that someone came to her door. I heard an angry exchange of words. When her visitors had departed – gaining no satisfaction, I was sure – she returned to me and ordered me to strip off my shirt. I thought I was in for another beating, but I was wrong. Until she looked at me then, I do not think she had any idea of what she had done. She said nothing but began to smooth over all the wounds on my body, arms, and legs some of the lotion she made up for cuts and grazes. She told me to go to bed and sleep, but I lay awake wondering what she was going to do with me. The dark silence later was broken by the sound of her sobbing, and it was only then that I realized what a dreadful thing I had done. That ewe would have borne a lamb in the spring, and her flock was pitifully small without my destroying it. I slid my money from its hiding place and crept across to her. "I am sorry, mistress. Truly, I am. Is it enough?" I asked, offering all I had. It was not, for she simply cried the more, and eventually I drifted into sleep.

'When the morning came I found I was too stiff and sore to move. I heard her rise and lay waiting for her to start screaming at me. She did not; she fetched me a cup of milk and told me that today I must stay in the hut; she would take out the sheep. I knew she no longer trusted me and was planning to get rid of me, but I was too sore and swollen to argue about it. And I knew that whatever she decided to do, I deserved it. I could not spin wool as she would have done, but when I felt able to rise I fetched in water and made up the fire and did what I could towards preparing a meal for her return.

'Men came to the door – the elder Bodlan and Rignis. Bodecus was with them. "Is that what she did to you?" Rignis asked, and I said no, the damage to my face was done by Bodecus, and the stripes they could see on my arms and legs had happened while we were fighting and I fell in a bramble. I hoped they would think it a fair exchange for what I had done to him. I stuck to my version despite Bodecus, and though they did not believe me, they could do nothing. Rignis drew me aside and said, "You won't run away, will you? It is far too dangerous, and now the winter is upon us. If you are ever frightened, ever, don't run away; come to me. Promise?" I heard Bodlan asking him why he was even putting such ideas in my head, and I could imagine that now Rignis would tell him I had already done so once. The friendship I thought I had formed with Bodecus was to be over. He was forbidden to come near me again.

'I took food out to Merriol, feeling ready to resume my duties, but she would have none of that and only complained that since I had brought enough food for an army I had better stop and eat with her. I told her of our visitors and what I had said. This angered her. "You had no call to do that. What I do to you is my business and not theirs, and I won't have you telling lies on my account. I suppose they came to complain about you hitting that boy Bodecus again? His father brought him round last night. I shall take you to sell in the spring when I take my wool down; someone there will take you off my hands." It was the first time she had mentioned getting rid of me without speaking of Bodenius. I was very worried and said nothing; I did not want to antagonize her again. That night she gave me back my money, saying it was of no use to her. "I shall never hit you again," she said. "Not like that – I won't beat you again like that. But don't get the idea you can run me ragged. There are other ways of dealing with you if you misbehave, so think on that."

'The broken-legged ewe continued to struggle after the rest of the flock to remind me of my wickedness long after my own wounds had healed. In the winter, when the weather became too severe to take the animals abroad, I made myself useful around the farm, rebuilding her tumbledown walls. At first this provoked no comment, but I fancied the amount of food put upon my dish was growing larger. Then, unexpectedly, she said, "Where did you learn to build stone walls?"

'"My brother has a farm," I told her. "I helped him." She wanted to know more, so I talked about my home. She listened in silence until I thought I had said enough, and then she said, "Your mother has help from two grown men and extra hands too," for I had told her that we used to hire slaves when there was much work to be done. "All I have is you. That Bodenius robbed me."

'"It is a bigger farm," I declared in defence.

'She told me then, "When my husband was alive, this farm thrived. He was the chief man among our people. We had slaves to work for us too. Now all I have are the sheep, a few fowl, and that poor cow. The walls are falling down, and there is barely a roof over my head. Every year my wool gets less as the flock gets smaller, and thanks to you, that ewe will have to be slaughtered! And all I have for help is a ten-year-old boy."

'I protested that I was sure I must be eleven. I was always older before the midwinter feast, and that had passed us by ages ago. There was actually a suggestion of a smile on her face at this – as if it made any difference to her plight at all. I was intrigued to learn that she had once had a husband though, and sons too. I had not imagined Merriol as anyone's mother. They, like their father, were both dead, but she did not tell me then how they had died.

'In the spring, when the lambs came and I knew what to do, for the first time she gave an indication she was pleased with me. We lost lambs, of course, and a ewe, but not from my neglect, and I felt proud of my achievement. The time came for her to go to Silurum market to sell the wool she had spun during the winter, and she showed me how fine it was, told me how much her spinning was sought after for its fineness and that she would get a good return for it. Nothing was said about her taking me; she gave me instructions about what I should do in her absence. It was clear that I was not going to be returned to Bodenius, and I was not at all sorry, though I would have liked to see him again so that he would know how I was getting on. She promised that if she saw him she would tell him for me, but I doubted that she would.

'After she had departed, I sought out Enemno and put to him a plan I had formed in my mind. He thought carefully and agreed to it. Daily I delivered the flock to his charge and then set about my business. I had noticed that an even more dilapidated hut existed not far away, and from that I could get the material to make some of the repairs her property was badly in need of.

'I had an audience, of course. The children who had been kept away from me began to gather and call to me. I ignored them as best I could, but Bodecus was among them. He intercepted me on my route and demanded to know by what right I took the stuff from the abandoned property. He was of course looking for another fight. I told him what I was doing, and to my surprise his manner changed entirely. He informed me he would have no idea how to repair a roof and that I must show him. As I probably had less idea myself, I doubted that this was a good idea, but in no time he had all the little children running to and fro carrying wood and reclaimed thatches for me. Then both he and I were on the roof doing the best we could to patch it up. I was glad to have Bodecus as a friend, though I knew Merriol would be very angry to find him there. I told him of this, but he said, "I have been told I must not fight with you anymore, and so my big brother, Young Bodlan, is to fight you instead."

'I did not want Merriol to return to find the evidence of yet another fight, and so we agreed it should take place that day in order that any bruises he inflicted might mend before she returned.

'I had not seen Young Bodlan before, and my heart sank when I saw him, for he was much older than us, as old as Tanodonus, though not a great deal taller than me. The fight was soon over. Bodecus was bending over me telling me that I might now have a broken nose like he did and that Bodlan had not got away unscathed. I kept my distance from Enemno when I collected the flock that night.

'The following day Bodecus came but did not stay. The soldiers were coming, and he and the other children were running to meet them. There was a string of forts throughout the hills where they lodged at night while undertaking their customary patrol of communities such as ours – to protect us, Bodecus told me. I, of course, knew better, but to learn that there were soldiers much closer to us than the fortress at Isca Silurum raised fears inside me again. He wanted me to go with them, but I would not. I left the repairs and went to join Enemno instead. I had barely reached him when he pointed down the hill. "You had best go back." I turned and could see that they were at her deserted farm, helping themselves. I could hear their shouting and laughter as they pursued her birds around the farmyard. I arrived breathless and very, very angry. "You can't do this." I screamed at them. "You can't take these things. We need them." I barely saw the coin the centurion tossed at my feet. "Who are you?" he asked. "I don't remember you."

'The children replied on my behalf. "Verluccus is a slave," they said helpfully. "He belongs to Merriol." And where was she? "Gone to market." I wished they would stop being so helpful.

'The centurion turned back to me. "We will take two sheep. Fetch them."

'"No," I said. The man was astonished.

'"What did you say?" he could not believe his own ears. I repeated, "No, we need them – all of them. We need everything."

'His voice hardened. "Two sheep. Go and fetch them now. Not old mutton either."

'"No more geese." I was beginning to bargain with him. I could see that some were still alive.

'"All the eggs, no more geese, two good sheep. That is it."

'"One sheep," I said, but I had gone too far. He made a step towards me.

'Bodecus urged, "You must, Verluccus. Rignis would tell you if he was here. There will be trouble if you don't."

'I had visions of my shirt being removed in whatever might follow, so I gave in. "Two sheep."

'"Five sheep now, and count yourself lucky." He indicated which of his men should go with me to pick them out. He did not need five sheep, of course; it was my punishment for defying him and another loss for Merriol.

'Bodecus would have me go with him and the other children and follow the soldiers back to their encampment, but I had no wish to go. There was order to be restored and geese to be retrieved. Soon Bodecus returned with brother Bodlan. "You are to come to our home," they said. "Our mother wants to see you." I refused to go, and to encourage them to leave me, I raised a stone and threw it at them. I remember only seeing Bodlan raise his arm.

'Bodecus said later that they thought he had killed me; I was quite unconscious. They fetched a cart and loaded me onto it and carried me to their home. When I came round I was in Bodecus' bed with my head wrapped up and a woman, his mother Elen, sitting beside me telling me what lovely blue eyes I had. My friend said he hoped she would now be satisfied, for she had kept on to him for ages to take me to her. I tried to rise but could not stand easily. "You have no right to keep me here," I told them angrily. "Let me go." They all laughed and said I was not a prisoner; I had a bad bump on the head. Bodlan, her husband, who had not gone to Silurum on this occasion, had gone to Merriol's farm and would do what was required. I must stay with them until I was well. I was truly most frightened, for someone – Elen, I supposed – had stripped my old shirt from me and was promising me one of young Bodlan's to replace it. "You won't tell anyone, will you?" I begged her when the opportunity came to speak to her alone.

'She knew exactly what I meant. "No, I won't tell anyone. Merriol knows, does she?"

'I nodded painfully. "She said no one should know of it. People would say she stole me."

'Her husband knew of it though; I heard them talking later. "Be content," he said. "We have enough mouths to feed already, and Merriol needs him, young as he is. He has survived the winter, and she has not taken him back as she swore she would. He will be all right now."

'"He is too defiant," Elen was saying. "He is in danger from the soldiers. Merriol should have warned him what to expect, not left him to find out that way. And there is that mark upon him. He made me promise not to tell anyone of it."

'"You should not have done that," said her husband. "We do not know what it means. I may have to talk to Rignis. We may all be in danger because he is here." I wished he had not known of it. I felt I could trust Elen not to say anything, but not him.

'That was how I met Bodyn, for she was Bodecus' sister. She wore around her neck even then a string of beads, amber and blue on a spiralled thread of copper. I had made up such necklets and armlets while I travelled from a stock of beads which Bodenius carried, and I guessed that her father had bought these from him some time in the past. Later I wore those beads, and they remained upon me always until they were stolen from me by Marcus Marcius and given to that girl, the sister of the Gaius.

'I left the next day, though Elen would have babied me for longer, and to be truthful there was a part of me which did not want to go. There was a surprise awaiting me at the farm, for the work I had commenced had been expertly finished by the men, and new and shining roofs now crowned all her buildings. They would have done it for her long before then had she not been so set against them, and I knew that she would not be pleased either by that or by my misbehaviour.

'I had some of the ground cleared and planted by the time she returned, and I had restored her pigpen in anticipation of it having a new occupant. I told her what had happened, and she went outside and counted the sheep. I showed her the coin and asked if that paid for what had been taken, and she cackled bitterly and said it did not. She blamed herself for not warning me but said that they had come earlier than usual and that it was the sign that a new commander had taken over the fortress at Isca Silurum. She also said that Bodlan had tried to detain her on her way to the farm and asked me if I had been fighting with Bodecus again, so I had to tell her about that too.

'The elder Bodlan did not wait for long. "You know why I am here?" he asked, and strangely, she allowed him to enter.

'"You tell me," she said. I listened to it all.

'"That boy has been marked as someone's property. He won't say how he came by the mark. That may be because it distresses him and there is nothing more to it than that. But when he first came here he told Rignis that he had run away from home. Perhaps that was not quite all the truth." His voice softened a little, "Merriol," he said, "no one here has suffered more than you; we all know that – your husband

and sons killed fighting the soldiers, your farm reduced to a ruin. You know we are all concerned for you. Did we not intercede for you so that you might at least have some help? He is a good boy, a nice lad, but his presence here could be endangering the whole community. Let us pay you for him and get you another instead, an older boy like you wanted in the first place."

'I was surprised at the calm in her voice. "How many know of it?" she asked.

"'At the moment, only my family. When I am better informed of what it means, I shall know better what to say to Rignis. He should decide what is to be done." He adopted a more persuasive voice. "If we were to hand him over voluntarily, his owner may show gratitude to us. He may have influence over the commander at Isca Silurum and persuade him you may be trusted again." She did not respond, and he said again, "We may be forced to choose between him and ourselves. Would you hand him over to the soldiers if it came to that?"

'That did provoke her; I heard anger in her voice. "I have lost my husband, my sons, my farm, my status. I would die sooner than hand that boy over to those monsters, and I would see him dead first."

'He tried to placate her. "There is no need for that; we could get him back to Bodenius. Just tell me how he came by that mark. Don't you see? It is your concealment of it, your unwillingness to tell us of how he came by it, that gives me most concern."

"'You just go away and forget that you ever saw it!" she shouted. "If you don't know about it, you cannot be blamed for not speaking up. It is my business and nobody else's, and if you had kept that young lad of yours away from him, you would certainly not have known of it." He left unwillingly, and I wondered for how long I was going to be safe.'

There was a necessary interruption at this point as Coridumnus, again had duties elsewhere. He excused himself for some time. 'You may continue until I retire,' he said on his return.

4

'I shall not go into great detail of my life with Merriol and Enemno, but something of it must be told, though other things have greater importance to me.

'It was our practice to take the sheep further afield in the summer, quite a long way up into the hills, and there we remained, living off the land. I learned a lot from Enemno, all about the plants – which were food and which were poison, which could be used as medicine, and when and how to gather them and cause no offence to the gods. It was with Enemno's help that I killed my first wolf and became truly adept with a sling. Enemno taught me the use of a spear also but swore me to secrecy because such weapons were forbidden to us, and he kept it hidden in our summer quarters, a deserted farmstead of long ago.

'Unlike Merriol, he observed all the seasons and the festive rites. At Lugnasad he sacrificed a lamb – one of his own, of course; I would not have dared to take one of Merriol's. One of her sheep did get lost, and she knew it, for she counted them when I drove them back down at the end of the summer.

'I was impatient to unroll the wolf skin and present it to her, but before I could do so, she took hold of me and led me to the pigpens. There were two new occupants. One we would eat in the winter; the other would produce more pigs. I could not help wondering what we should do if the soldiers took it into their heads to want pig meat next time they called but decided that she was probably a much better match for them than I was.

'I unrolled the pelt and laid it proudly before her as if I were a hunter and not a shepherd. She was pleased with my trophy and listened patiently to my unending chatter about my adventures with Enemno. In my excitement, I told her that she very nearly had a bearskin and would have done if I had my own spear.

'I was horrified at my indiscretion. I had all but sworn to Enemno that I would not betray him, and at once I had done so. I pretended that I had meant a spear of my own instead of just a knife and a sling, and as she made nothing of it, I supposed she believed me. However, when it was time to go away again, she bid me to look carefully around a certain tree before moving on. Enemno waited patiently while I did this and then joined in my delight and celebration at the discovery I made, for Merriol or someone on her behalf had hidden a spear there for me – not a child's toy but a proper man's spear. When I was able to thank her for it, she told me that the blacksmith had made it at great risk to himself and I must speak of it no more.

'That was the pattern of my life for two more years, but then when I returned from the hills with Enemno, Trenn came to her with a message. She asked me if I had done something she ought to know of, as she had been summoned to appear before the elders, but I could think of nothing. Neither of us dared to suggest it was about the mark on my shoulder. I had to wait impatiently for her return, but when she came she said they had spoken of other business, nothing to do with me.

'I did believe her, but afterwards mysterious people began to call as if suddenly she was moving back into the society of the community or as if they wished her to do so. She never allowed me within earshot of what was said, but when even Bodecus came down she made no objection but watched us together. We did not fight, of course; all that was over, and a firm friendship existed between us. I even asked if he might come into the hills with us, but that neither she nor Bodlan would countenance. I was very angry with her, I remember. For the first time I was aware of my potential strength; until that moment, I had not realized that I had outgrown her. I was a strong young man, and she was a weak and defenceless old woman. I behaved very badly, and when I saw real fear of me in her eyes, I was ashamed of myself. I ceased my ravings and tried to tell her how sorry I was. I had become so accustomed to thinking of her place as my home that I had forgotten what my position there was. I was sad that Bodecus might not come with me, but she was right that we might fight; Enemno would not wish him to be there. She told me to speak no more of it, so I did not; I went with Enemno and put that idea out of my mind.

'When we next returned, I had the skin of a bear to present to her. I had taken it alone, with boldness, and not allowed Enemno to assist me so that it was wholly my own. I could tell she was pleased to have it, and that night she spoke to me in a manner quite different from how she ever had done before.

'"You are growing into a man now, Verluccus, growing faster than I had thought. I noticed it when you came down the hill. You are as tall as Enemno now. Yes, you are a strong young man, and I am an old, old woman."

'I felt awful; she was remembering the dreadful things I had shouted at her. I tried again to tell her that I had not meant them then and did not think them now. I had come to look upon the farm as my home and had forgotten my true situation there. She smiled and said she was glad that I thought of it as my home but that I must hear her out, as there were things it was time that I knew.

'"You are fourteen years old now. It is more than four years since I brought you here. I thought then that you were a mistake, but you have served me well – that does not mean I might not have done better, but I was stuck with you and you were stuck with me. You know I am a widow. Once I was the proud wife of a prosperous farmer. We had sons, servants too, hands around the farm. My sons were older than you, of course, fine young men, ready to be married and raising families of their own. Some years ago, some years before I brought you here, I stood in the wreckage of my home beside the bodies of my two sons and saw my husband led away in chains to his execution.

'"In the centre of the village he; Engor, the blacksmith's father; and another man were cruelly put to death. The remaining men were all taken away and put to work for the Romans. After a little while, they allowed a few to return. Bodlan, Rignis, Enemno, Engor – these you know of; there are others too whom you have not met. I see your question; I will tell you. We have always resented the rule of Rome, the interference in our lives, their demands for taxes. My boys and some of the others spoke openly of raising arms against them. We thought they had listened to our counsel not to do so. We were too few, our community too isolated; it could only end in disaster. But no, secretly they were building up a store of arms in one of the outbuildings on this very farm. My sons were the ringleaders. That was why my husband was taken and put to death. He had been regarded as the head of the village. Rignis was made chief by the Romans. It was a joke about his name – it sounds like their name for king, you see. Poor Rignis; it was not his wish. They hold him accountable for all we do. That is why he is consulted on all things."

"'What happened?' I asked. "Was there a battle?"

"'It is easy to be provoked,' she said, "especially when you are looking for it. Hot-headed young men soon found an excuse, and we found ourselves fighting for our lives. The whole village suffered; our enemies made sure of that. They took my servants away and forbade me to replace them. I refused to give up my home as my neighbours urged me to do and struggled on alone. Rignis pleaded for me, and eventually the commander at Isca agreed that I could get a boy to help me. I asked Bodenius to find one. That was how I came by you. Now, as you know, they treat my home as if they owned it and never cease to search for weapons here."

"'Why are you telling me this?' I wanted to know.

"'You are a man now,' she answered. "You don't like the Romans, and I am afraid that you may get ideas like those sons of mine. You and Bodecus – when I see you together, you so remind me of my own boys. You must promise me you will never do as they did." I promised sincerely, and she went on. "I want you to understand why Bodecus and the other children are brought up to think of the Romans as our friends and protectors. They may remember something of the events but not a great deal. The older boys – young Bodlan and Trenn, for example – they will remember, but they obey their parents' wishes, and so we are allowed to live in peace."

'I told her that I understood and would do nothing to endanger her or anybody. "There is more," she said. "Do you remember when I was summoned to the council of elders? I said that the business did not concern you, but that was not true. It did concern you very much. It seems there are people among us who are beginning to take an interest in you. Some are even of the opinion that it is time you took a wife."

'She paused then to allow me to digest this astonishing piece of information. I was staggered. It was the last thing which would have come into my head, and she completely dumbfounded me. I heard her then say, "Oh yes, I have had foolish women come tripping to my door with their equally foolish daughters."

'I found my voice and heard it say, "Why should anyone want to marry me? I have nothing to offer a wife."

'"You think not?" she demanded in her old, cross voice, though I could tell she was not cross. "And is my farm nothing? Who then is to have it when I am gone if not you?"

'I cried like a baby. The prophecy which Bodenius had made was to come true. I was to be free and marry and own a farm. I had never dared voice it, though it had been a secret dream. It was a long time before I could talk coherently. It was she who broke the silence, telling me that I need not go with Enemno the next day but could spend it with Bodecus and follow Enemno later. She would not allow me to thank her but brushed the words aside, reminding me I had chores to do before any visiting took place.

'The following day I took great pains to do as much as possible before I departed. After all, Bodecus was not expecting me; there was no reason to hurry. Indeed, I might not be welcome. Merriol pointed that out, preparing me for rejection; Elen had not been among the women bringing their daughters to her. Both she and Bodlan had good reason not to wish me married into their family. But I was not going there to seek a wife; I was going to enjoy my friendship with Bodecus. Even so, it was a great surprise to me to discover that

Bodecus was not the idle boy I had assumed him to be. Like his father and elder brother, he was a skilled carpenter, and he was busy in the workshop making things they might sell in the Silurum market and to the soldiers. Elen would not hear of me going to disturb them; I must stay and allow her to feed me as though I were a starveling rather than the substantial person I had now grown to be. I ate her cakes and sweetmeats and told her of my life with Enemno.

'Bodecus thought it was wonderful that I should be in his home as a visitor. I must stay and share their meal. I looked at his father. He made no objection to this, and so we all sat down together. Bodecus was well aware of my new status and made many teasing and cryptic remarks concerning my appearance. "You've come courting, haven't you?" he demanded, and I felt my face burn. I denied it, of course, seeing the interest aroused in his cousin Caella's face and remembering Merriol's words of caution. His next remark clarified the situation. "You can have Caella if you want; I have got to marry her."

'"Why do you speak like that?" I asked. "She looks all right to me."

'"She is my cousin. She was betrothed to Merriol's son, but he is dead, so now I get her." He pulled a face at the unfortunate girl, and she pulled a similar one in return.

'"Eat your food and behave yourselves," Bodlan warned us, "or I shall make Bodecus return to his work for the rest of the day." This was great news; we could spend the afternoon together – a far too precious gift to be frittered away in teasing girls. Bodecus, however, had other ideas and continued with his face pulling and made grunting noises to imitate animals coupling. In vain I tried to divert his attention. Then he said, "Very well, if you do not wish to marry Caella – and who can blame you? – why don't you marry my sister Bodyn? Come here, Bodyn, so that Verluccus may inspect you."

'She ran from us, and caught in Bodecus' infectious sense of fun, I joined in his pursuit of her. We made a half-hearted attempt to find her but soon lost interest. We had more important things to do, and in any case I had no wish to be sent home by an angry Bodlan. It was not until quite late that we realized that since then nobody had seen her.

'After a search, we heard her calling from above. In her enthusiasm to flee us, she had climbed into a large ash tree and could not get down. Bodecus made as if to climb the tree, but for some reason which I could not understand I turned on him and said that it was I who was going to fetch her down and if he tried to oppose me he would be sorry.

'He backed off without question, and I saw in his face that I had frightened him just as once I had frightened Merriol. I shrugged it off and swung myself into the tree. Bodyn had climbed high and was now lodged precariously in the topmost branches that swayed in the wind and was too terrified to move. She seemed terrified of me too, having, I supposed, expected her brother or father to be her rescuer. Bodyn was a little younger than me but already had the shape of a woman coming upon her. She was slender and agile, with long black hair and a face pale as the moon. But her lips and cheeks were flushed with red, and her eyes were large and grey, dark like her mother's. Her cheeks were wet and smudged from her tears, but when I saw her I thought she was the most beautiful person I had ever set eyes on. At least some part of me did, for then I experienced a sensation I had never known before.

'I reached out to her and gently persuaded her to let go of the branch she was clinging to and to cling to me instead. When she did so and I felt her arms hug me, I wanted to hold her there forever; and I did, pretending the delay was merely to reassure her, but I did not think she minded it at all. Slowly and carefully I descended from the tree and restored her to her anxious parents. Her father took her into his arms and said he thought perhaps it was time I went home.

'I asked Bodecus what I had done to annoy his father, as it was I who had climbed the tree and rescued Bodyn. "Ha!" he said. "But what did you to her while you were up there?"

'I did not catch up with Enemno until we reached the grazing land, and there I tried to settle to my duties. But I felt differently now. I remembered what Merriol had said about my being married, and I began to daydream about being married to Bodyn – it was a wonderful daydream. My fellow shepherd did not question the new and silent me; I think he must have been grateful for the change. But my dreams became troubled. What if, while I was away, Bodyn became betrothed to somebody else – Trenn perhaps? Was Trenn married? I did not know. Worse than that, what if Merriol, during my absence, arranged for me to be married to somebody else? I must go to Merriol without delay and make sure she knew how I felt about Bodyn. Enemno must have thought me totally mad, but now I could not delay to explain to him. I just shouted that I had to run down to see Merriol and left him in charge of both our flocks. I ran the whole way and arrived at her farm breathless and ready to drop.

'The soldiers were there collecting our animals – their supper. I suppose that seeing me arrive in such haste, she might well have thought something was terribly wrong, but when I assured her that all was well and that I wanted to be married, her reaction was not at all one of relief but of anger. She was incredulous. "You want to be married? You left my sheep to the hazards of the wild beasts? You left Enemno to manage on his own? You get back up there at once! Married indeed! You won't be getting married while I am still alive."

'The centurion was translating all of this for the benefit of his men, and I afforded them a good deal of entertainment. "But you said I could," I argued. "You said I could marry."

'"I said nothing of the kind," she screamed at me. "Go on – be gone! Be gone before I give you a good beating." She raised her stick to me. I could not believe it – could not believe that she had changed towards me so much. I stood rooted to the spot and stared at her.

'The centurion stepped forward. "I'll deal with him for you," he offered. "He is too much of a handful for you to cope with." He was carrying a long stick. I was still rooted to the spot but now from terror. Merriol stepped between us. "It is kind of you to help me," she told him, "but he must not get the idea that I cannot manage him without your help. I should be in a poor fix if he thought that! I can deal with him."

'He offered her his stick, and she took it from him and raised it high above her head so that it crashed with all her might upon me. It struck me across the neck and throat; it really hurt me, but I still could not move. She struck again, shouting that I was a worthless, wicked boy and must go back to the sheep and do as I was told. I could hear the soldiers laughing. I heard the centurion saying he would take me off her hands. But now the voices were behind me, and I was running for the hills.'

5

'You must forgive my man,' said Coridumnus. 'He is concerned only for my welfare.' Verluccus' narrative had been interrupted by a steward entering the room and gently suggesting that the master ought to retire. Coridumnus stirred and rose stiffly. 'I realize that there is much left unsaid. I am willing to hear more tomorrow if you are willing to tell me. Alternatively, I could restore you to the young man who still waits somewhere nearby, though it is too late to commence a journey now.'

Verluccus leapt to his feet in horror. 'I have talked for too long and worn you out. You are not being paid to hear my story but to try to change my attitude. Say what you must, and let us be done with it.'

'On the contrary. I would hear more, for according to what you have said, you are now but fourteen years old, and there must be much between this point and your coming into the hands of Marcus Marcius. However, as you are aware, a certain young man is waiting with incredible patience, and he deserves to be told something. What may I say to him?'

'I have a need to tell you more. I want someone to know my story. But I cannot tell him or his kind. There is no one else if you will not listen. Say to him what you think fitting and obtain more time from him. I shall not take advantage of you.'

The next morning Coridumnus reported that Gaius Marcius had requested permission to sit silently within the room and listen to his tale.

'No.' Verluccus shook his head decidedly.

Coridumnus walked to the door and delivered his reply.

'Pray continue. You had told Merriol of your desire to be married, but her concern was more with the welfare of her sheep, I think?' he encouraged.

'Yes, I realized that her behaviour was much affected by the presence of the soldiers, but even so, she had said I might marry and had sworn she would never beat me again. I hated her, of course, and although I made my way back to her flock, I did so in a leisurely way, hoping stupidly that it would have been half devoured by wolves by the time I reached it. Gradually the pain began to ease and my foul temper to cool, and I saw that I was the one at fault. Enemno asked no questions, although he must have seen the welt, which lasted for several days, and we just carried on as if I had not been absent.

'Soon a visitor arrived in the shape of young Bodlan. I would have preferred to see Bodecus, but news of him and perhaps of Bodyn also was welcome enough. He had been sent by his father to discover whether or not I had returned to Enemno. It seemed that Bodlan, the father, had begun to make it his habit to call upon Merriol whenever the soldiers had visited her. He had found her sobbing into my sheepskins for what their presence had forced her to do to me. "Tell her I do understand," I begged him. "Tell her what Bodenius once told me – you have to let the Romans see what they expect to see." He departed then, promising to do so. I did not speak of it to Enemno. I think he understood well enough, and he was never the kind of man who would laugh at another's misfortune.

'Her first words to me on my return were: "You do understand why I had to beat you? The centurion would have done so if I had not."

'"Only because you were angry with me. Why did you say I could not marry? You had said I might do so."

'"I did not," she said firmly. "I told you that the elders said you should be betrothed. Understand this now and raise no further argument: while I am alive, I will have no other woman in my house.

I told the elders that, and that is final. Betrothal is one thing; being wed is another."

'My hopes instantly soared. "So if I promise not to get married while you are alive, I may be betrothed? I was only afraid that you might arrange for me to marry someone I did not wish to or that she might become betrothed to another."

"'And who might she be?" she demanded, and my face grew hot. "Bodecus' sister Bodyn." I told her. She shook her head. "Her father will never allow it, and you know why. You had best put that thought out of your mind." She spoke most kindly, and I knew she felt badly for me.

'I really did try to forget the idea. I knew what she had said was true. Once Bodlan had advised her to surrender me to the Romans. He would never allow his daughter to marry a slave and a runaway. There was, however, no question of my visiting Bodecus until the sheep could no longer graze outside her compound, and then she warned me again that I might not be welcome. "Her father was not pleased about your last visit there." I told her that it was because we had chased Bodyn up the tree, a tree which Bodecus had told me was sacred. Merriol was amused by this. "In that case the poor girl will probably have to marry you now. The elders were right; you will soon be getting around all the young girls. That is why they say your future wife should be decided quickly." I did not like the direction this conversation was taking. The only girls whom I knew lived in Bodlan's house, and the only one I was interested in was forbidden to me. I said nothing more about going to see Bodecus until we had a heavy snowfall, and then when I had done with feeding the animals, I asked again. She said I might go but cautioned me not to be disappointed if I was not made welcome.

'She was wrong. I was more chastised for not coming sooner than for coming when I did. Bodecus and his father were there, and a place was immediately made for me at the fireside. "We expected you sooner than this," Elen said.

'I muttered some explanation about thinking myself unwelcome. "And why was that?" demanded the father. "When have you been made unwelcome under my roof?" It was an uncomfortable question and unfair too.

'"Stop teasing the boy," said Elen, "You take no notice, Verluccus. You are always welcome in our home; you must know that. Join us at the feast of Imbolc this year. You have never come to any festival."

'I stole a glance at Bodyn. She was concentrating hard on the contents of her dish. "Merriol would not allow it when I suggested it before," I said regretfully, and I was urged to ask her again.

'"You never come to any of our feasts," said Bodecus. "Everybody else does. Bodyn will be there." I looked at Bodlan and saw him exchange a thought with Elen, but he did not intervene. Bodyn would not raise her eyes to me. I wished I knew what she was thinking, whether she wanted me to be there. Caella, on the other hand, was much in evidence, imposing herself on Bodecus and me when the wish of both of us was for our own company, and I began to understand why he was so rude to her, for little short of rudeness had any effect. It had been decided that she and Bodecus were to be married before the next feast of Beltane.

'Bodyn made it impossible for me to speak to her. She remained close to her mother for the whole time I was there and thus made me even more eager to know what her feelings were about me. I returned to Merriol no wiser than when I had set out. I told my mistress a little of how I had spent the day and casually mentioned that Elen had invited me to go to the midwinter feast. To my surprise, she responded, "Well, why not?"

'I was half-mad with joy and flung her into the air and caught her as though she were a child, so much stronger than her I now was. "Do you mean that? Do you really mean that? Please say you do and that you will come too."

'"Put me down, you great ox," she ordered. "Yes, I shall come if only to keep you in order. I suppose that means we must put on some finery?"

'I did not know how to respond to this, for of course I did not wish to be seen at a feast in my rags and sheepskins, and I thought then that I guessed why we never attended such festivals. But I was wrong.

She had me drag forward her great chest, and there within were the clothes she once had worn and the clothes of her dead husband and sons, put away and never touched. They were richly coloured clothes in the finest wool. She had not lied when she told me they had been wealthy.

'In the time that elapsed before Imbolc, she worked feverishly, transforming them into some new style to her liking, though they looked very good to me as they were. I was provided with a shirt and trousers of gold and brown and a cloak of fine brown wool pinned with a golden pin and a chain to wear around my neck, things which she had successfully hidden from the greedy eyes of the soldiers. For herself she had made a grey gown and a blue cloak which she mentioned was a colour which would look well on me but would have a dangerous effect on the girls we would encounter. What a changed person she was. The Merriol I first knew would not have made such jokes as that! You will think me vain to have mentioned this at all, but that feast was to me a most important occasion and I have no wish to forget it.

'She announced her intention to attend by sending me a day ahead with her contribution to the feast, a piglet and two geese. That in itself was a remarkable event in the community, and her return quite overshadowed my own arrival. I was not ignored though, as I might well have been, considering who and what I was. Rignis himself greeted Merriol and me with her and directed that Trenn must see to it that I met everybody. It would have been churlish on my part to refuse this, though I could see that it pleased Trenn no more than it did me. I only wanted to be with Bodecus – and Bodyn, of course.

'She kept her distance from me; she danced in the circle as I did, but I could not get near her, try as I might. She just was always that short step or two away, which I could have overcome only by the clumsiest of moves. For that reason, when the dawn streaked the sky and we at last broke up, I was not as happy as I ought to have been.

'For many the feast did not end then, though for us it did. I thanked Merriol for taking me; it was no fault of hers that Bodyn was not to be mine. "I see the flame of passion has died," she said dryly. "You did not speak to Bodyn at all – not once. I was watching you. Wasting time with that Bodecus. Why do you think I dressed you up?"

'"But you said her father would not allow it, and in any case, she did not speak to me," I defended, injured.

'"I don't understand you young people," she said. "I expect the poor girl was waiting for you to speak to her. You had plenty of the others ogling you." I told her not to speak so foolishly, to which she replied that I was still not too big to be given a clout and I had best get prepared to do some hard work.

'Oh how I had wasted my time! Had it not been Bodyn's mother who had suggested I go to the feast? My own pride and vanity had prevented me from taking advantage of the situation, and now I had lost my heart's desire. I wept.

'Elen came to Merriol's the next day. She came straight to the point. "I don't like to see my child unhappy." When Merriol realized I was listening, she set me work out of earshot, and I was forced to wait impatiently until our visitor had departed to learn why she had come. I convinced myself that Bodlan had sent her to tell me to keep away from their daughter, and yet when I sauntered casually back to Merriol, I found her looking very pleased with herself.

'"It seems you must go to the feast again tonight. You had best get those robes out again." I waited for more and heard the words I longed for. "You cannot go to your betrothed looking like that!" I could not allow her to say more.

'"Bodyn! It must be Bodyn! Do not say it is another." It was indeed Bodyn. She had wept for me as I for her, and Elen had come only to be assured that on Merriol's death I would be a free man. Their objection to their daughter marrying a slave was resolved by Merriol's refusal to allow me to marry during her lifetime. The fact that neither Bodyn nor I had exchanged a word with each other on the subject was an irrelevance. I did not think it vanity on my part to believe she must be as happy with the arrangement as I was. Had not Elen said her daughter had wept for me?

'A betrothal present fit for Bodyn was beyond the means of my purse, but Merriol had the answer. She delved deep into the bundle of clothing again and produced a dull-looking bag. From it poured jewels of gold and enamel, precious stones, rings, brooches, armlets, neck rings. I was truly amazed both at the sight of so much wealth and that she should have lived in such poverty for so long when she had no need to. More than that, I could not understand why the soldiers had never found it, for they often threw her belongings about when they came for their 'dues'.

'She laughed bitterly. "They search for weapons, not wealth in this house." She picked out a pretty gold ring, saying, "This will do for Bodyn; it is quite suitable for the purpose."

'"I cannot take that," I protested. "It is far too valuable for me to give her."

'"You foolish boy," she cried. "This is a betrothal gift. It will come home when she does." Then she became aggressive. "You remember this. These will belong to you when I am dead and gone, but no matter what the hardship you face, you must never part with them. I have sold none, not even the tiniest, and you must do likewise and even add to them if your means allows it. Bodyn was to marry my youngest son, and she would have borne my grandchildren; and though you are of different blood, it is you who are to be my heir. Perhaps your fortune will be better than mine and one day the master of this place may wear what he pleases with pride and dignity." I promised that I would do as she wished.

'"Yes," she said, "you are a good boy; I won't deny that." After considering me for a little while, she said, "The time has come for you to learn that which remains with me." She directed me to strip the fleeces from my cot and lift the great slab of stone on which I had slept every night I had been in her home. Beneath it was a cavity, and as I was bid, I reached into it and fetched out what I found. They were carefully wrapped in fleeces to keep them new: a sword and a spear. Here, under where I had slept, were the forbidden weapons which the soldiers had suspected her of and for which they so fruitlessly had searched. There was no shield, for that would not have fitted into so narrow a hiding place. I felt my jaw drop open as I gazed at them and felt the weight of the sword in my hands.

'"We all have them. At least I believe we all do; about Rignis I am not certain, but I expect that he does. It would not be fitting for us to be without our weapons. See the markings on them? These are the symbols of our tribe; they are more than mere weapons. That is something the Romans do not understand when they seek to take them from us. We keep them for the sake of our forebears and for our descendants. Now put them away and never speak of them again."

'It was no wonder that the soldiers had not found them, for the slab was heavy even for me to lift and impossible now for Merriol. I could not think what to say; I just held her close to me to let her know how much I appreciated everything she had done and given to me, something far more than any promise of freedom.

'We went to the feast again that night, and straightaway I went to Bodlan and his family. Bodyn, to my eyes, was radiant. She shone among them, among everyone present, brighter than all, as if a star had come to earth. I don't remember what she was wearing. It would not have made any difference if she had been dressed in rags – she would still have been the most beautiful person there. I endured the betrothal ceremony, wanting only that it should be finished and we might be let alone. I kissed her with much encouragement and goodwill and to many cheers, and she and I were gone from them into a world of our own. I loved her and she loved me, and I could not believe that the gods could have been so good to me. How little I had ever done for the gods. That was all in the past, and now I would make amends for all shortcomings. I made many rash promises in my immediate happiness.

'In the year that followed I saw young Bodlan married to Enemno's daughter Mona and Bodecus to Caella. I went reluctantly to the high pasture in the summer and grumbled at the slow pace of the sheep when we returned in the autumn.

'Merriol had begun to attend all the festivals and was again fully involved in the activities of the community, respecting the gods and making her sacrifices. I grew bold enough to suggest that she might get a second boy who could take the sheep off with Enemno and I could remain behind and make her land work properly for her. She would not have it. Nor would she have my further suggestion that Bodyn might move into our home and help spin her wool. She was immovable.

'"Do you want me to wish you dead?" I flung at her in one of my many outbursts when again she refused to allow us to be married.

'"You made me a promise," she reminded me. "You gave me your word."

'It was true; I had done so. I had promised that I would be good and obedient to her and patient for marriage. "I did not know what I was saying. You like Bodyn; I know you do. Why do you force me to keep my word when she could make your life so much easier?" I shouted in return, calling her unkind names which I had ceased to associate with her long before.

'"I do it", she said, "because you are both young, and to wait a few years for what you want will harm neither of you. I want you to learn an important lesson from this. Never, never make a promise lightly. Think hard about what someone is asking of you, and do not allow yourself to be bound by something you will later regret. Remember this: though much may be stolen from you, your word never can be."

'I was greatly impressed by such wisdom at the time, but since then I have had more and more reason to be grateful for it. That boy – he thinks he can take everything from me. But he cannot have my word against my will.' He spoke scornfully, tossing his head in the direction of the absent Gaius.

Coridumnus remained silent.

'I was never to marry Bodyn. It was no fault of Merriol; she could not have foreseen that dreadful event or prevented it. I had accepted that Bodyn and I must remain unwed, but we spent as much time together as we possibly could, and our love for each other was confirmed in every way bar marriage.

'The end of my life – I still think of it as the end of my life, though I was not killed by it. The end of that life came one hot day in midsummer when I was high up in the hills with Enemno. It was

222

the festival of Lugnasad, and the smell of smoke curled through the air even to our distant place; and Enemno and I agreed once again that it was always an event we were to miss. But then his expression changed; he had caught in the scent more than should be smelled. I smelled it also. I shouted to him that I would run on ahead and he should bring down the sheep, and heedless of what he might think, I ran.'

6

'My feet carried me more swiftly than they ever had before, but even so I was too late. As I grew nearer, when I reached a position from where I could expect to see some of the huts, all I could see was a dense fog of acrid smoke and all I could hear were the sounds of people crying out, screaming, calling to find one another. Then soldiers – I could see uniformed men rounding up the people into a column. My legs crumbled under the demands I made on them. I stumbled, fell, and slid much of the way. I was calling out, "Here I am – I am here." I knew it could only be Lucius Marcius who after all those years had discovered my hiding place and was punishing those he thought had hidden me.

'Suddenly my feet were dragged from under me and I fell, knocked senseless to the ground. I lay there winded. A man was lying on top of me, pressing me down, and his hand was across my mouth. I felt the point of a knife at my throat and heard a voice, quiet but menacing, warning me to be silent and lie still. There I was held, an unwilling observer of the destruction of a small and innocent community, until the column of prisoners had been marched far away by their captors.

'At first I supposed it must be one of our people who had got away and was trying to save me from the fate of our friends, but even so when I was released I turned in fury on the man who had held me fast. I beheld then such a sight as I had only heard of in stories. That such warriors really existed now that the Romans held sway throughout the land was a tale told around the fire and not really to be believed by grown men. The man's hair was stiff and limed so that it stood erect upon his head. He had stained his body with designs, and apart from his trousers, brightly checked in blue and yellow, he wore only jewellery. He was truly the most savage creature I had ever set eyes on.

'Murderous in appearance, the man rose and towered over me, his sword now where the knife blade had been, demanding to know who I was. But I was too frantic with concern for my Bodyn, for Merriol, and for everybody else to care for his threats. I scrambled to my feet and rounded on him. "Why did you prevent me? I could have saved those people."

'He scoffed at my claim, laughing incredulously. "Don't be a fool. What could a boy like you do? For what reason should the Romans seek you? It is us they were hunting. Those people are taken for their foolishness." At this he gave a signal, and from the very ground, or so it seemed to me, another four men, equal in appearance to him but until that moment totally concealed, leapt out.

'"Why are you hiding here?" I demanded to know. "Why aren't you down there fighting to save those people?" I got no answer, and now, heedless of their objection, I ran. The soldiers were fully departed. I reached Merriol's home first and found her. She was dead. By some means she had shifted the flagstone, and she had died with the sword in her hand, though there was no sign that she had used it. The spear was gone, however, and I hoped she had thrown it successfully.

'I ran to Bodlan's. The sight which I found there I shall never forget. He, young Bodlan, and Bodecus all were dead. They had fought to give Elen the time to do what she must. She was within. Her body lay across the threshold, but she had killed herself. She had made use of her carving knife and had fallen upon it. Inside were the bodies of Caella and Bodyn. They too had been stabbed, but I knew that it had been done by Elen before she killed herself. I knew why she had done it, and I was grateful to her for that; nothing could have saved my Bodyn's life. Of Mona, young Bodlan's wife, there was no sign; I supposed she had run to her father's home or else been taken prisoner.

'Do you recall that I said Bodyn had climbed a tree? It was near to her home, but it was the largest tree around; and for that reason, they had brought Rignis to it. They had nailed him to the tree and made him watch what was done to everybody. His body was slashed so that his guts fell before him. He was dead now; a spear was hanging from his heart.

'It was a Roman spear. The warriors pointed that out to me, how it was built so that it bent on impact and could not be thrown again.

'There were more dead too, bloody, terrible sights to my young eyes. I had never before encountered such practices. The warriors would have abandoned the place immediately, but furious with them that they had stood by and done nothing, I shamed them into helping to bury the dead.

'I returned to Bodyn the ring I had been given at our betrothal as a keepsake of myself. The ring which I had given to her was no longer on her hand. Nor was she wearing the necklace of beads. I buried her wearing my ring beside her family and said my farewell to her, swearing to all the gods that I would somehow avenge this terrible crime.

'I buried Merriol and put into the grave with her all of the jewels, taking care that the warriors should have no inkling of the contents of the pot which now contained them. Her sword I took for myself. I did not know whether I was welcome with the warriors or not, but somehow I knew I must find and kill the man responsible for this crime.

'We went then to Enemno's; he had reached his home. You may have thought the soldiers would have left it alone, considering that it was isolated from the others. But before they killed her, they had done to his wife what Elen's action had prevented being done to her and the young women. We buried her for him, but he was too demented with grief to leave her grave. I could have stayed and lived with Enemno, I suppose, but I had no wish to be idle. I left the sheep and the rest of the animals to him and went with the strangers.

'So, old man, never wonder why I hate the Romans. If you had been me – if you had seen what I saw, lost what I lost – you would never question why I became a warrior, why I did the things which I have done.'

Verluccus paused. Coridumnus could think of nothing to say. He reached out and put a comforting arm onto Verluccus' shoulder. 'Do you want to continue?'

'I would like you to know the rest, though I shall be brief. I was a man now, more than sixteen years old. I was tall and strong, but I was no warrior. I had much to learn.

'By the time night fell and we made camp, we had been joined by more small groups of similar men so that in all there were about two dozen of us. All except me were in high spirits, laughing and yarning among themselves as they recounted how they had thrown off and killed the Roman pursuers. There was the sound of laughter from one particular man which rang a memory in my ears that I could not place. I could not see who it was, as he was well within the innermost circle and some distance from where I was held. When all were assembled, they began dividing up their spoils by dicing for them – yes, they had helped themselves to whatever they could lay their hands upon, even stealing from the dead. Among these spoils I saw Bodyn's necklace and her gold ring. But I was not allowed to share or lay claim to these things, for I too was counted among their spoils and diced for. I was won by the man who had downed me in the first place, and he seemed to think that was fair and just. He sent me to fetch his meal from the pot and asked me what name I went under and what I could do to be useful to him. I told him I was of the Dobunni tribe, my name was Verluccus, I was the son of Cunobarrus but had been in that community as a slave and shepherd.

'The man drew his knife again and warned me that I should not take him for a fool and that I had better tell him my true name if I wished to live. I said again that I was Verluccus, the son of Cunobarrus. Another man heard this and accused me of being a liar. I denied it, said that I was telling the truth – that was my name and my father's name, and Cunobarrus was the name of a brother of mine also. Then the first man asked me how many brothers I had. I told him Cunobarrus and Cadrus, and I was about to add Colymmon and

Tanodonus also. I could not finish my words. This first man who had been so aggressive towards me suddenly paled and shrank from me, and so too did the second, and soon others were staring at me. "You had better not be lying," someone hissed in my ear, and I swore that I was not. Gradually a silence extended away from me, and all were staring at me. Even the laughter from the inner circle faded as my new owner entered it and spoke briefly to the leading men. I was at a loss to know why my name was so significant to these people and feared that whatever had made my captor tremble would be the worse for me.

'I was led forward then to be confronted by their chief, and I had to repeat my name and so on for the benefit of this man, the laughing man. He looked at me strangely as he heard me out and said, "Don't you know me, Verluccus? I am Cadrus – your brother Cadrus."

'I shall not detain you by repeating my whole story again as I then had to repeat it to my dear brother. I was overjoyed to find him and, through him, Cunobarrus too. I did tell him how disgusted I had been at the cowardice of his warriors who had lain hidden in the long grass and lifted no finger as they watched women and children murdered. He laughed even more loudly at that and said that if I went with him he would teach me the skills I would need to deal with the man who had perpetrated the crime. Drusus was his name, a Roman tribune, and he came from the fortress at Isca Silurum. As he said these things, all the men cheered and raised their weapons in salute to him, to Cadrus. My sword and knife were restored to me, and I was given a place within the inner circle. I told Cadrus that I wanted to have Bodyn's necklace and her gold ring from the men who had won them at dice, and he immediately ordered that they be handed over to me. I was amazed that these ferocious men did so without a quibble, so fearful of Cadrus they were, though he did give up small items from his share in token at their exchange. I bound the necklace around my wrist and strung the ring on a leather thong around my neck; it was too small for any of my fingers.'

It was time for Coridumnus to stretch his legs. He wondered what he now might say to Gaius to be of any help to him. It seemed to him that the boy was hoping to achieve the impossible. He had no idea of the depth of hatred which Verluccus carried within him. That he should be a gladiator as Lucius and Marcus Marcius desired seemed to Coridumnus too to be the best end for him.

'Do you have more to tell me?' he asked Verluccus while they walked around the garden. 'I can see now why you have a hatred for the Romans. You may think this young man has been the cause of your harm, but he was a young child at the time you were enslaved and has no idea of the consequences from that. If he now wishes to make amends in some way by making your lot easier, can you not accept that from him?'

'You think I should consign myself to him? After what I have told you? Is my lot to be his servant? I could lie to you and him and pretend, gain the opportunity to kill them, I suppose; then my death would follow. Or I could hold out and let his interest in me wane, in which case one day when the door to my prison opens it will be a soldier standing there with a blade or a noose for me. Or they may simply wall me up and forget about me. Before that happens I want someone – it must be you – to know the truth. The Romans have told many lies about Cunobarrus; I can put in the balance to them. I shall not lie to you and claim I have done no wrong. I have already told you that I have committed dreadful crimes, but at least you now know what drove me to that. Bear with me a little longer, and I shall be brief.'

He commenced as they made their walk and continued as they ate and into the late afternoon. 'I learned that Cunobarrus was the right-hand man of Belcon, the chief of their community. It was an exciting prospect to be meeting my eldest brother, to know that he was held in esteem by a warrior chieftain and that I would be joining him to make what I imagined would become an invincible trio of warrior brothers. How wrong I was!

'They lived in the style of our forefathers, the old style, on a high and well-concealed ancient site, well fortified. There were not so many of them, about a hundred, just men who had come together with a common purpose, together with their women and children, to defy the Romans and to live as free men, to pay no taxes to Rome, and to live unencumbered by Roman laws. Cunobarrus had a large part of the hillside, many huts, and several wives – or at least women. Cadrus lived with him. Word had gone ahead of us that a brother had been discovered, and there was a degree of interest in my arrival.

'I had been advised by Cadrus that I should kneel first and kiss the ground before Belcon, who would be sitting at the head of the assembly together with his sons Belacon and Belcadon. When I did, so the chieftain received my obeisance with warmth and told me how welcome was another member of the family of Cunobarrus. I had nothing to give him but the sword I had taken from Merriol, and so I pledged that, and he told me to carry it for him and bring good booty home to him. I was then permitted to turn to Cunobarrus.

'I saw cold eyes staring through me. There was no warmth from him, no friendly fraternal greeting. "How old are you?" he demanded, and I told him I was sixteen, which he must have known for himself anyway if he had thought at all about it. He so resembled my father in appearance – much more than did Cadrus. It was strange that he should have grown to be so like our father when he despised him so much. "How many men have you killed?" was his next question, and I had to admit that I had never killed any man. "Then what use are you? What can you do?" I said that I had been a shepherd but I wanted to become a warrior like him. He laughed then – not like Cadrus but sneering. He told me the only use I would be to him would be on his farm, and there I must go. He had no stinking sheep, he told me, only horses and cattle; I would have to make do serving them.

'I would have protested at this, but I saw Cadrus, his face not laughing for once, signalling that I had best obey and keep my mouth shut. Cunobarrus then demanded that the ring I had strung around my neck, Bodyn's gold ring, be given to him. I tried to protest, but it was useless, of course. He sent it away with a man to work it into something more to his liking. The beads I wore on my arm were beneath his interest, and I was allowed to keep them.

'For almost two years I was put to work on Cunobarrus' farm. Later I understood why, but at first it was very hard to do so. He kept a number of prisoners there – Britons, not Romans, for he never allowed a Roman to live; they were chained as slaves, and the only difference between their life and mine for those months was that they were chained and I was not. His cattle were very precious to him. Pure white creatures they were, and he would not have them reduced to the role of oxen, so we men pulled all his wagons and ploughed his fields, harnessed like animals. I hated my so-called brother for the way he treated me, but I was too well guarded to try to escape. I slept in the stable with his chariot ponies. He fought always on foot but kept them for racing and sport.

'After I had been there many months, perhaps near on a year, Cadrus began to visit me and I began too to be fed rather better than I had been. It was Cadrus who taught me the art of sword fighting; he would steal upon me and try to take me by surprise, and at first he was successful. Had I been in a serious battle, I would not have survived for long. But gradually my skill improved, and I began to believe that I was actually getting the better of him. This Cadrus was so different from the brother I remembered from childhood; now he was utterly devoted to Cunobarrus and would do anything for him, even to keeping his younger brother like an animal. But he showed me how to kill men, practising on the slaves with whom I had shared work and food, making it clear that to do so was my only way to get away from the farm. I never could master his skill, however. He could look a man in the eye – yes, I could do that, but he would laugh and joke with his victim so that he was lulled into believing his life was spared, and then he would plunge his knife between his ribs and laugh more loudly for having made the man a fool, or else he would open up a man's belly and let his guts spill out and leave him to die like that. Even later, when I had begun to kill men, I was never so skilled as Cadrus, and my tally was never so abundant. When I began to serve Belcon and took part in the raids, I screwed myself to hatred of them, my enemies, to think of them as evil beings to be done away with swiftly, so that Cadrus would complain I was too quick and should be less merciful. But the only one I truly sought to kill with no mercy was the man Drusus who had wiped out my community – my family as I had come to know them.

'So you may imagine my real joy when one day Cadrus descended to the farm full of the news that Drusus was taken captive and held awaiting my pleasure. I must fight him though; it was not to be a simple execution.

'He was waiting with a sword and a shield in his hands in a makeshift arena. It seemed as if the whole of Belcon's people were assembled to watch the fun. Belcon and his sons and Cunobarrus too were there.

'I came as I was, filthy and in the rags I toiled in, but I was provided likewise with a weapon and shield. I saw his face as I stepped forward; his eyes showed real fear of me. He shrank from me – this hardened soldier actually shrank from me, a youth who had scarcely drawn blood from a man. I was careful though. I remembered all the advice which Cadrus had given me even as we made our way up there. This man was a trained soldier, no stripling, experienced and hard, and I should not let my guard down.

'He fought ferociously. He knew he was doomed to die either by my hand or by that of another, but he had determined that if he could take out even one more of us before his time came then he would do so. Visions of what he had done – of my poor Bodyn, her mother and cousin, of Merriol, of Rignis. I remembered them all and soon saw defeat enter his eyes, and with immense relief – not to say elation – I plunged my sword into him and saw his life depart. A huge cheer deafened me and I turned, glowing with pleasure, to Cunobarrus.

'I was directed to cut off his head and present it to Belcon, and I did so. Then Cadrus, laughing as usual, approached bearing a steaming cup. It contained the man's blood. "Drink this," he told me. "Drink the blood and be one of us."

'I was appalled. I could not do it. I thought I should vomit. They all expected it of me, and I knew they all had done it themselves. I took the cup from him, and instead of drinking it, I tipped it so that the blood spilled down by chest and I bathed myself in it.

'My audience, and Cunobarrus, who I imagined would be furious with me, seemed delighted with what I had done. Immediately he named me "Verluccus the Bloodspiller." From that time onwards, that is the name by which I was known.'

Coridumnus was shocked, appalled, horrified by what he had heard but confused too.

'The Bloodspiller? You? We – that is, those of us who have heard tales of Cunobarrus from visitors who have come seeking healing – have always heard him named him as Bloodspiller himself. The name is synonymous with Cunobarrus. It was never thought there was a second man so called.'

'There was not,' said Verluccus with quiet pride. 'There is only one named Bloodspiller, and I am he.'

There was a long silence as Coridumnus contemplated the implications; he could not honestly return such a dangerous man into the custody of the naive Gaius.

'I want to finish my story. Will you hear me?'

'I have no stomach to hear more of such tales. You said earlier that you had committed many crimes. I beg you not to brag about them to me.'

'I shall not brag but tell you the simple truth. I want someone to know the truth against the lies which Marcus Marcius has put about. I shall cut the story short and concentrate only on the important parts so you will know how the death of Belcon and our betrayal came about.'

Coridumnus assented.

'The prisoner was not Drusus, of course, just some soldier they had captured and had decided to test me on. I passed the test, and so I was allowed to become one of Belcon's men and swore allegiance to him as had my brothers. Cunobarrus handed me over to Cadrus and said I must stick close to him and protect him with my life if need be; if Cadrus died, he had no wish to see me return alive. My name, Bloodspiller, was of course a joke at first, but I was determined to live up to it. It would become no joke and would instil cold terror in the heart of anyone who heard me utter it.

I became a member of Cunobarrus' household, enjoying the rich life he enjoyed and free to take such of his women as he was not at that time concerned with. Cadrus lived with us too and kept to one wife. Her name was Calla.

'I could not understand the way the women were attracted to Cunobarrus. I thought myself in every way as good as he, though dependent upon him for my wealth, of course. But it irritated me exceedingly that the women I took to my bed accepted me solely because I was his brother and they thought to please him by doing so. Feeling sore and rejected, I complained to Cadrus that I would have none of them until I could find a woman who did not love Cunobarrus. Until then I would sleep alone.

'His reaction was to laugh and say then I would remain alone for the rest of my life, for even Calla would go to Cunobarrus if he asked for her. This did not persuade me to feel differently.

'One day when we were attacking a small farm which had been settled in the Roman way, an abhorrence to us, we burst into a room to find a frightened woman about my own age trying to hide from us.

'Cadrus pointed to her and said, "Here, here is a woman for you who does not love Cunobarrus. You take her first."'

'While my companions watched, I did so. I took no pleasure from it, and she lay still as death until I was done with her. The others began to jostle for their turn, and suddenly I saw. I saw what I had done – saw as if from outside myself what I had become. For such a crime as this Elen had died to protect my Bodyn. To prevent Bodyn and Caella from suffering what I had just done to this young woman, Elen, that most loving mother, had killed her daughter and her niece with her own hand. I was ashamed of myself and furious with Cadrus, with them all. I rose, and with my sword I drove them from the room, shouting that she was to be mine and mine alone.

'The girl's name was Rosa. She was a slave in that household but Roman, and she became known as "the Roman woman". I kept her for my own, and she tolerated me, but she never had warmth towards me. That I can understand.

'I continued to obey the commands of Cadrus, of course, but my real desire was only to find the man called Drusus. I began to realize I had to make him seek me out, and so often when we had ambushed a small troop of soldiers I would let a wounded one escape to tell Drusus, whoever he was, that Bloodspiller was seeking him.'

'There are many men named Drusus,' said Coridumnus. 'It is a common enough Roman name.'

Verluccus laughed sardonically. 'I know. Sometimes I even thought it was a name plucked from the air to stand for any Roman and that I would never find the particular man which I was seeking.' He continued his story.

'Soon after I came by Rosa, a dreadful accident overcame Belcon while he, Cunobarrus, and Rogan, another of his leading men, were out sporting. He was crushed by his horse falling on him; and when they carried him back home, he had no feeling in any part of his body below the waist. He did not die then, but there was no cure for him. He took to his bed and conducted all his business from there, assembling us all around and giving us his instructions. No one questioned that he was still our leader, though he relied utterly on Cunobarrus and others, such as Rogan, to maintain his position.

'His sons Belacon and Belcadon came to me and proposed that I should hand over Rosa to their father so that she could give him some pleasure and care for him. Belcon had a wife, but they were not on good terms.

'I surrendered her; she was not a great loss to me, and she seemed glad enough to go with them. I told myself I did not mind that she was happier to be the handmaid of an impotent old man than the bed mate of the active and successful warrior that I now was.

'It was not long after this occurred that the woods were full of tasty mushrooms, and with the knowledge that I had gained from the instruction of Enemno, I was able to make a feast of them. Belcadon then approached me and asked me to gather more of them for his father; mushrooms had long been a delicacy he enjoyed. I did so gladly and delivered a huge number to him. He was delighted and insisted that we all share them, so many I had picked. Cunobarrus for once seemed pleased with me.

'We were placed on benches around his vast bed, and a board was set over it on which the food and drink would be laid out. Belacon and Belcadon were seated next to one another near to their father, but on his right hand, as usual, was Cunobarrus; next to him Rogan; then another – Lurgis, his name was; then Cadrus; and then me. Others were placed further, and so around to Belcadon. The mushrooms were to be served first, and because I had donated them I was to be given the first tasting. A slave carried them from man to man. They had been beautifully cooked and were quite delicious. I took my share, and the slave moved on from one to another until he reached Belacon.

'That young man declined them and would have passed the dish on, but his father insisted that he eat. "No, Father," he said, "you have invited too many to this feast, and there are barely enough left for you to enjoy. Verluccus picked them with only you in mind. Is that not so, Verluccus?"

'Belcon spoke, now in quiet anger. "Eat," he said.

'Belacon began to mutter incoherently, and instantly Belcadon snatched the plate and began to stuff his mouth with mushrooms. Cunobarrus was already on his feet. "What treachery is this?" he thundered. "Why will you not eat?"

'"Sit down, my right friend," said Belcon. "Your brother ate from the dish with confidence. There is nothing wrong with these mushrooms. Do you feel ill, Verluccus? Does anybody feel unwell?"

'Cunobarrus, still on his feet, and though he had not yet received the platter, answered, "No, I do not feel unwell, though I am sick at heart." He turned on me. "What does this mean, Verluccus? What have you done?"

'Now equally angry, I too was on my feet. "Yes, I picked them. Do you think me some fool who cannot tell good from poison? I picked only those which are safe to eat. You saw me eat. Do you think that from a cooked dish I could with any confidence have picked the good from the bad?" I glared across the bed at Belcon's sons.

Belcon spoke again. "If they were poisoned, it may be some time before the effect is noticed, but as Verluccus assures us he knew

what he was doing, there is nothing to fear. Let us eat our feast."
He took the dish and helped himself, offering them again to his
sons. Belcadon, who had snatched some of them, now looked really
worried.

'"You will all die! There is no remedy!" The speaker was Belacon.

'His brother rounded on him. "Shut up, you fool. It is a trick; you
are undone." He was such a coward that even now he was trying to
extricate himself from the guilt; he had quickly realized the plot had
been discovered, and that was why he had eaten them himself.

'"Come, Rosa." Belcon called to the girl, who went and stood
between him and his eldest son. He took her hand in his. "It is
thanks to the Roman woman, who saw the poisoned toadstools and
warned me of them, that none of you who ate has been poisoned. I
am mightily grieved that my own sons – yes, both of you – should do
this thing. Though I knew you were not sound men, I did not suspect
how evil you might be. You sought to murder your own father and,
by laying the blame on one you pretended to befriend, besmirch the
name of my most loyal and trustworthy Cunobarrus. You, Verluccus,
have been the innocent party in this, though as a father I would have
been happier to see you refuse to eat rather than my own sons. But
in eating you proved your innocence. So did all except my sons. Put
chains upon them and have them confined out of my sight."

'They had plotted it, of course, even when they persuaded me to
give up Rosa, thinking I would be jealous of Belcon's possession of
her and thus provide a plausible motive. But no woman after Bodyn
could rouse such feelings in me.

'Cunobarrus spoke to me only to say that I was an utter fool and
that like Belcon's sons, I should keep from his sight. That was the
beginning of the end. Belcon lost the will to live and ate very little.
Soon he would take only water, and his life ebbed away. He named
Cunobarrus as his heir, and Rogan, who might have quarrelled about
it, accepted this. Then he died. Rosa took poison and was buried not
far from him.

'It was then that Cunobarrus made the biggest mistake of his life.
Instead of executing the brothers as Rogan and others urged him to

do, he turned them out, drove them away, and told them they must fend for themselves. Because Belcon had not put them to death, he could not find it within him to do it. The result was – well, you know the result of that folly.'

He rose and stretched himself. 'I am done now. You have been very patient and heard me out. I suppose that boy is paying you to give me good advice. I will listen to what you say, but you will realize now the futility of his supposing he can ever be my master. He has no idea what he has taken on. You said you are not required to repeat to him my story. Old man, I have confided in you. Do not betray that trust. Advise him as you see fit, but do not betray my confidences.'

Coridumnus remained silent for so long that Verluccus rose and went across to him. 'I am so sorry. You have been put into a difficult situation. Take some rest. My talking has wearied you.'

He strode to the door and opened it to summon slaves to attend to their master. At the end of the long corridor, he could make out the form of Gaius.

A little later Coridumnus returned to the room. Verluccus had sat quietly within, making no attempt to leave. 'I suppose you must now do your duty to him and attempt to persuade me to see the error of my ways,' he said dryly as the counsellor resumed his seat.

'I must confess that I thought you had already done so. You are no stranger to violence; you have had ample opportunity to carry out the many threats you have made; and by your own admission, you find yourself constrained. You have no hatred of that young man. I can see that you hate Drusus, whoever he is, and if you ever find him, I pity him. You have reason also to hate Marcus Marcius; that too I grant you. But Gaius Marcius? No, I think you do not hate him.'

'He is born of that blood. He is the son of Lucius Marcius, who began all this. Perhaps if I had married Bodyn as I planned to do, if now I were living there with her family, a farmer in my own right, able perhaps to visit my own people once again, I might think, "Thank you, Lucius Marcius, for what you did. You did not intend it, but you brought into my life the best woman that ever walked the earth." But that is not the case. Through the brand he placed on me, I have been made a criminal. Gaius Marcius is his son and will become like his father. Yet despite knowing all of that, I have no quarrel with him. But it does not follow that I must be his slave.'

'Still you deny he has any lawful claim upon you? Can you not be mistaken in saying that you were abducted? You might have been sold to Lucius Marcius; such things are not so uncommon.'

Verluccus rose angrily to his feet. 'Never say such a thing – never. I was dragged from my mother's arms. She did not sell me. You may know of such people, but I do not!'

'Very well. But what of Marcus Marcius? He has an indisputable claim on you. To be made a slave is the misfortune of the defeated. He has the right to dispose of you as he will.'

'And but for Lucius' mark, I would now be a dead man! Is that what you are saying? But for Lucius marking me, I would not have been there in the first place!'

Coridumnus ignored the vehemence of the outburst. 'Can you be so certain? Two of your own brothers from that same place in Daruentum were there. They left their father's house of their own free will. Might that not have been the case with you?'

Verluccus shook his head decidedly. 'My only desire was to be a farmer. I loved Tanodonus and wanted nothing more than to be always helping him. I would never have left home.'

Coridumnus could see that he was getting nowhere. 'I am immensely moved by your story and deeply touched by your willingness to impart it to me. It cannot change your circumstances, however. Gaius Marcius is awaiting you. If you have any compassion for him at all, think of a small and lonely boy who asked his father to allow him a playmate.'

'Playmate? He got a slave.'

'He got what he was given. I doubt he had any choice and indeed whether he would have chosen to make you his slave; he is every bit as much a victim of his father's practices as are you. Can you not forgive him and allow him to offer you his protection?'

'His protection?' he sneered. 'Is that what he is trying to do? Protect me?'

'Surely you must realize that even his patience, and a great deal of patience he has for one so young, must soon be exhausted?'

'Then he should set me free.'

'That, sadly, cannot be. He would not be allowed to do so.'

He thought for a while and then said, 'I am not ready yet. He has to pay for what he has done to me. I must have something.'

'You are waiting for him to beg your forgiveness?'

'No, not that. A sign perhaps. Just something; I don't know what. I want him to realize he does not possess me by the will of his gods as he thinks – that simply because he is Roman the world is as he orders it. When the time is ready, I shall know. You are not to tell him – not yet. I shall decide when the time is right.'

'In the legal sense then, you do accept that he is your master? Not by any virtue of superiority over you but because he owns you? Even if only because you were given to him as a captive by his uncle?' Verluccus remained silent but assented by a deep sigh of resignation and the merest nod of his head.

'It is time to return you to him. However, it is impossible to start a journey through the woods now. You must remain another night, I think.'

In the morning Coridumnus returned. 'Have you thought about the matter? Are you ready to receive your master?'

'I will not say those stupid words. The time is not right. I am not yet ready.'

'I shall bring him in. Do not insist that he have the chains put upon you again, I beg you.'

'I must if he makes it a condition of my response to that bloody silly question. He is such a fool he cannot see beyond the nose on his face.'

'I know, I know,' the old man sympathized, 'but he cares greatly for you. Why else would he go to such lengths on your behalf? I have had men bring slaves here for healing often enough but not for them to be counselled. I think a gesture from you is overdue to him.' He left Verluccus to ponder this and went to summon Gaius.

'Well?' demanded the young man. 'Have you brought him to

reason? Will he now accept that he is my slave and do as I bid him? No, I can see for myself.' The dumb mutiny was still on Verluccus' face. He asked the vital question and was rewarded with the slave thrusting forward his wrists for the chains to be refastened. The smith was sent for, and Verluccus was secured upon the chariot which Felix had prepared and brought forward.

'Come with me. I have some ointment for that wound on his head. It will help it to heal more quickly.' Coridumnus led Gaius off in search of it, and the young man guessed it was merely a ruse so that they might speak privately.

'You must not blame yourself for failure, good man,' said Gaius. 'I have left a fat purse with your steward; I hope it is recompense for the time I have wasted. Verluccus won't need ointment on his head now; he is doomed.'

'He stayed and spoke at length with me with no chains upon him. He told me a great deal. I am not at liberty to repeat to you what he told me, but I do not think I am betraying a confidence when I say that he has not been so long in the company of Cunobarrus as you believe. You may yet detect some softening of his stance, some change in his attitude towards you. Be ready for it, and do not let it pass by. It may be a very small thing, some tiny gesture of conciliation. Watch for it and reciprocate. I feel all is not lost, but much depends upon you. He needs to trust you and have you put your trust in him. If he should make that move and you fail him, he will be lost to you forever. However, should he submit himself to your authority, believe me, you will be a very privileged man. I feel honoured that he has imparted to me secrets which I doubt he will ever speak of again.'

Some Druidic nonsense, Gaius supposed.

Verluccus was waiting in the chariot, watching them intently. He called out to Coridumnus, 'Remember what I said. If you have betrayed my confidence, then you are accursed.'

Gaius sighed. Coridumnus had been misled; Verluccus was exactly the same as when they had arrived four days before.

Gaius elected to ride Cervus and consigned the driving to Felix, who though by no means expert had a slightly better hand on the reins than his master. They hurried away, and to the relief of both were soon rattling quickly along the good road to Glevum.

They were overtaken by a rider coming out of Corinium. It was Titus, who had been in search of them. Cautiously, though delighted to see his friend, Gaius asked if he had seen his father.

'I did,' said Titus. 'I very nearly betrayed you. Only from his surprise at seeing me and asking me how you were did I realize you were not with him. You did not take him to the gladiator school either.' He spoke of Verluccus. 'I checked there, but more discreetly.' He grinned. 'So what have you been up to?'

His face was a picture as Gaius explained the purpose of his journey.

'And so you have achieved nothing. Do as my father advises: give him a good flogging,' said the centurion's son. 'I have felt his stick often enough to know that it is the best way to make someone obedient.' He offered to take the reins from Felix and drive the team home.

'You are a very good driver,' a voice said from beside him. 'Better than either of those two.' The skilled hands of Titus had made a world of difference to the motion of the horses. Now, instead of trying to battle with one another, they moved as one. He laughed, understanding the gist of what was said if not every word of it. He turned to Gaius, who was riding close beside him.

'I think I was just served a compliment on my driving skills. From him.' He gestured towards Verluccus. 'I bet he could drive this vehicle well.'

'He may be able to, but I cannot allow it,' Gaius responded. 'Tell me why you were looking for me. You were looking for me?'

Titus grinned. 'I nearly forgot. Yes, I have a message from Antonius to bring you back quickly. He has had to bring forward the date we go to camp. The mothers of some of the younger boys have ganged up on him and said the weather is deteriorating. They want their darling sons back home before the snow comes.'

Afterwards Gaius could have kicked himself. That was it – that was the gesture which Coridumnus had told him to watch for, his compliment to Titus. And he had ignored it, dismissed it as irrelevant. Between them they might have been able to lodge him so that Verluccus could hold the reins, control the horses. It was too late now.

That they were to go to camp earlier than planned was devastating news.

In Glevum again he closed the door on Verluccus and told Felix to find him some food. He delivered a letter from Coridumnus to Anicetus and went in search of Antonius to be given his orders.

It meant the end for Verluccus. Though Lucius was still absent, he knew he must resign him and just hope that when his father took possession of him Verluccus would show some change of heart and be spared. Before he left with the boys, he would visit him for the last time and tell him his fate. That, as master, was his duty. He was glad he did not need to see him until then.

7

─────────── ✺ ───────────

Verluccus had forgotten how grim his cell was, how closely the walls oppressed him. What a miserable, dark, and inhospitable place it was compared with the room he had been provided by Coridumnus. The little oil lamp had long since extinguished itself and was not renewed; the stale water was not replenished. He thought about what Coridumnus had said and about the futility of standing out against Gaius. The boy had all the advantages and could keep him there for eternity if he chose to. If he yielded to him, then he might at least see something of his old home, perhaps even see Tanodonus again. He wondered if his mother was still alive.

He came to a decision. The next time Felix came, he would not abuse him; he would ask him if he knew these things.

Unfortunately Felix was either unwilling or unable to supply the answer. 'I cannot tell you,' he replied. 'Only the farm bailiff has any dealings with the natives.'

'Then tell your master I wish to speak to him.' His mind was settled. Concession or not from Gaius, he would not spend a further night in this hell-hole.

'My master is not at your beck and call,' answered the boy primly, speaking more bravely than he had done before. The presence of a watchful soldier helped to boost his confidence.

'You really are devoted to him, aren't you?' He could not resist the sneer; Felix irritated him too successfully. 'Tell me what makes you a willing slave to such a cruel master?'

'My master is not cruel. No one knows him better than I do. I have been raised and educated with him; indeed, he relies greatly on me to assist with those lessons he finds most difficult. Often the work which the tutor praises the most is that which I have done the greater part of. When he has his own household, I shall be his steward just as my father Palatus is to his father. He will not be able to manage his affairs without me.'

'And me? Supposing that I was to do as he wished? What then would be required of me?'

There was a brief silence as Felix absorbed the intent behind the words, and even in the darkness with the boy's features concealed, Verluccus sensed a change come upon him. After a moment Felix said with a sneer, 'At one time he toyed with the idea that you might replace me. Of course he now realizes the stupidity of such an idea. I suppose he might have found you something to do – with horses, perhaps – and then, when no one would have remarked on it, quietly got rid of you.'

'I don't consider working with horses a degrading task. A horse has nobility whatever its breeding. Tell your master I want to speak to him. He has not come near me since we returned from Corinium, and I wish to say something privately to him.'

'I do not give my master orders,' said Felix and made to shut the door.

Verluccus jammed himself against it.

'If you have thoughts now of giving in to him, I can tell you that you are too late,' said Felix. 'He has washed his hands of you. He is resolved to do his duty and tell you your fate himself and will come in his own time, but his mind is fixed. You are dead meat. Better he had never set eyes on you than to have suffered the misery you brought him. Better Marcus Marcius had finished you off when he had the chance. But then, as we all know, he did not make such a good job of that as he bragged, did he?'

'What do you mean?'

The bait had been offered, and Verluccus had bitten on it. Felix was delighted. He was skilled at manipulating Gaius, but he had never before got the better of Verluccus; and he had a lot of old scores to settle.

'Have you not noticed his absence? Do you suppose he could resist coming to gloat over your captivity if he were still in Glevum? He has been gone many days. It seems he was not so successful at killing Cunobarrus as he would have us believe.'

'What do you mean?' Verluccus had flung the door open and had the young slave by the throat of his tunic. 'Are you telling me Cunobarrus is still alive? Alive now? Out there, somewhere, fighting on, being hunted by Marcus Marcius?'

Felix cringed in fear. 'I was not supposed to tell you that; it was to be kept secret from you.'

He threw the boy bodily onto the flagged pavement and heard the door slam upon him as he groped his way back to his pallet. Was it true? It was true that he had seen nothing of Marcus, but then he had seen nothing of Lucius either. Suppose it was another – not Cunobarrus? No, no other would assume his brother's name. He had not seen Cunobarrus die; that much was true. Cadrus certainly had died, still with his happy laugh upon his lips, but Cunobarrus? And yet he had seen his brother's jewellery in Marcus' tent. And yet Marcus Marcius believed it. He would not have gone as hastily as he had without certainty in his mind. He raised his hands and thanked the gods for preserving his brother's life.

'He can have me. Now he can have me. Protect Cunobarrus and keep him out of Marcus' deadly reach. I will do as he wishes. I will submit to this boy and serve him and be whatever kind of slave he wants, and I pray that you, for your part, gods, will safeguard my brother and keep him alive.' In the darkness, he spoke the words aloud.

As the dawn rose the following morning and the boy soldiers were assembling, Felix warned his master to expect trouble from Verluccus. The slave was bitter and angry that he had been locked up again; he was in a very dangerous mood. It would be wiser not to face him alone; he should take Titus or someone else with him.

Gaius had steeled himself to this task. Sick to the stomach with misery at what he considered his duty, he heaved open the door for the final time. The onslaught of hostility did not greet him. Instead of the sulking and bitter captive he had been warned to expect, he found not the hostile enemy but a grinning and joyful man who came forward as if to welcome an old friend, his arms extended.

'Why are you looking so pleased with yourself?' Some insight of genius made him strongly suspect he knew the answer; Felix must have spoken out of turn.

His suspicion was confirmed. Verluccus positively whooped with joy. 'He is alive! Alive and free! Do not deny the truth of it. Marcus Marcius has failed; your mighty Roman eagles are no match for that British harrier! Marcus Marcius failed, and Cunobarrus lives!'

'My uncle will soon rectify that; he will not be free for long.' The purpose of his visit was momentarily forgotten.

'He only discovered his whereabouts before through treachery. Your uncle will never be given such a chance again. No, he will never take Cunobarrus.'

'You are so confident! You have such belief in him. I think he had a good disciple in you. Did you call him master?'

'Master? Cunobarrus? No, I called him brother.'

'Oh? A brotherhood was it? A brotherhood of criminals!'

'A brotherhood? Yes, a brotherhood if you like to call it so. Three brothers: Cunobarrus, Cadrus, and myself – we three brothers. What better, stronger bond than three of one blood? Three brothers together, united as one for our cause, to purge our land of Romans.' Despite his good intentions, the bragging was irresistible.

Gaius felt his breath desert him. 'That's absurd. You took an oath of brotherhood; that is all. You are Verluccus from Daruentum.' He was not ready to believe what he was hearing.

'And so too were my brothers, sons like me of my father, who also was named Cunobarrus. Those brothers, Cunobarrus and Cadrus, left home many years ago, and I had the good fortune to meet them again. Do not pretend you did not know Cunobarrus was my brother. Why else keep this knowledge from me?'

Gaius was conscious of his jaw having dropped open. *He is serious! He really is the brother of Cunobarrus!* Aloud he said, 'What a prize! And to think Marcus brought you to us and does not even know what he did. How truly marvellous! I must write to him and tell him what he has missed. He may yet send for you to help seek out that renegade.'

Verluccus saw he had made a colossal blunder. 'I will not do that. I would die before I did such a thing.' He could see now he had not thought it through. This was Roman reasoning. He had been an utter fool. Irrationally he felt betrayed by Gaius' attitude.

But already the boy was nodding his understanding. 'Yes, I do believe you would. It will not happen. I shall not tell him.' He had no right to raise the man's hopes. How could he keep such news from his father? Lucius would not hesitate to do his duty.

He knew one thing for certain, however. He would not, could not, carry out the purpose for which he had come. If Verluccus had behaved as Felix had said he would, if he had ranted and raved and sworn, then he might have gladly told him his end was come. But now, seeing this happy face in the morning light, to do so was impossible.

'I have to go to the youth camp to assist with the boys. Now I shall have you returned to the farm. I'll arrange an armed escort for you.'

'There's no need to do so.'

So quietly were the words spoken that Gaius was sure he had not heard correctly. 'What was that? What did you say?'

'I said there will be no requirement for an armed escort – or for chains. I shall not run.'

'I don't understand.'

'You once said that you would believe me if I gave you my word. Now I do so. I'm giving myself to you. Your dog I shall be. I shall be obedient to your bidding as that one-eyed hound is to Victor's. That is what you crave, is it not? A cur and not a warrior? I shall do what you ask. I submit myself now to your authority and pledge my obedience to your bidding. There: I have said it. I have said what you require.' He paused and added, 'And I keep to my word.'

There was a long silence. Gaius knew that he ought to move, shift himself, say something, make some acknowledgement of the capitulation. There was a huge lump in his throat, and he felt sure he would cry. Anything he said would have been nothing but a squeak.

The waiting Verluccus misunderstood his hesitation. 'I suppose you doubt me because I say this at such a moment? You think it is a trick of mine and I say it to deceive you in order to take advantage of your trust and go to join my brother? What can I do or say to convince you that it is not so? All I can say is that to do such a thing is not my intention, and it is not in my heart. I had come to this decision before I knew that he was alive; indeed, I told Felix I wished to speak with you. Ask him if you do not believe me. But I do pray most earnestly that the gods will protect Cunobarrus, and I gladly give up hope of my freedom if that is what they want in exchange for his.'

'My uncle will stop at nothing to remedy his error.'

'Cunobarrus will live and die by the sword; it is his way. If he does not kill Marcus first and he is killed or captured, that must be the will of the gods. Now that I have given you my promise, I shall not revoke it. No matter what happens.'

'Felix!' Gaius called to the boy, who was hovering fearfully not far from them. 'Felix, put together the bigarum and prepare to take Verluccus down to Daruentum.' He turned to Verluccus. 'I do believe you, and I value immeasurably what you have now done; truly, I do. And to show that I do trust you, I am sending you down to my home only with Felix. You may not enter the house until my father approves you, so go back to the outhouse you shared with Polyphemus and lie low. I shall give Felix instructions about what to do, and he will bring you food as he does now. You must not do anything to upset the household. As soon as I can get a message to Father and he hears your pledge of obedience, you will be with me all of the time. I have to go to camp with the boys, but I will get away when I can and come to see that all is well.'

He hurried away to detain Felix and briefly give him his instructions.

Within the hour all chains were gone and Verluccus was standing beside the nervous young slave as he guided the two-horse chariot through the city gate and into the countryside.

BOOK IV

SERVING GAIUS

1

For a little distance there was a silence between them. Verluccus knew that the skinny boy who was holding the reins, and not unskilfully, was absolutely terrified of him. The chariot jolted considerably when they left the official road and took the Daruentum trackway, and at each jolt Felix would gasp and cringe as if the discomfort presaged a blow or threat from the man looming beside him.

Finally Verluccus, privately acknowledging that he had given the boy cause to fear him, decided that it was time to make amends for his past conduct and said, 'You have no need to fear me, though I could manage these beasts better than you. I have sworn to Gaius that I will serve him even as you do, if that is what he wishes. And I shall do you no harm. Tell me what will be expected of me.'

Felix remained silent, concentrating on his task. It was only after he had negotiated a tricky incline that he said, 'I cannot help you. To start with, you will have to learn Latin. Nothing else, unless Greek, is permitted in the house, for fear of plots. Those unable to learn have to work outside under Victor's whip.'

'Who better to help me than you who can speak both our native tongue and Latin?' Verluccus was beginning to find his avowed intent difficult, even to dealing civilly with Felix. 'We could commence even now,' he added, determined not to let Gaius down.

Felix frowned. 'I've been given no such instructions,' he said. 'If our master had wished it so, then he would have told me.' He wheeled the chariot to a halt beside a roadside tombstone and pointed. 'Here lies the man who might have succeeded in teaching you to be useful. He was Gaius' tutor and the freedman of Lucius Marcius. It was he who started the school at Glevum. He was a highly intellectual man, a very wise and trustworthy man. That is the sort of servant which Lucius wishes his son to have, the kind which I too would be. Let us descend and see what the letters say.'

'You know I can't read,' Verluccus protested, but he jumped down, glad to stretch his legs and expecting Felix to follow.

'You are to go now.' The boy was gathering up the reins and turning the ponies.

'Go? Go where? What do you mean?'

'Go wherever you wish to go. You are freed. My orders were to bring you here and release you.'

Completely baffled by this unexpected turn of events and not sure that he was understanding what he was being told, Verluccus scratched his head. 'Those were not my orders. I was told to wait in the outhouse for Gaius.'

'Of course,' said the other smoothly. 'Gaius must not lie to his father. Lucius Marcius will ask him what instructions he gave to you, not to me. Why do you suppose you are with me only and no armed escort? I am to tell him you escaped.'

'Is that not a lie?' He was puzzled, half-elated and half-dubious. Had Gaius really intended this? To give him freedom? It did not make sense.

Already the whip had descended onto the horses' rumps, and they were heading down the track towards the farm. Too late he realized that he had been made an utter fool of.

He was angry more with himself than with Felix. What a fool the lad must think him to be taken in by his lies. And yet were they lies? Perhaps Gaius was seeking to protect him from Lucius, knowing that Lucius would certainly hand him over to Marcus Marcius now that he knew he was the brother of Cunobarrus. Yes, that was it. Or not. No, Gaius, believing he would make his way to Cunobarrus, which he had not the slightest intention of doing, was having him watched and followed. Hadn't Gaius declared him a prize when he told him of their relationship, said he must tell his father? No, Lucius still had been absent when they left Glevum, and Gaius had been totally amazed at his revelation. There had been no time for him to make elaborate plans.

The thoughts whirled around in his brain until he took grip of himself and started to take stock of his situation. He was now close to realizing his heart's desire, near to his old home, just a few strides away if he took that path. It was so tempting to go there now, directly, to do nothing else but go back to his home and to his family. To embrace his mother again and to work the land beside his brothers. And yet he would put them in the gravest danger if he did so, for surely theirs would be the first place to be searched as soon as Felix raised the alarm. No, he remembered Coridumnus' counsel that if he wished to see them again it must be through the good offices of his master, not through antagonizing him.

And there was another thing. Could he break his word so readily? Would he not despise himself if he so easily broke the promise he had made so genuinely to Gaius? It was something of a revelation to him to find he could not do that, and he wondered if his new demeanour was perhaps not more despicable. Cunobarrus would most certainly consider it so.

But he could not remain where he was. He came to the conclusion that now he had two options – either to make his way on foot back to Glevum and search out Gaius, who would perhaps even now be setting out on the march towards him, or to make his own way to the farm and there await the boy's arrival as he had been instructed. If Gaius did not come to him, it would mean that Felix had either told the truth or, more likely, was believed above him. This would be a test of Gaius' trust in him. And what if Felix had told the truth? He put the consequences of that to the back of his mind. What on earth had possessed him to give a modicum of credibility to anything Felix said?

He thought of what he might do in Felix's place. What would Felix say had happened? He would drive to the house and report that his prisoner had escaped from his custody. He would need to claim that he had been overpowered. And surely it would serve Felix's interests better to say that when he had made a run for it they were much closer to the house than they were so that if by chance he was taken quickly it would appear that he had at least made some distance. He wondered dismally if Felix was as cunning as he was giving him credit for and decided that he probably was.

He took the trouble then to retreat into the undergrowth and conceal himself while he worked out a plan of action. Running to the house in pursuit of Felix would be folly. Gaius had said most positively that he must not reveal himself to the family before Lucius had approved him. There was only one thing for it. He must somehow gain entry to the farm secretly and conceal himself until Gaius arrived.

Though the trees had now shed most of their leaves, he felt secure among them and moved swiftly along using the familiar skills. Soon he was within the outskirts of Colymmon's hill and, to his delight, saw that brother there, still tending his precious sheep just as if no time had passed. It was a reassuring sight; it meant that there was stability at home. If Colymmon was still alive, then all must be well; he could not fend for himself.

He picked nuts and berries and made a meal for himself and for later and lay hidden where he could safely observe the comings and goings at the farm below.

Surprisingly, for he had anticipated great concern at his supposed escape, there was no noticeable activity below him, and he discovered that he was mildly vexed that the potential danger of his being at large was of such little consequence to the occupants of the house. Not until the small troop of boys playing at soldiers trumpeted their arrival and began the business of setting up camp did someone – not Felix – hurry from the farm to report the news. He tried to make out Gaius, to see if he could tell from his reaction what his thoughts might be.

The messenger was sent swiftly back to the farm, and a horse was saddled. Somebody was on his way to Glevum. The boys were divided. Some continued to make camp. Older ones became search parties. He smiled to himself. They had no hope of finding him; he was far too skilled. And he prayed that they should not; he would probably kill one of them before he could stop himself.

He was disappointed; they made no attempt to come in his direction. All indications were that they supposed he must be heading towards the river Sabrina or back to Glevum and its only bridge. For a long time nobody, not even Gaius, went near to the farm.

Soon men on horseback arrived and went directly to the encampment. One looked like Lucius; he had supposed him still in Corinium.

Distraught at the ghastly news that the boy had brought from his home, Gaius insisted to Antonius Secundus that his father, Lucius Marcius, must be sent for no matter where he was. It had to be done. Whatever doubts the tribune might have about the necessity for it and whatever other course of action he deemed necessary when Gaius told him that Verluccus was aware that Cunobarrus, his erstwhile leader, was alive and at large, Gaius could not bring himself to tell him of their relationship.

Lucius arrived in haste on a borrowed horse, his own Ravus being too exhausted from their journey from Corinium for a further gallop. He had arrived in the city moments after Antonius' messenger and had departed from it immediately to determine what more he could about this catastrophe and deal with his feckless son. The rousing of a search party from the fort had almost confirmed his worst fears, but relief that Gaius was unharmed was quickly replaced by blind rage at his son's arrant disobedience and recklessness.

His son stood before him, a picture of guilt and shame, quaking visibly before the unbridled fury of a man Gaius barely recognized as his beloved, gentle father. They were in the supposed privacy of the principia tent, but they might just have well have been in the centre of the forum.

'This creature!' raged Lucius, storming to and from before him so that he actually felt the ground beneath him vibrate. 'This creature yet again has made an utter fool of me, of you, of us all. And as if his escaping is not bad enough on its own, now I learn from you that you, my own son, having discovered he is more than a mere follower of Cunobarrus, that he is in fact the brother of him, the brother of the criminal that even now your own uncle is scouring the countryside in search of, have let him go!'

Gaius made as if to protest that it was not so. An angry hand rose to silence him.

'Do not speak. I'll hear no whining. You have as good as let him go! You unchained him! Unchained him!' Lucius' voice rose to such a pitch and his face grew so red that his son was sure he would suffer a stroke. 'You sent a known criminal; a violent, dangerous barbarian; a known killer, to your own unprotected home with no greater guard than Felix! You stupid, deceitful, duplicitous, underhand, treacherous – yes, treacherous – young idiot. Not a word! Not one word did you say of who he was to Antonius, to Draco. Why, Gaius? Why?'

'He gave me his word; I believed him. I trusted him.' How feeble that sounded now.

'You trusted him! Bah! Did I not say he should not be trusted until I approved it? What must I do to instil obedience into you? You deserve a good thrashing for this.' He reached out to take a staff from Antonius, determined to mete out the punishment himself.

'Father,' Gaius begged, 'let me go with the men who are searching for him. With my own hand I will do what must be done when he is captured.'

'Gaius Marcius,' said his father coldly, 'you have not the slightest conception of what he is capable.' He turned to Antonius. 'Call those children back before he kills them all. Leave the task to the cohort I have had turned out; those men will do what is required.' To his son he said as Antonius departed, 'Aemilius Lepidus Virens was an experienced soldier. Even he, with all his ability and resources, was not able to recapture Verluccus when he was merely a child. You know what became of Virens. Your so-called trustworthy slave killed him! Do you seriously think Tribune Antonius and these children stand the slightest chance of tracking him now, a man seasoned in the skills of living off the land? Now I shall go to my home and find out what state your poor mother is in. You remain within the precincts of this camp and submit yourself to the punishment you are due.' He threw the stick away in disgust and strode from the tent.

On hearing the news, Aelia had secured herself within the house and provided the male slaves with weapons, certain that the runaway would come to attack them before he had any thought of rejoining Cunobarrus. Lucius calmed her and reassured her and bade Irene take care of Gaia and her mother.

He told himself he was looking for Victor when he opened the outhouse door and looked inside. The slave was not there; of course he was not there. How ridiculous to feel that pang of disappointment when only Polyphemus rose, wriggling an excited body and curling a welcoming grin of his lips at the honour of the master's rare visit.

Victor approached him in haste, seeking instruction.

'Bring Polyphemus and Felix. The boy can show the dog from where to begin his hunt; Felix knows the place. And don't mind if Polyphemus does his worst; it will be for the best. I have been a very foolish father, pandering to the whims of a son such as mine. No more; this will end today.'

Felix took them to the fork in the road, and they expected the hound to go straight towards the native settlement. It was what Lucius had dreaded – almost as much as he feared Marcus being confronted by both Cunobarrus and Verluccus. He started to say they should await men from the cohort to reinforce them, but he was too late. Polyphemus was loosed, and his nose was raised to the wind.

The dog's age had not dimmed his enthusiasm for a hunt, be it for man or beast. He plunged excitedly into the brush, not in the direction of Daruentum or back to the farm but into the depths of the woodland behind, gladly giving tongue. He quickly left the men far behind, but they could easily follow his excited baying as he called them to follow him.

The boar was trapped. It turned on its tormentor and charged,

259

and the old dog, not so agile as he once had been, felt the tusks tear at his flesh. He died in Victor's arms and was buried where he fell. 'Did he kill him?' one of his men asked, fearfully, and he had to be reassured that a boar had disposed of the great hunting dog, not an unarmed man.

Verluccus heard the distant baying and the final yelp. He knew that cry and what it meant. The problem of what to do about a noisy and aggressive dog had been solved for him.

By sunset no good news had been reported. Lucius went to his home, and Gaius remained as ordered within the camp.

Later, when all was quiet except for the occasional shriek of a vixen and the hooting of owls, a tall figure clambered with great stealth over the boundary wall and silently dropped into the garden. He remembered how with fear and trembling and a fast-beating heart he long ago had climbed out from almost that very same place. The irony of the situation was not lost on him. He crouched for a long time listening to be sure no one was about and waited for a scudding cloud to obscure the moon. The door did not creak as he eased his body through it. He settled himself in the vacated kennel and slept.

Gaius wasn't sleeping. He shared a tent with Calpurnius Drusus, not a youth he cared for greatly, and six of the younger boys. He had taken his turn at the watch with Calpurnius, but now that turn was completed and Titus Justinius and his squad of boys replaced them. He watched Drusus go to his bed and lingered to speak to Titus.

'I have to go down to the farm, Titus. Will you cover for me?' He nodded to a third lad who withdrew to patrol the camp perimeter. 'Or at least turn a blind eye?'

Titus sucked in his breath and shook his head in warning. 'You know what your father said. Why do you defy him so? He has already instructed that Antonius must give you the worst fatigues he can dream up. You were lucky he did not thrash you on the spot. If we were not here, he would have thrashed you; I am sure of it. What is the point of going to your home where your father will surely kill you? Is that what you want?'

'I need to see for myself. You were not there, Titus, when he pledged me his word. I cannot believe he was so devious.'

Titus sighed. He believed himself more realistic than Gaius. But even he could voice a doubt.

'It puzzles me,' he said, peering at Gaius through the firelight. 'If he escaped, why didn't he kill Felix or at least disable him? If it were me in his position, I would have waited only until we were out of sight of others and then killed Felix, broken his neck or something, thrown him in a ditch, and kept the chariot or at least ridden off on one of the ponies. I certainly wouldn't have come all this way before I did something. Don't you think that's odd?'

'Of course!' Why had he not seen it? Why had his father not seen it? They had both believed Felix without giving a thought to what Verluccus might do if he intended to escape them. 'Titus, I love you. You are so right! Now I must go home. I shall be there and back before Gnaeus Petronius there makes it round the perimeter.' He was gone before his friend could protest.

It was impossible to get in without waking the porters. He tapped quietly at the gate and called out so that they would know his voice, and they opened the gate yawning, sleepily unprepared for the disturbance. Clearly they did not expect the runaway to attack the family.

He walked towards the outbuildings, and his courage failed him. He turned aside and went instead to the shrine and poured a libation and spoke a prayer. There was nothing further he could do; the truth had to be confronted and no longer delayed. Steadying himself and steeling himself for the worst, he stepped determinedly towards the looming door.

The man within had heard him coming. His sleep was light, and he was alert to the many nocturnal sounds. Now came the booted tread of a soldier. He was on his feet and in ambush even as the door was heaved open.

He came out of the darkness as soon as he was certain. 'I did not know your footsteps,' he apologized, a pale face stark in the moon's light. Gaius felt the wetness of tears on his own and was glad to be in the shadow.

'Felix reported that you had escaped.' He could barely hear his own voice.

'As you can see, I have not.'

'No one seemed to know you were here. Men are out searching for you.'

'But you are not with them.'

'No.' Gaius' voice was low with shame. Verluccus grasped the situation.

'I gave you my word. You must trust me. I shall not lie to you or deceive you.'

'Yes, it is true. I was taken in by Felix. I am sorry.'

'What story has he given of my escape?' They were walking back to the encampment past the open-mouthed porters.

'Felix said you quarrelled about who might drive the chariot. He said he almost had you here when you ran off.'

'He is very crafty, that one. The truth is he abandoned me near a tombstone further up that way. I hope he did not say we fought? I do have a reputation to uphold.'

Gaius could smile at that. He took him across to where Titus and Gnaeus stood watching their approach with interest. Titus grinned.

'I think I should wake Tribune Antonius. Don't you? We do not want to annoy your father any more by delaying what must be.'

The tribune looked them up and down. He really did not know what to do – whether to send to the farm and have Lucius woken in the middle of the night or whether to let the matter wait until morning, another four hours away. What should he do with the slave? He seemed safe enough, apparently docile and amenable.

'Can you control him, Gaius? Will he be safe here until your father can be told?'

262

'Of course he is safe, Tribune Antonius. It has all been a misunderstanding; he did not run away. Felix had it wrong; he gets things wrong sometimes. Felix is a very nervous boy, and as you can see, Verluccus is a very large man.'

'That's as may be. Your father will be even more angry with you and angry with me now for failing to prevent this further disobedience on your part. More so, I think, if he is not told immediately that the slave is recaptured.'

'Not recaptured,' Gaius corrected him firmly. 'He did not escape. There is no need to disturb my father. Better send someone to Glevum though so that the hunt is called off.'

'Yes, yes, quite right. Titus, see to it. Have a man roused at the farm and sent directly.'

Titus saluted and ran to the farm himself.

Despite Antonius' intention not to wake Lucius, the disturbance of the youngster's arrival brought the head of the household angrily to his door, shouting for Palatus to come quickly. 'By Hercules, what is going on now?' he demanded, seeing an agitated Titus on his doorstep.

Titus apologized profusely. The porters, having seen Verluccus led away by Gaius and now seeing Titus come haring towards them, had drawn the wrong conclusion and believed harm had been done. They had decided to alert the household to the danger at large.

'Nothing, sir, really. That is …' There was nothing for it but to tell him. 'We have Verluccus up at the camp. He is with Gaius and Tribune Antonius.'

'You did well to wake me. Is he secured? Send to Glevum and let them know we have him.'

He would hear nothing from Titus, convinced that there was nothing more to be said, and hastened to dress in outdoor garments.

'What is this, Publius Antonius? He roared at the unfortunate tribune. 'Knowing what you do about this runaway, you let him stand here unsecured?' But for Gaius' intervention, he would have had the porters seize him at once.

'Father, Verluccus did not escape. He was where I told him to wait for me – in the outhouse. See for yourself; he is not a danger to anyone.'

'Don't boast to me of your further disobedience.' His father shook with anger. 'Did I not order you remain within the camp? And still you continue to lie to me. I myself looked in that outhouse. He was not there.'

Verluccus could not understand a word of it, but he recognized that Gaius was in serious trouble with his father. He whispered to Gaius, 'Let me tell him what happened. He is blaming you for my deeds.'

'You be silent!' Lucius glared with distaste upon the creature who stood as if a guard protectively next to his son. He was unshaven, unclean, and an ignorant brute. His hair was growing upon his scalp again, straw coloured with a shock of white emerging along the line of the still-unhealed head wound. But despite all of this, there was something about him which shook Lucius – the way he looked him straight in the face, his apparent concern for Gaius a shield against the teeth of a father's righteous anger. 'How dare you stand and defy me? Prostrate yourself and plead for your life,' he barked, determined to maintain discipline.

It was more than Marcus had demanded of him, but it was not unexpected. Verluccus spread himself before Lucius and said, 'Lord, be merciful to me. I know in your eyes I am a criminal.'

It was sufficient for a reprieve, Lucius decided. It was chilling to discover just how easily the confessed criminal had breached the security of his home, a security supposedly provided by the porters and other trusted slaves, and had entered almost into the house itself. He supposed he would have done even that had Gaius told him to wait in his own sleeping chamber. He sent the porters home, their failure as clear in their minds as it was in his – they would have to be replaced and soon. Verluccus could have slaughtered them all had he chosen to – Lucius, Aelia, Gaia, Quintus, everybody. But he had not done so. He had not escaped either, though the temptation to do so must have been great.

'Very well, Gaius. He may remain,' he decided. 'Not here; I shall take him to the farm with me. He may occupy Polyphemus' kennel until he has made an official pledge of obedience and loyalty. By official I mean that I shall require it said before the whole household. In the meantime, I shall make Victor responsible for him. You need have no fear that he will be maltreated. Order him now that he is to do it.' Gaius did so and was relieved and proud to see that Verluccus dipped his head respectfully.

'And now, my disobedient son. I have already told Antonius he should not be nervous of giving you fatigues. I see no alternative left to him now but to reduce you from whatever rank you are privileged to hold. Somehow, somehow, I shall get it through to you that I will not have this continual disobedience. If this wild and villainous barbarian can be obedient to your will, why can you not be to that of your father?'

His son could think of no way to satisfy him, and after waiting in vain for an answer, Lucius shook his head in despair and dismissed him.

2

It was some days before Gaius met Verluccus again. Lucius had already invited guests to dinner. Calpurnius Drusus and his wife and their son Drusus, whom Lucius erroneously supposed to be a pal of Gaius; Cloelius Draco and his wife Lydia and their daughter Cloelia; and finally Publius Antonius Secundus had been added to the list, as Lucius now felt indebted to him. Had Gaius been permitted to nominate a guest, he would have asked for Titus Justinius Severus, but Gaius was still short of his father's goodwill. He had returned with the youth corps to Glevum and then had been forced to wait and accompany the guests to his home, and knowing that he must do something to improve his standing in his father's eyes, he did not demur but apologized to Titus for the slight he considered it to be to his friend. Titus assured him that he experienced no snub at missing the opportunity to dine with the younger Calpurnius, a sentiment well comprehended by Gaius.

The slave he found in Polyphemus' kennel was a very different man from the Verluccus he had come to know. Gaius winced at the neatly trimmed hair and the shaven face, the clean garments on loan from Victor until somebody could make him a tunic of his own.

He wanted him to make his loyal vows quickly so that he might sooner come into the house.

'You think him capable of serving at table?' asked his astonished father. 'Very well. Allow him to make a total fool of you if you must. Perhaps our guests will find amusement in the procedure. I shall require him to say his piece tonight before we eat.'

Gaius was appalled. His father intended to humiliate Verluccus not only before the family but before guests too. 'Verluccus said you were cruel, but I defended you. Do not do this to him, Father. You will be no better than Uncle Marcus. Let him make his pledge when only family are present.'

'How dare you! You insolent whelp! No better than my own brother indeed! Would I were half the man he is! A fine slave you have acquired who defames a father to his son. You agreed to my conditions; now they are called in. If he cannot or will not obey, you lose him. I will have no argument.'

'What is he to do?'

'I will give you the signal, and he will be sent to the head of the triclinium. He must bow his head and state – I would prefer it in Latin but we cannot wait until he has grasped sufficient of that – he must state that he is your slave and an object of my household. He will swear to be loyal, truthful, and obedient to all instruction by whosoever, to keep himself clean, and not to be in any way offensive. I suggest you tell him now.'

Gaius thought that extremely unfair. Other slaves were not required to make such avowals; but then, he admitted to himself, no other slave had been as abusive as Verluccus. But further argument would not help his cause; instead his time would be better spent teaching Verluccus to say at least as much as was required in Latin. That surely would gain Lucius' approval, and of course he would explain to him what it was he was actually saying.

'We are dining formally tonight,' Gaius told him, using the forbidden British tongue. 'Can I trust you not to throw my dinner over me?'

'I shall do my best, provided you do not provoke me,' Verluccus answered, grinning as he remembered his previous appearance in the dining room.

When Verluccus said things like that, spoke as though he were a free man, Gaius warmed to him; it was the casual friendship he had long ago sought. But it could not be allowed – not now. 'Verluccus,' he said quietly, 'I know you mean no harm by such remarks, but they will not do. Moreover, my father will not accept you in this household until you have made a pledge of loyalty to me and indicated your total acceptance of your position as my slave with no demur. He will signal when he is ready to hear you. Go forward as he indicates and speak as I guide you.'

He signed that Verluccus should take a post next to his dining couch and attended to what his father had to say.

Verluccus gazed at the company as they took their places. The men had been bathing, and the scent of the sweet oils permeated the room. *How womanish they are,* he thought, eyeing them slyly. He recognized Antonius, the tribune who organized the boy soldiers, but not the man next to him, Cloelius Draco. But Draco knew him and marvelled to his wife how very different the slave now was from that which Marcus Marcius had brought to town. Lydia giggled and nudged her daughter. She hoped that the girl would not waste the time she was to spend in the company of Gaius Marcius.

The decurion Calpurnius was another guest whom he did not know. He knew of his son though, although he was not aware of it. He knew that someone had gesticulated and shouted obscenities about him across the forum when he had been chained outside his cell. He just did not know it was this man's son.

Calpurnius was on the same couch as Gaius and Lucius. On the wicker chairs were seated a woman who might be his wife; next were Gaius' mother and a very unhappy-looking girl who could only be Gaius' sister.

He was roused from this reverie by the impatient voice which indicated it was not the first time Gaius had spoken.

He stood where he was directed, wondering what would be demanded of him. 'What do you require of me, master?' he appealed to Gaius for help.

'My dear guests,' Lucius intervened, 'there is of course a reading to follow to entertain you. First I have a small domestic matter which must be dealt with if you will indulge me. Palatus, fetch in the household slaves.' Only when all were crowded into the triclinium did he permit Gaius to continue.

'Verluccus,' said Gaius, 'state your name and status.'

Verluccus stared at him. Was he serious? He saw the frown on Gaius' face as he delayed and plunged into what he supposed was required. 'I am Verluccus, the son of Cunobarrus of Daruentum. I was a warrior known as –'

But already a horrified Gaius had risen to his feet and stopped him. 'No, no. You are Verluccus, slave of Gaius Marcius in the household of Lucius Marcius Abellus. Remember what I told you you must say. Say that now.'

There was an expectant silence as he struggled to recall the desired formula and finally recited it perfectly. Lucius nodded grimly.

There was tittering and sniggering among the guests. 'Ha!' Cloelius Draco applauded the achievement. 'A wonderful job your son has brought about. I don't know how he's pulled it off, but he's a credit to you. You must be a proud father. A fine son you have. Don't you agree, Lydia?' His wife cringed in embarrassment at her husband's stridency.

'I think our guests are ready to hear Felix reading from the Aeneid now, don't you, Lucius?' his wife asked pointedly, and so the floor was given over and a more accomplished Latin tongue graced their ears.

'You did that on purpose,' Gaius accused later.

Verluccus grinned. 'Would it not have been more to your credit to have a famed warrior subjugate himself and pledge his loyal obedience to you?'

'I was humiliated.'

'That's funny,' said Verluccus. 'I thought your purpose was to humiliate me.'

Gaius could not joke about it. 'That's not fair. You know I have every respect for you.'

'Your father would not like to hear you say that; it is I who am supposed to have every respect for you.'

'Well, you do, don't you?' The grin he received was answer enough.

The following day, after the family and their guests had performed the morning rites, Lucius called Gaius into his study for a serious and private chat. He hated being on bad terms with the youth and wanted desperately for the rift between them to heal.

Gaius' heart sank. He had no doubt what was to be the subject of the discussion and all too vividly recalled his father's recent anger with him.

Lucius came straight to the point. 'Son, have you given thought to what employment Verluccus is to have?'

'Why, Father, what an absurd question. You know he is to replace Felix. He has done all that was required of him, has he not? Why won't you accept him as I do?'

'I have accepted him – as a slave in my household. I remain very uneasy about it. Last night, before you stopped him, he was about to boast of his crimes as if you should be proud to own a creature who has committed such evil as he has done. Oh, yes, he repeated the words you put into his mouth. Yes, he is tame enough and wise enough to do that, but did he know what he was saying? I consider him devious. I do not like the way he has insinuated himself into this household.'

'The way you speak, one might think he craved only to be our slave and had done all that he could to have us possess him. That was not the case, but now that he has submitted to his fate, he has made a clear and honest pledge, and yes, I did explain what those words meant.'

'He clearly prefers to be in my house to death in the arena.'

'Now there you are wrong. He does not know that was his alternative. I did not need to threaten him with that.'

'Then I suggest you tell him the facts, and speedily too, before he picks up slave gossip.'

Gaius laughed. 'There is no danger of that; he really does not understand a word of Latin.' He collected himself. 'But I shall tell him without delay. I am sorry, sir.' He hoped the conciliatory tone would soothe his father.

'Which brings me back to the reason I wish to speak to you. Surely you can see how totally unsuited he is to be a personal servant? How ill he compares with Felix?'

'Father, how can you say that? It is true he has a lot to learn, but he has far better qualities than Felix.'

'Then be so good as to tell me what they are, for in truth I have to say I cannot see them,' responded Lucius patiently.

'Well, for a start, he is both courageous and honest. Two qualities which you must agree Felix has not displayed.'

'You amaze me, Gaius. You are speaking of a slave whom we both know has come from a den of thieves and the gods know what else. You call him honest! Do you know what the word means? And in what way is Felix dishonest? How does he lack courage?'

'He reported that Verluccus had escaped. That was not true. And when Verluccus was violent towards me – in the early days,' he added hastily, realizing he had made a grave error. 'In the early days, when Verluccus raged a bit, Felix took shelter behind me.'

'My understanding is that he reported merely that he and Verluccus had quarrelled. Some disagreement over who should drive the chariot. He was forced to abandon him for his own safety. I consider your favourite far more devious for sneaking into the farm under cover of night rather than reporting himself at the gate. That action I do not like. And as for Felix being timid, of course he is; he is not required to be brave. What need do you have of a bodyguard? Where do you acquire such fanciful notions? You need someone who can make your life run smoothly, who can remove from you the need to bother about the small essentials. Felix is an excellent slave, and later, when you have your own household, as your steward, he will be an embellishment to it. Take my advice and keep them both – Felix as your attendant and Verluccus in the arena, a trained gladiator as Victor was. In that place he may put the courage you esteem so highly to its best use. Son,' he pleaded, trying to meet the boy half-way, 'don't let this mulishness of yours ruin your life! From what I have observed so far, unless you take steps to rectify the matter, you will live in a perpetual state of Saturnalia!'

'Father, I know that Felix lied about the way they parted company. If you will allow me to call Verluccus here, you may hear the truth.'

His exasperated father agreed. Verluccus was waiting outside the door. Gaius wondered if Lucius would have disapproved even of that.

'Verluccus, my father requires to hear from you how you and Felix came to part company. Do you know what Felix has said of it?'

'He reported that we had quarrelled; we had not.' Belatedly he added, 'Master.'

'Continue.'

'Master,' he began. Would he ever get used to this? 'Master, I asked Felix to tell me what would be expected of me in the household. He said that I would be required to speak Latin. I asked him if he would teach me. He said he could not. He stopped by a tombstone, and at his suggestion, I got out of the chariot to look at the letters on it. Then he said that he was acting on your instructions and that I was made free.'

Lucius' face was a picture. Gaius was delighted.

Verluccus continued, 'I argued and said that my orders were to wait for you with the hound in the place I had been before. He just drove off and abandoned me. I realized immediately that it could not be true, so I waited until nightfall and came over the wall.'

'Why did you not come to the gate and report your arrival?' demanded Lucius curtly.

That was a flaw. Verluccus shifted his feet. This merely added to Lucius' belief in the shiftiness of his nature. 'Master, I am aware that Felix is highly regarded in this household. I wished my first contact to be with your son. I knew he would come to the place he had told me to wait for him. I was confident he would not doubt me.'

Both father and son knew it was a confidence misplaced. 'There is another thing,' said Lucius. 'You claim that the criminal Cunobarrus is your brother. How can that be?'

'He is my mother's son, fathered by my father.'

'Don't be impertinent with me.' Lucius misunderstood Verluccus' genuine belief he had given the answer required. 'Knowing then that he was alive, why did you not take the chance you had to return to him? Why did you come here rather than go to join him? Is the oath you have made to serve my son to be as lightly discarded as that which you must have made to him?'

'Even before I learned he was alive, I'd made my decision to resign myself to your son. I don't deny I did toy with the idea of joining or trying to join Cunobarrus again when I was told he was alive, but I saw that in giving thanks to the gods for his life I had nothing to sacrifice in exchange but my freedom – if the gods will accept it. As for my allegiance to him, I owed him duty as his brother warrior and served him well. More than that was not required of me.' He shrugged apologetically.

'You cannot make such a bargain with the gods – your enslavement for his freedom. You are a slave regardless of that, and he will be taken, dead or alive. Marcus Marcius will stop at nothing until he has him.'

Gaius had said the same thing. He thought how alike they were these two, so alike and yet so different. One cruel, the other kind. 'I do not claim to have made a bargain. I only offer myself for him. The gods may reject such a poor sacrifice, but I can pray that he continues to live in freedom.'

'And what of the oaths, the vows you made to him? You did make vows of loyalty to him, did you not? Do not those vows which you made to Cunobarrus require your bodily service for as long as you live?'

He had never made such a vow to Cunobarrus. He had to Belcon, but that man was dead now. Cunobarrus had taken his loyalty for granted. 'Cunobarrus would not consider my return to be an asset to him,' he said, remembering the contempt his brother held him in.

That was an interesting admission. Intrigued by such candour, Lucius' approach mellowed somewhat. 'Do you know where Cunobarrus is?' he asked.

'No, I do not, my lord, no more than does Marcus Marcius. But even if I did, I would not assist anyone who intended harm to him. You may do as you will with me.'

The softened tone was replaced by a cool sneer. 'And you will serve my son? Replace Felix? Go, go and find something useful to do until your master requires you.' He turned to Gaius and answered the question his son directed to him. 'On the contrary, I do believe he spoke the truth. But we have owned Felix for a great deal longer than him, and Felix has served me and you most loyally with love and devotion. How painful it must be for him to be displaced, summarily ousted in favour of such as that. If he has tried to get rid of Verluccus, is that not understandable? I can forgive him for this mendacity. His reading as we dined yesterday was most impressive; he is truly an asset to my household. As for Verluccus, it is to his credit that he did not escape when given the opportunity, but he remains a hazard. Consider how he will react when news arrives from Marcus that he has destroyed Cunobarrus.'

'He is used to the vagaries of war, and he knows how high the odds are stacked against any who oppose the legions.'

'Son, I wish I had your optimism! However, I consent: you may keep him. Felix must serve your brother, I think – lucky Quintus. You are an utter fool to so casually discard the merit and usefulness of such a fellow. As for that one, keep him busy, keep him clean, and make certain he learns some useful language. You know how nervous your mother is if she hears the British tongue; she thinks the slaves are plotting against her. I do not trust him; I doubt if I ever shall. Let me say this: the day I lie naked on a slab and allow him beside me stropping a razor, then you will know he has my trust! In the meantime, he is to be allowed access to no weapon, no blade, no tool. He has hands like shovels, and if necessary, he can make use of them. These are my express commands, and I will in these be obeyed.' He paused, and Gaius thought the interview concluded, but then he spoke again. 'I am sorry that you have elected not to take my advice in this. I have been extremely lenient and indulgent towards you in the hope, the seemingly vain hope, that you may in time realize what is the best thing to be done with him. What I fear above everything is that the influence he appears to have over you will prove detrimental to your character and ruin your life. I have never limited your freedom, despite my position. Is it too much to expect my son to set a good example?'

His son conceded that he had acted rashly in the past and would endeavour henceforth to do all he could to make amends.

Verluccus was provided with a space on the floor in Gaius'

bedroom and a pallet to sleep on. Something was consuming him though, and he had to discover more. He ventured to raise the matter with Gaius. He had to find out, though how he would deal with the situation now he feared to answer.

'Your father's guest is named Drusus?' he asked as casually as he could, reminding himself again what Coridumnus had said – that it was a common enough name among the Romans.

'You mean Calpurnius? Yes, his name is Calpurnius Drusus, and so is his son's; he bunks with me in the *contuburnium,* the lads I share space with in the camp.'

'Then he is a friend of yours?'

'By no means, though Father wishes it. I prefer Titus Justinius Severus, and Titus has been a good friend to you also.' Gaius remembered his friend's observations at the campfire. 'What is it to you?'

'I was wondering if I was responsible for his lameness,' he lied. 'He is a veteran, is he not?'

'I think you can be at ease about that.' Gaius grinned. 'I know he brought that injury from Gaul. He has not been active in this land – only deskbound until he retired.'

Verluccus was surprised how greatly relieved he was to learn this; Calpurnius had not seemed the kind of man who could be responsible for such havoc as his enemy Drusus had wreaked, and his son was far too young.

Gaius outlined the tasks Verluccus would be expected to do, which for the time being were to rise before his master and bring him clean water to rinse his hands and face and bread and fruit for his breakfast. While Gaius was then away to greet his parents and attend the shrine, Verluccus should tidy and clean the room they slept in.

It was, they both knew, women's work, but Gaius was anxious to be able to say Verluccus was demonstrating his preparedness to bend and make himself useful.

Lucius organized a hunting party to entertain his guests. Among the slaves who accompanied them were his personal Hardalius and Victor for the treat; Gaius understood he was not to suggest that Verluccus should attend.

'Try not to be an annoyance to anybody,' Gaius warned him as he departed. 'If someone gives you a task, whatever it is, do it. If I consider it wrong, I shall take it up when I return.'

There was no more he could usefully do in Gaius' room, and still the hunters were active, their whoops and shouts clearly audible across the valley.

Agricola spotted him idly listening. 'Make yourself useful,' he advised him. 'Help stoke the fires while the women are bathing and fetch more fuel. The men will require the bath suite when they return.'

It was more agreeable to work than to do nothing. He was given a saw and reduced logs to more manageable sizes. Agricola nodded his approval. 'You're a useful fellow,' he said. 'I could do with you helping me and Victor.'

Of all the work that might have been demanded of him, he thought working alongside Agricola the most attractive. But he knew that Gaius would have none of that, so he just shrugged and kept his thoughts to himself.

The hunters returned in triumph with a good young boar and venison. Gaius wanted to know how he had spent his morning, and so he told him.

'Father would not approve of the saw,' said Gaius. 'Let's hope he does not find out.'

'Does he think I'm going to saw everybody's heads off?' Verluccus asked, faintly amused.

'Of course not. It's Mother and –' He broke off.

'You should tell me, I think. You know I would not harm your family. Those things I said – they were empty threats to provoke you.'

'Of course. I know that. No, it's my sister. I have agreed that if she objects to your being here, I shall give you up. You killed the man she was going to marry.'

'Give me up to your father? To be killed?'

'He won't put you to death – not now. But he would send you away to work on another of his properties, far away from Gaia.'

Far away from Daruentum and any possibility of seeing his own people again. Verluccus sensed that he would have to do something pleasing to Lucius to be granted such a privilege; annoying the womenfolk would not be to his advantage.

But the relative safety of working on the farm was denied him, for Agricola unwisely praised his efforts to Lucius, who ruled that such access to implements was dangerous and forbade it.

3

─────── ⟰ ───────

The guests remained, and within a few days Gaia celebrated her fifteenth birthday. Her father had brought from Corinium a stripey kitten, a gift for her from her dear sister Marcia. Marcia, Verluccus learned, was very well and blooming and in her second pregnancy, and though the child was due in February, not a good month for giving birth, it appeared that all would be well. He had never seen a tamed cat before and was fascinated by its friendliness. The fluffy kitten bloated itself with milk and titbits and was promptly named Orca, a rotund vessel. From her brother Gaius she received writing materials, and from her mother a fine wool gown of palest amber. Cloelius and Lydia gave her a fine bronze mirror, Cloelia a hair comb, and Calpurnius and his wife and son presented a pretty set of matching enamelled brooches. From Antonius she received a phial of rose perfume, a very expensive present.

Despite all of these gifts and the amusement which the little cat provided for everyone else, and despite the girl's protest that she did truly love it, Gaia's face remained as downcast as ever.

At dinner she wore her new gown and a gold headband which her parents had given to her and which gleamed between the dark, ever-escaping curls. Gaia's hair never would remain constrained like her mother's.

The gown suited her well, and she might have been beautiful had she but tried even a little, Verluccus decided. But her face remained glum, and she barely spoke and only toyed with her food as if becoming fifteen were the worst thing in the world that could have happened to her.

Standing now behind Gaius' couch, Verluccus could see her clearly, and he had the grace to acknowledge to himself that he was the likely cause of such total misery. He wondered if he could do something to comfort her, if there were any words she wanted to hear from him which would cheer her, would make her smile again; but ever mindful of Gaius' warnings not to give the women cause to complain, he always kept as close to his master as he could and a respectful distance from everybody else.

Since it appeared to him that as far as mother and daughter were concerned he did not exist – neither of them ever required any service from him, not even to pick up something which had fallen before his eyes, and would signal for anyone but him to perform the task – he considered it safe enough to observe the girl from the distance of his present position.

There were beads around her neck, bright and shiny blue and amber, and he was reminded of his own beads which had been given to her. He wondered where they now were, for these were not them. They could have been, but they were strung together differently and he puzzled as to the arrangement of them. After some considered thought, however, he realized that the necklace consisted of the same beads, but the rewiring had put them in a different and less attractive order.

Suddenly, and for no comprehensible reason, Gaia rose to her feet and rushed out of the room. Hastily Delia went in pursuit, and an alarmed Aelia would have gone also if her husband had not stayed her and reminded her of their guests.

After a few minutes Delia returned and spoke softly to Gaius, 'Your sister begs you to go to her.'

After a few moments, unsure what he ought to do, Verluccus followed them from the room. Aelia and Lucius exchanged concerned glances but tacitly allowed him to go.

He collected the scattered beads as he went and entered her bedchamber still picking them up from the floor.

Gaius had found her sobbing piteously into her bed. She had

ripped away the necklace and scattered the beads about the floor. Delia had tried to restore it to her, but she would have none of it.

'What is it, sweet girl? Why are you so upset?' her brother asked.

'He hates me; he hates me. Those beads – I feel his eyes burning into me, loathing me for my having them. Gaius, he hates me. I cannot bear to wear them ever again.' The words came stilted between her sobbing.

He put an arm around her to comfort her. 'Nonsense. That is not true. Gaia, please, please don't say this. You know what Father will do.'

By now Verluccus had entered the bedchamber. He knelt and began to collect together those beads which were in view and offered them to Gaia, taking care to say nothing. She shook her head and shrank from him. He poured them onto a small table and began to hunt for more.

'You had best go,' Gaius directed. 'Return to the dining room. I shall be in shortly.'

He dared to speak. 'I did not mean to frighten your sister. I noticed the beads had been strung together wrongly. They are meant to be in threes, not singly – three amber, three blue. Like that all around. Would it please your sister if I rewired them for her?'

He was conscious that not only Gaius but his sister also understood what he was saying.

'Does he not mind my having it, my wearing it?' she asked her brother, clinging to him and staring fearfully at the huge slave. She could not bring herself to say it must have once been worn by Verluccus' wife and Marcus must have killed her.

Verluccus shook his head; drew a deep breath; and, still kneeling before her, said, 'I know I have made you unhappy. If it is true that I killed the man whom you would have married, I did not know that then. He was an enemy of mine, and we were fighting in a battle. Please forgive me for causing you this grief.'

To his dismay, she simply started to cry even more and was inconsolable.

'Return and wait by my dining couch as I ordered you,' said Gaius. 'Delia, go and fetch my mother.'

After some time Aelia returned to the triclinium with her daughter. She apologized to their guests for her behaviour but gave no explanation. For the first time, Gaia bore a smile on her face, but it was a fixed and polite smile, put there at her mother's insistence.

The following morning their visitors departed, taking with them generous portions from the hunt for their own tables.

Gaia had told Aelia that Verluccus had asked to be forgiven for killing Virens. While it was not the strict truth, she knew that it was the best thing to say to her mother. Aelia had not been particularly impressed even so and warned her daughter against encouraging the use of native tongues.

After the departure of the guests, Aelia called Gaia into Lucius' study. Gaia had to wait his return from his morning tour of the farm. She was cuddling Orca and looking idly out of the window, watching for the first glimpse of Lucius, having more than half an idea of what he was going to say to her. Outside she could see Verluccus. He was striding along the terrace, presumably on some errand for Gaius or perhaps in search of him. Behind the tall slave, quite alone and unattended, was little Quintus, stretching out to match the steps of the slave as he followed on.

Verluccus suddenly stopped as if aware he was being followed and turned quickly; Quintus froze. Verluccus resumed his steps, and so did Quintus. Again Verluccus stopped and turned, and the child again froze. The pattern was repeated, and instead of continuing on whatever errand he had been sent, Verluccus now began to walk around the garden, stopping and turning, playing with the little boy. Gaia began to giggle.

'What are you laughing at?' Aelia wondered, looking for amusement. She glanced outside and saw enough. She flew to the door, calling for Felix to cease neglecting his duty and to fetch his master in from the cold.

'Verluccus was only playing with him,' said Gaia. 'It was harmless fun.'

'He is not here to have fun,' snapped her mother. 'There will be plenty of fun for the slaves at the Saturnalia; let him have it then if he must. Ah, here is your father.'

'My darling child,' Lucius said to her, drawing a chair up beside hers and taking her by the hands. 'Your mother and I do not wish you to be so unhappy. We were going to wait a little while until I had positive news before telling you this, but we have come to the conclusion it is better that I tell you now. I want to see a smile on that pretty face of yours again.'

It is marriage, she thought dismally. *I do not know anybody. It must be Calpurnius Drusus. It will have been arranged while his parents were here. What can I say? I do not want to marry him. He is no older than Gaius. And I know Gaius cannot stand him. After I am married, my brother will never speak to me again.* She composed herself and prepared for the worst.

'I wrote a letter of consolation to Decimus Aemilius, Virens' father. I am aware he has another son, Glaucus, and I have proposed that, should he be free and should it be acceptable to him and to his father, he will become your husband. What do you say to that? Of course, he may not be free; you must be prepared for that.'

Gaia looked at her mother, who was nodding encouragingly. 'How old is Glaucus?' she asked faintly. 'Have I ever met him?'

'No, darling,' said Aelia. 'As far as we know, he has not visited Britain. He is younger than Virens, but we think he must be in his early twenties now. We remember Virens speaking of him. Are you pleased?'

'I do not know; it is a bit of a surprise. I had thought you were going to say Calpurnius Drusus.'

Her parents were dismayed. 'I did not know you harboured such ideas,' said Aelia. 'I would not have suggested him.'

'No, no, I don't want to marry him!' cried the girl hastily. 'I was wondering how I could say so. That is all.'

'And what of Aemilius Glaucus? Does this news cheer you up?'

'I think it may, when I have got used to the idea.' She smiled wanly, hoping it was enough to satisfy her parents.

She had to tell her news to Gaius first. Victor told her he was at the stables with Cervus. There she found the stable hand slouching outside and looking sulky. He pulled himself upright at her arrival and made a slight bow. She acknowledged it and frowned in puzzlement as she stepped within, calling cheerfully for Gaius.

The man attending to Cervus was Verluccus.

'Oh!' It had to happen sooner or later – another encounter. She said in a language he could understand, 'I was looking for my brother. Where is your master?'

He put down the grooming brush and moved towards the door as if he would take her to him. 'It is all right, Verluccus,' she said. 'If I speak to you in the British language, you may answer me likewise.'

'He has gone to the farmhouse to see Agricola. Mistress,' he added as a polite afterthought.

She called to the sulking groom, 'Go and find Master Gaius; tell him I am here,' and then to Verluccus, 'Why are you grooming my brother's horse when we keep stable hands to do that?'

He took up the brush again. 'That man has no idea. This fine horse should be treated better than he is.'

'Are you saying your master neglects it? You should mind your tongue.'

'I beg your pardon, mistress.' He was trying really hard not to offend her. It was good to see her looking more cheerful, and he wondered if he dared to say so. 'My master does not neglect his horse. I know he cares for Cervus very much. But –'

He got no further, for suddenly Cervus let water. Gaia was in great danger of being splashed and marooned by the enormous puddle and having to walk through it to reach the door. He was beside her in an instant and had swung her from where she stood through the air and onto the threshold.

'I am so sorry, my lady – mistress. Truly, I do beg your pardon.' He was scarlet with embarrassment that he had actually touched her, put his arms around her, and lifted her from the ground and not at all unconscious of what a delightful sensation it had been.

To his surprise, she laughed. 'Verluccus, there is no need. Really, I do assure you. You have done nothing wrong. I would far rather be grabbed hold of by you, however roughly, than pissed on by Cervus!'

Gaius, arriving at that moment, however, had seen things differently. His sister explained how she had been rescued, and then he laughed with her. 'How good it is to see you happy again,' he told her. She gave him her news.

He hugged her and said how delighted he was for her. He had no doubt that Glaucus would wish to be husband to such a beautiful creature. 'If he is in Rome,' he said, 'when we return there after the winter, you will surely be married to him.' They walked off arm in arm, leaving his slave to complete his task and show the stable hand what he might better achieve if he put his mind to it.

But for the rest of that day and for a considerable time afterwards, the memory brought a stupid grin to Verluccus' face, and the words she had spoken to him were happily and frequently repeated in his head. No one else would have thought them a compliment or even praise, but he treasured those phrases as though they were words of love. 'I would far rather be grabbed hold of by you, however roughly, than pissed on by Cervus,' she had said.

4

He had heard of the Saturnalia. Even though he was excluded by language, the air of excitement generated among the slaves as the day grew closer was tangible. He remembered with sadness the midwinter feasts he had enjoyed with Merriol and the later loud and drunken excesses in Belconia. How such celebrations were conducted by the Romans he did not then know, but it involved a great deal of preparation by the cooks.

He was woken on the first day of the festival by the voice of Gaius, who was standing over him and already dressed, saying, 'Wake up, you idle wretch. Today you are to be my slave.'

He scrambled hastily to his feet, full of worried apologies. 'I thought I already was.'

'Ha,' chortled Gaius, clearly delighted with him. 'That is Father's joke, you see! He says that my life is a permanent state of Saturnalia. And you know what feast commences today?'

Of course he did. Verluccus grinned. For once he could appreciate one of Lucius' jokes; he was acutely conscious of the gulf of knowledge and usefulness to his master which existed between himself and Felix. But he was not prepared by any means for the madness and chaos which seemed to infect the whole household apart from himself. To see Aelia waiting upon the women who normally were at her beck and call, and to all appearances enjoying the experience; to see Palatus striding around the house joyously shouting, 'Heugh Saturnalia!' and demanding service from Lucius; to see Delia raising an imperious finger to Gaia – it was too much. He was out of his depth. He had steeled himself to perform duties abhorrent to him when he had submitted to Gaius' authority, but this he could neither comprehend nor enjoy.

The only person in the household who seemed to share his confusion was Quintus. The child summoned the attention of the only slave prepared to obey him; and Verluccus, taking advantage, perhaps, of the licence allowed that day, went to see what he wanted. He knelt down to give the child his ear. It seemed he had to be a horse, and so he capered madly around the room while the excited child hung on grimly, whacking his buttock with a toy sword he had received from someone as a gift. Unfortunately he did not hold on tightly enough, and as his mount reared on command, he slid down its back and landed heavily on the floor, raising a healthy shriek to prove that he was in no way harmed. Before any assistance could reach him, however, he had meted out due punishment. A series of blows landed on their mark. Verluccus covered his head with his arms and waited for rescue.

Felix arrived first, laughing at the spectacle. Only on Aelia's intervention did he make the child desist and the punishment cease.

Verluccus became aware that the person suddenly kneeling down on the floor beside him was Gaia. She called for someone to fetch a cloth and a basin.

His head was filled with the scent of roses, and he could see clear dark eyes immediately above his own and eyebrows, black and fine, frowning in anxiety for him; she was so close to him – her body, her breasts so near to own his rapid chest. He experienced a sudden and almost unbearable desire to raise a hand and to touch her. He felt nothing of the injury done to his head and the stream of blood from the opened wound which caused her such concern. All he knew was that his lips were burning to kiss those which hovered so close to his own, and the knowledge both thrilled and terrified him. Her mouth was so close – he needed turn only a fraction, raise his head barely more than an inch or so, and his lips could brush hers. And then she moved, raised her head, and turned to see if the basin had arrived. He closed his eyes and sighed with relief. This would not do; he must not have such thoughts, such desires for Gaia Marcia. Had it been noticed? She seemed unaffected by his proximity and concerned only to staunch the wound. He lay with his eyes shut until he felt the cold, damp touch of a sponge upon his head.

'Mistress,' he said, carefully pushing her hand away and reaching to take the sponge from her, 'I cannot allow you to do this; it is not right.'

'Today it is.' Laughing eyes met his, and he melted.

'I beg you. It is only a scratch. It does not hurt.'

'Are you ordering me to cease, my lord?'

'Ordering you? No. Yes. Please, my lady, this is not fair.' He could see Gaius' face beyond hers, grinning down on him.

'I think my sister has you cold! You must submit. What did you to Quintus to merit such punishment?'

'He fell off my back. I think his mount was over enthusiastic.'

'That is quite wicked of you, Verluccus, to throw your poor rider. Tell the truth! You thought that since it was the Saturnalia you could do as you wished even with him. There are limits, you know.' She was laughing at him, teasing him.

Nobody was prepared to listen to him. It was agreed that he had taken advantage of the child, but it was a joke to them all. Quintus was not hurt, and nobody, not even Aelia, was really angry with him.

'If you will permit me,'– he rose to his feet shaking, not from the wound on his head but from the discovery he had made – 'lady, I think I must go and lie down. Master Quintus has a strong right arm, stronger than I had realized.' He backed carefully out of the room.

'So much for my gladiator,' sighed Lucius as the victim withdrew. 'Felled by a four-year-old! A Roman four-year-old, it is true, a match for a British barbarian any day. What say you, Gaius? You will not be boasting about this, I think? Hail the hero! And pour more wine for young Felix. His cup is dry.' He swung Quintus high into the air and paraded around the dining room with the crowing child on his shoulders.

For a moment Verluccus wondered if the blow to his head was worse than he had supposed and he had stumbled into the wrong room; either that or he was seeing things. On Gaius' bed were two figures so fully engaged with themselves that they were unaware of his entrance. He recognized them as slaves Florus and Vera.

'Are you mad? In here where Gaius sleeps?' Vera had disengaged herself. She withdrew from the room giggling and dragging her dishevelled gown around her as if a sudden modesty had come upon her.

'We didn't expect an interruption.' Her lover shrugged. 'We only sought a little privacy. What happened to you?'

Verluccus told him he had annoyed Quintus and had been bashed over the head for it.

'Oh, I'd best be gone; Gaius will be along any moment to see how you are. You are so very precious to him!' he said meaningfully.

Verluccus took him by the throat and lifted him with one arm so that his toes dangled clear of the floor. 'Let us get something clear. I am not that precious to him. If you don't want this little episode spoken of, you will make sure everybody who thinks differently knows this.'

Florus raised his hands. 'Fine, fine, I understand if I was mistaken and I will rectify it, but you cannot blame anyone for thinking it the way you and Gaius carry on. And nor can you threaten me with this. All right, maybe we should not have been in here, but – me and Vera – they all know about it. There is no objection to that so long as no guest desires Vera's delightful services. If Lucius' household increases, the gain is his. If you want to get into Lucius' favour, do as I do and get a girl pregnant – with a boy child, if you can. But choose another girl, not Vera.'

Perhaps he should; perhaps that was the problem. Perhaps if he was otherwise occupied, the desire he was suffering for Gaia Marcia would desist. But the idea was abhorrent. To make a slave for Lucius? To create a child of his own that would be born into slavery? He shook his aching head. 'Just go away.'

Gaius arrived very late and slightly tipsy.

'It's that old wound in your head, isn't it?' He saw that it was still bloody. 'I still have that ointment which Coridumnus gave me. I had not realized it was so serious. I let you go because you made such a poor pass at enjoying the festival.'

'The injury is nothing, truly. I have never had much use for wine. Beer – now that is my drink. I can drink beer with the best of them.' He hoped Gaius would let the subject drop.

All but he were still carrying on as stupidly the following day, but he sensed that the pleasure was wearing thin for Lucius and his wife, as they took themselves off into the master's study for much of the time. By the third day, in that household, at least, order and normality were resumed, and he put aside the pretence of a damaged head to bring himself to face Gaia again.

If he had thought she would forget the incident so soon, he was mistaken. She looked with concern at the bruise emerging on his forehead as Gaius pointed it out. 'Gaia thinks I must have beaten you for your misbehaviour to Quintus. No, sister, this is our little brother's handiwork entirely. Not bad, eh? I shall of course lay claim to it when I return to Glevum. That will impress my colleagues, I think, don't you?'

'Don't remain angry with Quintus, Gaius. I shall see that he apologizes to Verluccus.'

'That you must not! Have Quintus Marcius, the son of Lucius and grandson of Quintus the elder, apologize to a slave? One who bears the name of such uncles as Marcus Marcius and his own namesake, Quintus Marcius? And father has made him such a hero for it! No, girl, no indeed. I shall tell Verluccus that the next time he is struck by anyone he must strike back. Then when his assailant is proclaimed a hero he may be entitled to the honour.'

'Don't be bitter, dear Gaius. I have never before known Father allow a slave to be abused by one of us. I am sure he does not know how serious this is. He too will insist that Quintus make amends when he sees Verluccus' poor face.'

Lucius did indeed insist that the apology be given. Verluccus tried to imagine Cunobarrus having an apology offered to one of the poor wretches he had kept as slaves and found the task beyond him. He bowed gingerly and denied that he had suffered any real harm, though the evidence against Quintus was plain for all to see.

The shortest day came and went, and the family honoured the rebirth of the sun. It was time for Lucius to return to Glevum, where the veterans would be holding their annual parade to rededicate the altars and renew their vows to the emperor Trajan.

Gaius, he decreed, must go too and resume his schooling, if only to keep him from getting into mischief. The threat of snow which had so concerned the mothers had turned out to be nothing more than a light dusting, and that had quickly disappeared to be replaced by a crisp frost that made the track firm underfoot.

The old warhorse Ravus drummed along the track in pursuit of Cervus as if he too were a colt. Well to the rear the bigarum rumbled, bearing Hardalius and Verluccus, who ensured that the reins were in his safe hands. Between these two there was no ill feeling but no conversation either, as Hardalius stuck rigidly to the rules of the house and would speak only Latin or Greek, both languages he was very proud to be literate in.

The chariot was left far behind and Gaius on Cervus had gone so far ahead that no one witnessed the accident. They rounded a bend and came upon Lucius struggling to free himself from the fallen Ravus.

'He's dead; get him off me,' Lucius complained as the shocked slaves approached him.

The two heaved and struggled with the dead weight until Lucius was freed and mercifully discovered that nothing was broken.

'Did someone attack you?' Hardalius asked, looking around nervously.

'No, I expected too much of the poor old thing, should have retired him years ago.' Lucius was on his feet surveying the carcass when Gaius, noticing the sudden lack of drumming hooves behind him, returned to find the cause.

'What happened? Father, are you all right?' He could see that he was, though the horse was done for. Lucius was still dazed from his fall. 'Yes, I'm fine,' he assured his son. 'I should have realized; poor old brute. I have had him for far too long, and expecting him to race that colt of yours was asking too much. Send Verluccus back to the farm to get it shifted. I shall continue in the chariot. Don't fuss, Gaius. I have suffered no harm whatsoever. Be sure he does not give cause for alarm to your mother.' He dusted himself down and looked at his loyal old horse sadly. 'I have no doubt, you know, he was happy the moment he died. In his younger days he would certainly have given Cervus a run for his money.'

Resuming his lessons without the assistance of Felix was hard. Verluccus was of no use whatsoever to Gaius in this respect, unless carrying his books and writing tablets could be considered useful. What made life more difficult was that the boys who had mocked his slave when he was chained and imprisoned now demanded to see what kind of a warrior he was and wanted to have fights arranged for their entertainment. Remembering his father's explicit direction on Verluccus possessing weapons, he could only refuse. His friends could not understand his reluctance, especially as even the veterans expressed their interest in such an event, particularly the soldiers who had participated in guarding him. Even Verluccus was baffled by his refusal, pointing out that even if weapons were forbidden he would happily wrestle with bare hands against any man they put up.

He was sitting outside the schoolroom where Gaius had said he should wait for him, idly watching the people passing by with more than half a hope that one of them might be his brother Tanodonus, when a familiar voice interrupted him.

'The master wants you.' Hardalius was standing next to him and used one of the few phrases he had become familiar with. But

Hardalius meant Lucius, who was observing him from within the basilica.

Lucius had diligently cleared a backlog of demands and petitions and now considered that some personal amusement was due to him. He was in the company of the elder Calpurnius and some other men Verluccus did not know; they all seemed to be in a rare good humour, and he had the feeling they had been discussing him. He went to Lucius quickly and bowed warily. Something was afoot.

After a few unintelligible words to him in Latin, Lucius gave up. 'You barely understand a word I say!' he said in the British language.

'I must seem very stupid to you, master.'

'Stupid? No, I don't think you are that. I blame my son for this state of affairs. However, that is not what I want you for today. My friend Calpurnius Drusus here thinks you could give us a show. I, however, think that you make more than a show of us already.' He paused to allow his friends to enjoy his joke. 'Let me make this clear to you: no fighting and no wrestling. Is that clear enough to you?'

'Yes, my lord.'

'Good. Now there is another matter which you must attend to. Thanks to you, I am now in need of a horse.'

He could think of nothing to say. He knew exactly what was meant. He stood dumbly, his face hot with shame, and wondered not how it was that Lucius knew of his curses but why he treated them so lightly. Calpurnius, standing a little beyond him, was enjoying the situation very much. 'I said a lot of things when I was angry. Believe me, I did not think this would come to pass.' He supposed, rightly, that the soldiers had passed the titbit on to Lucius.

'You rained curses down upon me and my family. Do not attempt to deny it. I have it on excellent authority. No, not from my son. Your master would not betray your shameful behaviour to me. You shouted your curses so loudly that not only those within the fortress but the whole town could hear you. Now you are called to account and must make amends.'

He was clearly relishing Verluccus' discomfiture.

'What is required of me?'

'The least you can do is replace that which you have deprived me of.'

Since the slave was now at a total loss to see how he could do such a thing, Lucius took pity on him. 'My friend Calpurnius persuades me that all you Brits are good judges of horseflesh. What experience do you have in this regard? Can I entrust you to pick out a decent mount to replace Ravus?'

What experience? He thought of the years he had spent slaving away in his brother's stables. Cunobarrus had derisively styled him his master of the horses. 'I was master of horse to Cunobarrus,' he answered. 'I know a little.'

They were obviously impressed by this – far more than they had any right to be.

'It comes down to these two,' said Lucius, leading him to the market horse lines where the dealer was patiently awaiting his decision. 'The decurion and I are of different minds and would welcome an expert opinion.' It was impossible to tell whether he was being sarcastic.

They were both fine animals. He reckoned they were eight years old. Both were geldings, very tall and suitable for riding. One might have been the mirror image of Cervus, as red as polished copper with a jet-black mane and tail; the second horse was almost pure white. He doubted Lucius would choose such a showy animal; he suspected that he would prefer to take the one which so well matched Cervus.

He took his time, hoping that Lucius would be pleased with the care he took but sure that the red was the one he must recommend. There was no fault to be found with either; it was purely a matter of taste.

'May I ride them?'

That, he discovered, was expected of him.

'Well?' demanded Lucius when he had tried them both. 'What do you say? Which is your choice?'

'The white one.' He spoke with firm certainty; he had no doubt about it – not now that he had ridden them both. There was something about the red which was more than mere spirit; he had experienced a feeling when he was seated on it which had sent shivers up his spine. When he dismounted, he went to look it in the eye to see if he might have imagined it, and probably he had. But he knew that this was an animal he would never trust.

Lucius and his companion laughed as if that were the decision they had expected of him. A coin was exchanged. 'Now, boy, you owe me even more. I bet Calpurnius you would not have the impudence to offer me that showy grey. Why do you deny me the red? What objection do you have to one that would be a match for Cervus? Perhaps you do not wish to see me outride my son?'

'He has a hard mouth,' he said, giving an answer which was more adequate than the truth.

Lucius tried both horses. 'His mouth is not so hard. I've known worse,' he announced, still favouring the red.

'I think he is unsound.'

'Hard in the mouth one moment and now unsound? I did not notice any unsoundness about him.'

'I experienced something I cannot name when I rode him. I think he would be treacherous,' he told Lucius finally, having his suspicion forced out of him.

'You think him treacherous! But I *know* you to be treacherous,' Lucius pointed out levelly. 'And yet I tolerate you around my house. I even entrust my eldest son to you. The red horse you say is dangerous and warn me of it. Why should I not suppose that it is the white which is a dangerous animal and that you would put me in the saddle of something which would try to kill me?'

'My lord, I am not treacherous,' he replied vehemently. 'I did say things against you when I was in anger, it is true. Are you really surprised that at first I resisted what appears to be my fate? That anger should be my reaction to being captured and returned to you? I have made my promise to your son, and it was truly meant and will be kept; you need not consider me a danger in your household. You did me the honour of asking my opinion about something which is important to you, and I have given it honestly. I have said the white, because it is the better horse and one which I would choose for myself. Buy the red if you will, but I beg you not to allow my master on it.'

Lucius studied him for a while. There was no doubt of his sincerity. He made his decision quickly. 'The white it will be.'

Gaius, when he discovered this, was delighted. 'Now that you have seen for yourself how good Verluccus can be, can you not soften a little more towards him?'

'I have never denied he can be useful. I just do not think you are realistic about what use he is best put to. He has learned nothing of our language beyond a few essential phrases. Do you give him instruction? No, I thought not. And incidentally,' he added wryly, 'I have no confidence in his assertion that the red horse is dangerous, but he forbade me to allow you to ride it if I bought it and so that was that.'

Gaius put his arms around his father and hugged him; it was a long time since he had done so. 'And that, Father, is why I love you. I know you don't think half as badly towards him as you pretend.'

Candidus, the shining one, as he was promptly named, performed beautifully and demonstrated a satisfactory turn of speed, so Lucius had no regrets whatsoever about his decision. In any case, it was too late to change his mind now, for Calpurnius promptly bought the red gelding for young Drusus. Lucius felt a cautionary word to Gaius was called for. He wanted no repetition of the incident when, almost as soon as he was given Cervus, Gaius and some other youngsters had raced their horses through the streets of Glevum, causing great anger among the townsfolk and bringing irate citizens with claims for compensation to his door. Gaius assured his father that he had learned his lesson and such behaviour would not be repeated.

Gaia was laughing, laughing aloud. It was a full and hearty laugh; it was good to hear it: at last he had made her happy. He glowed with pleasure at the part he had played in this. It was as if he were seeing the goddess Epona come to earth.

She was at the farm gate sitting astride Candidus before her audience of parents, brothers, and slaves and demonstrating what a beautifully behaved horse it was. Verluccus was holding Cervus' bridle to restrain his jealousy that so much attention should be meted out to the newcomer. Aelia had an arm protectively around Quintus, while Felix hovered in the background with Palatus and Delia. Lucius and Gaius were standing side by side, watching indulgently as the girl, barefoot and legs bared from where her gown was caught up, her hair struggling free from its bindings, was parading before them all on Candidus, trotting and walking the horse with a masterful hand.

Lucius turned to his wife and informed her fondly, 'I shall have to divorce you, Aelia. You have raised my youngest daughter to be a ruffian, and no man will marry her now.'

'Let's see what he can really do!' Gaia called out, turning the horse away from them. 'I'll race you to the top of the hill, Gaius!'

Her brother dashed to take Cervus' bridle and remount him, but their father stopped him. 'No, I don't want you racing against her, son. Verluccus, you take Cervus and see that my girl comes to no harm.'

He needed no second instruction. 'Some Latin he understands more readily than other,' Lucius dryly observed as Cervus thundered in the direction taken by Gaia.

She took the sheep track, trees crowded overhead, and he had to duck to avoid them as his determined mount pursued its rival. The girl in front of them was quite fearless, an excellent rider, urging her horse forwards without hesitation. He supposed she must have learnt to ride as a child alongside her brother, but since he had never before seen her on the back of an animal, he supposed that such things were no longer considered appropriate behaviour for her.

On the hilltop she paused to give the animal a breather, and turning to greet the one who followed, she saw that it was not her brother but Verluccus. The disappointment was plain in her face. She reined Candidus back and allowed him to reach her.

'I heard Cervus behind me, but I supposed Gaius to be on his back. I should have known I could not keep so far ahead of anyone but a slave. Why have you come?'

He was apologetic. 'Your father thinks you need protection.'

'From what?' she asked coolly, clearly annoyed that her fun was spoiled. 'Wild animals? Robbers? I think in that case he has sent the wrong protector!'

She was instantly sorry for what she had said and told him so. He said there was no need – she spoke the truth; he was the only robber for miles around. But he had given all that up now and hoped she would try to forget the crimes he had committed in the past.

She indicated that they ought to move the horses forward; Candidus was sweating and must not catch cold. She told Verluccus how beautiful the horse was, and he agreed, delighted that in this way he had given her so much pleasure. He wondered if it would be acceptable to her to say how beautiful she was and what a fine rider but knew he must not and so held his tongue.

'You should canter Cervus beside me,' she granted. 'I think he does not care for being left behind.'

She rode to the edge of the hill and waved to the people standing below. 'They look tiny, don't they? My father, such an important man, and yet to any bird who flies up here he must seem to be no bigger than a worm.'

For some reason, for it was not a particularly funny thing to say, they began to laugh – to laugh together, sharing an intimacy which was unspoken. She was so easy in his company, so unafraid of him, that he knew she no longer held the killing of Virens against him, even if she had no more feelings towards him than towards any slave of the household. He longed to touch her there and then, to put his arms around her and to kiss her. He wondered if he alone from the household felt this way towards her; if others did not, then why not? And if they did, then how did they cope? He told himself it was not the inevitable consequences he would suffer that prevented him from action but the terror he would create in her.

She had not noticed anything untoward. She was busy with the horse and the view surrounding them, oblivious to the feelings he was experiencing at that moment. And fortunately for them both, Cervus' antics and desire to race precluded any danger of physical contact.

He decided to be bold. 'I have something for you.' He had intended asking Gaius to give it to her, but now seemed an opportune moment. He reached into his tunic and withdrew the necklet from where he had pinned it. 'Your brother obtained the wire for me, and I have rethreaded the beads as they should be in the right order. Please take it.'

She looked at the necklet and then at him. The horses were not prepared to allow them close enough for him to pass it across.

'Verluccus,' she asked gently, 'do you really not mind my having it? Does it not pain you that it should be worn by the niece of the man who killed your wife?'

He knew that whether or not he minded was irrelevant. 'It belongs to you now. It was given to you by your uncle; please take it,' he tried to reassure her. 'The girl who wore it before you was not my wife. And you need not feel concerned; she was not killed by your uncle – nor by any Roman.'

The words he used might have been physical blows, so quickly the expression on her face changed. She shrank from him, drew Candidus further from him, repelled by what she had heard. She turned away without a word, kicking Candidus into a gallop. She charged across the hilltop, taking the scattered debris of the ancient roundhouses in skilful leaps, and without a pause plunged down the slope and through the trees with a recklessness which terrified him; he thought at first that the horse was bolting. Even with Cervus beneath him, he was hard pressed to come near to her. But on the trackway below she reined Candidus in and resumed a more dignified pace to canter back to her waiting parents. They asked her why she was crying, and she said that the wind had caught her eyes.

Whatever had upset her she kept to herself. Nobody acted towards him in any way differently, and the cool distance which she maintained between them was unremarkable. He secreted the beads under the floor of Gaius' room and decided to be wise and devote himself entirely to attending to and anticipating his master's wishes.

5

Much to Gaius' delight, Titus arrived unexpectedly; but the news he brought made Lucius frown.

'Calpurnius Drusus is speaking of a race. He has that red horse your father rejected. It is very fast; you should see it shift itself. You will take up the challenge?'

There was no question but that he would. Lucius sighed and shook his head and said he had best not tell his mother. Privately he was delighted with the news; for Gaius to have an interest beyond Verluccus was a welcome development. His only word of caution was that the race should not be through the town.

Only a few days later they had set the course. It was to be around the open and flat and very fast field used for chariot racing. Bonus, Titus' slave, made it quite clear that such a competition was of no consequence. Chariot racing, such as his master indulged in – now that was racing. His master, he assured Verluccus, was quite without fear. Nobody had such nerve as Titus Justinius in handling a quadriga. Verluccus acknowledged that he believed him. He was holding Cervus, leading him about and watching the other horse being led towards them.

'Pity about Agasus,' said Bonus, noticing that Verluccus was looking at a tall lad who was leading the red, now renamed Rex. 'He was crushed, killed, in the stable. It was an accident, of course; the boy must have been very stupid. Now Placidus is having to act as groom until Drusus can find a replacement. He is not at all happy about it. If Gaius wins the race, I expect Drusus will use Placidus' incompetence as an excuse for failure.'

The horsemen were mounted and quickly away. They disappeared from sight in a hail of clods thrown up by their hooves and with shouts of encouragement ringing in their ears. 'They have decided to extend the circuit and loop around beyond the trees so that they give the animals a longer run and have to jump some fallen logs; you can't do that with a chariot, but with the horses running free it's a good test,' Bonus translated a piece of information which was being passed around. 'They will do that twice. Is Cervus really as fit as he ought to be?'

'I've made sure that he is,' confirmed Verluccus with certainty. 'Have no doubt about that, and if you have any money to bet, put it on the right one.' Bonus and Titus assured him that they had.

'You don't remember me, do you?' The tall lad named Placidus was speaking to him. He admitted that he did not, but there was something familiar about him even so.

'It was thanks to you that I got a thrashing from Aelia Paula and from Victor and was sold to Calpurnius. Ah, I see you do remember me. It's hard to recognize you too. But I know you. You were once the little shit who ran away from Gaius. I'll bet Palatus is giving you a hard time, considering the punishment he was given too.'

'Palatus was thrashed? Because I ran away?' He did not know whether to be glad or sorry.

'No, stupid, not thrashed. He had to give up that slave girl Melissa to Cordatus. Oh, you would not know them either, would you? And it was not because you ran away but because of marking you. You still have that mark, don't you? You will always have that – unless Lucius sells you to someone who wants his own symbol upon you.' The young slave was bitter; he deeply resented the fact that he had been sold to Calpurnius and that after recapture Verluccus had achieved such a privileged position, which he thought should have been his. He held Verluccus responsible for all that had subsequently happened to him including his temporary demotion to stable hand.

Titus dragged Verluccus away. 'Bonus, tell him to ignore Placidus. I don't know what that was all about, but now is neither the time nor the place to settle old scores.'

Verluccus barely had time to digest the significance of what he had heard before shouts from the watchers indicated that the riders were in view again.

But there were no riders – just one horse and that riderless. It was a red horse, but no one could be sure which one. He found himself praying that it was not Cervus, and very shortly that prayer was answered as another shout heralded the sighting of Cervus, Gaius still aboard. He said a swift thanks to all the gods he had invoked and let others run after the loose animal, waiting instead for Gaius to reach him.

They found the body without much searching. Drusus was lying under the trees where he had been swept from the horse's back, the cuts and bruises from branches plain for all to see. Gaius was shaking his head in disbelief, in bewildered shock. He tried to tell them what had happened. He had thought Drusus was taking a shortcut, cheating; he had veered off course and into denser forest. Until then they had been neck and neck, though within the woodland Gaius had been keeping Cervus in check, not wanting him to have his head on the uneven ground. He had supposed Drusus had beaten him home, and he was going to accuse him of cheating and demand a second race. He had not wanted this – not Drusus dead.

The frightened boys consoled him while someone went to find Calpurnius and break the news to him and to fetch a board to carry the dead boy home. It was just an accident, they tried to tell Gaius; it could as easily have been him lying there.

Verluccus was sure it was no accident; he had no doubt whatsoever. Calpurnius Drusus had chosen to cut under the trees to take a shortcut. He recalled the sensation he had experienced when he sat on the animal himself, and his thoughts went to Gaia and her mad dash down the hillside, how Candidus had leapt piles of stones and fallen trees without a pause and how she had ducked and tunnelled her way through the swinging branches, taking the straightest course rather than the winding track. A sweat broke out on his brow as he contemplated what might have been if Lucius had stubbornly refused his advice and bought the one they called Rex instead. He sent up a silent prayer of thanks to the man for putting his trust in him.

There was nothing suspicious about Rex. It quietly allowed itself to be led away by a sobbing Placidus. Calpurnius had arrived and was in a state of shock and disbelief, and the boys were standing impotently around their lifeless companion, awestruck by the calamity and unsure what next to do.

The sudden death was a sobering experience for them all. At the inquest it was decided that the fatality was accidental, but Gaius knew that not only Calpurnius but also his own father would hold him responsible for the boy's death. He even heard Lucius sigh that poor Calpurnius now had no son, no heir, not even a daughter to his name; and he thought how much less it would have pained his own father had it been he who had died and not Drusus, for Lucius would still have had an heir in Quintus and two daughters. Gaius would allow no one to console him and said that the fact that he disliked Drusus intensely did not mean that he wished him dead, though many might think it. Verluccus could do nothing but wait and hope that in time reason would prevail. He seemed to be alone in blaming the animal for the death.

Lucius, in guilt-ridden belief that he might have prevented the disaster, now stated his intention of buying the animal himself in order to remove the painful sight of it from his dear friend. In desperation, Verluccus sought out Bonus and begged him to recruit the assistance of Titus. 'Get your master to inquire deeper about this animal, I beg you,' he said. 'I know the horse was at fault, but no one will listen to me.'

He heard nothing more. He would not leave Gaius' side again. Some days later, however, Lucius sent for him, and reluctantly he attended.

'When I first was told that you had been putting it about that the horse was guilty of a crime, I thought, *Preposterous native superstition.*' Lucius raised a hand. 'Be silent. I know – a clumsy stable lad was crushed. That is of no significance. However, young Titus Justinius has come to me with information – you even have the gall to send your betters on errands – which changes my whole perception of this incident. I do not see how it could have been known to you, but it appears that the accident with which its previous owner met and which put the horse on the market was identical to that experienced by Calpurnius Drusus. The animal carried its rider under low branches to unseat him and then kicked him to death. You told me that the red was treacherous.' Lucius uttered his admission reluctantly. 'How you knew that I do not understand, but on your advice I did not buy it; had I done so, that tragedy would not have happened. Calpurnius Drusus would still be alive. The tragedy, however, would have been in my family. My daughter rode Candidus. Had I bought the red one, she would no doubt have done likewise with unthinkable consequences. For that I am indebted to you. I just want you to know that.'

He nodded to the slave, who now had relief written across his face. 'I have bought the animal from Calpurnius to save him further pain and already given instructions that it is to be destroyed. You may inform my son of this. The news may assuage his grief somewhat.'

Verluccus had his hand on the door handle before it struck him that never again might he have such an opportunity to raise with Lucius an issue that was troubling him.

'Master, may I ask you something?'

'A reward? I suppose so; you do deserve something.' He turned, beckoning a slave to bring his cash box.

'Not so much a reward as – I heard something from Placidus which puzzles me. May I ask if he once belonged to you?'

Lucius confirmed the truth of this.

'I have always thought – that is, I know it was Palatus who burned me, but I have always believed it was at your command. It seems that the hatred I bore towards you, which always centred on that action and on my abduction, may have been misplaced. I may be a slave, but that does not mean I need be unjust. Will you please tell me the truth of it?'

It was a humbling experience for Lucius. He looked regretfully at Verluccus for a long time, and then he invited him to come into the room again. As it was not possible for the slave to sit in his presence, he rose and walked to the window. 'Did Placidus tell you also that I had Palatus punished for what he did? Yes? The truth is something which I did not wish you to know, and I thought I had made sure it would not become known to you.' He broke off, wondering about the wisdom of continuing, and then decided the truth was probably necessary.

'Your master was a sick child – dying, we feared. He had discovered you and wanted you and only you; and I, to this day, do not know why. Perhaps he can explain it, because it baffles me. At the point when it seemed he must die, when all remedies had failed, when the augurs said it must be so, I sent Palatus to buy you. I thought your parents would be glad of the money and to know that a son of theirs would have a home such as I could give him. Palatus managed to make a total mess of the enterprise and then added greater damage by – by that injury he did to you. If, on discovering it, I seemed angry, it was with Palatus, not with you. Running away as you did was a most foolish act. You can see now how your life might have been as Gaius' dear companion. Yes, as a slave but close within the family, educated and loved as if a son. Now you know the truth. I forbade your being told it for fear you would harm Palatus; as you now know, I punished him at the time, and in my household it is I who decide to whom and how punishment is given. I will not allow you to wreak any kind of revenge on that good servant.'

'Then you admit it? I was stolen and not bought? I should not be a slave?' It seemed to him a simple truth.

'I admit nothing of the sort. You are conveniently forgetting your crimes. But for my son's intervention, you would have been put to death in the arena by now. Instead you are condemned to slavery – for life.' He paused to ensure his words were clear. 'See, the situation is this: you belong either to my son, as I gave you to him, and you are of my household; or else you belong to the State and I must return you to my brother Marcus Marcius to be dealt with for your criminal past. Convince me I have no right to own you, and you go to Marcus Marcius without delay. I think on reflection you will agree that the former option is the more to be preferred?'

It was no more nor less than Coridumnus had said, but it hurt like a physical blow; for a moment his hopes had been raised again. When he had made his pledge to serve Gaius, he had made it unreservedly, expecting it to be a lifetime's duty. But this was a rude awakening to the reality of his commitment.

'Then I do have a favour to beg of you, master.'

Lucius heard him in silence. How he wished Verluccus had asked for something easier to grant. To refuse what must seem a simple reward from one to whom he was undoubtedly indebted must seem at the very least churlish parsimony. 'I cannot allow it, Verluccus,' he said finally. 'I can no more bear it now that your people should know what was done to you in my name than at the time when it was done. I have to forbid you any contact with them. Never again ask that you should have licence to visit them; forget you have any relationships beyond my household. It may be better for me to send Gaius to Rome and you with him now, before the rest of us, and remove you from this temptation. But I shall tell you this: I have Agricola's assurance that those people do not suffer hardship from your absence. Casual labour is always available to them when the harvest must be gathered. I see to it that they always get a fair price for what they sell, and they are not cheated by any tax farmer. More than that I cannot do. This is a discreet matter, of course; they are unaware of my patrimony. Return now to your master and tell him what I have told you about the horse. And let me hear no more whining from you about imagined injustice. I have shown you much kindness in speaking to you in this way; another master would have raised a stick at such effrontery.' He let Verluccus close the door behind him before he sat and put his head into his hands.

Gaius had to pay a penalty – at least it seemed to him to be a penalty; Lucius insisted on it. It was the intention of Calpurnius and his wife to sell up and move to Londinium. They could not bear to see their son's friends grow into men and know he would not be among them. Until they departed, Lucius would spare them the further pain of 'seeing Gaius strutting around on Cervus'. That was how his father put it. Cervus must be sent down to the farm, and Gaius must make do without him.

6

Lucius invited Gaius to bring friends to his home to enjoy a boar hunt. Boar were now so plentiful that they were becoming a nuisance. Titus Justinius; Tribune Publius Antonius; and a boy who had been a closer friend of Drusus than of Gaius, Gnaeus Petronius, came. So did Cloelius Draco and, for Aelia and Gaia's sake, Lydia and Cloelia.

Again Verluccus was excluded from the select slaves who accompanied the sportsmen. In view of what Lucius had said to him, he was not surprised. He consoled himself with discreetly observing Gaia as she and the other women amused themselves spinning and weaving and playing board games after their morning bathing. He wondered if Gaia had been told about Rex and his own part in protecting her, but she gave no such indication; in fact she remained towards him as distant and cool as the day he had offered the beads to her, choosing an alternative slave to retrieve a dropped counter or fetch refreshment when he could easily have supplied the service. When the men returned, of course he was needed by Gaius, though Lucius would not have him in the bath suite. He would gladly have dealt with the horses, but others were deputed to those tasks, so he tried to look useful even though he knew just how far he was from achieving that.

After four days Cloelius and his family departed with a variety of spoils, though the others stayed on. It was a tearful parting for Gaia from her friend, and an invitation was extended to her to visit Cloelia in the not-too-distant future, which she gladly accepted.

So successful had the hunters been that they decided not only to have mercy on the wildlife surrounding them but to allow the visiting slaves a holiday from labour. Bonus asked him whether there was any particular slave girl to whom Verluccus had attached himself so as not to tread on his toes. He received a blunt answer.

The young men exercised themselves with throwing balls from one to another in the pasture below the garden, and Verluccus, having opted out of the type of sport his fellow slaves were engaged in, had undertaken to provide any service the masters might demand. However, nothing more was required of him but to stand around on the terrace and await instructions. It was not such a tedious duty as it might have been, because with her companion having left, Gaia had sought other entertainment and had placed herself further along in the garden at a vantage point from which she could observe the activities in the field without being in plain sight of the young men. She was in Verluccus' view, however, and he could easily glance her way and enjoy that view without suspicion. He only wished she would demand some service of him in order that he might draw closer to her, fetch her a drink or something to eat, a wrap to place around her – though that would have detracted from the pleasure of seeing how the breeze drew her gown close to her body in a very interesting manner.

He was lost in these daydreams when Aelia's voice calling to her daughter roused him and he drew himself up. Aelia always made him feel inept and clumsy, and he tried very hard not to place himself in her way.

The girl below them had heard her name being called, but she was not ready to leave her amusement. For the first time she showed that she knew he had been watching her and placed her fingers to her lips for him not to give her away.

Aelia came upon him. 'Gaia?' she demanded. 'Do you know where my daughter is?'

He shook his head, hoping she might think he did not understand her, and she shook her fist at the uselessness of him.

The little cat, however, had been carried outside by its mistress and ignored when the athletes took her eye; now it heard the voice of one who paid it greater attention, provided it with a warm lap, and fed it more frequently. It ran mewing towards Aelia, and she looked in that direction to see what Verluccus must have been able to see all along: her daughter.

She also could see that her daughter had been watching the young men. She called out to them, and Gaius came running towards her. Verluccus watched her hiss angry words into her son's ear before snatching her daughter by the hand and marching her back into the house.

'You lied to my mother, Verluccus. I cannot have it. Not even for my sister's sake. You do not realize how fragile her toleration of you is. I have apologized to her on your behalf, but an apology from you too would be a good idea.'

He promised to rectify the matter as soon as he could and went for the drinks the young men required.

The opportunity for his apology came quite quickly. After their exercise, the young men elected to use the bath suite for a lazy afternoon. Verluccus was not required and could do whatever he pleased, he was told by his master, and he had in mind to visit Cervus and groom him. Titus, Petronius, and Gaius were sauntering in the direction of the baths unhurriedly. Lucius and Antonius had elected not to join them and were still in the house. Quintus, however, had decided to go too and was determinedly accompanying them but being ignored, as the three boys had more entertaining thoughts to share between themselves and were laughing and making crude jokes.

Suddenly Quintus was running ahead of them, triumphantly waving aloft a hunting knife which he had filched from Titus' belongings.

With great good nature, the knife's owner obliged him in a chase while his two companions lent vocal encouragement both to hunter and hunted as they circuited the garden. Quintus was on the point of being captured when, inspired by Mischief, as Titus afterwards put it, he threw the weapon as high and as far as he could. It winged through the air in a perfect arc and, as they watched, descended, embedding itself deep into the midden pile awaiting attention from the farm labourers.

There was only one present who could possibly be required to retrieve such an object from such a place.

'And when you have it, go and clean yourself. I do not need you while I am bathing,' Gaius happily informed him.

He retrieved the knife and was on his way to clean it and himself when he came upon Aelia. She appeared to be alone; he seized the moment.

'Lady, mistress.' He blocked her way and spoke his few carefully rehearsed words of apology.

Her reaction to this was extraordinary even for what he might have expected from Aelia. She began to scream. She stood stock still and opened her mouth and screamed and screamed and screamed. When footsteps ran towards them, she pointed to him, enraged. 'He has a knife; he threatened me. Lucius! Lucius! Gaius! Oh, where is that wretched son of ours?'

Victor quickly knocked him to the floor, and two men sat on him while they hastily bound him with whatever came to hand. The knife had been wrenched from his grasp and he lay before them all. Victor, pressing his foot upon his neck for good measure, wondered what he could have said or done to cause such a commotion.

'He tried to kill me! He came at me with a knife demanding that I apologize to him. For what I do not know! I always said he was unstable. I cannot have it, Lucius. I cannot have it!' The shaking woman was led away by her concerned husband and Gaia, who had come running to the scene.

'He is as good as dead now,' said Titus grimly to Gaius, as they too arrived haste from the bath house. 'Your mother is distraught. What possessed him?'

Gaius was mystified. 'Let him up, Victor, so I may question him.'

But Victor would not. 'With respect, Master Gaius, I will do the questioning. Your father will expect no less.'

He meant a flogging, possibly worse. Gaius went to plead his case.

He could explain Verluccus having the knife easily enough. The threat to his mother was harder to defend. But he did manage to persuade Lucius that he need not be beaten to be persuaded to tell the truth.

'It was just a misunderstanding, Father. I ordered him to apologize to Mother; ask Gaia if this is not so. She will vouch for what he did that day and why.'

'Only your useless slave could make such a poor attempt to speak Latin as to turn an apology into a threat,' his father told him when he had spoken to Gaia. 'I will talk to your mother, but she heard what he said and the manner in which he said it. How do you think she must have felt seeing him approach her with all that filth upon him and a knife in hand, demanding an apology? Any reasonable woman would have reacted as she did.'

She was lying down on the bed attempting to recover from the shock of it when Lucius returned to her.

'There was a time, you know, Aelia my treasure, when you would have laughed at such a thing as this. I do not believe the slave meant harm, but I will bow to you. You know as well as I do how much importance our son places upon him, and I do not believe the slave harbours ill will towards us. But if despite this you say he must go, I will sell him today.'

'I know, my darling. I feel so foolish now. I was taken by surprise; I should have taken into account that whatever Latin he used, it would be sure to be quite wrong. And our daughter is by no means blameless in this.' She scolded Gaia, who had come to beg on her brother's behalf. 'You must do what you think best, Lucius. I do not insist he be sold, but something must be done. He disgraces us all. If Gaius cannot or will not have him trained properly, then you must do so. If you will do that, I shall not demand more.'

'You agreed to my terms,' Lucius told his son, 'and now your debt is called in.' He raised his hand to silence the protest. 'You surrender Verluccus to me.'

'What do you intend?' Gaius was white-faced and fearful. He had tried all means of appeal, but his mother had said it was out of her hands now; his father would do what was best, and he should accept that. 'Is there nothing I can do or say to make you change your mind?'

'For you? Return to school. I know it is a waste of that good man's time, but it will keep you occupied and away from *him*. You can study the works of Vitruvius on architecture, the philosophical works of Cicero, and the Iliad again – Julius Caesar on the Gallic wars too, if it pleases you – and endeavour to improve your Greek, if nothing else. I shall supply the books. Antonius will divert you in your leisure time. The alternative is that I send Verluccus away from here – to Corinium perhaps.'

'No, no. Please. I'll go to school. Don't send him away if you have some alternative in mind.'

'For him, yes: proper training to become useful and worth something.'

'You mean to sell him?' Gaius felt sick.

'That is up to you. Any more trouble from you, yes. And any at all from him, yes to that too.'

'May I speak to him?'

'Only Latin. He has to learn. If you had made a little more effort in that respect, this situation would not have arisen.'

'There is one good thing about it,' said Gaius, trying to make the best of the situation. 'At least Cervus will be properly looked after. Verluccus can exercise him until Calpurnius is gone.'

'It is not for you to say what he will be required to do, Gaius, but you can forget any idea of his exercising Cervus. I have forbidden him contact with the natives, and he knows why. Victor and Palatus will devise a regime for him, and that may include cleaning out the stables; it may send him onto the land to work the plough. It is no concern of yours. I suggest that when our guests depart tomorrow you go with them. I see no point in prolonging your pain. Enjoy the company of Titus while you can. Antonius tells me he soon will be enlisting in the army; he has a promising future. There is a young man who respects his father and follows in his footsteps.'

There was no point in arguing about it further. He went to his mother and kissed her and thanked her for being so understanding. Verluccus would be no trouble to her whatsoever. She would soon appreciate him as much as he did.

'I doubt very much if that will be so,' said Lucius. 'In any case your mother will be absent for some time. Marcia is almost due to have her child, and I am taking Aelia to Corinium to assist her. I am not forbidding you to return home from time to time to assure yourself that all is as it should be, but the house will be in good hands.'

'I shall be running the house, Gaius,' his sister told him. 'Please remember that.' She smirked, relishing the rare prospect of power.

'Yes, I am leaving Gaia in charge here. Palatus will not let her down. Gaia is to come to Corinium only after the baby is safely delivered.' Aelia did not think it a good thing for the girl to witness the horrors of birthing. 'The experience will be good for your sister, since we hope it is not too long before she has a household of her own.'

Lucius firmly denied Gaius further use of Verluccus. He was locked in a room at the farmhouse for the night and not allowed out until his master had departed. Gaius hoped the few words he had managed to convey to him were understood. He had to admit that his father certainly had a point.

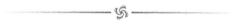

There was no point in Aelia delaying her departure. The winter had so far proved to be quite uncharacteristically mild in that there had been no substantial snow, though the frosts had often been so heavy that the landscape was quite frequently glittering and white. But a heavy fall of snow would certainly block the road to Corinium.

She was wrapped in furs and the warmest garments obtainable, and provided with a heated brick, and packed into the carriage Lucius had acquired especially for her together with half a boar and a number of other home-made delicacies. Accompanying her were not only her husband and his Hardalius and her own Chloe but also Quintus and Felix. To expect Gaia to cope with the child she deemed was unfair, and in any case he would be able to play happily with his little nephew Julius.

'The master has permitted me to tell you this much in the British tongue so that there will be no excuse of misunderstanding,' Palatus told him. He had Victor beside him and Agricola also for good measure. The steward was still apprehensive of Verluccus' sentiments towards him, but Lucius had reassured him that he need fear nothing; and if there was any problem whatsoever, Victor had his full authority to deal with it, sparing no deserved punishment, even death. He did not, however, expect on his return to hear a catalogue of trivial complaints. The slave must be given a proper chance to become a useful member of the household, and minor transgressions should either be overlooked or dealt with judiciously and fairly.

'You will continue to sleep in master Gaius' chamber until I'm instructed differently. You will rise before the sun and leave it in a tidy condition. Fetch water for the house from the spring. Report then to Victor. He will send you with milk to the cook for the cheese making. The cook will give you whey to take to the nursing women, infants, and any sick slaves. After that you will do whatever Victor requires for himself or for Agricola. He will decide if and when you eat. After midday you report to me for domestic instruction, duties around the house, and I must try to teach you Latin. May the gods help me. When you retire to your bed at night, you may continue to make yourself useful while your master is absent by using whatever energy you may have left in increasing his household.' Palatus actually chuckled. 'Have you any questions?'

He held his tongue and shook his head. Palatus walked away, and he was left with Victor and Agricola. He needed to be on good terms with the farm manager, as he was his only link with his family.

But Agricola addressed him first, still in his own tongue, almost apologetically. 'Look, I know what Palatus said –'

Verluccus interrupted vehemently. 'That I will not do! I will not get more slaves for them! That I will not do!' He was seething with anger.

'You are mistaken,' Agricola said hurriedly. 'I was not talking about that, and you do Palatus an injustice; I am sure he meant it as a kindness. No, what I was going to say is I do not think I can find suitable work for you on the farm at the moment. The work of the farm slaves is hard and dirty. Palatus will expect you to be clean when you report to him. Can I trust you to keep yourself out of trouble until you are due to return to Palatus? Victor will be working the men on the land.'

He was amazed. 'Agricola, I am not afraid of hard work; farm work is something I do know and can do well. There must be something which I can turn my hand to. Just tell me what you require and leave me. You may trust me to work without supervision.'

'Well.' Agricola scratched his head doubtfully. 'There is something. Down by the stream there is a tree which the autumn storms brought down. It's fairly dammed up the water. I have it in mind to cut it up for the fuel stack, but I haven't yet had a man to spare for it. See what you can do with that. You will need an axe and a saw and some baskets to fetch it in.' He led him to the tool store. 'I am putting you on trust to go no further than where the tree lies. The master has warned me that I am not to allow you any contact with the natives, so if any approach, you must drive them away. And no matter how much you have shifted, when the time comes, do not be late reporting to Palatus.'

'That's enough,' Victor intervened. 'He should know what he's here for by now. Set to work.'

It was a colossal tree, a beech, and it had partially dammed the stream where it had fallen so that a pool had formed and diverted water gurgled noisily through a narrow runnel. The roots, dislodged from the ground by a combination of badger activity and the loosening of soil by storm water running off the steep bank, were now starkly exposed and stood higher up the bank than its branches – an upside-down tree. The absence of its canopy had already been taken advantage of although it was but January, and wild vegetation had begun creeping into the lighted space. The tree had been damaged and not merely by the fall; several branches had already been attacked by someone – possibly even his own brother, he thought, gloomily surveying it and wondering about his sudden enthusiasm for hard work. The task was enormous; the tree was not only tall but wide too, and now limbs which once branched horizontally were vertical, stretching high above him.

Victor, seeing him heading for the stream, had followed and now watched until he was satisfied that work was genuinely being done. Then he left him to it and went to drive the less enthusiastic to their labours.

Verluccus quickly developed a routine, taking one limb at a time and reducing that into portable loads which he then shouldered and delivered to build a new stack of green wood at the farm.

He was hailed on one such journey by Victor, who called to him to eat, and a dish of stewed meat and vegetables was thrust into his hands. He could have eaten twice as much, but he had barely finished it when he was told, 'To Palatus with you; clean yourself first,' and shortly afterwards reported to the steward.

When he finally returned to his room, he found that he was not alone. A young slave girl was waiting for him, clean and sweet smelling. In any other circumstances he would have welcomed her. He tried not to take his anger out on her. 'Go, Vernia,' he said, hoping he did not seem too unkind. 'I do not want you.'

That night he dreamed of limbs and of branches and of twigs and of leaves and of trees crashing down on him. He felt the pain as he was struck and woke in horror to find Victor standing over him prepared to wield his stick for a third time.

He derided himself. *I have grown so soft! There was a time when no one would have come upon me in my sleep and taken me unawares. Now after one day's work I am so exhausted I cannot even rise.* He delivered the water and milk as expected and left hastily for the tree, anxious not to incur further wrath from Victor.

'Where is Victor?' a frowning Gaia demanded of the stable hand tending to Cervus. He pointed to where men were spreading dung onto the fields. She could not see Verluccus among them. Agricola was not in the farm; from the girl who lived with him she discovered he had gone to Glevum market with some calves.

The sense of concern she had felt when Palatus reported that Victor had beaten Verluccus for failing to rise was intensifying. Palatus had dutifully recorded the fact for her father's benefit, but as temporary mistress of the house, she had received the report. Palatus was scrupulously correct in his behaviour towards her; he felt that the standard she would one day expect in her own home would reflect on him. But he was not nearly as concerned about the whereabouts of one particular slave as was she. Suppose he had run away? The beating from Victor might have been enough to make him do that. The feeling that she had let her parents down so badly and so quickly was overwhelming.

'Do you know Verluccus? Know where he is?' she asked Agricola's girl, who shrugged and pointed down the hill, from where the sound of a saw came.

She experienced a sense of relief. Of course there would be others working with him; there was no need for further concern. She allowed the girl to lead her inside and display the cloth she had been weaving. It was well done, and she praised the girl and promised she would tell her father what a good worker she was. There were other girls within working at looms, and she found it necessary to comment favourably on all of their work before she was shown to the door.

The sound of sawing had ceased; all had gone quiet. She again wondered if she should be concerned. Then she saw him; he was striding towards the wood store with a basket of logs. It was only relief, she told herself, that feeling which took her breath yet illogically warmed and comforted her so that she suddenly found herself smiling; it was only relief that he was still where he should be. She did not speak to him but returned to the house to ensure the kitchen staff were working as they should.

She told herself not to be a coward. She told herself it was her responsibility, her duty. Agricola was at the market; Victor was supervising the field hands. She could send Palatus down there. No, that would not be appropriate. She called for Delia to bring her warm cloak to her; she would have to go down and see for herself that he was not shirking.

He heard the approach of footsteps lighter than Victor's. No one could walk silently through the mess of leaves and twigs, and the women made no attempt to do so. The bright green gown she was wearing seemed to flare like a torch beneath the dullness of her cloak. Verluccus, sweating freely from his exertions, had pulled off his tunic, and it hung on a convenient bough. He had resisted the temptation to remove his woollen trews as well, and now he was exceedingly thankful for that foresight.

He continued working, and she stood in silence, approving the growing pile.

'I think we should rename you Hercules,' she finally observed.

He was very wary; always he seemed to upset her. 'By Hercules' was an oath Lucius often used and meant nothing more to him than that. He smiled politely but continued working.

'He lived a long time ago; he was very strong, and he had to perform twelve very laborious tasks.' She was very careful only to speak Latin.

He paused and smiled again, nodded, and turned back to his own labours.

'Help me up there.' She was indicating the broad, smooth trunk bridging the stream. He looked at Delia for guidance and, at her shrug, offered his hand to Gaia.

It needed slightly more than a mere hand to assist her. He had the great pleasure of lifting her by the waist until she was secure. She scrambled into a comfortable position and studied him. It was increasingly difficult to concentrate on work in such circumstances.

Suddenly as he was lowering his axe she screamed, and he saw the flash of brown as the little cat Orca darted at play among the tangle of wood below him. It had followed its mistress secretly from the house and had just revealed itself. It scampered free and ran along the trunk to the safety of Gaia's arms.

That night his nightmare consisted of his chopping the cat into pieces. He could see it clearly as he lowered his axe again and again, and though he wished to halt its fall he was helpless to prevent it. Gaia was there, screaming at him to stop. He woke with a start, and when the first birds called, he rose.

Agricola said that it was not necessary. Her father trusted him implicitly, Lucius had left him in charge of the farm, and she need not concern herself. Her mother never questioned him; her mother never saw the need to accompany him around the farm. When she was married, her husband would not expect it of her. Victor assured her that all of the slaves were working satisfactorily and that Verluccus was doing a really good job on the tree.

Palatus advised them to let her amuse herself. Her level of interest would wane if they did. If they tried to dissuade her, she would prove as stubborn as her brother and complain about them to her parents. They took his advice, and Agricola wasted precious time conducting her around the farm and explaining its activities to her until finally – it seem to her finally – there was nothing left to tell her about but the source of fuel. He explained that for the time being a tree was being dismembered. She must see for herself, she told him, as if she had not been down the previous day. Of course she could find it herself, she told him; Delia was with her. He must go and continue with his own chores; she knew they must have been delayed through her interference.

Again Verluccus had removed his tunic. Sweat was glistening on his body from his exertions and running down his reddened face. For what he had done this seemed a harsh punishment. She wondered if he blamed her for it as she did herself.

'I have secured Orca in the house,' she announced, since he ignored her presence.

He paused from the sawing and said carefully that he was relieved. He feared he might hurt the creature. He felt her eyes studying him and wondered what it was that she wanted to say but dared not ask. He wondered if he ought to put his tunic on, if the sight of his body offended her, if it was to do with the necklet, and why that had upset her so.

'I should like to sit up there.' She pointed to a broad, smooth bough bridging the water. That was a command he was happy to comply with. He swung her from her feet and placed her near to where he was working. Delia made no such request but chose one of the grounded branches and took the opportunity to close her eyes.

There was no need to do noisy sawing or chopping for a while; he took pity on Delia and dropped to the ground in order to load his basket.

'Come here. Come up here, Verluccus. I want you to see something.' Gaia beckoned to him, half turning away, looking into the water.

'I have to work, mistress; Victor keeps count of how much wood I take each day. Do you want me to get a beating?'

'When I bid you come here, you come here!' Her voice sharpened; she sounded ominously like her mother. 'I want you to catch this fish for me.'

He doubted that there was a fish. How angry was she likely to become, he wondered, if he refused to play whatever game she wanted? He decided it was too risky to upset her yet again.

He leaned across the trunk and gazed into the water where she had indicated, seeing no movement.

'There: what is that if not a fish?'

It was nothing but a stone. He told her so and began to raise himself.

Something cool and firm that could only be her hand was in the centre of his back, pressing him to be still. He felt the surge of blood and heat in his head and groin at her touch. He held his breath, wondering what to do. His heart began to pound more quickly than from the exertion of wood cutting, and he felt again that pleasurable ache drawing upon his mouth and the movement of a part of him which he could not halt. He found a voice.

'Please don't do that; I am filthy. Let me up.'

'Verluccus, these marks on your back. Someone once gave you a terrible beating. Who did this? This has not been done since your return to us. Was that too done by Palatus? Did my uncle do this to you?'

He had forgotten that the evidence of Merriol's assault upon him might even now be visible. He turned, rising towards her as he did so, and his face brushed past her cheek, his lips near to hers. He jerked back, clear of her and of all danger of putting into action that which he most sorely desired to do.

'Gaia Marcia!' It was Delia's horrified voice. A small log struck him, and he deflected it to the ground to join it himself a moment later. He helped Gaia down. She was annoyed with Delia for her interference. She shrugged away the woman's concern.

'I want to know, Verluccus. Did my uncle do that to you?'

He resorted to his own tongue. 'No, no, it was long ago. Not Palatus or your uncle.' He resigned himself to having to tell her. 'I belonged to an old woman; it was she who did it. I had behaved very badly.'

'I want to know. Tell me.'

'Verluccus must do his work, mistress,' chided Delia. 'It is not fair of you to interrupt it as you do. He will get another thrashing, this time from Victor.' She wanted to remove her mistress as rapidly as possible.

'Yes, of course.' Large brown eyes looked at him with regret. He felt turmoil inside him. 'Tonight you must tell me. After dinner, instead of talking with Palatus, you shall talk to me.'

He would have to tell her – have to tell her something. If Gaius had asked, he would have refused him, and Gaius would have allowed it to drop. But Gaia would not; refusing to tell Gaia something could spell unwelcome trouble. He suspected that if she was crossed or thwarted in any way she could be as volatile as her mother. Deciding what to tell her preoccupied his mind for much of the afternoon; he was grateful that his task, routine cleaning around the house, was undemanding.

But before the evening came Delia sought him out and drew him aside.

'You have really upset my mistress now,' she accused him. 'Now she is refusing to marry Decimus Aemilius Glaucus. It is all your doing.'

He laughed. He laughed aloud, supposing her to be joking, loving the crazy idea that Gaia should prefer him to the unknown Aemilius Glaucus. But Delia was not laughing. She was perfectly serious.

'You are not joking, are you?' he asked. He experienced a sudden dryness in his mouth. She shook her head in answer, her features grim.

He was mystified. 'How can I possibly be accountable for this? I have not seen her since this morning.'

'It was your behaviour, your conduct towards her. I had to warn her how dangerous it is for her to allow you to be so close. Now she is refusing to be married.'

'I see. You do not want me to come near her, to tell her about the stripes on my back? I am more than happy to stay away, but you will have to explain my absence.'

'Oh no,' said Delia. 'That is not it. On the contrary, come to her you must. You must persuade her to change her mind about marriage.'

'Don't be ridiculous, woman. I cannot do that. That is woman's work. Let Irene talk to her since her mother is not here.' He dismissed her with a gesture.

She would not go. 'You would have Irene know of what you did to her?'

He was stopped in his tracks. 'I did nothing.' These women were dangerous.

'I saw you kiss her – or at least try to. Had I not been there, you would have. You, a filthy slave, kissing, molesting my young lady! Do not deny that you wanted to do so. If you try to deny it, I have a gown of hers with your muddy sweat upon it which will say you did more. I will not hesitate to use it.'

'But Gaia will deny it. I did nothing to her. She would never claim I molested her. You are a stupid woman. Leave me alone.' He turned away, for once hoping that either Victor or Palatus would come upon them and complain he was shirking his work. Neither did.

Delia would not give up. 'That will cut no ice if she is refusing to marry. Her parents know how she loves her brother and what value he places on you. They will readily believe she denies it merely for his sake.'

He was defeated. 'What can you have said to persuade her against marriage on the basis of what took place today? I did nothing.' It was true that he had wanted to kiss her, he acknowledged privately, but Gaia had not been aware of it; he was far too subtle.

'It was my duty to warn her how dangerous you are, how vulnerable she is – of how alike are men and beasts.' Finally, because a silence had grown, she added, 'Perhaps I made it more than I needed to. But it's done now, and you must undo it.'

'Then you undo it,' he said. 'It's not for me to do. And why the hurry? She will change her mind by tomorrow when she has slept on it. The desire to be a wife is too strong in her.'

'I cannot take that risk. Her father may return home at any time. He only travelled to Corinium as company for Aelia. He might well be back in Glevum already. Gaius himself may come home. If she announces she will not be wed, I shall tell them the reason why; then you are done for.'

And that was not so hard to believe. He remembered how he had once horrified Gaius with his boastful intentions towards the girl. The boy might just be persuaded he had deceived them all and had now begun putting his threats into effect. 'Why are you so anxious she should be married that you would destroy me? What harm have I ever done to you? Or is it just that you are fearful you will be blamed for this damage?'

'When Gaia marries, she will make me free. Her father and mother did that with Cordatus and Irene. I know she will do likewise. She has as good as made me the promise,' said Delia.

Supposing that it was this particular young man whom Gaia must have some objection to, he felt great sadness for her. That Delia, who always seemed so loyal and loving towards her mistress, should be prepared to cast her into an unhappy marriage to a total stranger simply for her own ends was shocking to him. 'What is it you expect me to do?' he asked, resigned.

'Tonight after dinner I shall tell Palatus we have no need of him and send him away. He will be glad enough to go. Then you tell her what she wants to know about you, but make sure you are nice to her. Let her realize that her fears of you are unfounded.'

'Is that all? We are talking about the fears you have put into her head?' After the fuss she had made, it seemed so simple.

'You must talk to her about the difference between men and slaves. Bring her to see what is right and what is wrong – that when she comes to her husband, she must be chaste. If she seems afraid, explain how things are in marriage. Do it in such a way that will make her desire for it to come about.'

This was definitely women's work. He wondered what horrors Delia could have put into her mind.

'What has been done to you, Delia,' he mused, 'to make such a task beyond you?'

'It was a long time ago,' she said, 'before I came into this household.'

Gaia had continued to make use of the triclinium despite the absence of her family in order to 'maintain standards' as she put it to Palatus. Her only company was the freedwoman Irene, who was very frail and aged. She suffered even more greatly than Aelia from painful bones and ate very little. It was her habit to retire to her bed very early.

Palatus watched him assist Delia in serving the meal. Normally his part would have been to remove himself afterwards with the discarded dishes and not return, going elsewhere with Palatus for his Latin lessons; but tonight another boy was sent to remove the dishes, and Palatus withdrew shortly after Irene. As Delia had indicated, he seemed happy enough to leave Verluccus to practise his interesting version of Latin on their mistress.

Verluccus could detect no change in Gaia. If the situation was as Delia described it, she concealed it very well and behaved perfectly properly and coolly towards him, speaking with kind encouragement when she had to ask for something he had overlooked.

She told him he should sit on one of the nearer couches and commence his story, speaking in his own tongue with her permission.

She heard him in silence and growing wonder. He began the tale at a point after he had reached Merriol's home but glossed over the manner of his arriving there.

'Gaius does not know of this, does he?' All of her family believed Verluccus had been a warrior for much longer than he had – for most of the years of his absence from them. She felt somehow privileged by the revelation. Verluccus admitted Gaius did not know and asked her to respect his confidence. He had reached the point where he had received the injury and Merriol had wept for the pain she had caused to him.

Tears were streaming down Gaia's face.

'I did not mean to make you cry. I always seem to make you unhappy. Please do not cry.' He moved across to her and thoughtlessly put his hand out to touch her arm. It was slender and soft, decorated with bracelets. 'You must believe me,' he said. 'I would not harm you for the world.'

She raised her head, and her eyes, swimming with tears, searched his own for truth. 'Not me perhaps. What of that girl you killed? The one you robbed of her beads?'

'You thought I killed Bodyn? Why? I did not say that. Why do you believe I killed her?' He tried to remember what he had said which could have put such an idea into her head.

'You said no Roman killed her. You took her beads as a trophy.'

'No, no, it wasn't like that.' Without thinking of what he was doing, he wrapped his arms around her and held her close to him. 'It wasn't like you think. I will tell you if you wish, but it is not a pretty tale. Are you prepared to hear of violence and horror?'

If Delia was still in the room, they were unconscious of her. She nodded, steeling herself to hear a dreadful story.

'What Delia said is true then,' she said finally. 'Men do do horrible, terrible things.' She shuddered. 'I wonder if my mother would have had the courage of Elen.'

'Your mother, your family – you all are safe from such things.' He did not say, 'You are the Romans,' but she understood his meaning.

'I can understand now. I can understand why you joined up with those criminals, why you became like them. I can even understand why you killed Virens. Was it his men who did that dreadful thing?'

'No, no, I do not think that.' He would not reveal the name of the one he held responsible for it. Even at that moment he could not risk her betraying his intention to seek out and kill the one named Drusus. He had satisfied himself it was not the elder Calpurnius Drusus long since, and it certainly could not have been the younger.

His arms enfolded her tightly again, and he allowed his lips surreptitiously to caress the coils of her fragrant hair, it was soft, softer even than that of the kitten. He had known it would be so.

'I would never allow anyone or anything hurt you, Gaia Marcia.' He had never used her name directly to her before. 'I would die, gladly, to prevent harm coming to you.'

She said nothing, made no sound other than a sigh of contentment, and did not try to push him from her. He kissed her hair gently, comfortingly. He could hear only the sounds of their breathing and could feel the excited beating of her heart. He knew he should disengage himself from her though it was unbearably hard to let her go.

She broke the silence. 'This girl Bodyn – tell me, what was she like? What did you love about her?'

'Bodyn? Hmm.' He thought for a moment. 'Bodyn was older than you, nearer to my age. She was small like you, but her hair was straight and very black, black and shiny as coal, and her face was very white, and her cheeks were bright like blooms.' He smoothed the escaping hair. 'If she had tied her hair up, it would have stayed in place and not struggled free like these determined curls. Her eyes were grey, not brown like yours, and she laughed more than you do. I think it is I who make you unhappy.' It seemed a good enough excuse to plant another kiss on the teasing curls.

'Oh,' she said somewhat glumly. 'I suppose she was very beautiful?'

'Pretty, yes, very pretty. But very young inside herself; we both were young in that way. Although she was older than you, she was … not so knowing. Not so … womanly as you are. And no, not so beautiful.'

It had grown very late. Delia was sleeping; her steady breathing punctuated by the occasional grunt told them so. He remembered her injunction and sighed, turning the girl's chin gently with the cup of his hand so that she looked again into his eyes. He longed more than ever to rest his lips on hers.

'Delia says you are refusing to be married. That cannot be?'

She nodded miserably. 'She said you were horrible, that it was your nature because you are a man and would do … that thing to me. That which you say Elen killed her daughters to save them from.'

'Delia is very stupid. She does not know how much I cherish you. I will not hurt you. But that is no reason for you not to marry.'

'She said it is the way of all men, that thing. She said men are like animals when they are roused and …' Whatever it was, she could not put it into words.

'Gaia, Gaia, look at me. Look at me.' He tilted her head up again to face him. 'Don't you think that you might want "that thing" just as much as your husband? Don't you see how happy – that is, how much your mother loves your father? They only want you to be married so that you too will know the kind of love they share. Delia only said those stupid things because she guesses I have fallen in love with you, and she fears I may let my passion for you get the better of me.'

'Have you? Have you fallen in love with me? Do you love me, Verluccus?' She turned her body and placed her hands upon his shoulders so that he had no choice but to release his embrace.

Her eyes were looking deeply into his, and his insides were turning revolutions. He looked down.

'I adore you,' he whispered honestly. 'To me you are like a goddess. The sight of you gladdens my eyes. I think of you all the day long. I long to hear your voice, for you to require something of me so that you speak to me and I may do a service for you. Sometimes I wonder how else I might have known you had I never come into this household – if I never had more than sight of you from afar, some haughty, distant lady.'

'Haughty? I am haughty?'

'No, no,' he answered hastily. 'I mean I might have thought that from not knowing the real Gaia. That is, if I –' He found it impossible to continue.

'You mean if you were not a slave?'

She did right to say it. He forced himself to reply, 'That is what Delia meant. A slave may not touch you – not in that way. No man should, slave or free. No man other than your husband. Your parents have raised you, guarded and protected, for the delight of that lucky man and for your own happiness as a wife and mother. Others – other men, I mean, for slaves do not count – may only watch and envy the good fortune of such a man, and he in his turn must do all within his power to make you as happy as he.'

'And would you envy that man?' she whispered.

He thought he would cry but would not deny it, so he kept silent, tortured by his feelings for her.

He knew what she did then was meant only as a kindness, a

consolation to him, but when she moved nearer and pressed her lips onto his cheek, he was undone.

He cradled her head gently in a massive hand and drew her onto his lips, gently parting hers with his own. She made no resistance but encircled him with her arms, and his senses enflamed him.

His body arched, and he was across her, his free hand reaching into her gown. By nature she responded to his embrace and his kiss. Delia was forgotten as she dozed beside them.

Now suddenly Delia was awake – and loudly too, with such a shriek that they instantly split apart and rose fearfully to their feet to meet her accusing rage.

The door was thrown open and Florus appeared. Behind him were others of the household, alarmed by Delia's shouts.

Gaia collected her wits. 'A mouse.' She was pointing at the chair vacated by Delia. 'A mouse climbed onto Delia and startled her; there is no harm done. Go – go and find the cat. Find Orca. We shall shut her in here tonight.' She wrapped her arms around Delia as if to comfort her and signed to Verluccus that he should go too as if to find the cat.

He followed the others and heard her rounding on the girl. 'What did I say? Did I not warn you what would happen? I fell asleep, and I have let your parents down. I dread to think what might have been had I not woken when I did.'

He did not sleep for a long time. There had been no need for Delia to behave as she had done; he would have done no more than steal that one kiss, no more than that, and set her down again.

He almost believed it himself.

There was a movement in the doorway; a figure entered the room and crouched beside him. It was the girl Vernia. 'Delia says you are wanting me.' She giggled, preparing to share his blanket.

'Delia is wrong,' he said crossly. 'Go back to your own bed.'

7

Gaia did not come to the tree the following day; she was not seen there again.

He needed desperately to speak to her. He convinced himself it would be to offer her an apology and beg her forgiveness. All of the time he thought about her and the events of the previous day, and the timber took great punishment, and the stack of wood grew very quickly. When he came to work in the house, Gaia was always elsewhere. He dared trust no one but Delia to act as his emissary, and Delia remained as elusive as Gaia. Never before had he so looked forward to the evening meals.

She was there, but so was Palatus, overseeing his every move. She allowed him to place food before her. But she would not look at him, and he knew she hated him. It was now only a matter of waiting for Lucius' return for her to make a complaint about his behaviour. What would she say? Would she claim he had tried to rape her? And if she did, would that be so very far from the truth? As sad in his heart as she was in her face, he cleared the dishes and took instruction from Palatus as before.

There were a further five days of pain and doubt before Gaius returned. His sister, maintaining the custom she had begun, conducted him around the farm as though it were her own but made inclement weather the very good reason for not accompanying him to the tree where Verluccus was still working.

'Palatus and Victor both give excellent reports of you. Father cannot help but be pleased,' his master assured him. So Gaia had said nothing to her brother. He tried to assume his old casual attitude towards Gaius, but now, speaking in circumspect Latin, there was little easiness and soon he indicated that the tree required his undivided attention.

'Verluccus, you are not here for a punishment. And you certainly need not continue to do this work now I am at home,' protested his master, chiding him for being too lean and promising to make sure he was better fed. 'I am taking Cervus out for a gallop, and I want you to come with me. This can wait. It will go nowhere, and we have no shortage of fuel now. I shall tell Victor I am testing your progress.'

'I am taking Gaia to Glevum with me,' he announced as they walked the horses back through the cold drizzle. 'She complains that she is bored with having no better company than slaves and ancient Irene. She is very much changed. I think having this authority has gone to her head. I find not my little sister any more but a grown woman.' The explanation was plain enough to Gaius. 'She is very short with me, I suppose because we have not yet had word back from old Aemilius.' He rubbed his face reflectively. 'Do you know what? In fun I said Glaucus could not be interested in her or else we would surely have had word from him by now, and she slapped my face! The Gaia I left here a few days ago would not have done that. That Gaia would have burst into tears and run from the room.'

'Then your intention was to cause her hurt rather than yourself,' answered Verluccus, wondering if it had been Gaius' idea that she should go to Glevum or his sister's. 'I do not understand you.'

'It was nothing but harmless fun,' protested the other. 'And Glaucus may reject the proposition. He may have other ideas. Even if he is free to do so, he may not want to marry Gaia.'

'How could anybody not want to marry Gaia?' Verluccus marvelled unguardedly. Fortunately it was said only to Gaius, who slapped him on the back in appreciation.

'Ha! But you have seen her! Poor Glaucus has no idea what may be in store for him.'

———— ⑤ ————

The next day it seemed a worse idea that Gaia should leave the house, for the rain had turned to sleet and fell like rods of ice. She was warmly wrapped in copious layers completed by a thick travelling cloak, but she and Delia had to ride in the bigarum and brave the elements. Gaius rode alongside her on the plain horse which he had to make do with in the absence of Cervus, who was still banished from the town. He had made no mention of how he had managed without Verluccus; but Verluccus, knowing what little use he was, supposed it really made small difference to his master.

It was from Palatus that he learned the young lady had gone so that she might enjoy the company of Cloelia and be on hand to travel as soon as word arrived from Corinium that a new nephew or niece had arrived.

The house was gloomy and silent, empty without her. Palatus ensured that the slaves worked hard, continued as if the owners were present, and kept the hypocaust at a comfortable temperature; but Irene took her meals in her room, and the triclinium was closed up. Palatus, Victor, and Agricola took advantage of the vacated baths, and Verluccus learned the art of the carefully applied razor and strigil.

Eventually there was but one limb left on the tree. When that was gone, only the trunk would remain and Victor would bring down a team of farm slaves, criminals like himself but considered less trustworthy and always supervised, to help reduce what remained to manageable proportions.

After some five days there was an overnight snowfall, and they woke to a whitened world. He had cut enough wood to see them through, and Victor said his gang could deal with the rest. Verluccus' work would be to replenish the stokers, clear a path to the shrine so that Palatus could lead the household to prayers, and then clear wherever else snow had blocked a walkway. He gladly fell on the bowl of porridge awaiting him when these chores were considered done.

Victor, not wishing to see him idle during what remained of the morning, gave him work to do in the smithy, and he was grateful for a job close to a fire. Afterwards he reported to Palatus for more domestic training and the pursuit of Latin.

He was with Palatus in the evening when Penelope burst in. She had taken food to Irene and had found the old woman had died. She had been dead for some time, her life taken from her during the cold night, but nobody had been near before Penelope. A sense of guilt and fear pervaded them all. They acknowledged their neglect of the freedwoman, who was in a sense deputy to their owners in their absence. In another household, such a fear might have been justified; in that of Lucius Marcius it seemed unreal.

Palatus instructed that a pyre be built and that she should be prepared for her funeral. A small cortege of slaves conducted her to her cremation while the rest gathered around. Palatus said what he considered appropriate, and the pyre was lit.

He drew Verluccus aside. 'I am sending you to Glevum. Gaius Marcius will be there, and he can decide what we should do with Irene's ashes. I shall give you a tablet to take explaining what we have done. You will have to go on foot. Find yourself a spade to cut through any snowdrifts you encounter, and take some food from the kitchen to warm you on the way. I am placing my trust that you will carry out this errand and not abscond.'

Verluccus wondered when he would be given a task to do without that proviso. He assured Palatus that he would go as quickly as he could to Glevum and deliver his message to Gaius.

He travelled more easily than they had expected, for although there were occasional drifts to confront, in many cases the wind which had caused those had also swept his path clear, and he had little use for his spade. He enjoyed the bread and weak wine they had given to him and experienced a real sense of freedom for a few hours.

He found Gaius easily enough. He was not at school but exercising in the gymnasium. He was surprised and delighted to see Verluccus but saddened by his news. 'You must come and tell Father. He will decide what should be done.'

'I thought your father was in Corinium?' He experienced a sense of foreboding at having to deliver the news to Lucius and wondered if the fear expressed by the other slaves might be justified. Another sense was disappointment that a possible opportunity to see Gaia again, and to learn from Delia if not from her what his standing was, was to be removed from him.

'Father returned just before the snow fell, which was very fortunate.' Gaius led him to the house of Cloelius. From nearby there came the sound of girlish laughter, and then as they made to enter the house the two girls came rushing past them, one pursuing the other with handfuls of snow, heedless of the tall cloaked man beside her brother.

Lucius took the tablets. Agricola had sent his report as well, and his face darkened as he read what Palatus had written.

'This is shocking news, quite shocking. Shameful that she should have been so alone. My wife will be really distressed to learn it. For this at least you may be exonerated – you would have no business in going to her room.'

He sent Gaius to bring his sister. She came nervously not only because her brother had broken the news to her but also because she saw who the messenger was, and her face reddened, as did his own. It was impossible to speak in such circumstances; he heard her express her grief at the death of the freedwoman.

Lucius asked him, 'You say the road is passable?'

'I encountered no difficulty, my lord; nor would a horseman. It might prove difficult for a vehicle.' He supposed Lucius meant to bring them all home.

'Then you may take a pony and return. I shall write my instructions.' He scraped Palatus' letters from the wax and began to write. 'Go to the kitchen and get a meal.'

Verluccus glanced at Gaia, but she had no eyes for him. He spoke to Lucius, 'My lord, may I advise the cook how many will be returning?' Would one of them be Gaia? He hoped so.

The question did not please Lucius. 'You may tell the cook that when the day comes that there is no meal for a casual visitor, let alone family, he will find himself in the marketplace and not buying supplies,' he said.

'Yes, my lord.' He followed Hardalius to the kitchen, and when he had eaten a decent meal returned as directed for Lucius' messages.

'Agricola writes that you have been doing some metalworking,' Lucius said to him in a less displeased voice. 'I shall write now that I wish you to continue; train to be a smith. A smith would be useful to us. Your training by Palatus is to continue also. Your language is better, much improved, but not nearly satisfactory – much too slow. As for your leaving the farm, I pardon your excursion to Glevum in this instance and those who sent you because of the nature of your business, but it must not be repeated. Nor shall I restore you to your life of idleness. My son is now served by a new and very satisfactory well-educated boy.'

He felt as if he had been struck a blow, and yet reason told him that it ought to be so. Gaius would have replaced him; he ought to have been pleased that it had been necessary. He kept his composure and turned questioning eyes on the young man. Gaia saw his expression.

'You had not told him, had you?' she accused her brother.

Lucius frowned at his imprudent daughter. 'Go to Cloelia and amuse yourself; this is your brother's business.' He turned to Gaius. 'Where is Placidus? I hope you are not keeping him concealed.'

Gaius was almost apologetic. 'Father bought Placidus off old Calpurnius. He used to belong to us. Calpurnius and his wife are gone to Londinium, and I will now be able to have Cervus again.' He walked with Verluccus as far as the city gate. 'As soon as father gives me the word that he is satisfied with you, I shall have you to serve me again; don't fret. Placidus is only a stopgap. If you put your mind to it, your return to me need not be so long in coming. Just do everything asked of you and let father receive good reports.' He held the horse they had found for him to return on.

'I am sure Placidus will do much better for you than I,' he said with a surliness which was quite unworthy and, turning the horse briskly, trotted towards the slushy track and Daruentum.

Palatus didn't reveal what Lucius had written to him, but it was not so difficult to guess. He fetched from the outhouse the urn containing Irene's ashes and placed it in what had been her sleeping chamber. Whatever plans he had to use the room, perhaps for himself, were frustrated; and the household knew the presence of the old woman's ashes within the house was a rebuke for them. The urn remained there until Lucius brought his wife and children home and conducted a respectful burial of the freedwoman, placing the urn in the ground not far from that of Cordatus. But that took place a good while later.

The talk in the household now seemed to consist solely of who next might be freed. It was a long time since a freedom had been granted – not since Melissa, in fact, and she was no longer there. Palatus was confident it would be him; he had the trust and approval of both master and mistress. But equally confident was Victor, who felt he had a much greater claim, having served Lucius for longer. Agricola too was not without hope. When the family returned to Rome as they intended, it would make better sense for Lucius to leave the farm in the charge of a freedman than of a slave. Nobody present considered Delia, who Verluccus knew would most certainly expect to have it granted to her. He himself had no hope or expectation of it. He idly toyed with the idea that Gaius might free him one day, were he able to, but Lucius never would; Lucius still considered him marginally less dangerous than the poor creatures he kept to work the land. Penelope, who allied herself with Victor, had no expectations either, but she said Chloe might – she was Aelia's maid and well past thirty now. It would be fitting for Aelia to grant freedom to Chloe after Irene.

It was a depressingly logical argument. He wondered what Delia might do if it were denied to her.

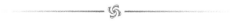

Almost another whole month passed. By this time he had repaired and made so many implements that Victor was selling them in the market at Glevum, where they were consider of good quality and so keenly sought that Victor was finding it difficult to supply sufficient raw material for him.

Towards the end of February Catullus, a slave from Marcia's house, arrived with the news they had all been anxious for. On the nones, the fifth day of February, his mistress had given birth to a healthy girl, tiny but lusty, and all was well with them both. He had delivered his message to Lucius, and he with Gaia had now gone to Corinium to meet the new arrival. Catullus had been sent him to the farm so that all of them should know, but as Palatus was not slow to point out to him, he must have hung around in Glevum for much longer than necessary.

Catullus had never been to Lucius' house before. He was suitably impressed by what he found there and took careful note in order that he might brag about it when he returned home. He seemed in no hurry to do this and would have settled himself in until the return of Lucius had he been allowed to do so, but he was reminded of where his home was and duly packed off with a flurry of good wishes for mother and child, congratulations to the father, and a supply of more tangible gifts from the aspiring freedmen and their supporters – from Penelope a soft wrap, from Palatus preserved fruits, and from Agricola a side of ham. Victor sent some of Verluccus' handiwork, a stand for hanging oil lamps to light the baby's room. A heavily laden Catullus reluctantly departed.

It was not until the middle of March that the family returned. Verluccus was overjoyed to see Gaia again, and while he worked in the smithy his whistled imitation of birdsong could faintly be heard between the ringing strokes of the hammer. So high then were his spirits that even the arrival of long-awaited news could not totally depress him.

Not only was Decimus Lepidus Aemilius Glaucus actually willing to marry Gaia but he seemed to be delighted with the idea. *As well he ought,* thought Verluccus sourly.

But the best news of all for Gaia was that he was not in Rome but in Britain. In Eboracum in fact, on the staff of the provincial governor, Neratius Marcellus, no less. The delay in hearing from him had been caused by his father's letter having to be forwarded on to him, and because it was not State business, it had not received his prompt attention.

He had heard of the daughter of Lucius Marcius through his elder brother, who had often expressed his impatience for her to become of a suitable age for marriage. Had Lucius not made the suggestion, he might well have ventured to propose it himself.

No better result could have been dreamed of.

The house was ablaze, lit by the unquenchable happiness of the bride to be.

BOOK V

SERVING MARCUS

1

'Why', a wry Lucius wondered aloud, 'do I get the feeling that we have been inspected?' He was standing at the gate with his arms around his wife as they bade farewell to the slave who had come from Decimus Lepidus Aemilius Glaucus. 'I trust we have not been found wanting!'

Aelia fingered the string of gold around her throat, a gift for her from the young man. She remembered Virens, how charming he had been, how dreadful that he had died, and in such circumstances. Now there seemed to be hope again. It was quite beguiling that the first gift had been sent to her; it reassured her that Glaucus would be as gallant as his brother. Brothers, as she well knew, need not necessarily be alike. It was wonderful for Gaia that they should have heard again from him so quickly. His betrothal ring was now gleaming bright upon her daughter's hand and been brought to the attention of the whole household.

Gaia hoped the report Glaucus would receive of her would be pleasing to him. That he would be satisfied with her lineage she had no doubt whatsoever.

'Is there nothing we can do about him?' Aelia asked her husband, indicating the general direction of the smithy from which the sound of metalworking rang clearly. 'He is much improved now and, according to Victor, has some real ability there, but can you imagine what Aemilius Glaucus will think to discover that we not only retain as unshackled labour the criminal who butchered his brother but that our son prizes him above any other? Gaius will by now have appreciated the better qualities of Placidus. Let us try again to persuade our son

341

to sell him; he could realize a good price now he has been trained to be useful.'

Lucius turned to their daughter. 'I would not ask you to lie to or to deceive Glaucus, Gaia, but I see no need for him to be told of Verluccus' background. I am really impressed with his improvement and had intended to restore the boy to Gaius when he next returns. I hope that he might agree to make some different use of him, perhaps permanently on the farm. Your mother is right. Placidus does very well for Gaius at present, but I doubt if we could persuade your brother to part with Verluccus altogether.'

She was torn. She remembered that he had indeed killed Virens. Marcus had made the allegation, and Verluccus had as good as admitted it. But she knew also what he had told her of his life and of how he had come to join Cunobarrus; that was something which not even Gaius knew about him. She also knew he had said that he adored and cherished her. It had been wrong of him to do so; it had been wrong of him to kiss her as he had. But she could not feel but tenderly towards him. Had he not also said he would gladly give his life for her? That was all her concern for him was, of course – mere female tenderness and nothing more. Delia had explained it all, and now she understood how she had been in error in allowing him to presume upon her innocence.

'What would Glaucus do? Could he insist that Gaius surrender Verluccus? That he be put to death? I do not want that, Father, Mother. No, I see no need for him to know anything about Verluccus. He will have no reason to ask for the antecedents of our slaves unless he intends the purchase of them.'

'And there is no likelihood of that happening to Verluccus,' acknowledged Lucius, pleased with her response. 'However, it is my intention that this estate is to be your dowry, so a number of the slaves will go to Glaucus. I know how fond you are of the place, and I can think of no better custodian when we are departed. Does that please you?'

She put her arms around her father and hugged him. 'How wonderful! How good of you. You know how much I love this house.

342

I had not thought about a dowry, but of course Glaucus will. He cannot help but be delighted.'

'He does not yet know. The marriage terms are not yet discussed. And if he is anything but delighted to have you even if you were to go to him with nothing at all, he would be a sad man indeed and not fit to be your husband.'

Not six days later, that same emissary accosted Lucius when he was emerging from the council chamber in the basilica with his fellow decurions. The slave revealed that his master's freedman Demetrius was awaiting him in the praetorium, craving an audience.

Slightly concerned, Lucius immediately made his way there; he hoped that whatever had caused this rapid turnaround could easily be remedied.

The man who greeted him effusively was a tall and splendidly attired Greek. *Sleek* was the word which came to Lucius' mind. The freedman was a very well-educated Greek who apologized if the slave had disturbed Lucius Marcius; the fellow had been clearly instructed to await his emergence. Lucius assured him that it had been so. Demetrius announced that Decimus Lepidus Aemilius Glaucus had sent him with documents which he hoped would achieve a satisfactory arrangement of the marriage between himself and Gaia Marcia. Lucius was impressed. He had not anticipated such a quick turnaround. He immediately changed his plans for the day and took the freedman to his house.

There were more gifts now – for Aelia, for Gaia, for Lucius, for Gaius, and for Quintus too, his existence having been discovered in the slave's earlier reconnoitre. Lucius was as dazzled as his wife by the young man's consideration. The idea that the farm should be passed to Gaia was inspired; the freedman was clearly impressed and happily assented to a tour of the estate in order that Lucius might point out its advantages.

But Demetrius was not sent for nothing. Soon Palatus was

summoned to the study to produce the records both of the farm and of the household. Decimus Lepidus Aemilius Glaucus would need to know which slaves he would acquire with the property.

'Agricola of course. He is a very able manager. I would recommend that he be freed; if your patron has no intention of settling locally, to have a freedman in charge of the farm rather than a slave is advantageous.'

Demetrius agreed. 'I do not anticipate Aemilius would have any difficulty with that suggestion. The farm staff as they are will be most useful. I see you have already started ploughing; you are planting wheat?'

'Yes, emmer. It grows well in these parts.' Lucius' knowledge of farming had grown considerably.

'Excellent! Now, the overseer. Is he really necessary, bearing in mind the excellence of Agricola? I do not think Aemilius will expect to fill the bellies of the idle.'

'I can assure you that Victor is by no means idle. But neither is he available. I intend him to become my next freedman, and he will return with my family to Italy. I do, however, recommend that Aemilius Glaucus obtain another in his place; I have found to have such a man invaluable.'

'The smith – he is not listed here,' the freedman complained. 'We – that is, Decimus Lepidus Aemilius Glaucus will certainly require a smith.'

Lucius was puzzled. 'We have no smith. The work necessary can accomplished by Agricola.'

'I saw another – that one.' He pointed through the window at Verluccus, who was crossing the garden, making himself useful in spreading dung on the ground. 'He was working in the smithy. He appeared competent.'

'Ah, I see your mistake,' said Lucius, not displeased. 'Verluccus belongs to my son. He makes himself useful around the place but is not part of the farm and will not be transferred as part of the household. I do intend that my daughter shall have one or two slaves as she chooses, but those who serve my family particularly closely will be taken with us to Rome. Gaia will of course have Delia; she will be granted her freedom before the marriage as my gift, a reward for loyal service. Gaia will be quite delighted about that.' Lucius had intended this, as he was unsure of his future son-in-law's attitude in such matters. Once the marriage was completed, Gaia would be subject to his will and rule. However, from the response to his suggestion concerning Agricola, it seemed there would be no need to be concerned.

'On the grounds that she has borne three children or on grounds of age?'

'Er, on grounds of age.' Lucius had no idea how old Delia was. He looked to Palatus for support. The steward nodded confirmation. 'She is more than thirty.'

'I am advised by Vera that she is with child,' Palatus said quietly. 'If I might make a suggestion, she should go also. She could prove very useful to your daughter.'

'Excellent!' said Demetrius, grasping his point immediately. 'Apart from the menials, which I presume you will not be removing to Rome, what else will there be?'

Lucius pondered. 'Scribonus, my amanuensis – I keep him more or less permanently in Glevum – is not part of the estate. He is a useful fellow, but I am prepared to sell him. Hardalius can do such of that as is necessary for me until I reach our new home. Rufus, the young lad – what is he, about eight or nine?' Palatus confirmed that he was almost nine. 'Gaia may have him; he is a promising youngster, and I should be sorry to have to send him elsewhere. In respect of the younger children, I would prefer that they go to whoever has their mothers. I shall certainly keep Palatus, Hardalius, and Penelope; she is the mother of Rufus, but Victor has a special attachment to her. My wife will retain Chloe, and Felix takes care of Quintus. Gaius will retain Placidus and Verluccus. I think we can manage without the others while we are travelling.'

'Florus, Argus, and Lepulla?' Palatus asked. He thought his master too generous.

'Well, of course I shall continue to live in the house until we depart, but once Gaia is married there is no need to linger. We shall travel better with fewer. I do not want to burden our hosts where we lodge along the way with a great number to accommodate, and they will be better off with Gaia than sold on the open market. The porters and stokers, of course, like the cook and kitchen hands, will remain.'

'I am sure that arrangement will be acceptable to Aemilius. There will be a rent to pay, of course, as the house legally will be his by that time.'

Somewhat shocked to hear this, Lucius spluttered an acceptance of the proposition but equally argued that a suitable price ought to be paid for the last three named slaves, and the deal was agreed.

'Now here is another matter,' said Demetrius. 'As you know, Decimus Lepidus Aemilius Glaucus is on the staff of the provincial governor, Lucius Neratius Marcellus. You will not be surprised to learn that in due time he will be carrying out an audit of this region. My patron has persuaded Neratius to bring forward that audit and to make Glevum his centre of operations rather than Corinium. You will see that he is eager for this marriage to be transacted. From my knowledge of him, I can assert with confidence that he would also prefer a house, in keeping with his standing, in Glevum Colonia or at least much closer to the fortress than this place. He would be exceedingly obliged if you could assist in securing such premises for him, and if your daughter could select and furnish it with property and staff as you both think fit for her husband and herself. I realize that you anticipate some slight delay after the marriage before your departure, but obviously if Gaia Marcia is to have the slaves you have indicated, then that would assist considerably in establishing their home.'

Lucius was delighted to hear this as would be Aelia and Gaia. 'What will my son-in-law contribute?'

'Decimus Lepidus Aemilius Glaucus keeps a small household. Myself, the boy you saw, and a mere handful of others. They are all exceptionally well trained, of course, but it is essentially a man's household. There are no females. Your daughter is bringing two plus her freedwoman, which should satisfy her initially, but she will also need a steward like your excellent Palatus.'

Palatus beamed with pleasure. Lucius noted that Demetrius did not consider himself to be Glaucus' steward. He wondered what his position was; broaching marriages for his patron could hardly be considered a full-time occupation.

'How highly our future son-in-law must be regarded by the governor,' said Aelia when Lucius told her what had taken place. 'I think he must be an exceptional young man. I am overwhelmed with happiness for Gaia that she should be his wife.' She told her daughter the good news, and Gaia too was overwhelmed.

There was only one possible house available, and Lucius found himself not for the first time marvelling at the ingenuity of the gods, who had brought about the departure of Calpurnius from it.

It would have to do; building a new one was out of the question. Lucius hoped it would be acceptable to its new owner. It was a lesser property than the mansio and was situated not far from the eastern wall of the colonia but in what was generally considered to be the better area of the town. It was in a reasonable state of decoration, and he quickly installed painters and carpenters to carry out remedial work and a mosaicist to lay a new floor where damage had been caused by some subsidence. The sense of urgency which Victor managed to instil into the workers soon wrought what was generally considered to be little short of a miracle. When news arrived that the governor was resting in Ratae and would be with them in a very few days, only the floor remained unfinished, but it was well on its way.

They had celebrated the freedoms granted to Delia and Victor with a party, to which Cloelius Draco and his wife and daughter, Antonius, Titus, Publius Petronius, and some further decurions were invited as formal witnesses. Palatus had been sufficiently discreet with the knowledge he had become privy to for it to be a wonderful surprise not only for the two in question but also for all the rest of the household.

Verluccus eyed Delia sourly. He remembered how deviously she had acted towards her mistress, and he found it a great deal easier to congratulate Victor on his good fortune than the maid. It was on this day too that Lucius restored Verluccus to a delighted and grateful Gaius, who promptly dismissed Placidus and told him that Palatus would find him useful employment; he no longer required his services.

Gaia, glad for her freedwoman, delighted with the dowry and with the news concerning Vera, should have been much happier than she was, thought Verluccus, who as usual took every opportunity to gladden his eye by the sight of her.

But the impending arrival and the meeting with her intended was affecting every day; the strain was telling. And now, learning that Glaucus was so close and their first encounter so imminent, she retired to her chamber and the consolation of an understanding mother, a quaking mass of nerves.

Verluccus attended his master and accompanied him and Lucius to Glevum in good time to be satisfied that all preparation was completed for the arrival of the governor. It was assumed that he would occupy the praetorium, and the available barracks had been hastily cleaned out and refurbished to accommodate such escort as might be deemed essential for the progress of such a notable. A reception committee consisting of the town councillors and a detachment of veterans was assembled to greet him and assure him of his welcome. It was also a peculiar enough event to bring natives from the surrounding district into town, and traders almost went so far as to pronounce themselves well satisfied with the impact of his visit.

Although Gaius was not on the official reception committee, he did wangle a good viewpoint for himself and Verluccus; but while the young Roman's attention was taken up with his first sighting of the provincial governor and other notables, Verluccus' eyes were seeking only one man.

Quite close to Neratius Marcellus was a finely built young tribune of immaculate appearance. His hair was fair and wavy and very stylishly trimmed and his skin considerably more fair than that of

Lucius' family. With depressing accuracy, Verluccus identified him as the long-awaited bridegroom.

In a most agreeable mood, Neratius expressed satisfaction with the condition of the praetorium and his private accommodation within it. A bath would now be taken, to which Lucius was invited so that he and his intended son-in-law might meet and relax together. Gaius and thus Verluccus were not invited to join the guests.

When they dined that evening, however, a place was found for Gaius on his father's couch.

Glaucus' toga had been expertly folded by his dresser, though when he lay down he discarded it quite casually for the boy behind to rescue. Underneath it he wore a tunic dyed a deep red and trimmed with a golden braid.

He was lying quite close to Lucius and talking animatedly with him – about Gaia, Verluccus decided, though he could not hear a word of what they said. He was straining to glimpse the colour of the man's eyes. He had been made aware that the name Glaucus meant that they would be blue like his own. In fact Gaius had once said that his mother had toyed with the idea that it should be Verluccus' name. How glad she must now be that it was not, though no doubt it could have been discarded as easily as it was invested.

They were light blue and piercing.

They had been suddenly revealed by the man himself when he raised his head, frowning and staring back, confronting the impertinent slave.

Ashamed that he had let Gaius down, Verluccus hastily dipped his head and took a step backwards.

The following morning Lucius was able to conduct Glaucus to the newly refurbished town house. The party included Gaius but not Demetrius, he having been left to discharge services on behalf of his patron.

They were accompanied by a high-spirited but not unfriendly

mob of townsfolk and visitors who blocked their path, seeking a closer view and probably the ear too of one of Neratius' entourage, and the way had to be cleared for them by Glaucus' escort and the judicial application of staves which they had thoughtfully chosen to bring along. It amazed Verluccus. Never, to the best of his recollection, had it been necessary for Lucius to adopt such a practice.

The house was satisfactory. Glaucus understood the constraints under which Lucius had laboured, how short a time had been available in which to prepare it, and no doubt a great deal had been necessary. He intended to waste no time then in settling in and instructed his slaves to collect and arrange his possessions. It was therefore necessary for Verluccus and Hardalius to secure the return path to the praetorium, a novel experience for both of them.

Glaucus had expressed his desire to meet Gaia Marcia at the earliest opportunity, but that could not be before the following day was concluded, as a banquet had been arranged with the best entertainment the colonia could muster. Verluccus joined with the other slaves and served his master at the table and watched with enjoyment the gyrations of the dancers, though the songs and readings which followed were lost on him.

During the meal he became aware of Glaucus eyeing him thoughtfully from time to time and discovered that he was actually grateful to have received sufficient training not to heap great embarrassment upon Gaius and his father.

2

They were expected, of course. Aelia knew that the next time her husband came home he would be bringing Glaucus with him. She could barely contain her own nervousness, and poor Gaia was in danger of becoming ill with terror.

Aelia remembered her own marriage to Lucius. It had been different for her. She knew him already, but even so, when the day came she experienced that same thrill of desire and terror which she recognized in a heightened manner in Gaia's wide-eyed and pallid face and quickened heart. 'He cannot fail to adore you, child,' she assured her for the umpteenth time. 'Nobody could.'

Verluccus studied their meeting. He watched anxiously as they came face to face for the first time. He saw the man betray both pleasure and relief – relief, no doubt, that reports he had received were truthful; and who, setting eyes upon such a gem, could experience anything but pleasure?

As soon as he arrived he had charmed both Lucius and Aelia with effusive compliments on their home and on Aelia's beauty, compliments which reminded her so much of her dear Virens, and they had told him how much they had loved his brother. Lucius had drawn Gaia forward, and her nervousness had become modesty. Their hands touched. Glaucus bent and kissed her gently on the cheek and drew her into his arms. He made some remark about the betrothal ring which she was wearing, and his lips brushed her fingers. Now she was happy. Her face was again alight, and confidence oozed from her; she felt loved. Gaius was laughing and demanding that wine be brought, and the household were clapping their hands with joy. The wedding was a certainty.

There was no hindrance. There was no secret wife now discovered. The farm and estate met with proper approval, and the terms of the settlement were ratified; the wedding was being prepared. There was not a single flaw. Even the gods were in approval, and the auspices indicated that delay was unnecessary. Verluccus chided himself for his meanness of spirit and told himself yet again that if this was what represented happiness for his beloved girl, then he must be happy for her. To dream that anything else, anything which might involve him, should come to be was worse than stupid; it was pathetic.

Despite Demetrius' best efforts, however, he had been unable to secure a steward suitable for the new household. Palatus, Lucius had to make very clear, was not available. He could not manage without him, he said, and he would be accompanying them to Rome. For once he was resistant even to Gaia's cajolery.

'Then what about that one.' Glaucus indicated Verluccus. 'I am sure your brother could be persuaded to part with him if I made an offer interesting enough. He seems able.'

Verluccus was attending on Gaius, observant and alert to his master's whim. He heard the question clearly, and for a moment he felt a flush of pleasure at the compliment. In a further moment it was dashed most cruelly by none other than Gaia herself.

'Him? Verluccus?' There was incredulity in her voice and scorn. 'Oh no, Glaucus! He would not do at all. He may look all right, but believe me, you would soon regret it. The boy is illiterate, and his command of Latin is only passable; he certainly knows no Greek. Verluccus would be utterly useless as a steward in *our* household.'

He felt as if a blade had pierced his guts. It was Gaius who came to his defence.

'What my sister says does have some truth, Aemilius Glaucus. Verluccus cannot read or write, and he does not speak Greek. But she knows full well that to me he is invaluable. There is no question of my disposing of him – not to you or to anyone. I am certain that my sister spoke as she did to discourage you so that there would be no disagreement between us as brothers-in-law, but she knows also that her remarks will have caused pain to one who is utterly devoted not only to his master but to his master's family, including herself. Your new household will not enjoy the service of any slave more loyal and diligent and conscientious than my Verluccus.'

'I apologize to you, Gaius Marcius; I intended no offence. I had noticed that he looks pleasing and has good manners. Of course, looks are only superficial, and I bow to my betrothed's superior knowledge.'

The lightness with which he responded soothed Gaius to a great degree towards Glaucus if not towards his sister. Had Glaucus not been present, he would have insisted that she apologize to Verluccus, but he had learned enough of the man in the short time he had known him to understand that his attitude towards slaves was less indulgent than that of Lucius. And Gaia was in no mood to humour her brother; she clearly was more intent on impressing her future husband.

Lucius and Aelia had come to the conclusion that with the marriage accomplished they would have no further need to occupy the farm. Any business remaining in Glevum Lucius could finalize by accepting the hospitality of Draco and his wife; and Aelia, with Gaius and Quintus and the remnants of their household, could then move to Corinium and lodge with Marcia, where the precious days remaining could be spent with her darling grandchildren, little Julius and his new sister Julia. The wedding was to take place in April, a good month, not as good as June but definitely better than May. How fortunate that Glaucus had arrived when he did.

For the first time ever, Aelia regretted that her home was as distant as it was from the town. She even considered requesting use of the praetorium for the wedding. But Gaia said no, she wished to marry at the farm even if it must be a less public ceremony than might be desired and even if a longer journey afterwards to her new home was therefore necessary.

Glaucus and his companions returned to Glevum on the eve of the wedding, and the family's guests had begun to arrive. Marcia, who was to perform the duties of matron of honour; her husband; and her children had come in good time, and she was much involved in the preparations. Cloelius, Lydia, and Cloelia came. Calpurnius in distant Londinium had been invited but sent his regrets, and sad memories came with them. Others who were not so close would arrive on the morning of the wedding itself, so the house became full and noisy and busy.

Verluccus was not required to participate in any of the preparations, but work was found for him in the forge, 'out of our way' as Aelia put it, when Gaius was engaged with his father in entertaining their male visitors with hunting expeditions.

On the eve of the wedding, Gaia and the women spent most of the day gathering spring flowers, primroses, oxlips, cowslips, bluebells, violets, and tree blossoms to decorate the whole of the house, the household shrines, and the altar to Mercury. Some of the guests had brought good-luck symbols in the form of phalluses, and these too were adorned with flowers.

That evening when all were returned and Verluccus was attending Gaius, Gaia was dressed in her wedding clothes. 'All traditional', Gaius told him 'to confirm that the omens are good.'

Her garment was a simple white tunic, quite straight but bound at the waist with a woollen rope from wool she had spun herself. 'That's for Glaucus to undo,' Gaius remarked to no one in particular and succeeded in making his sister blush. A headdress of flame-coloured gauze was placed on her head secured by a coronet of flowers which now concealed the somewhat elaborate arrangement of her hair, and she wore smart new shoes of matching colour.

There had been no opportunity to speak to Gaia since those cruel words he had heard her say of him; she cast not a glance in his direction, laughing and smiling at the rest of the company and twirling around in her wedding dress, the loveliest and happiest bride to be there ever was.

Wrong though it may have been, had he not told her that he loved her, adored her? Surely she had some pity for him? But there was no chance for him to cross the divide, and he knew that if she did not choose to contrive some means to speak to him he was never going to be able to speak to her again. He wanted simply to do that, somewhere private, together, to reaffirm his feelings for her and tell her he would always be her protector, given the chance.

The day of the wedding began early, and he had to prepare Gaius in his finest tunic and place the circlet of flowers on his head. All of the men were dressed as he, and they took their places in the atrium. Gaia again was clad in her wedding finery and attended by her sister Marcia and little Quintus and Julius, both in smart white tunics and floral circlets on their heads.

Cloelius, who held position as a priest, had announced that the auspices were good, and on cue Glaucus and his party arrived.

Verluccus watched the ceremony. It seemed to him that a transaction was taking place, and then Lucius passed his daughter from his hand into that of Decimus Lepidus Aemilius Glaucus and Gaia Marcia became a married woman.

The house erupted with applause, laughter, and merriment. A feast had been prepared in the triclinium, and they all fell upon the food as if starved, Verluccus thought. He tried not to think so sourly; he knew Gaius was likely to notice indiscretions, and he had almost wept at the climax of the ceremony. He served at the table and almost had the chance to serve her, but he was forestalled by another and the chance was gone.

And then they were leaving the house. There was some affectation of Glaucus dragging his wife from her mother's arms, but it was all in good fun. The household followed after them all the way into Glevum, for the continuance of the wedding was to take place when Glaucus got her to their new home. Not knowing much of the ritual to come, Verluccus wondered at what point the party was to break up so that bride and groom could go to their bed together.

There was again a great reception and much food and entertainment, and the newlyweds were honoured with the presence of the provincial governor, Neratius Marcellus, who expressed highly complimentary remarks about the bride's beauty, much to her parents' pride. But the household slaves including Verluccus were excluded from this, so she was gone. He tried not to care; he knew he must not.

The following morning it became clear that soon the remaining family would be departing too as soon as Neratius Marcellus relieved Lucius of his responsibilities.

Gaia's marriage and his loss of her had so consumed Verluccus' attention that the realization of what this meant for him came as more than a shock.

He sought Agricola to beg a favour from him, supposing it to be his only hope. The farm bailiff, however, was not in an accommodating mood, being less than happy at not being freed by the newlyweds and at having no overseer to assist him now that Victor was a freedman.

'I even suggested to Gaia Marcia that she ask her brother about you remaining here,' he admitted, 'but she said there was no question of that.'

'Can you get a message to my brother Tanodonus?' Verluccus wanted to know. 'Can you tell him how things are with me? I shall never see him again, I know. Lucius will not let me go there myself. If we had been here longer, I might have convinced him that I can be trusted –'

Agricola shook his head. 'I wish you had not asked me that. I am bound to report this to Lucius Marcius. In any case, Tanodonus will have no truck with me. He is a very bitter man. I can tell you though that all is well with them.' He shrugged. 'Perhaps I need not speak to Lucius. I am owned by Aemilius Glaucus and his wife now and not by him. But it is better to leave it as it is now. If they think you are lost to them, what good would it do to tell them that you have been living beside them for the best part of a year? Best leave well alone.'

Gaius was approaching them.

'Come on, Verluccus. I need to get to Glevum to say farewell to Titus Justinius. Father has given him a letter of recommendation, and he is off to Isca Silurum to join the Second Augusta. I don't want to miss him. Bid farewell to Agricola now, for we shall not return here.'

Verluccus made a last appeal to the bailiff. 'Please … if you see any way …?'

At Cordatus' tombstone, Gaius paused. 'I wish to bid farewell to him, and to Irene, of course,' he added hastily. Her stone was not yet in place – a matter for Gaia to attend to.

'I am taking Verluccus to Rome,' Gaius told the departed. 'We shall at last see all those wonderful things which you used to tell me of. I remember so well everything you taught me. Father and Mother will come by shortly and bid you farewell too, but when we are gone, my sister Gaia will take care of you both.'

3

Lucius and his family took lodgings in the home of Cloelius Draco; there was no question of anybody intruding on the newlyweds. Verluccus, who had dreaded such an encounter, was heartily relieved to learn this. So he assured himself.

Neratius Marcellus accepted Lucius' report with good humour and wished him well for his journey, reminding him, as if he needed reminding, that entertainment in the arena had been laid on by his host and that Lucius and his family were to be his guests. As Lucius had contributed a goodly sum towards this, he was inclined to think that their situations were reversed, but it was no matter; a final party before their departure was not to be declined.

Gaia, of course, was now seated with the wives of the honoured guests behind their menfolk and Verluccus with the slaves many rows behind. He saw her being teased by her relations and responding with laughter, glowing and radiant with happiness, but he was unable to hear what was being said and resigned himself instead to observing the forthcoming entertainment.

He had learned that it would commence with the execution of a number of criminals; then there would be some animals – bears, wolves, and dogs – to fight; and then a gladiator show to round the day off. He was excited to know he would be watching professional gladiators in action, brought, Gaius had told him, from their training school in Corinium.

He had helped with the litters on which the family travelled through the uncomfortable streets to the amphitheatre. Victor, who was walking alongside Lucius, expressed some regret that his fighting days were over; and Verluccus was subjected to some good-natured ribbing about how close he had come to performing in it until Lucius, with thoughts of Virens awakened, warned against continuing in that vein.

Gaia pulled her wrap more closely around her head and neck, and he remembered what had happened before when he had stared too hard. Too late to do anything about them, he now remembered that her beads were still beneath the floor of what had been Gaius' room. He wondered if they ever would be discovered and what would be made of their being there. Nothing like the truth; that was certain.

'The first show is of some criminals who are condemned. Should Neratius Marcellus feel so inclined, he may grant clemency to one or more,' one of Publius Julius' slaves told them.

'There is no chance of that!' A more knowledgeable one from the governor's household was able to put them right. 'He would not be here so early in the day except to see to it that they do all die.'

Eventually, after the ceremony due to his position, Neratius Marcellus opened the proceedings, and the first performance began. The participants had been set in pairs and given weapons with which they were ordered to fight for their lives. That, the first speaker indicated, was the joke, for the winner from each pair would be matched against another survivor until none were left standing.

The pair immediately in front of Neratius' party consisted of a skinny youth who had apparently murdered his master and an aged man who had been caught stealing slaves. Both were armed with swords and shields but no armour. It was plain to see that neither of them had held such weapons before, and very soon both threw down their weighty shields, each apparently seeking a quicker death.

But already Verluccus was moving forwards, heedless of this being noticed and frowned upon by those around him. He reached the barrier and called out to the old man, 'Bodenius? Bodenius? Is it you? It is I, Magnus.' Then he turned to Neratius Marcellus and begged, 'Please spare that old man. Let me fight in his place.'

Men, soldiers, thinking Neratius' life at risk, were closing in on him. He leapt the barrier and crashed heavily into the arena, winding himself and bringing the fighting to a temporary halt.

When he felt able to dismiss the idea that an assassination attempt had been intended and then the possibility that this was some bizarre piece of theatre designed by the gladiator trainer, Neratius turned to Lucius. 'Isn't that one of your household?'

Lucius was speechless with shame and anger. He could only nod his head and stammer an apology.

'No, not at all. Let us see what transpires.' Neratius signalled that the proceedings should recommence.

By now Verluccus had taken the sword from the old man and was embracing him. 'Bodenius, Bodenius, don't you know me? I am Magnus, the boy you took to Merriol.'

'They got you too then?' was all the old man could say, his face suddenly distorted in alarm.

Instantly Verluccus whipped around, and the sword had despatched the skinny boy who had thought his only chance of survival had come when the tall slave turned his back to him. His body lay twitching in the sand. Half the crowd seemed puzzled; half, believing like Neratius that this had been set up, now cheered exultantly. The governor had to demand silence to hear what the slave had to say for himself.

But Verluccus was not there to fight; he wished to speak. 'Yes, they got me. I have been taken back by those I ran away from. It is not so bad.' He wrapped his arms around Bodenius, noticing how frail and weak the man was. 'I owe you so much. You delivered me to a good life. Now let me save you.' He turned to Neratius and called out, 'My lord, please grant this old man his life. Let me fight in his place. Please let him live; be merciful to an old man with few years left.'

'A few minutes left, if I am any judge.' Neratius' aside brought laughter from his cronies. 'Kill him,' he ordered. 'Kill him now.'

'No,' Verluccus pleaded again, to no avail.

'No, I shall not spare his life; he is condemned. But I may spare yours if you please me. You may kill the others if you can, but you must despatch him first.' He turned with a chuckle to Lucius. 'I think

360

he might just manage it – to wipe out all comers. He is clearly far superior to his opponents.'

It was Bodenius who stopped him from pleading again. 'No, Verluccus. You must not interfere. Today I am to go. I am awaited. I have prepared myself in my mind for this. You do wrong to delay me. Let it be by your hand, for I know it will be swift and clean, and I will depart in peace. All I ask is that if you are able – if at the end of the day you are spared – you take my head and give it to the waters, the great Sabrina river. Take my head there and cast it into the water, if you are spared.'

Neither the crowd nor Neratius were impressed by this delay and show of affection. Cheers became jeers.

Bodenius knelt, exposing his neck. The sword whirled, a flash in the sunlight, a head dropped heavily into the sand, and a frail body crumpled to the ground.

Gaius had said nothing. He was paralysed with shock, and Gaia thought she must faint or be sick; she did not know which.

There was a deathly silence. Nobody had foreseen such a thing. It was a strange and terrible thing which he had done, something ritualistic, and they were not sure how to react. The crowd looked to Neratius for guidance.

Verluccus had already picked up the head and held it to his breast, heedless of the blood soaking his tunic. He looked at Neratius and then at the arena gate. Neratius nodded, and the gates opened. He was allowed to pass unimpeded.

It was Glaucus who acted. He turned to men of the governor's guard. 'Follow him and observe him closely. When he has disposed of that head, secure him and report to me everything which occurs.'

Lucius turned on his son. 'I am shamed and disgraced by this slave of yours; after all I have done for him, this is how he rewards me. Before Neratius Marcellus himself he has managed to make a spectacle of himself, to make our family a subject of ridicule. Let us be thankful that we are done with him and depart from this place with dignity.'

'No, no, do not go,' Neratius interrupted. 'You are by no means ridiculed and far from disgraced. Decimus Lepidus Aemilius Glaucus has the matter in hand. It is surely an incident of no significance. Let us enjoy what else is placed before us and let the men deal with the slave as the tribune instructs.' He motioned that they must resume their seats and signalled that the entertainment should continue.

At the end of the day Gaius and his father parted with bitter feelings. Lucius no longer could control his son, and the son refused to budge an inch from British soil while he might do something to save the life of his slave. Headstrong and stubborn as ever, Gaius insisted he must remain in Glevum and try to secure Verluccus' release. It was a flimsy hope, but he could not abandon him without at least attempting something. His mother, certain that she would never again see her precious eldest boy, quarrelled with both him and Lucius, and it was left to Marcia to show some care and feeling for her shocked younger sister.

4

He knew the soldiers were with him but fearful to touch him while he carried the head. Someone had flung a sack at him, and he had wrapped it carefully within. He trudged steadily back into the town, talking to Bodenius the whole of the time, telling him what had happened to him since they had first parted and what had eventually happened to Merriol and how he had joined up with his brothers and fought alongside them until he had been captured and returned to Lucius Marcius. He even told him of how he had fallen hopelessly in love with Lucius' daughter Gaia, now the wife of Aemilius Glaucus.

The soldiers kept their distance, awed and distrustful of what they were witnessing, but as soon as the head splashed below the bridge into its watery grave, they seized him. He could see in their eyes a superstitious fear of what he might be, but a greater fear of their commander overruled their doubts, and soon he was secured in the pit, a prison emptied by the games from which he had so recently emerged.

Gaius obtained a bed in the home of Gaia and his brother-in-law. If he could bring influence to bear, then he would do so; but if he could not, then from here he would learn sooner what was to be done.

'I have no interest in him, Glaucus,' Neratius Marcellus replied in answer to his tribune's request. 'You may interrogate him first if it amuses you, but give him back to that rash boy. I have no wish to part so devoted a lover from the object of his attention.'

'You do not think him a magician then, my lord?' Everybody else seemed of that opinion.

'I think the old man might have been; he is dead now.' He shrugged. 'The slave is due to go to Rome and can do no harm. Let him be taken away from here. Do not bother me again with such trivia.' He waved dismissively, and Glaucus, unused to such peremptory treatment, nodded with a scowl to Demetrius that he might have Verluccus brought from his dungeon and restored to his owner.

'I want to know who that old man was,' demanded Gaius when the gate was opened. 'How you came to know him – why you declared yourself to be Magnus. Is that the name you used when you were with Cunobarrus?'

Verluccus' back was sore from the attention he had been given in anticipation of a questioning. Slaves never told the truth unless they were flogged; it was a well-known fact. He moved painfully from the darkness into the light and the reception committee of Demetrius and Gaius.

'Master, it was before I was with Cunobarrus. He helped me when I ran away. I owed him much; he will never know how much. No, I did not use a Roman name when I was a warrior.' He was tired and hungry and thirsty, but first Gaius was owed an apology. 'What I did was on impulse. I regarded that man as if he were my grandfather; he gave me help and succour when I was in desperate need. You may consider my act foolish and rash, and if it has caused you or your father embarrassment, then I am sorry. Bodenius wanted his head to be returned to the river; he thought he had some kinship with it. That is all.'

'People are thinking you and he were Druids.'

'You cannot think that of me!' he protested, shocked at the notion. 'As for him – I do not know.' He shrugged. 'He went to the shrines along the road and showed me how to make offerings. I do not think that is how the Druids performed their rites.'

'Decimus Lepidus Aemilius Glaucus has persuaded Neratius Marcellus to act towards your slave with great leniency,' Demetrius told Gaius. 'It is my duty to report these facts to him. He has admitted to being a runaway; some former owner must have a claim on him.'

'You are mistaken, Demetrius. It was from us that Verluccus ran away, and he was recaptured by my uncle when he stormed Cunobarrus' fort at Belconia. My uncle is Marcus Marcius, commander at Isca Silurum.'

Demetrius knew full well of his relationship, he assured Gaius. Nevertheless, he had a duty to his patron; he should know the facts. He allowed Verluccus to be taken to Glaucus' house and hurried in search of his patron.

It was most interesting news to Glaucus. He came home rapidly to confirm that Demetrius' story was true.

'What's this, Gaius? Your slave is a runaway? And what is all this about Cunobarrus? He knows him? He fought beside him?' Was the youth really so stupid he did not comprehend the significance of this knowledge? What was Marcus Marcius about, neglecting such intelligence?

'Oh, it is nothing, Glaucus,' said Gaius airily. 'It was our family that Verluccus ran away from. While he was at large, he met up with Cunobarrus and discovered he was his brother – yes, his real brother of the same blood. A brand he bears on his back identified him to my uncle, and so he was restored to us. If you think Verluccus can assist with recapturing Cunobarrus, you are mistaken; he has had no contact with him since he was taken into captivity again. And Father forbids him any contact with the remnants of his own family, those who remain at Daruentum.' He spoke with a mixture of pride and happy confidence.

His sister, her presence ignored, groaned with fear.

'I can scarcely believe my own ears.' Glaucus was astounded. 'And this is known by your father? This is known by Marcus Marcius, is it? He knows all this and does nothing?'

'My father certainly knows. We discovered the whole of it after my uncle had left. He will have written of it to him. He must consider there is no useful purpose which can be served by Verluccus in his pursuit of Cunobarrus.'

'I think we will let Neratius Marcellus be the judge of that!' Glaucus seethed. 'Have you no idea how much time and money and effort has been wasted by your uncle in searching for that criminal while the remedy to it all has been enjoying the liberties of your bed? It is time you got your priorities right.'

'How dare you!' Gaius, blazing with anger, squared up to his brother-in-law. 'That is not why I keep Verluccus. He is not my bedfellow!'

Glaucus, enraged by Gaius' fatuity and irresponsibility, lost for further words, stormed from the house in search of Neratius.

'Oh Gaius!' cried his sister. 'How could you be so stupid?'

'Stupid?' He had thought himself clever. 'I did not tell him about how Verluccus killed Virens. That would have been stupid. You will see; Verluccus can be no help in finding Cunobarrus.'

Verluccus was not even told why he was summarily returned to the cell, and Gaius was forbidden contact with him while he was 'warmed up' in preparation for a proper interrogation.

He fell on his knees before Neratius. 'You are too enthusiastic, Glaucus,' commented the governor. 'Put him away and see to it he is fit to answer my questions when I receive a reply from Marcus Marcius. In the meantime, find out, discreetly, what is known of this family in Daruentum.'

'Agricola can tell you,' Gaius supplied. 'He has knowledge of all the local natives through his business on the farm.' He was anxious to appear cooperative and was certain the man would receive a report which would impress.

5

─────── ✺ ───────

'I do not know where Cunobarrus is. How can I? They told me he was dead.' Verluccus had been put before a governor better informed than previously.

'When you address me, you will say "my lord".' Neratius peered thoughtfully at his victim. 'But you know as well as I do he is not dead. Somehow he escaped from death on that occasion. You are better placed than anyone to help find him.'

'I do not know where Cunobarrus is, my lord.'

'And you believe you need not help me to find him, don't you?' He sighed. He knew the type, bloody minded and stubborn to the end. Flogging would do no good. 'What if I told you that I have the means to make you help me find him? To help Marcus Marcius find him?'

He shook his head, his guts churning at the mention of Marcus Marcius. 'Nothing you can do could induce me to betray my brother to you even if I did know where he is. But I do not, so your efforts would be doubly wasted. My lord.'

'What if I mentioned the name Tanodonus to you?'

Verluccus was puzzled. 'Tanodonus does not know where Cunobarrus is. He could not possibly know anything useful to you, my lord.'

'I think he might persuade you to … be cooperative. No? A taste of what you have already experienced – perhaps a little more? Would not that persuade you to loosen your tongue? Shall I bring him in, or are you already of a fresh mind?'

The reaction this produced was sufficient to convince Neratius that the scheme would work. He gave a kindly smile.

'Not now – later, perhaps.' He had not yet sent to have the brother fetched from his home. Then he said to his men, 'Take him away and get him fit to travel. Marcus Marcius has suggested a good use he can be put to.'

He stood grasping the bars and listening intently. There were no sounds other than the occasional footsteps of a guard and the scuttling feet and squeaks of rats, company which his other cell had been mercifully free of. The place was dimly lit and malodorous and perfectly secure; there was no possibility of escape. But the silence told him one thing: Tanodonus was not present. It would have been pointless to keep them out of earshot of each other. They intended him to hear, possibly even witness, the torture they intended to inflict on Tanodonus. He had to act speedily. When the guards changed duty, he was always visited, so if he was going to do something, it must be done immediately.

But he did not have the skill to break his own neck and was found hanging against the wall, choking into the home-made rope of plaited strips of shirt, and cut down alive. From that time on he was not left alone.

Gaius was by no means idle. Daily he pestered his brother-in-law to obtain him an audience with the governor, and eventually it was granted to him. Neratius was in little mood to hear him. He told him that Verluccus was no longer in Glevum. His slave had been sent early that same day to where he would be more useful – to the eager hands of Marcus Marcius.

Marcus' response had exonerated him. He had not known of the relationship between the renegade Cunobarrus and the slave other than that he had been a follower. Lucius Marcius had not informed him of it their kinship. Marcus had outlined a proposition to Neratius, and the governor had written back with his consent. 'Marcus Marcius', he told the youth, 'has an imaginative scheme in mind to which I have agreed; we might just as well try that as anything else.'

'Then let me go to him also,' pleaded Gaius. 'I can be of assistance. I know my uncle will have no success with Verluccus; Verluccus hates him. You do not know how hard he can be, how obstinate. He would not save this brother Tanodonus if it meant he had to betray Cunobarrus – not for Marcus. But he would do so for me; I could persuade him.'

'The commander of the Second Augusta', replied Neratius, emphasizing that he was not interested in Gaius' relationship to him, 'has my personal authority to act as he thinks fit. This is State business, and I shall not allow any whining pup to interfere with it. If you have nothing useful to contribute, then I suggest you make tracks to rejoin your parents. Your slave is now in the service of the emperor. I think you will not see him again.'

'But my lord, I can help you; you do not know Verluccus as I do. I know how to persuade him to talk. For me he would confess things which no amount of torture, either of him or of his brother, would produce. Allow me to go to Marcus Marcius as your agent. I shall find out what you want to know.'

'What a shameless cur you are! Do you suppose that some caressing from you, some kisses, some urging to tell them this or that, will save his skin? He will talk; of that you may be certain. But yes, you may go. For the embarrassment which you have caused to him, I shall let Marcus Marcius deal with you. You may learn a valuable lesson from him in the interrogation of prisoners. As for your father, his conduct is reprehensible, and I have to give serious thought as to what report I should make to Caesar Trajan about this neglect. Withdraw; your presence is an offence to me.'

6

Verluccus was certain that Tanodonus must already be in Marcus' hands. He made his own journey there bound fast in a four-horse chariot, agonized in mind and body over what he might do to withstand what was to come and how, somehow, to protect Tanodonus. He knew how indebted he was to Lucius that this had not come about before, and he knew also that if it had not been for his mad impulse to try to save Bodenius it need not have happened at all.

Marcus read the documents from Neratius Marcellus with satisfaction. He smiled at the dejected prisoner standing before him, his wrists and ankles bloody from determined but fruitless efforts to escape.

'I see he caused you some trouble,' he said to the escort and then to Verluccus, cheerfully, 'Well, thief, we meet again. You seem reluctant to be my guest. Why is that?'

'Where is he? What have you done with him, you bastard?' He had come to the end of a demoralizing journey during which he had twice attempted to kill himself and once had made a brief run for it. The escort were relieved men when they entered the fortress gate of Isca Silurum with him still alive and cursing.

Marcus sighed. 'I see your manners are not improved. I will be addressed by you as "my lord" or "master" or "commander"; you may choose as you wish. I am open to anything useful you wish to say to me. As for him – by that I suppose you mean my lever, this brother of yours from Daruentum? I do not think we need him. Do we? Are you not amenable to a reasonable proposition? No, I doubt it in your present condition. No man should sit down to dine in such a state.'

When he was taken to the bathhouse and felt skilled hands massaging and scraping his skin and gentle lotion soothing the damage to his back, he tried not to admit that he felt any pleasure from it. To be so lulled was treacherous to Tann. To succumb to such seduction, to such inducement to think kindly of his persecutor – as it was clearly intended he should – was rank disloyalty. But then again, knowing he was being softened up, rest and refreshment would give him strength to contend with whatever was to follow.

When he was considered presentable he was hurried at double speed back to the legate.

Marcus grinned his approval. 'That is much better. Not even you can have liked being as you were.' He motioned him to a table prepared for eating with chairs drawn up and invited him to take a seat. 'My tribunes consider having you in their dining room an insult; they think themselves too grand to entertain a slave at their table. I said that I considered you to be a potential ally, but they still demur. Do sit down. We shall be served by Tertius; I expect you remember him?'

The guards had left him, and he stood before his hated captor bewildered. Could Tertius alone really prevent him from killing Marcus? But what if he did kill him? That would certainly signal the end of Tanodonus. It took yet another command from Marcus and some encouragement from the slave to make him sit at the table; the manners he had learned from Palatus had become ingrained. The tempting food assailed his nostrils, and he allowed the fowl and cuts of boar to be loaded onto his dish. He ate.

Marcus was delighted; his plan was working perfectly.

Verluccus knew himself now to be a total traitor, sitting with his brothers' enemy, his own enemy, eating his food while elsewhere, somewhere else within the same fortress, his innocent Tanodonus, bewildered and frightened, probably already suffering the usual preparation, awaited a cruel and pointless death.

His conscience got the better of him. He spat out the meat and rose to his feet. 'My brother – where is he?'

'That', said Marcus courteously, 'is what you are here to tell me.' He motioned him to sit again.

He confronted his tormentor furiously. 'I mean Tanodonus, you bastard! Where is he? What have you and your loathsome bootlickers done to him?'

'Oh! Oh, *that* brother.' Marcus shrugged dismissively, quite unconcerned. 'Tano – whatever his name is – is not here; not at present. I have not yet sent for him. And if you cooperate with me, there will be no need to do so. Will there? But if it becomes clear that he needs to participate in our discussions, then he certainly shall do so. Have no doubt about that. But I think you are more amenable to reason and can see the logic in Tanodotamus never knowing what an important part he plays in this mission.' He motioned to Tertius that the plate should be replenished. 'Please eat. I have a task for you for which you will need your strength – or to sustain you when you suffer the consequences of defying me,' he added, and then he apologized and said Verluccus should not mind his odd sense of humour. His sister-in-law never could understand it either.

When he had eaten his fill, Marcus offered him wine, but he refused and would take only water. 'You have a good appetite.' Marcus nodded, pleased with the progress he had so quickly made. 'Neratius spoke highly of you. He was most impressed, most confident that we could work together. I must admit that when you arrived I thought his judgement mistaken.'

Verluccus hurled his dish across the room. 'Get it over with. Your food chokes me; I have no desire to assist you. If you have been told by Neratius Marcellus that I will help you, then he is a liar. He has no reason to speak well of me.'

To his amazement, Marcus' response was to throw his head back and roar with laughter. 'Ah, wonderful, wonderful – I knew you would not let me down. I have laid money on it. Only you would have the nerve to stand in front of me and call the governor of Britain a liar. Marvellous!'

Had the man spoken well of him? He could not believe it.

Tertius brought sweet delicacies, honeyed fruit, and cakes, and Verluccus was urged to try them. He threw the dish of them across the room.

'Why am I here? What do you propose to do to me?' Verluccus eyed Marcus with unalloyed suspicion.

'Immediately? Nothing – nothing other than to talk with you and enjoy your company and learn more about you. When I am ready, I shall tell you what your task is. Now, what of that young man, your master? Neratius tells me he has been very possessive of you, a very fond master. I wonder – can I use your love for him to persuade you to do my will?'

He denied it hotly. 'What you suggest to be the case is thought by some; I know that. It is not so. Beyond that I will not discuss my master with you.'

'And you are right not to do so. He has made an excellent slave of you, far better than I thought possible. I had you in mind to be a gladiator; from what Neratius tells me, you were much of the same mind yourself. But no, now you speak a passable Latin, and you are so well trained that it is uncomfortable for you to sit with your betters. I expect you can serve at table as well as – who was that boy? You remember – when you launched yourself across the dining table onto Gaius as though ballistic? Now you can do all of those things as well as young … Felix, can you not? The muscles though – how did you come by those? Not from Gaius' training, I am sure.'

Despite himself, Verluccus knew he smiled as he remembered hurling himself across Aelia's triclinium. Against all that he expected, against the best of his intentions, he was being charmed by the man he thought his greatest, or perhaps second greatest, enemy. He told Marcus about his role as a labourer on the farm and how he had come by it. The pleasure which he gave to Marcus as he described producing the knife and frightening Aelia he would not have believed had he not seen it for himself.

'I want to know what you expect of me,' he demanded of Marcus.

'What is your purpose in bringing me here? You know I do not know where Cunobarrus is; I too thought him dead.'

'But now both you and I know that he is not. As for what I expect of you, it is this – simply this: I have a proposition to put to Cunobarrus, and I want you to deliver my message to him.'

It was a trick, it had to be. He eyed the man with the greatest suspicion.

'What is the matter now?' Marcus asked in feigned surprise. 'You wanted me to tell you why you are brought here, and now you know. You are to go and find Cunobarrus and deliver my message to him. Here, drink this wine and go to your bed, and in the morning I shall pack you off. You do not need me to refresh your mind to the consequences of a refusal, do you?'

He had seen Tertius dropping what could only be a drug into the cup and refused it.

Marcus drew from it himself. 'For what reason would I poison you?' he demanded, handing the cup to him. 'It contains only herbs to help you to sleep. You will need to sleep tonight and be ready in the morning to commence your journey.'

He drank. If it would help him, then why refuse it? He allowed himself to be led by another slave to a secure sleeping cubicle.

Melissa was waiting. Scented with his favourite perfume and lying in the bed they shared, she was smiling at his frown and ready to soothe away his worries with her caresses. He allowed her practised fingers to undo the knots in his neck and back, but he was in no mood for gentleness. He took her swiftly and fiercely, and she was wise enough not to protest.

In the morning Marcus took report from the guard who had sat through the night with his prisoner. He wanted to know if Verluccus had asked to be given his instructions.

'He slept heavily at first,' he was told. 'But he woke early and asked if he could go to make an offering.'

'And? Did you allow that?'

The man had not.

'You should have done so. I do not come between men, even slaves, and their gods. And we might have learned something.'

'He did offer prayers within the room. I heard what he said.'

'And? It was?'

'He spoke in his own tongue. I could not make it out properly, but I heard the name Tanodonus and a girl's name, another slave, I suppose – Gaia.'

Marcus creased his brow. It was difficult to tell if he was annoyed or merely puzzled. 'Mmm, you are mistaken. It would have been Gaius; his master's name is Gaius.'

'No, Commander, unless he is in love with his master – the way he spoke it. But it was the feminine. I am not mistaken; I have learned many of the British terms of love, and he spoke the female name.'

'Well, forget it. And he has said nothing else? Since he woke he has asked you no questions?'

The soldier said that he had not. He had been relieved by another, who might have more to report.

'Have him brought to me now.' He gave another man fuller instructions.

What is the fool thinking about? Lusting after his master's sister when he ought to be concentrating on more immediate matters? The potential of another lever did not escape Marcus' mind.

'Have you seen anything yet of my fortress, my troops? I hope you have. The Second Augusta – a full legion and all at my disposal. It is important that you understand that.' He had a breakfast of bread and cold meats laid before them.

'I saw something,' his prisoner answered reluctantly. He had wondered about the circuitous route his escort had led him on their way to Marcus that morning. He had seen the great war machinery; they had made no attempt to conceal it from him. 'There are many men and weapons here as I would expect.'

'And have you thought about what I said to you last night?'

'You spoke nonsense in order to trick me. I do not know what you have in mind, but it is surely not to let me out of here alive.'

'There you are wrong. I do indeed. I want you to go out there, to find Cunobarrus, and to bring him to me. What about it? Will you do that for me, Verluccus?' he said in a conversational way. He almost added, 'for old times' sake,' but Prudence held his tongue.

The idea of Cunobarrus being foolish enough to stage an attack on a legionary fortress was so ludicrous that despite himself he began to laugh.

'I do not consider it funny.' Marcus broke open a loaf.

'You seriously believe that Cunobarrus is so stupid that he would attack this place? That I should go out there and tell him of your layout and encourage him to think he can overthrow a legion? And you think he will come here in order to rescue Tanodonus? You are crazy. If that is the best plan you have, you will never capture him.'

'That is not my plan. No, indeed not. But if you are willing to suggest how I might capture him, then I am prepared to listen.' He spoke encouragingly, conversationally, charmingly.

'No, I shall not help you. I do not know where he is in any case.'

'Perhaps you should listen to what I have in mind?' He did not wait for an answer. 'I want you to go out there and find Cunobarrus and persuade him to come here to talk to me. Just to parley, nothing more – no tricks. I have a proposition for him, but I cannot reach him to make it. You could do that and help both him and me. Now what do you say?'

There was a long silence broken only by Tertius quietly moving around them. He looked at Marcus Marcius in bewilderment. Was the man really speaking of opening his gate to him, letting him out, allowing him to walk away freely? He need not go to Cunobarrus. He need not go back to Gaius. He could just walk out, give whatever escort he was provided with the slip, and never be seen by any of them ever again.

'I want an answer.'

It was as if the hard grey eyes read his mind. In the continuing silence, the Roman added, 'I should be disappointed if you chose to remain at large and not return. Your young master would be also; I gather there is a mutual fondness? But you should know what would be the outcome of such treachery.'

Verluccus continued to stare at him dumbly.

There was a bowl of boiled pigeon eggs on his desk. Marcus liked to peel and eat them occasionally as a snack. He took out three and placed one at one end of the table and the other two at the other. Between these he tipped the remaining eggs so that the bowl was emptied. At first Verluccus took the bulk of the eggs to represent Roman troops, but suddenly and with a ferocity which he had concealed successfully until now, Marcus hammered a fist down upon the solitary egg so that it was flattened instantly. For a few furious moments, both his fists thundered in rapid succession until there was nothing but a mess of broken eggs and shells in the centre of the table. Then he dealt with the two remaining eggs, separately. One, like the others, he squashed flat, but from the final one he only took a large bite before he restored it to the bowl.

'Do you follow?' He pointed with a blade to the mess of squashed eggs, turning to Tertius for a towel to wipe his hands on.

Verluccus understood perfectly, or he thought he did, but because he still did not speak, Marcus felt a more detailed explanation necessary. 'Very well. You force me to describe the events which will proceed. If, having been turned out of here, you do not fetch Cunobarrus to me but align yourself with him instead and revert to your old practices, your brother, Tanodonus, I will crucify.' He pointed to the squashed mess which had been the solitary egg. 'Then, until I lay my hands on the both of you, be you with Cunobarrus or in any other place in this world, I shall, with the exception only of loyal Romans, kill every man, woman, and child who stands between me and my objective. When I have Cunobarrus, I shall kill him; but you I shall not kill, for you are a slave and the property of my nephew, and I shall send you back to your master and reward him for the service he has rendered to the State in loaning you to me.'

Deathly pale, Verluccus found his voice. 'I cannot help you. I have no idea where Cunobarrus is. How can I? I supposed you intended to torture me – I was expecting that – but what you demand I cannot do. Have pity if not on me then on Tanodonus, who is innocent of any crime, and on all those people. Resolve your dispute with Cunobarrus where it belongs, on the battlefield, but do not slaughter innocent people along the way.'

There was one escape route. He reached across the table to a knife, but he was too slow and Marcus had his arm pinned down before he could grasp the weapon.

'Listen, you fool. What I described will come about if you do not obey me. Hear now what my requirements are. You may find it easier to agree to them than you suppose. I have a proposition to put to Cunobarrus. Bring him here to hear it from me. If he hears and declines the terms I offer, then as certain as my name is Marcus Marcius Phillipianus, son of Quintus Marcius Phillipianus, commander of the Second Legion Augusta, I swear by any god you may demand that he may leave here without a hair of his head harmed, and we will settle it in accordance with your advice – out there. Now, boy, tell me – where there is difficulty in that? I am not asking you to betray him, to surrender him; whether or not he comes must be his decision. I only want this simple message delivered to him directly and to him alone. If you do it, I will reward you with whatever is within my power to do.'

'A slave wants only one thing – his freedom! Do you seriously believe I would trade my brother for my freedom? To enslave him instead of me? And even if I was of that mind, do you seriously believe I could persuade Cunobarrus to come here? Do you think he would give a shit about Tanodonus or any of the other people you propose to kill? Cunobarrus despises Tann. He would laugh at your threats. Why, if he knew of them, he would be more likely to defy you simply for the satisfaction of knowing he could cause the Romans themselves to kill a man who has done nothing other than be a model subject for the whole of his life. You have no idea what kind of a man Cunobarrus is.'

'Apparently not!' said Marcus dryly. 'But I am learning fast.

What you choose to tell him – your reason for going to him – I leave to you, but go you shall.'

'It would achieve nothing. Cunobarrus will not exchange himself for me. There is nothing I could do or say to him which would induce him to do so.'

'You mistake my intention, boy. You are not a hostage for him. All I require from you is that you persuade him to come here to me. You must return also. At that, your task will be fulfilled. He and I alone will parley. If he chooses to reject my proposition, which will include a pardon for him, then he may freely return from whence he came, and we will settle our differences with bloodshed – with the one exception that as a reward for what you have done I shall spare Tanodonus and any not directly involved in the conflict. As for your freedom, I should have to negotiate that with your master.'

'I cannot believe you have the authority to do this. How do I know you can do this thing? What authority do you have to allow this enemy of the State, as you call him, to come and go unimpeded? And even if you have the power at this moment, what guarantee do I have that even if I could persuade him to come here you would still be in command and not have been supplanted by a new commander? This is an idea you have dreamed up since you learned of my kinship to Cunobarrus. You knew I was one of his warriors. You knew that I was alive. But until you learned I was his brother, you did nothing.'

Fortunately for Verluccus, Marcus' sense of humour got the better of him. 'Me lose my authority here? Be deprived of my position? What whispers have you heard during your morning stroll? Are my tribunes plotting against me? Do you smell mutiny? Or have your picked up a titbit of gossip from Neratius' court that I am to be replaced? Forgive me, boy, but you do amuse me greatly, and believe me, I would much rather keep you here for private entertainment than send you packing. Be satisfied when I say that I have the authority to deal with Cunobarrus in this way, yes, from Neratius Marcellus. And if it makes you happier, he is empowered by Trajan himself to govern this country as he sees fit. But you are right. Now I know from where Cunobarrus comes, I have a plan which can remove him from his place, and I suspect that it may not be unwelcome to him. Discovering the relationship between you and him and of your filial affection for this Tanodonus does give me a new advantage which I intend to exploit to the utmost. Your choice is simple: do what I wish or suffer the consequences.'

Verluccus was shaking his head. 'In your eyes Cunobarrus is a criminal who has terrorized your provincials. He has stolen your gold and killed many of your men for the cause in which he believes. He knows you can only wish to see him dead. I can see no reason why you should wish to pardon him, since he does not come to beg it from you.'

'You have certainly spoken the truth, for that is what he is – a common criminal, pure scum. I see no cause, no justice, in his nefarious activities. He has become a thorn in my flesh, and the fact that his existence continues despite my best efforts offends and disgusts me. Do not provoke my anger by reminding me of his atrocities. Personally I have no desire for him to live but even less for him to become some sort of folk hero, emulated by a dozen other renegades. Accept my word that he will be treated as I say. I want him out of this territory and forgotten; and now, through you and his family, I have the means to do just that – to return him to live among the peaceful Dobunni tribe from whence he came.'

'Cunobarrus is to go free? To live freely in Daruentum?' This was more astonishing than any of Marcus' threats.

'Verluccus, listen.' Marcus leaned forward. 'If I disclose my proposition to you, can I trust you not to blurt it out the moment you are reunited with him? You must allow me to judge when and how to speak it.' Verluccus nodded, unconscious that he appeared to be assenting to his errand, and Marcus continued. 'I shall require from him a fourfold commitment. One, he persuades his followers to lay down their arms and wage no more war on the State and the innocent. Two, he surrenders the train of gold which he stole. Three, he returns to live in Daruentum and lives a peaceful existence without trying to stir up dissension among the people there. Lastly and most importantly, he swears an oath of loyalty to our Emperor Trajan and the gods. None too difficult, I would have thought.'

'I cannot agree to it. No,' he added hastily, 'what I mean is I need to think more about it before I give you my answer. Allow me more time to think and pray.'

Marcus, who thought he had agreed, rose in fury and began to stride to and fro before him. He swung upon him and said tartly, 'I can see I have been too generous with you. I could have had you flogged and doubled all the way here and flogged again. I could even now be twisting the limbs of this Tanodonus out of their sockets, but no, I have bathed you and fed you at my very table, a slave and a criminal despised by my own tribunes. I have given you rest and decent garments and shown you what my might of arms is and even offered to spare the life not only of Tanodonus but of Cunobarrus too, and yet you are either too stubborn or too stupid to seize what to any man's reckoning must be a tremendous lenity. What kind of a fool are you? Have I not said, "Bring Cunobarrus to me and Tanodonus' life is spared"?'

'I am agonized that you would have me trade one brother for the other.'

'I have no patience left. You have until noon to decide whether Tanodonus and the rest of them live or die.' An exasperated Marcus summoned a guard. 'Take him to a secure place and keep him there.' He turned and stamped from the building in search of another on whom to vent his wrath.

'Verluccus!' A familiar voice called to him as he was led outside, and he was able to turn long enough to see Titus hurrying towards him. He had forgotten that the young man had enlisted with the army. The lad was barred from him by the more experienced guard but immediately hailed by Marcus, who had paused and turned at hearing his shout. Titus hurried to obey, fearing that whatever misfortune had overtaken Verluccus was also about to happen to him.

'Titus Justinius the younger, Commander. Recently arrived from Glevum. I came with a letter of recommendation from Lucius Marcius,' he announced himself.

'I see. You know my nephew then, and him?' he nodded towards the departing Verluccus. 'Does he trust you? Can you persuade him that my word is trustworthy?'

'Commander, your word is legendary.' This was a bewildering conversation for a raw recruit to be having with his commanding officer.

'Then go to him now; he lacks your certainty. Persuade him that if I say I will do a thing, I will do it.'

He turned on his heel and re-entered the principia, barking for his tribunes to attend him. 'Vitellius, Assinius, Servius! Which of you dogs is plotting against me? Who among you is scheming to have me unseated?'

The tribunes turned startled eyes upon him to hear him add, 'That damned brute. I swear I had his agreement – I had him here in my palm – and then up jumps another reason why he should not go. "What happens if I bring him to you and you are no longer legate?" he inquires.' He mimicked the native's accent. 'And so I demand to know – who among you is plotting against me?'

They made no attempt to deny it and laughed with him. 'I know what I should do if Cunobarrus were lured here – on whatever pretext,' answered Drusus Vitellius. 'I should lop his head off and post it on a stick outside. He would not pass within these gates alive. And nor would he,' he added, signifying Verluccus. 'I think you must pay up, Legate; you have lost your *sesterces.'*

'Not yet. I am reprieved until noon!' He was in a better humour than he ought to have been, he told himself.

Before the deadline he found time to return to the praetorium and to Melissa. In the previous night, anxiety had made him short and rough with her, and he wished her to know it was not any fault of hers. He found her working wool in her room and sent her maid out so that they might be alone.

'You are a goose,' the ex-slave told the commander of the Second Augusta, loving him all the more for his concern for her. 'I know how much this enterprise means to you. I would help you if you would let me.'

She ought to have forgotten all about the slave, but when they lay together after their love making, she said, tracing a lazy pattern on his chest, 'What if I spoke to him? Could I help? He might listen to me; I could tell him what a good man you are.'

He chortled. 'He is not setting eyes on you, woman! You are mine and mine alone.' And he feasted on her again.

'If he does what you want, how will you reward him?'

'Will you not be silenced? What does any slave want? I will set him free,' he asserted with confidence, and she shook her head.

'You cannot do it, Marcus; it is not in your power. Gaius would never consent to it.'

'Then I shall write at once and demand his price. If this boy does that which I want, I shall buy him from Gaius; and then I will be able to set him free or not as I please.'

She shook her head. 'I know Gaius better than you do. He will not part with Verluccus. For nine years – nine long years, Marcus – even though he was still only a child, he secretively moped and yearned and prayed to have Verluccus restored to him. People dismissed his faith that the gods would deliver him as foolish nonsense, but they were wrong. Gaius will not part with Verluccus – not for any price.'

'I must give him something.' He frowned, annoyed by the distraction. 'I cannot expect that he will do what I want, perhaps achieve a successful conclusion, and have nothing for himself.' He lay in silence considering and eliminating other options. Of course his nephew would free the slave if he ordered him to do so.

'I have something that would please him,' she said lightly, and he sat up in amazement.

'You, him? No, no, no! I told you he is not setting eyes on you.' Surely she was teasing him?

'You are an oaf! You really are an oaf.' She kissed him fondly. 'What do you think I mean? Would I – could I – want any man but you?' She kissed him again to emphasize his error, and not for the first time he wondered how he had lived for as long as he had without knowing her.

'Wait here,' she instructed. 'I shall show it to you.'

She placed the bundle between them on the bed and bade him open it.

'I gave these to Aelia. How is it that you have them?' he demanded.

'You must not be cross. Promise me you will not be cross.' She knew how he must react. 'They were given to me with the best of intentions, but I do not need them. You could restore them to Verluccus.'

He guessed immediately. 'That interfering woman! She thought to give you the means of escaping from me! I will not have it; I will not have it. You must rid yourself of them without delay. How dare she so persist against me?' He hurled them across the room so that they crashed into the furthest wall. 'It appals me – appals me! – that for all of this time I might have carelessly said some word, done some unwitting act which you thought cruel, and you could have upped and gone from me and been lost to me. I am glad you do not want them, but it hurts me that you have kept them so long from me and secretly. I thought you loved me.'

He had forgotten how offensively he had treated her on their first encounter. She did not remind him but instead assured him, 'I do. I do love you; you know that I do. Give them to Verluccus. Gaius would be proud to see him wear them.'

'I would not shame him by having him decked out so, displayed like some pampered toy. When he wore those he was a warrior and they were fitting. In his present condition they would make him look like a whore. No, they will not do. But rid yourself of them just the same.'

Titus, admitted to the guardhouse, was sympathetic but more eager to ask after his friend Gaius than to carry out Marcus' bidding.

'You will have been allowed here for a purpose, Titus Justinius,' said Verluccus flatly. 'You might as well tell me what it is. It can't be worse than what Marcus Marcius has threatened me with already.'

'Only that I am to tell you how reliable his word is. Has he promised you something?'

'Oh yes, indeed he has,' said the other bitterly.

'I am not privy to what it is, but I know enough about him to be able to say with certainty that if he has said a thing will be so, then so it will be.'

'Titus Justinius, I am brought to a position where I must do his bidding. That I do know! My problem is not whether I do it or not, or whether he will carry out his threats, but how I can achieve what he expects of me. Unless I bring Cunobarrus here, another brother, Tanodonus, who lives in Daruentum, is to be crucified. To be assured that Marcus Marcius will carry out his threat is no comfort to me. What I need to know is this: how can I persuade Cunobarrus to surrender himself as Marcus Marcius wishes? Neither you nor he has the faintest idea of how Cunobarrus reasons. He will not listen to me, and Tanodonus, a man innocent of any crime, will be put to death.'

Titus had not expected to hear this. He wished to be helpful and so, after some moments' thought, said, 'Verluccus, do you swear to me that you will do your utmost to bring about the will of the legate?'

'Reluctantly, yes; I see no alternative. I must. Yes, I so swear.'

'Then I swear to you that if you don't come back, I will broach with Marcus Marcius all the representations my heart can furnish on your behalf so that he may know that your failure was not wilful and that what he demanded was beyond your power. I will speak of your sincerity of purpose and desire to save Tanodonus and the hopelessness of your mission. It is not much, but it is the best offer I can make to help you.' Titus had experienced a sudden and sickening realization that he might well be among those detailed to be this Tanodonus' execution squad. He hoped he did not betray his feelings to Verluccus. It seemed that he had not.

'I am not unconscious of the manner in which your wisdom has helped me in the past, Titus Justinius,' Verluccus said, remembering things that Gaius had told him when he had been thought to have run away from Felix and also of his assistance in obtaining the antecedents of Rex. 'I think this is my last chance to tell you I am grateful to you for those kindnesses. Marcus Marcius has a good man in you. I hope he appreciates your abilities. You are right; what you promise to do is the best I can hope for. Will you return to him and tell him he has me? I don't know how I am going to deliver what he wants, but I genuinely shall try to do so.'

—— ⟨§⟩ ——

'You are ready to go then? Good.' Marcus was studiously trying to contain his glee. 'I hope that young man has not misled you. The terms remain as I spoke them.'

He confirmed that he accepted them and that no, Titus Justinius had only impressed upon him how reliable the legate's promises were.

Marcus nodded happily. 'I have someone anxious to meet you.'

The door opened, and a grizzled centurion marched briskly in and saluted his commander before being told to stand easy.

'Centurion Gnaeus Cassius,' Marcus named him. 'Cassio has volunteered to accompany you.'

Verluccus looked the man over. 'He is more foolish than brave then, for he undoubtedly goes to his death. I have no need of an escort. If I say I shall do as you wish, then to the best of my ability I shall do it. My word, albeit obtained by coercion and the word of a slave, is as good as yours. You have no need to sacrifice him as your spy.'

'Don't be so touchy!' he was rebuked. 'Cassio has volunteered to accompany you for his own reasons which, in due time, he may feel able to disclose to you. But as you will discover, a hostage may be required in exchange for Cunobarrus, and this brave and foolhardy man is prepared to be that hostage.'

Verluccus glared at the centurion. 'Him? For Cunobarrus? At the very least he would expect a tribune. He will not think a mere Centurion a fair exchange for himself.'

Marcus smiled grimly. 'I believe you may be wrong. Cunobarrus will not doubt the worth of this man even if you do. Now collect what you require for four nights and depart.'

Verluccus gasped with horror. 'That is not enough time. I have no idea where to start looking for Cunobarrus. I must have longer – a month at least.'

'It is more than enough time,' he was assured. 'But as today is the fourteenth of April, I will give you until the twentieth and not one day more. You will know it by the fullness of the moon. You must return by then – that is twelve days before the kalends of May – if you have any hope of saving this Tanodonus. Cassio can lead you for the first part, and after one night in the open, Cunobarrus' men will find you. How long they let you live depends on your resourcefulness. I have great hopes, and so too does Gnaeus Cassius.'

Verluccus set the pace, moving over the rough terrain as though pursued, and the centurion, though not wearing his armour, clad merely in his tunic and cloak with a pack of essentials, was hard pressed to keep up with him. By the time night fell, they were many miles distant from Marcus.

7

Gaius had ridden like a man possessed. He had abandoned the tired
Cervus at a mansio along the way, and retrieving him was another
duty he must fulfil after retrieving his unfortunate slave.

The despatch from Neratius Marcellus gained his admission into
the fortress, but he was left to kick his heels outside the principia until
his uncle was pleased to receive him.

'I think', said Marcus pointedly, 'that a little discipline along the
lines being learned by your friend Titus Justinius would do you no
harm.'

Gaius regretted not bothering to clean up before presenting
himself. He flushed and saluted belatedly. 'I came in haste. Where is
Verluccus? May I see him? You have not …?'

'The slave is employed on State business. Take yourself off to the
praetorium, where you will find Melissa; she will be pleased to have
news of your family. You may tell her I shall dine with you both this
evening,' he told him, and reluctantly the young man obeyed.

By the time Marcus arrived (in no bad frame of mind), Melissa had
sought refuge in her room to escape the youth's relentless badgering
about the whereabouts and condition of his slave. Now, considerably
agitated and fearful of bad news, he turned on his uncle.

'Where is Verluccus? Your woman would tell me nothing.'

'Let us be clear about one thing, young man,' said Marcus coldly.
'If you are referring to Melissa, and I cannot think you mean any
other, you will remember you speak of my wife.'

'Melissa is not your wife. Your wife', Gaius almost spat the words,
'is my aunt Claudia who, you may remember, is the mother of your

only son, my cousin Marcus. Melissa is your concubine, an ex-slave who once belonged to our steward, and he won her in a game of dice. Since then she was also bedded by my father's freedman – and previously by the gods know whom!'

He recoiled from the stinging blow across his cheek which had dashed him across the room.

'Melissa is more wife to me than Claudia ever was, though she gave me a son. I love Melissa, and you will do well to remember that. Through her good offices, you may obtain favour with me. Now, if you wish a place at my hearth, you will apologize to her.'

He did so immediately, having known even as the scornful words poured from his lips that he behaved badly to one he had no quarrel with. 'I am anxious for what my uncle has done to Verluccus,' he explained lamely.

'Neratius has written that you thought you might be useful to me,' Marcus told him later. 'There is but one way in which you may perform me a service. I had intended to write to you on this. If Verluccus succeeds in the mission I have sent him on, I must reward him. I would like to grant him his freedom; it will be deserved. Sell him to me now so that I may do so. Name your price.' He was fully prepared to be generous.

Gaius was outraged. 'You had no business offering him his freedom. No wonder he has done what you wanted! He is not of an age to be freed, but even if he were, I would not set him free or allow you to do so. Not for any price will I sell him. Why, I have only just regained him after nine years of waiting, and now you coolly inform me that you have turned him loose on some pointless enterprise whereby he may resume his old ways. You have incited and encouraged him to break promises he made when he submitted to my government and have as good as stolen him from me!'

'You are a self-centred little shit!' Marcus shouted at him angrily. 'I have not promised Verluccus his freedom. On the contrary, I have made it clear to him that gift lies with his master. You could buy yourself a dozen men with what I would pay for him, or you could manumit him yourself and take his thanks and have the service of a loyal freedman. I can only suppose you fear he would not serve you were he free to choose.'

That was exactly what Gaius did fear, but he would not admit it to his uncle. 'The whole argument is pointless.' He scowled. 'You have loosed my slave, and neither I nor you will see him again.'

'Time will be the arbiter of that,' snapped Marcus. He despised the boy. 'You may remain here if you can behave yourself, or I shall have you escorted back to Glevum. If you choose to remain, you are to be confined to the praetorium; and if you upset Melissa, I will personally see to it that you are whipped for your insolence. When this is over, I shall write to your father and tell him exactly what I think of you, so you have until then to mend your ways and impress me.'

8

For a long time all communication between Verluccus and Cassio was confined to essentials. Verluccus supposed the centurion despised him and wondered what had driven him to volunteer for such a task. The man was a hardbitten soldier whom he may well have confronted or fled from in his previous exploits. He wanted to believe Marcus that his role was not dishonourable, but it was not easy to do so. Cassio, for his part, was content not to press for conversation and seemed to be trying to avoid giving the impression he was in charge of their expedition, deferring to Verluccus on all decisions as to which direction was best whenever there was a fork or a junction in their track.

When they had made camp that night and had agreed to take turns at the watch, sharing their hot meal, Verluccus ventured to question him.

'What crime in Marcus' eyes have you committed, Centurion, that you must do this in order to redeem yourself? For you surely have a death wish.'

Cassio studied his young companion; he had hoped that the meal might provide the moment when the icy treatment meted out to him thawed a little. 'In my time I have committed many crimes of one sort or another, but I have survived. I have a reason for coming. It is, I believe, an honourable reason, and before it is over you will learn what it is. But this is not the time. I can tell you it is certainly no death wish.'

'And is it honourable in Roman terms to murder Cunobarrus? Is that what your purpose is?'

Cassio laughed, relieved to discover what the difficulty was and that it was not a personal hatred of him. 'I said I have no death wish! No, what Marcus has told you will have been the truth, and I have no orders to do other than to offer myself as hostage in his absence and to obey your direction.'

'Even though I am a slave and you a centurion?'

'As you say, even so. In this territory your knowledge is superior to mine, and I am prepared to act even as your slave if necessary in order to achieve our goal. My knowledge of Celtic is, as you have already discovered, limited. But I am not too proud and ignorant to call you my master in the field where you are so. Or to ask you to use my name – Cassio.'

'Tell me then, Cassio, why is Marcus so desperate to secure Cunobarrus that he offers what must be repugnant to him, a pardon and freedom to one he considers a vile criminal?'

'I see no problem in telling you that – if you can be discreet?' He received Verluccus' surprised assent. 'There is need of the Second in the north of Britain, and until he can be assured that Isca and the territory it protects are safe, he dare not go. Your villainous brother and his followers are in danger of costing the legion its reputation.'

For the first time the whole enterprise seemed to make sense. He could understand why Marcus had not felt able to tell him this. How galling it must be for him, and how Cunobarrus would whoop to learn of it.

He told Cassio, 'I value your trust in me that you tell me such a secret; I do not know why you should. I am truly touched and grateful for your manner towards me. If I entrust something now to you, will you agree not to reveal it to Cunobarrus?' Cassio agreed, wondering at the wisdom of this, and Verluccus went on. 'Marcus has made my innocent brother hostage. If Cunobarrus were to discover this, he would do his damnedest to have Tanodonus murdered by the Romans. He despises anyone who submits to the Roman yoke. I beg you not to reveal it; it will play no part in what I say to him.'

Cassio could see the extent of the difficulty they now faced. How Verluccus was going to convince a man of such strong persuasion he could not imagine, and his confidence in the outcome of their enterprise began to wane. But he replied robustly, 'Say no more; I shall take my lead from you in all things. What do you think will happen when they take us? Are they watching us now, do you suppose?' He scanned the horizon from the promontory they had reached.

'If we are moving in the right direction and in the right territory – which, you may well know already, is nowhere near where we were previously – then there is a good chance that they have already made quarry of us. They will observe us and try to gauge our intentions and then ambush us. That is what we want, is it not? If you would then live longer, do not speak; let me do the talking. I might at least get us as far as Cunobarrus, if we are lucky.'

'Surely his men will recognize you?'

'What men? Marcus killed all who were in Belcon's camp. I have even doubted that this is Cunobarrus.'

'Oh, it is him all right. I think that is what alarms Marcus the most – that so soon after wiping out all who followed him, he has collected more of the same persuasion and continued to strike terror so that tax gatherers cannot function and slaves break out of their mines to join him.' Cassio dug into his belt and produced a knife. 'I think it is time to reveal why I volunteered to come. Do not be alarmed; it would make no sense for me to kill you.'

'Then what?' The knife Cassio was holding had a hilt bound with leather strips. He began to unwind the bindings.

'You may hate me for this; perhaps you have often cursed me. Have you ever wondered about the man who found you half-dead and handed you over to Marcus?'

The knife was unbound. He had it in his hands again, and tears were in his eyes. He could not speak.

'Of course you recognize it. I had to conceal it from you, but if we are ambushed, it will be taken from me. Give me instead the knife they gave you from supply and keep this for yourself. I know that my actions reduced you to servitude again, but perhaps it has not been wholly bad? My motive for accompanying you is out of respect and, yes, admiration for you as a warrior and because Marcus respects you – oh yes, he does. And let me tell you he saw to it that I was punished for not killing you on sight! Denied retirement and denied the spoils. Doing this may redeem my fortune.'

'There is no hope of that for you, Cassio,' he said sadly.

It was ambush country. It would surely happen at any moment. There had been a sense that some silent being or beings were watching their movements just as Verluccus had said they would. They had both felt the hair rising on the backs of their necks, had wondered about a sudden bird call, a suspicious movement and then an equally suspicious stillness when they paused to verify their suspicions. There was no habitation here, no life except for wheeling birds and the occasional rustle of a disturbed animal that they had approached too closely; their hearts were pounding at the waiting.

If they had not wanted to be taken, they would never have chosen the steep, short route which made them so vulnerable. As they did so, Verluccus imagined himself in the position of those who must be watching, considering what such careless travellers could be about, either total fools or decoys. But time pressed them into the action, and Cassio ascended first. Verluccus heard the brief scuffle and knew he was taken and it would not be the centurion's hand that was reaching to haul him upwards. As he was dragged over the ridge and pressed flat on the shelved cliff, he wondered if they had already killed his companion. There was no time to be lost if either of them was to be spared.

'How dare you?' He struggled to free himself, defying the vice-like grip and murderous expression which leered at him. 'Who dares to strike the brother of Cunobarrus? You lay your hand on me at your peril! I am Verluccus the Bloodspiller seeking his brother. Take me and my slave to Cunobarrus now or explain to him how you came to slaughter his brother, Verluccus the Bloodspiller.'

His familiarity with their language and his words gave them pause; he was not released, and the hold on him did not relax. 'Cunobarrus has no brother,' he was told.

Another voice said, 'Kill them; they have no gold.'

'I tell you I am the brother of Cunobarrus.' He raised his voice angrily. 'I am Verluccus the Bloodspiller. See if he does not know me.' He tried to ignore the expression which mention of his warrior name brought to Cassio's face. He remembered how Coridumnus had reacted to it.

Their captors debated the matter. Another man said, 'You are lying, whoever you are. We know Verluccus was killed at Belconia as was Canodranus. Cunobarrus has told us so himself.'

'My brother Cadrus – not Canodranus as you incorrectly name him – was killed there, and I avenged his death before I too was struck down; but I, Verluccus, was taken captive, and my life was spared because I was a runaway slave. I can prove I am Verluccus. Did you know he bore a mark placed there by the Romans? Has Cunobarrus told you that? Send to him to inquire if you doubt it.'

The brand was enough to raise doubt among them. There was much scratching of their heads and hesitation. He was allowed to rise to his feet. He pulled Cassio up also. 'He is my slave and companion. The man who harms him is answerable to me. Now take us to Cunobarrus.'

Cassio muttered quietly as they were hurried along the track. 'Is that true? You are the one they called Bloodspiller? We thought it a name for Cunobarrus.'

'Tell your man to be silent.' He did so and managed to confirm it was true; he was that man indeed. The name obviously meant something to Cassio; Verluccus knew it must end his companion's respect for him.

They travelled quickly for the whole of that day, west and north alternately, deep into country where no Roman boot had ever trod, until the men bade them cease running and rest. It was obviously a rendezvous place, a place where a decision as to whether they would live or die would be made. They made camp, and another precious night was wasted.

At daybreak a man came running along the line of a narrow stream; they were urged forward again, but now his status had clearly changed and the weapon threatening him was sheathed and the chains binding them were loosened though not removed.

They rose a few hundred more feet and rounded a bend to see in the valley a scatter of roundhouses of various sizes and a throng of curious people already come to the head of the main track. A man walked towards them. It was not Cunobarrus, and yet he proclaimed himself to be. So it was true – his brother was not alive; an impostor had claimed his name. He thrust a sword into Verluccus' hand.

'You claim to be Verluccus the Bloodspiller, the spiller of Roman blood. Kill that Roman now. He has no business being alive in my presence.'

'Cassio is here to serve me. Verluccus has killed enough Romans not to have to prove it by slaughtering his own slave. If you were Cunobarrus, you would know that. Is this some kind of a test, or is he really dead and you a pretender?'

'You are right.' The man nodded. 'I am not Cunobarrus. I am Deldon, son of Rogan.' He turned to the waiting crowd. 'He cannot know me, as I was raised elsewhere with my mother. I say he should be taken before Cunobarrus, who can confirm or disprove his claim.'

With the crowd's vocal assent, they were urged forward again.

They were driven between a group of huts until they reached the most spacious. This was no fortified camp such as Belcon had occupied but a community of families such as he had lived in with Merriol. Children crowded around them, curious about the Roman in their midst and unable to quite believe it without poking and prodding Cassio with their toy weapons.

The doors of a large roundhouse were pulled aside, and suddenly Cunobarrus loomed large before them. Even to Verluccus he was a daunting sight. His garments as ever were bright and gaudy reds, yellows, and greens. Around his neck in torcs and chains and on his hands and made into brooches he flaunted his gold. He paused and stared at the newcomers without expression.

Unsure of his standing, Verluccus waited for some indication of acceptance or rejection.

It came suddenly and fulsomely. Never before had Cunobarrus

gone so far towards him. The huge man flung open his arms and took a step forward, his face beaming with undisguised pleasure. Overcome with emotion which he could scarcely understand, Verluccus ran into the welcoming arms, and they hugged each other in silence.

Finally Cunobarrus said, 'Welcome, Verluccus. Welcome, welcome, Verluccus. You are three times welcome. I could not believe it when they said someone was coming who claimed to be my brother. I said he was an impostor, for I knew you to be butchered. But it is true – you are here and you are alive, though disfigured.' He looked critically at his trim haircut. 'Soon your hair will grow again and you will be Verluccus the Bloodspiller as you were. And you are not empty-handed.' He began to walk around Cassio, prodding and feeling his body as if considering his worth, and the man stood still, watchful, fearing to display fear.

'He is sound but old. Is he handy with a sword, do you think? Shall the boys have some fun with him?'

'Brother, Cassio serves me. I will not relinquish him – not even to you.'

'Then what gift have you brought me?'

'My bags are plundered by your men. I have what I stand in, nothing else. And Cassio is my companion and aide, not a slave. Brother!' He tried to draw Cunobarrus aside. 'There is a purpose in my coming here which I would impart to you privately.'

'Privately? Privately!' He raised his head, and his voice to denounce the very idea. 'We keep no secrets from our friends. There is nothing I am prepared to speak of which they cannot hear. Do not provoke my anger, brother – not so soon. My love for you is as strong as ever, but I owe my life and loyalty to Dolbactan and his people. You remember Rogan? Here is his kinsman, Dolbactan, my host and yours.'

He was presented with some pride to the head of the village. *So,* he thought, *again Cunobarrus is not chief man.*

Dolbactan was almost as effusive as Cunobarrus. He was a dark-haired man, a little shorter in stature but very muscular and strong. He too, unless it was his practice always to wear his colourful robes, had dressed carefully for the occasion. He put out a welcoming hand. 'Verluccus the Bloodspiller, brother of my good friend Cunobarrus, you are most welcome here. Tonight we feast to celebrate your arrival and you shall tell us your story – this reason which you say has brought you here. Tomorrow we shall find another place in which to celebrate your homecoming so that it will be known abroad.' He laughed uproariously. His meaning was clear to Verluccus; he wondered if Cassio understood it.

They were accommodated in a guest house, and Verluccus too was provided with fine garments, British clothes. He was allowed to keep Cassio with him, but it was made clear that he was suffered only as a slave and nothing more. He apologized to his companion as soon as they had some privacy.

'Verluccus, I assure you I am grateful to be alive now.' He grew more serious. 'This situation is not what Marcus supposes. I cannot believe that from this small town such a terror is unleashed as the Romans have of Cunobarrus. There must be a fortified camp elsewhere.'

'It may be so, but I doubt it. There will certainly be warriors here – not so many, perhaps, but ruthless enough and more in number than show themselves. Did you catch what he meant about tomorrow?'

Cassio shook his head.

'He means to set up a raid to celebrate my return – for me to demonstrate my ability, my famed skills in blood spilling. If I am to achieve Marcus' purpose, I must speak tonight. If only Cunobarrus would hear me privately.'

They gloomily agreed there was little likelihood of that.

'If I cannot speak to Cunobarrus alone, how can I deliver Marcus' message to him? He will not listen to me.'

'You must find a way. Find the words. I fear that if you warn him in public of the bloodshed which Marcus promises, his pride will prevent him accepting the offer. Tell him rather –'

He was interrupted by the man sent to attend them. 'None of that tongue here. Speak our language or be silent.'

Cassio lowered his voice. 'Tell him instead how good life is for all under Roman rule. Describe the benefits which people here could enjoy from trade and from adopting Roman customs.'

Verluccus shook his head. 'Cassio, do not be misled by the appearance of this place; these men are warriors. This is not a small settled community as it may appear to a casual observer. And you do not know my brother. The benefits you describe – these are the very things he despises. Your laws and your fine towns and your gods are an anathema to him. Pray that when the time comes and I must speak, the words I choose are fitting.'

Cassio looked at his transformed companion now in brightly coloured and checked trousers and robes. 'So! This is Verluccus the Bloodspiller! Not a name by which Marcus Marcius knows you. Remember why you are here, and do not be swayed to return to your old ways.'

'Why I am here? I shall not forget that! My brother Tanodonus' life is at stake.' He gripped his companion. 'Cunobarrus is in a bragging mood and given to exaggeration. Tonight you will hear tell of things which I have done and cannot deny – my crimes you will consider them. Here they will be considered brave deeds committed in a just cause. Do not despise me because my designs were opposed to yours. I had good reason to act as I did, and if need be, I would do so again. If I cannot achieve our purpose in time to save Tanodonus, then I must stay and rejoin Cunobarrus.'

'Is it so easy? Is the improvement of you so easily undone? Are a few layers of gaudy wool all that is required to turn you again into a barbarian savage? Do not forget the trust which Marcus has placed in you.' There was scorn in the centurion's voice.

'Cassio, my mind is in turmoil. Do not you turn on me. I tell you my brother Tanodonus is more important to me than Cunobarrus or you or any whim of Marcus Marcius. For him alone I am here, though I know now the task is hopeless.'

'I have no quarrel with you,' replied his companion hastily. 'I too am on edge. This oppressive weather hanging over us may help the temper of Cunobarrus, but it troubles me. A storm is long overdue.'

The evening air was heavy and sticky, and unusually, the land had been without rain for many days; men were talking of the weight of the sky above being upon them and complaining that their heads were pained by it. Verluccus was glad to see the feast table was laid in the open, a series of long benches set in a square to accommodate what seemed to be all the men and adult women. He and Cassio were conducted to where a heavily bejewelled Dolbactan sat, outshining even Cunobarrus.

'Sit next to me and eat,' the man said, indicating the only available seat. He had been welcomed again and presented to the assembly. There was no place for Cassio. He must wait for his master to throw scraps to him.

Sick at heart, he barely touched his food. *How much of this do you follow, Cassio?* he wondered as he heard Cunobarrus, with a great deal of embellishment and much fiction, spin a tale of a brutal and vicious barbarian – reputedly Verluccus less than a year before. Cunobarrus told of how Verluccus had come to him as a green and timid youth and had been hardened and schooled so that he might seek out his enemy, the vicious Drusus, and avenge his loved ones. He turned and looked at Cassio when Drusus' name arose and saw there enough reaction to tell him that the man probably knew who his enemy was. From him he might yet learn his true identity and finish what he had sworn to do.

Eventually the saga was at an end. He was expected to speak. He rose and turned to the expectant faces. 'My brother exaggerates my deeds when he praises me,' he said with modesty. 'It was, as I recall, not quite so, though in substance all that he has said is true. For my part I am amazed to find the brother I thought dead alive and glad to see it. May I know how he was saved?'

'We would know also how you are alive from that carnage,' said Cunobarrus. 'For myself, I was saved by Bodrogan.' He pointed to a man whom Verluccus recognized as a son of Rogan. 'Rogan had sent his son and a few handpicked men to right my folly, to track down and kill the sons of Belcon. Unfortunately they failed to catch them before they reached the Romans. But it placed them safe from the massacre. As for me, in the heat of battle, when my blood was hot and coursing,

I looked at our brave warriors all stripped and fearless, and I was clad in all my fine robes. I stripped them and my gold from me and threw it down and fought in the style of our forefathers, shielded by the gods alone, slaying our enemies with my sword. I fell, of course.' He bared his breast to reveal a livid scar. 'But I was not killed and was found alive, as were a few others, by Bodrogan. He brought us here to safety in the house of Dolbactan. You know, my brother, how I love finery and gold, but on that occasion to be without it saved my life, for I was unrecognized by my enemies and so was preserved to wreak revenge. The Romans stole my gold and so many lives, and so as soon as I was strong – and since – with men from Dolbactan, I show the Romans that Cunobarrus lives. I purloined a train of ingots and brought them here.' He flaunted the chains and rings with which he decorated his body, and his words were applauded with much foot stamping and table banging.

'And now, brother Verluccus, tell us how you survived, how you came to live again, and how you are come to us now.'

It was the moment he had been dreading. There could be no further delay. He rose doubtfully to his feet. 'My Lord Dolbactan, I beg you to forgive my poor speechmaking. I am not a storyteller; I do not have the gift to weave as good a tale as my brother does. My own tale will be brief.' He paused and looked at the faces gazing at him in expectation, and he knew beyond a shadow of doubt that nothing of what he had come to tell them would be welcome to their ears, least of all to the ears of Cunobarrus. He looked at the overhanging sky for inspiration and prayed silently for the dark and threatening clouds to burst, for a torrent to fall upon them and break up their feasting. It was not to be.

'My brother Cunobarrus has told you many things of me, but for his pride's sake and mine, one thing he has left unsaid. It is a sorry thing to tell, but it must be told, as it is central to the reason why I too survived the slaughter of Belcon's fort. This is not a thing which was concealed from my fellow warriors, but my actions made it forgotten. I will be brief.

'When I was a child, it was my misfortune to be made a slave on the whim of a Roman boy who took a fancy to me. Within one day I ran away, but by then a brand had been burned upon me to show the world that I was the property of this man, the boy's father. After many years I was reunited with my brothers Cunobarrus and Cadrus, and I became the warrior you have heard described, Verluccus the Bloodspiller.

'At Belconia, when the Romans were collecting their dead and wounded, they chanced on me and found this mark, which they recognized, and so I was restored to the man who claimed to own me. Since that time I have been a slave.'

'But no longer!' Cunobarrus shouted, hammering on the table. 'By good fortune you are escaped and come to join us again.' He called for more beer to be served for all. 'Tell now how you killed your master and found your way to us!'

Verluccus took a long drink of the brew and a deep breath. So much depended on what he next said. This was not how he had envisaged it might be, and that had been difficult enough. He looked at Cunobarrus in desperation, hoping that his brother would realize he was in a predicament and rescue him – a foolish and pointless hope.

'Lord Dolbactan, Cunobarrus, warriors, friends, I am not a free man.' The faint undertone of approval died, the silence interrupted by the murmur of those asking for confirmation of what they had heard. Heads and eyes turned from him to Cassio and then to him again. 'I am not here as a free man or as a runaway slave. I am here on an embassy to my brother Cunobarrus for the Roman legate at Isca Silurum, Marcus Marcius.'

No one spoke. A breath was drawn sharply. A dog whined quietly. There was the sudden sound of a knife splitting wood. He knew that all eyes were turned to Cunobarrus for him to guide their response, and he also knew that the man who had driven his knife into the table was Cunobarrus. There was an expression on Cunobarrus' face as dark as the thunderclouds above them. It was Dolbactan who broke the long silence.

'Continue. We will hear this message which you have brought from the Romans.'

What should he say now? He wanted to turn and ask Cassio for assistance, but already Bodrogan was clambering to his feet, about to mount the table itself, staring beyond him, glaring at the Roman. A single utterance from Cassio would have been his death sentence. Already the mission was a failure.

He began again. 'My lord, I have told you that my life was spared because the mark on my back was recognized. This was so because the man who attacked Belconia and slaughtered all bar we few was Marcus Marcius, and he was – is – the brother of the man who first enslaved me, Lucius Marcius.'

'We know who he is!' hissed Cunobarrus between clenched teeth.

'And you come on an embassy for such a man!' Bodrogan cried out. 'You are alive, but my father and mother are dead!' He spat at him across the table.

'Silence! Silence!' roared Dolbactan. 'Speak, boy, or be damned. Cunobarrus, let him speak.'

He was making a hopeless hash of this. 'I was restored to Gaius Marcius as I have said, and though I resisted at first, I saw that I had no choice but to submit to my new condition. Then I heard that Cunobarrus was alive. I gave thanks to the gods for sparing him and accepted that my lot was to be a slave. So it has been since – until our relationship was discovered. Then I was flogged and sent to be tortured by Marcus Marcius so that he might discover your whereabouts from me.'

'So you admit it – you are a filthy traitor.' It was a voice from the body of the audience, one he did not recognize, but it spoke the thoughts of many.

'I arrived at Isca in chains and terror, punished for my struggles to free myself, expecting worse and fearing I could not withstand what must follow. There was nothing I could tell them even if I was willing, which I was not. So I came face to face with our sworn enemy, he whom you hate above all men. From him, instead of abuse, I received better treatment than at any time since my capture. Despite all that he must know or suspect of me, he showed me respect. This was not for my sake but for the sake of the respect he has for my warrior brother, Cunobarrus.' It was somewhat short of Marcus' opinion of Cunobarrus, he was sure, but telling the absolute truth would not help him now.

He was forced to continue into the hostile and extended silence.

'Only recently, he had discovered my relationship to Cunobarrus. He saw that the message he wants to reach him could be delivered through me. That is why I have come – to give Cunobarrus his message and for no other reason.'

'The message.' 'Marcius sends us a message.' 'You have not yet told us what it is.' Various derisory voices spoke from around him.

He knew it was too soon. He tried a different approach. Force of arms they might respect.

'While I was in his camp I saw his army. He commands a whole legion, thousands of men, well trained, well equipped, and auxiliaries too. A thousand and more of them. They strain to find you! There are men who fight with swords, with spears, with arrows, with dogs, men on horse and men on foot. They have huge machines of war. They await only his command to move, and they will, as surely as the sun sets and rises again, come upon you and leave not a living soul in the whole of this country until Cunobarrus is killed or taken. He will not give up. If you will not accept his offer, that is what he threatens to do. Are you prepared to be the cause of so much carnage?'

'Is this his message?' Cunobarrus was scornful. 'We know that, don't we, men? We know what he thinks he would do. But we are secure here. He cannot find us; his so-called army is quickly at a loss in our hills. These men you see here are not his only enemy. We have men freed from his mines, and now they lie like foxes in their earths; but when we send out the call to arms they will be like a pack of wolves. We have no fear of Marcus and his army.'

'This offer you speak of – may we know it?' It was Dolbactan who asked the question.

'Marcus knows nothing of you, Lord Dolbactan; it is Cunobarrus whom he invites to parley with him, to go to his fortress at Isca in trust and confidence that he will not be harmed and there talk terms of peace with him. If you and he, Brother, cannot come to terms, he will allow you safe passage to return here; then what must follow will follow.'

It was too much. The tension snapped. Cunobarrus broke into loud guffaws and bellows of raucous laughter, hammering with delight upon the board in front of him, and so too did everyone else bar Verluccus and Cassio. Sick to his stomach at his utter failure, he could only sink his head into his hands and wait for the uproar to cease.

'Ah, Brother! That was brilliant! You had us all believing you. I had not realized what a good storyteller you are! I never took you for a practical joker. Now, just to round it off, tell us that your slave is really Marcus Marcius brought to us in disguise.'

'It is no joke, Brother; it is the truth. Marcus Marcius would have you go down to him at Isca Silurum, where he would put a proposition to you. Cassio volunteered to come as proof of his good intent, a hostage until you return.'

Cunobarrus had sobered somewhat. 'I'll not go to him. Let him do his worst. He may comb this land from tomorrow until the sky falls upon us, but he will not find me.'

Dolbactan leaned forward with interest. 'What is the nature of his proposition? Do you know what he has in mind?'

'Essentially it is that Cunobarrus give up this way of life and urge his followers to be peaceable and accept the rule of law. He wants his gold back too; and Cunobarrus must return to live with the Dobunni, his own tribe. If he will do this, his life and those whom the Romans call criminals will be spared.'

'This is rubbish!' shouted his brother. 'What a simpleton you are, as ever, to fall for his lies. He knows he cannot get his hands on me, and he thinks to have me betrayed by you, you spineless idiot. He has seen the last of you and of this stooge. I will be the slave of no Roman.'

'I am assured you will not be a slave but live fully pardoned as a free man in Daruentum.'

'No man in Daruentum is free! They are all slaves as much as you are. And I have no need of pardon from Marcus Marcius or any other. I have heard enough of this. Dolbactan, send him away – return him to the guest house. I will speak to him and turn him again into the warrior I made him before. He will serve you as I do.'

Dolbactan eyed him shrewdly. 'When did this Roman expect to see you again? He must have set a limit on this enterprise?'

'By the Roman calendar, the twentieth day of April. That will be the next full moon. We have wasted more than two of our precious days already and have but three left. If Cunobarrus does not put in an appearance at Isca, then Marcus will come on the rampage and, without mercy, destroy every man, woman and child who stands between him and his object, Cunobarrus. None but Roman citizens are to be spared. With the men he has at his disposal, this is no idle threat; this land will be sodden from blood and charred from fire. He has the means, and he will not rest until he achieves his end. Even the bravest of your warriors will be no match for such as him. But if he can make peace with Cunobarrus, he will allow all here to live in peace, in the Roman way. Here he will have no interest in building a city, his patrols will rarely venture onto this land if you do not attack his citizens, and if the taxes they impose are paid you will govern yourselves through your own leaders.' He had no need to hear what their response would be; even as he spoke the latter words, he knew how limp and feeble they must sound.

'Rubbish!' expostulated Cunobarrus, now joining Bodrogan on the table, yelling to din the uproar and be heard. 'Let him come with his army. That is exactly what we want. Oh, he has promised well! This threat will rid our land of Romans forever. Let him come! Long we have tried and long we have failed to unite our tribes to rise as one. Can you not see how much hatred this plan of his will inspire throughout our land? Who would tolerate such despotic rule? We should hasten and prepare beacons to inflame this country and rouse support for us. Spread the word! Oh, excellent, excellent!' He clapped his hands together, moving along the board to encourage the hesitant to support his vision, and soon he had the whole company urging

Dolbactan to agree: 'Death to all Romans! Kill the Roman! Kill the Roman! Death, death, death.'

Dolbactan, who seemed impassive to the encouragement, leaned forward. 'Take your slave and get yourself into the guest house. I will take counsel about what we do with you.'

'I am sorry, Cassio.' In the guest house Verluccus spoke in a quiet undertone in Latin. 'I tried to tell Marcus I could not sway Cunobarrus. This was a pointless exercise. You can see how it is. Those things you heard said of me, if you understood – they are not all true, and those which are have much exaggeration. I do not want to return to that way of life except to kill one man. I saw it in your face when Cunobarrus mentioned his name. You know who Drusus is, don't you?'

'There are many men named Drusus; I cannot say,' replied the Centurion. 'You may return to that life or not as you choose, and I shall die; but Marcus will avenge my death. I am here to serve the Emperor as I swore to do when I first became a soldier. If you have any influence with these people, let my death be fitting; that is all I ask. But I have not entirely given up hope.' He rallied himself and stood. 'I do not feel entirely deserted by my gods. Let us pray in silence for our deliverance from this.'

They fell into silent contemplation, thinking about those whom they loved and of dear comradeships which they would never enjoy again. He tried to think of Tanodonus and of how he would suffer and not know for what reason, but it was the face of Gaia which floated before his eyes. Unconscious of the movement, his hand swept his face, trying to brush away the memory of her kiss and the renewed sensation of longing for her.

Well before it was dawn, Cunobarrus entered their hut. It was a more sober and thoughtful Cunobarrus than they had seen the night before. They both awoke instantly at his disturbance, expecting news of their fate.

'How much of our language does he understand?' he asked. 'I do not speak Roman.' He spat to cleanse his mouth after the use of such an obscenity.

'Cassio understood sufficient last night to know he will not leave here alive.'

'Good,' said his brother abruptly. He seemed hesitant and then sat and spoke frankly. 'I believe that a man should die with a sword in his hand. I kill my enemies when my blood is up, but I fight clean and for a reason. I am a warrior, and I would pass over as a warrior.'

They were puzzled as to his meaning. He continued.

'You know we approach the feast of Beltane, and Dolbactan has invited the priests to oversee the ceremony.' Verluccus sensed the chilling warning in his voice. 'Verluccus, you know it is not my practice. I believe in the gods, yes, but only so far as we cause them offence or gain their approval and I keep the seasons as is fitting. That was nonsense when we played that joke on you about drinking blood and you spilled it down your body. It was a stupid trick, a game played on an innocent … you know it is not our practice to drink the blood of men, but we had determined your name was to be Blood Drinker. Instead, you … well, enough of that. But these priests … it is decided … this oppressive air that will not disperse or break into a storm is an ill omen. But it can be dispersed. And as the storm can be driven away, so too can be our enemies, the Romans – by magic. I have tried to reason with Dolbactan, but in this I am outnumbered, out-talked. I have no desire to see this man live, but I would sooner put a sword in his hand and give him a chance to defend himself.'

'What do you mean, Brother? What is to happen to Cassio?'

'Dolbactan has determined that the priests will reveal the will of the gods through your Roman's death. He will submit to the priest's knife, and his belly will be split open so that his innards may be read in the manner the Romans do with cattle; thus his death throes will make all plain, and my fate too will be decided. Tell him when he is offered the cup to drink deeply; it will aid him.'

'You must do something to prevent it. Give us back our weapons; let us flee from this place.'

'Prevent it? I'll not prevent the death of any Roman. If I restored your weapons to you, it would be so that you could kill yourselves. Fleeing is not for you. You are in my custody, and I will not betray my trust. I am accepted in this community only because of the gold I gave to Dolbactan and the further wealth I promise him. Though he sits on his pile of gold, no amount of it will overcome his beliefs. I am not here to free your man or give him an easier death, only to prepare him to steel himself and know his fate. His Roman garments will be taken from him and burned before his eyes. He will be bathed and anointed and garbed in sacred vestments and taken to the sacred grove. It is there that he will be given to the gods. If the gods are pleased with this gift, this oppressive air will clear, the sun will shine again, and the Romans may be driven from this land as the clouds are cleared from the sky. Only when this is done can the feast of Beltane proceed.' Cunobarrus' voice made it clear what he thought of such superstition.

He could say no more, for the hut was suddenly filled with Dolbactan's men. They shouldered Cunobarrus and Verluccus aside and seized Cassio and dragged him away struggling and fighting. Cunobarrus held Verluccus firmly to prevent his following. Verluccus called to Cassio in Latin, 'May your gods sustain you.'

They were alone now, and Cunobarrus turned to him angrily. 'Now tell me by what means this Marcus Marcius has persuaded you to betray me, your own brother and fellow warrior. You could have killed that soldier – he is no match for you – and come here alone or made good your escape from your enslavement, but you did not. You cannot have supposed that I would willingly cast this life aside to enslave myself to his kind, so he must have offered some palatable inducement to make you betray me. Speak, or I swear I shall run you through myself.'

'No palatable inducement, I assure you. I tried to tell him you would reject his offer, though I do believe he meant exactly what he promised. But he has threatened the life of one who is dear to my heart if you will not come to an agreement with him to let you return freely and await his onslaught; I found myself unable to do other than deliver his message. I can save the other one if you allow me to flee from here and return to him now.'

'And does such a threat not tell you what kind of a man he is? He would not allow such as me to go from his fortress alive.' Cunobarrus did not pursue the identity of his brother's dear one but went on, 'I will not allow you to return to him. I have to show Dolbactan and these people where my loyalties lie, even if you have become a traitor. You, if they choose to let you live, must become one of us again.'

Verluccus said a silent prayer of farewell to Tanodonus, for he knew Marcus would have no compunction about carrying out his threat. He felt utterly sickened by his situation and had for that moment forgotten Cassio's predicament.

'I will take you now to view the ceremony. Do not attempt to intervene; it will be done as it must be done, and you must hope that the thirst of the gods is satisfied with one and that your death will not follow.'

He wanted to say, 'Why do you live with and support such people?' but the answer was obvious. Instead he said, 'It would have been better that I died at Belconia as I should have done, for I bring nothing but misery and unhappiness wherever I go.'

'That is true; it would have been better if you had died then and Cadrus had lived instead. But you did not, so stop your whining and follow me.' And Cunobarrus strode from the hut with no further word.

They crossed a mile or so of open land upon which already the beacons were constructed in readiness for the spring purification rites in which their cattle would be driven between the fires. Then they plunged into woods again where ash trees grew densely, and suddenly there was a clearing, a wide arena of evenly grown ash saplings. At the far end beneath a large and spreading mother ash was an ancient stone, and beside this a man clad in priestly robes was standing with his attendants, waiting.

From behind them he heard the sound of voices chanting in unison some mysterious incantation, and in a little while a procession came towards the ash grove. Cassio was at the head of it, his arms held by Deldon and Bodrogan. He was decked in the robe Cunobarrus had described and adorned with wreaths of flowers, a circlet on his head and swathes of them strung around his neck, and even as they moved, more folk pressed even more of these floral chains upon him. It looked to Verluccus as if he had been decked out for a marriage instead of a killing.

Cassio looked straight ahead with his jaw grimly set, and Cunobarrus held his brother in an iron grip to prevent any action which might interfere with the ceremony. Verluccus could only watch in dreadful fascination as the procession broke, and only the victim and his escort reached the priest.

The omens were not good. Even as they stood there, the thunder continued to rumble ever closer, yet the rain did not fall. Verluccus was certain he must soon follow Cassio to his death.

The priest turned to his acolyte and took from the proffered gaudy cushion a large steel knife with a golden hilt. He held it aloft as Deldon and Bodrogan pushed the sacrificial offering, now stripped of his robe, onto his knees and pulled back his head to expose his throat.

The flash of lightning and the simultaneous crack of thunder shook the ground beneath them. Brilliance lit the grove, and the mother ash was riven by flame. To Verluccus it was as if Belenos himself had come to the grove to accept his offering.

But it was the priest who was lit up. A spectacular fire ran from the lofted knife and into the ground. Cassio and those who held him slumped lifeless to the earth as the boughs of the ancient ash broke away and crashed indiscriminately on those below.

Verluccus was the first to recover. He broke from his brother and raced across the clearing. He dropped onto his knees beside Cassio's inert body. He pummelled and struggled with him and begged him to live, shaking and jerking life into his body again, even kissing his face, breathing into him, begging him to come back to him. Beyond that he had no awareness of what else was happening – of the removal of the still-smouldering body of the priest and his dead acolytes, of the gradual awakening of the awestruck crowd, of the torrent of rain which was falling upon them.

He did not know for how long he had fought, but suddenly the eyes beneath his own fluttered and opened, and pale and as ashen as the trees surrounding them, Cassio breathed again and spoke to him.

'What in the name of Jupiter ...?' He wiped the kiss from his mouth, more angry than relieved to be brought to life again.

'I thought you were dead.'

Cassio lay back on the ground and tried to take in what had happened to him.

'I think they call it necrophilia,' he said at last. He had obviously become utterly deranged.

'Don't you remember what they did? I was trying to make you live again.'

Cassio lay still, absorbing what Verluccus was telling him, and then he said in awe, 'It was Jupiter! I saw Jupiter. Verluccus, I saw Jupiter. For me, simple Gnaeus Cassius, a mere centurion, the great god Jupiter, best and greatest of all gods, brought down the priest. He hurled down a thunderbolt from heaven and saved my life. I cannot believe this thing. I am alive, aren't I? Confirm I am alive. Not dead – not dead and you too in the underworld beside me?'

'No, you are not dead. It is the priests who are dead. And if this was the act of Jupiter, then Jupiter be praised.'

People were beginning to move about; Verluccus and Cassio rose and turned to find Dolbactan and Cunobarrus beside them trembling with awe at Cassio's deliverance.

'Your god is powerful,' said Dolbactan. 'Here is the rain falling which has been hanging overhead as if contained in a great belly. Our priests have been destroyed by your god and abandoned us. Return to my home and let me honour you appropriately. We will consider again the message which you brought to us.'

9

─────────── ✺ ───────────

The death of the priest and his acolytes had a profound effect on Dolbactan. He wished to know more of Marcus' offer – what his own status would be and what his chances were of retaining the position he held among his people. Verluccus could not answer him. Marcus Marcius did not know of Dolbactan, only of Cunobarrus, and it was only Cunobarrus to whom he was prepared to talk. Cunobarrus still argued against it; but he no longer had the support of Deldon or Bodrogan, who also had been maimed by the falling boughs, and he knew his was a lost cause. So Cunobarrus had to go, and Cassio, held as hostage for him, was received into Dolbactan's hut and treated as an honoured guest.

The brothers did not travel alone. Verluccus had emphasized Marcus' time constraint; even now he doubted that he could return in the allotted time. But they were provided with a war chariot in which to travel and accompanied by a fitting escort. Even so, Cunobarrus would have delayed given the chance.

'I think you do not want to be there in time,' Verluccus accused him.

The response was surly. 'No. I do not want to be there at all. But I shall be. It is your doing that I take this road. The gods have abandoned me and the priests deserted me. The man I once called brother has deprived me of men, of wealth, of my dignity and brought about that I should debase myself before my enemies as a slave. I want neither his company nor his conversation. He should be silent and stay behind me where I need not look upon him.'

'Cunobarrus, Brother,' Verluccus answered, 'you comply with all that Marcus Marcius demanded by coming to him as you do. He is willing to let you return to that place if you cannot come to terms. I know you think I have betrayed you – perhaps you are right – but I did it not to save my own skin but that of others. If he and you cannot agree, I will cast aside all oaths I have made to the Romans – yes, even of my allegiance to my master, and fight beside you if you will have me.'

He received no acknowledgement even that he had been heard, and for the rest of their journey Cunobarrus spoke to him only when absolute necessity demanded it.

10

The triclinium door opened, and a soldier saluted. Four faces turned as one.

'Men have been sighted, Commander – a chariot and escorting men approaching.'

Marcus was visibly relieved. The day had come when he must send off the execution squad, and he had greatly hoped he would have no need to. They were all ready to go; Vitellius had said his nod only was awaited.

'What number of men? Give a proper report or none at all.' Vitellius spoke angrily. It did not necessarily follow that the bet he had with Marcus was lost.

'A crowd of natives, bold as crows. They are making their way towards us without subterfuge, a dozen or more all told.'

'I will have only Cunobarrus and Verluccus admitted – Cassio also, of course, should he be among them. The others must remain outside the gate. Bring those two to the principium. Open the gate; admit them freely and pass the word: there will be order. No insults, no obstruction. Bring him speedily to the principium, and I will greet him there.'

'No wonder he makes fools of us.' Vitellius grinned, acknowledging his own error and observing the progress of the two men along the main street. 'Look at him – look at them both! See how gaudily they are attired, how boldly they march towards us, and look how he flaunts before your eyes the gold he stole from us!' Cunobarrus was wearing his personal regalia.

'Who is to be present at your conference?' Assinius had spoken little during the exchanges, waiting no doubt to see which way the wind finally blew.

'Myself only. Send for a man from the town to be our interpreter. My British tongue is fair, but he will have no Latin, and I want no misunderstanding about our position, about any agreement we arrive at. Be swift and have a wise choice made.'

Nearly in sight of the fortress Cunobarrus had produced fresh robes from their packs and dressed himself carefully, bidding Verluccus do likewise. They would not crawl before the Romans in abject submission, wet and bedraggled from the rain, but stride in with pride like men come to talk to equals on equal terms and shame the Romans, if they were capable of shame, into treating them with dignity. After so much procrastination, the spring in Cunobarrus' step was remarkable to see.

The road they were directed to use as they entered the gate was very straight and seemed very long. Walking a pace behind his brother, Verluccus thought he would remember forever every step of the way. Their path was lined with both men in arms and men off duty come out of curiosity to see them. Despite the directive that they must respect their visitor, there were not a few who had comments to pass about the sight of the notorious criminal being granted free access to their fortress and welcomed by their commander as if a visitor of some distinction.

'So this is him? Bloody Cunobarrus, spiller of honest men's blood,' Vitellius had muttered to Marcus as they passed through the gateway. 'You allow him to stride forward as though in triumph. A triumph for you to get him thus far. And I see the slave has also reverted to barbarian dress. Are you going to permit that? Now his usefulness to you is over, why not give him to the lads to play with? I have got a few recruits who could do with some real practice – and take on the other one too.' Marcus frowned in vain to hush him, but he would not be silenced. 'You know my views on this; they are not disguised. I would not fete Cunobarrus! Were I in command here, things would be different! Once I got him within my reach, I would not let him go. I would remind him of his crimes and of the misery he has wrought, and then I would match him and that brother of his, one against the other, to the death. And then I would chop the head off the survivor and stick both of them up above that very gate as trophies. What will you wager now on Cunobarrus with a net and trident against the slave armed with a sword?'

'That is enough of such talk. I will not break my word, and I will not allow you to do so either. While I am in command and Cunobarrus is here, he is to be treated with honour like any guest. And Verluccus also; my nephew will remain confined within my house until our business is done. This brief period of pseudo freedom may be all that I can reward Verluccus with.'

'All, Marcus Marcius?' said the other. 'I trust this freedom does not include the officers' mess and private quarters? You are allowing the third scoundrel, the one at Daruentum, to live. Is that not reward enough?'

There was no time for further speech; Cunobarrus was very close. It was true; he was flaunting the gold which he had stolen from them – that or some other come by equally criminal means. The two men reached Marcus and Vitellius and the other tribunes, and Cunobarrus was greeted cordially – more cordially than he deserved or anticipated. Marcus invited him to enter the offices.

A centurion stepped forward and detained Verluccus. 'You are not required while they talk; you may wander at will. That is the commander's express wish. But do not enter the praetorium nor other private places. I think Titus Justinius knows you?' He raised his hand and signalled for Titus to step forward. 'Soldier, you are responsible for his good conduct. Keep him by you. He is not required as an interpreter; that has been arranged. The other criminal is being treated royally; you may assure him of that. Now keep him from my sight, for like Tribune Vitellius, I am not as forgiving as our commander.'

'A meal, I think? What do you say?' said Titus, and Verluccus nodded; he was very hungry. 'Can you tell me what happened, or are you under penalty to remain silent about it?'

'I don't think I should speak of what my mission was. As you can see, I have brought Cunobarrus here. Be content to know what I told you previously and don't press me for more. I don't know how much I may or may not say.' He wondered if Titus would object to his free way of talking, but it seemed to be all right. He supposed if others joined them he must be more circumspect.

He did not see Cunobarrus again that night. Titus provided him with hot food at the cook house and shortly afterwards took him to the guest room where he had slept before. He slept fitfully, assuring himself that all must be well by virtue of the fact that he had not been placed in chains and beaten up. And now, relieved of his fear for Tanodonus, he dreamed again of Gaia.

Titus came for him the next morning with the news that he was assigned to entertain him; 'to escort and keep him guarded' was the way he had described his duties to his barrack mates. He told them he had been chosen because the slave's master was a personal friend of his. The other young soldiers seemed to think he ought to feel insulted, and he supposed that perhaps he ought. He suggested that a visit to see who was drilling in the amphitheatre might be interesting.

Men had been practising in the arena, but almost as soon as Titus and his charge entered they were formed up into orderly lines and marched away. Verluccus wondered about this. Was it because his knowledge of their tactics might make him more dangerous? He knew well enough how they fought, he mused, smiling to himself; he had personal experience of it. Some other young men came to join him and Titus, thawing a little towards him since he appeared to behave in a respectful enough manner. For a little while they sat side by side, Titus drawn into conversation with them and Verluccus feeling self-conscious and ill placed. After a lengthy period when absolutely nothing happened and the boys amused themselves in telling dirty stories, other seats began gradually to fill; more action seemed to be anticipated.

A bull thundered in, snorting and irritated, and a few bold youths jumped down and began to tease it so that it became more enraged and started running wildly at them, scattering them in good-humoured panic. The temptation to join in the fun was great in Titus, but he restrained himself and confined his enthusiasm to shouting for his mess mates to do better. Eventually the beast was expelled and more lads entered, again with dummy swords, and began sparring against each other. It was a casual type of drill – no serious tactical deployment, just arm strengthening exercises and feinting for recruits even greener than Titus. Verluccus became engrossed in their training, enjoying the errors they made, criticizing and admiring and shouting encouragement and censure on equal terms with the young soldier spectators, his opinion and judgement accepted as if as valid as their own. He knew that they had momentarily forgotten that he was a slave.

At the furthest end there was a sudden stir, and a group of tribunes entered and took places at the best seats. Titus identified them for Verluccus. 'Equestrian Tribunes Decimus Assinius Varus and Gnaeus Servius and Senatorial Tribune Drusus Vitellius, deputy to Marcus Marcius.' He saw that they took note of where he was sitting, and his enthusiasm faltered under their gaze. 'They must be bored', added Titus, 'to find entertainment in boys' games. Drusus Vitellius is the best swordsman in the legion.'

Verluccus had already caught his breath, wondering if he had misheard. 'Did you say Drusus? Which is he?'

He pointed to one of the men. 'Why, Tribune Vitellius, Drusus Vitellius. Everyone calls him Drusus – not directly to his face, of course, but that is what he is known as when not formally addressed.' He saw an expression on the slave's face which chilled him. He felt the hairs on his neck rise. *What have I said?* he wondered. Verluccus' eyes were concentrating on the group of tribunes.

From the group one man rose and made his way to the exit. He reappeared shortly afterwards at the contenders' entry, to the delight of the participants and spectators alike.

A cry went up from Titus' companions – 'Drusus, Drusus, Drusus' – and, sword upon shield, a rhythm was struck. The tribune raised an arm in acknowledgement and took up a sword and began to demonstrate how it ought to be handled, how it ought to be thrust. One by one, each of the young soldiers received what would have been a fatal blow and fell dramatically before him. It was great good fun, but now they were all 'dead', and he turned to seek a better opponent, inviting one of his fellow tribunes to spar with him.

But already Titus had been unceremoniously upended and disarmed. He was on the floor, winded and wondering what had hit him and horribly aware that his sword had been removed from its sheath and was in Verluccus' hands. As Titus regained his feet, he saw Verluccus below him bounding across the arena floor, waving the weapon on high and screaming hatred at the surprised tribune, who was still armed only with a wooden practice sword.

Drusus had seen the movement even as he heard the war cry. He recovered his senses rapidly and threw down the dummy weapon, drawing his own sword from its sheath, a momentary thrill of horror exchanged for sheer delight. This was more than he had dreamed of and was not of his own doing – there were witnesses enough to vouch for that to Marcus Marcius.

He deflected the first savage assault skilfully, and the barbarian drew back, his eyes burning with hatred for him. They began to circle each other, cautiously trying to gauge the other's strengths and weaknesses. No one needed to wonder what their intent was. It was plain enough: each was determined to kill the other, though the gods alone knew for what reason.

Somebody thought to send for Marcus; here was something he should know. He was virtually alone with another equally unstable barbarian.

There were a few feints, and the spectators were treated to a display of the superiority of Roman skill and power against the wild and furious passes of an undisciplined Celt. A hush fell over the whole stadium, broken only by the scuffling feet, the panting breath, and the clang of striking metal.

It was inevitable that Drusus must win; he had his own familiar weapon and was in excellent condition and highly trained. But he did not find his victory easy. As he parried the blind fury of his opponent, he acknowledged that had the challenger been properly trained and fit and unhampered by the robes he was still clad in, the victory might easily have gone against him.

It was exhaustion; lack of practice; and the strange, short Roman sword that beat Verluccus. He no longer had the stamina he had once possessed, and eventually he sank to his knees, gasping for breath, waiting for the edge of metal to pierce his flesh and wondering if he would know when it came and where it would enter, wondering if indeed it had already fallen and he was even now killed.

He was sobbing tears of frustration. If he was still alive, then Drusus should not be, and so he had failed; he had done all that was humanly possible to avenge those deaths and clear himself of the guilt that he had not died with them, but it was not enough.

Drusus' heart was pounding. His chest was heaving. Still mystified by the attack, he gazed down at his beaten assailant and the waiting neck. There was no appeal for mercy, no effort to clutch his knees. He glanced across the arena and saw Marcus and Cunobarrus bearing down upon him. He drew breath and raised his sword. It swung down and, just in time, it turned. The flat side of the weapon crashed against the exposed skull, and the defeated man fell in a crumpled heap.

'By Hercules, explain yourself!' Marcus demanded. 'Can I not turn my back on you? How has this come about? I need to know, Vitellius, and quickly too.'

Cunobarrus was examining his brother, relieved to find that though the wound on his head was severe, he was not dead.

'Are you mad? Can I not trust you, Vitellius?' He turned to find that a stretcher party had arrived. 'Lift him carefully and carry him into the infirmary.'

Vitellius protested his innocence. 'Ask anyone – this was not of my choosing. He came from the seats like something possessed. Who gave him the sword, I should like to know?'

An embarrassed Titus had run up to them. 'I did not give it to him; it was taken from me. I had no idea he would do such a thing. It came about when he learned your name was Drusus.'

A heavy stick descended onto the young man's back. 'That is for allowing your sword to be taken,' said his centurion, who had heard it all.

'You also need to see the surgeon,' Marcus coldly informed Vitellius. 'Your arm is bleeding.'

Vitellius grinned. 'No one has drawn blood from me since I was a youth. I knew he had the makings of a sword fighter; he just needs training. And I want to know what objection he has to my name.' He left them and followed his victim into the infirmary building.

'Tribune.' One of the stretcher bearers approached Vitellius. 'I took this from him. I know this knife; it belongs to Centurion Gnaeus Cassius. I fear there is treachery here.'

'Are you certain?' Vitellius took the knife. The initials G.C. Cassius had carved into the ornamented hilt were pointed out to him.

'Tell me, Cunobarrus, what shape was Gnaeus Cassius in when you last saw him?' With a respectable dressing on his upper arm, he had rejoined Marcus and the barbarian at the bedside of the still-unconscious Verluccus.

'He was having the time of his life, his every whim being attended to by our fairest young women. I doubt he will voluntarily return to you when he may. That knife, once the property of my own father, was given up by him in friendship and restored to its rightful owner. You will know how Cassius came by it.'

'I hope you speak truly, Cunobarrus,' Marcus said dryly. 'Now can you explain your brother's actions?'

Verluccus was coming round. The wound had been staunched and dressed, and his head was swathed in a bloody bandage. When he discovered he was still alive, he spoke to his brother first.

'That was him – at last I have found Drusus. I had to do it. I cannot help what takes place between you and Marcus, but I had to do what I did. He has left me living, but I do not want to live longer in this world. Why did he not kill me as he ought to have done when he defeated me?'

Cunobarrus scowled. 'You are so stupid. There is more at stake here than your petty quarrel.'

He turned to the interpreter, but Marcus said, 'I heard what was said, but I do not understand it. What is this thing between Verluccus and the tribune?'

'He is my sworn enemy,' said Verluccus. 'I cannot rest while he lives. I am sworn to kill him for the atrocities he did to my people.'

'Flattered as I am to be given credit for it,' drawled Vitellius, 'I have to confess that I was not at Belconia but here in charge of Isca at the time.' Not for the first time, he reflected that if he and not Virens had accompanied Marcus on that occasion, he would not have been such a fool as to get himself killed, and he most certainly would not have allowed Cunobarrus to escape with his life. 'And if Cunobarrus can come to terms with what took place and accept the offer made by our commander, why cannot you?'

Cunobarrus answered for him. 'My brother is not speaking of Belconia but of another place where he once lived. It was because of what took place there that Verluccus came to us. Then he was a green and callow boy in need of drilling. I trained him to hate his enemy and used your name, your existence, to keep his hatred alive.'

'And what am I supposed to have done to his people? Who were they? I have never come across him before.' Vitellius was by no means dismayed to learn how hated he was by the barbarians.

Verluccus spoke up, painfully aware of the wound in his head. 'Do not deny your part in it! Rignis nailed to a tree, Bodecus and his father and brother butchered, the girl I was to wed killed by her own mother to protect her from worse, and worse done to many women. I was the shepherd of Merriol and away in the hills with Enemno when you came. It was the smoke from the burning houses which brought me home in time to see you depart with those you had reduced into slavery. It was the men you hunted who told me the name of the one responsible – Drusus.'

'Ah!' Enlightenment had dawned in Vitellius, who was nodding in sober agreement. 'I remember Rignis and his friends. And the blame for that is laid on me, is it? All that you have described did indeed happen – except that the survivors were not reduced into slavery but resettled in Venta Silurum, and the killing was done neither by me nor by my men. That butchery was done by the maniac, the one we knew as the Laughing Man! By him and his band of filthy murderers! I was leading a small patrol in pursuit of him when we came upon that carnage.'

'You are lying.' How his head hurt him. 'You left the dead unburied, and it was a Roman spear in Rignis' body. I saw it with my own eyes.'

'A spear through his heart? A merciful end to his suffering; we could not cut him down alive because they had pierced his belly and secured him to the tree. I had the survivors hastened to safety while I pursued the Laughing Man until we lost track of him. When we returned, the burying was done – by you, presumably. You must know of the Laughing Man? Ask him if this is not the truth. I am not responsible for those deaths. Your hatred for me has been perverse.'

He did not need to ask Cunobarrus. He could see it in his face. It had all been a lie. What a total fool they had made of him. Cadrus, not Drusus, was responsible for Bodyn's death.

Cunobarrus answered the unasked question. 'Cadrus was a worthy brother to me and did what he believed in just as I did. Do not think yourself better than he. It was his wish that you should be made one of us, much against my judgement; even then I saw you for what you really are – a worthy slave. It was he who taught you how to fight, and because of him you survived when I might well have left you to rot on my farm. We made you into a warrior. We turned a simple shepherd boy into the feared and respected Verluccus the Bloodspiller. Those people, that old hag, that Rignis – all of them gave sustenance to our enemies and would have alerted them that day too had Cadrus not acted as he did. Since then you have done no different from Cadrus. You gained a name more feared than his, and you were proud enough to crow it over the corpses of your enemies. Now, thanks to your treachery, I am defeated and given up to the Romans. Our cause is subverted, and so our enmity has to be put aside, for I am resigned to the truce I have made with Marcus

424

Marcius. If he is a man of his word, he will keep it. Nothing which has happened between you and Drusus, if he is prepared to forget your anger and assault upon him, should change our agreement.'

'And you think I can so easily forget what has been done to me?' he cried. He had his hands again upon his knife. 'Everything I have done, all of my crimes – yes, crimes – have been based upon a lie. Would I were dead now and could seek Cadrus out wherever he is gone to!'

He groped his way to his feet and, swaying unsteadily, lunged at his brother. Cunobarrus pulled the knife from his grasp and flung him back onto the pallet, where he lay still and for a long time so silent that Peritus was required to reassure them that his injury was superficial.

Marcus drew Vitellius aside and demanded to know how he stood on this issue. He had been wronged, and he might rightly claim Verluccus' life for his attack.

'On the contrary, strange as it may sound coming from me,' he answered, 'to have clashed swords with the Bloodspiller is a diversion I scarcely expected to enjoy. I count this scratch now an honourable battle scar. He is already punished for his crimes by enslavement. I think it wrong that the other is to enjoy freedom, but for the price of our progress, I am prepared to accept the decision you have made because I know that it has Neratius' approval. I shall make no trouble for you.'

They returned to where the invalid was still glowering hatefully at his brother. Cunobarrus seemed oblivious to the turmoil he was now causing and turned, nodding at the Romans. 'So all is happily agreed? He has no further price to pay for his foolishness?'

'I need an oath from Verluccus that he will not raise his hand against you.' *What craziness is this,* Marcus wondered as he spoke, *that I am actually pleading for these two not to kill each other?*

There was a long and thoughtful silence from Verluccus before he nodded his consent.

'And for the service he has rendered you, what reward is he to be given? My brother, foolish though he is and for all his faults against me, has served his Roman masters well. Free him so he may return with me to Daruentum,' Cunobarrus pressed.

'I am not empowered to do so. His master alone has that privilege, and it is his master's decision; he is not to be set free.' It was bitter for Marcus to have to admit himself so helpless.

'Gaius Marcius is here? May I see him?'

How had he figured that out? There was no point in denying it. 'He is in the praetorium, and you may go to him if you are fit to stand,' said Marcus. 'But take my word; he has already been asked for what you wish, and it has been refused.'

He needed some support, and it was forthcoming from Titus, who somehow had inveigled his way past his centurion again and joined them in the infirmary. The young soldier was living dangerously, but he had decided that if he was to receive any more punishment, it might as well be for something he had consciously done.

Verluccus should have heeded Marcus' warning. He confidently hurried to his master, even knelt before him, and felt a repossessing hand touch him and bid him rise. But the words were not what he expected to hear.

'My uncle has much to thank you for,' said the boy coolly. 'He will, I am sure, be generous to you. You are undoubtedly due some reward from him. Some decent clothes, perhaps?' He looked with concern at the fresh head wound. 'I hope your injury will not delay our departure.'

Even Titus was shocked. 'I had thought you might free him,' he said, 'Everyone thinks he deserves it.'

'Why should I?' answered Gaius. 'This work has not been done on my behalf. In any case, even if his crimes are excused, he is not of age. Verluccus is coming to Rome with me. I intend that he shall experience the great wonders of the city, sights such as you and I have never set eyes on. He should count himself fortunate he is able to enjoy such a privilege.' He turned to the slave. 'Go now and lie down, Verluccus, and rest your head; my uncle has slaves enough who can attend to my needs.'

Titus shook his head. 'You are not the man I thought you, Gaius.

I have to go; I only came to assist Verluccus since he is still groggy. Now there are duties awaiting me. I may not see you again, so I wish you well and hope that you learn to treat him better than you do now.'

'I don't know what you mean,' his friend replied indignantly. 'Verluccus has the easiest of lives with me. I saved his life! Marcus and Father would happily have seen him executed. And no one can say I work him to death. On the contrary, little is required of him. He is well fed, well clothed, and given great licence. We may never meet again, Titus, and I am sorry we are to part on bad terms, but it is you who have changed, not I.'

Titus left them. There was nothing that he could do, and he had problems of his own. He surrendered himself at the guardhouse to receive his punishment.

'Verluccus is to join us at dinner,' Marcus announced to his nephew. 'If you do not like the idea, eat elsewhere. Since you deny me the power to reward him as I think he deserves, it is my intention that while he is within my jurisdiction he is to enjoy such freedom as I am able to bestow. And here, should you need reminding, I am the law. Furthermore, he will return with me when Cunobarrus takes me to this Dolbactan who, it seems, has the gold which I am to have restored. There he will be treated as equally as any freed man. Again, if that does not please you, remain here until he returns, for if you come with us, you signal your obedience to my command.'

'I shall come with you. And you are right – it is not fitting that he feed at the same table as me. I shall dine elsewhere,' Gaius responded sulkily. He should not be treated like this; his father and mother would be disgusted at Marcus' behaviour. He supposed it was what was termed barrack-room conduct, something which Titus also had very quickly adopted.

11

With Cunobarrus as their guide, it took the men a respectable length of time to reach Dolbactan. The number of men which Marcus would take had plagued Verluccus' mind greatly. To take too many would make the Romans look foolish; to take too few would be insulting and even dangerous. He was greatly relieved to learn that the escort would consist of one cohort only, ignorant of the fact that Marcus had a contingency plan in readiness for treachery.

A guard of honour had been assembled for their arrival with Dolbactan at its head, and the community even managed to look welcoming, though Verluccus could not believe the smiles and greetings which the soldiers received were sincere. There would be a surrender of weapons – that would be a basic requirement – but he knew it would be a sham just as in Merriol's village. He wondered if Marcus would realize this.

His position was lowly now. It was not made apparent that he was no longer in the great man's favour, but Verluccus could see Marcus must have no further use for him and so kept his distance from the officials conducting the business. As soon as he could, he sought out Cassio.

His experience with Gaius, who surreptitiously watched almost his every move, had decided him what he must do. He found the centurion within the tent designated as the principium, for the army was encamped outside the village at a site which afterwards was intended to become a fortlet, and at first he hesitated to enter for fear of rejection. The duty guard recognized him and directed him to go inside.

Cassio had resumed his centurion's garb, but his welcome was warm. 'Verluccus; I am glad you have come. What news? Are you a free man now?'

He had to admit that he was not. Gaius Marcius had denied it to him; in fact, he had followed him not only to Isca Silurum but here also. He saw the uneasiness among the soldiers. Cassio's comrade they would welcome; they were not comfortable to entertain a slave.

He took the knife from his belt and handed it to Cassio. 'I have only come to give you this. I shall not be allowed to keep it. I can think of no one I would prefer to have it than you. Most of your men believe you are its rightful owner. They thought I had killed you for it.'

'Poor Verluccus!' He peered at the recent wound. 'Is that why you were bashed on the head?'

He had forgotten about it. 'Oh. No, no, Tribune Drusus Vitellius did that when I was fighting with him.'

Cassio grinned at such impudence. There was no way Vitellius would lower himself to fight with a slave. In a moment, though, he remembered that Verluccus had been particularly interested in him. He shook his head and dismissed the thought. If he had raised a sword with Drusus, he would not have lived to tell the tale. He turned to their audience.

'Meet Verluccus the Bloodspiller! I have been telling you how he saved my life. This man, though he is a slave, is my good friend and must be made welcome by you whenever he seeks me out. I do not wish to hear of his being abused or ill treated. And friends, be wary – it may be his own blood you see spilled now, but I have learned things about this man which would terrify you.'

'We have seen it for ourselves, Cassio. He took a sword in anger to Vitellius, and he wounded him. And he lives to tell the tale.'

Cassio paled. 'When you said that I thought you were joking. You have made yourself a serious enemy in Vitellius. I fear for you. He will let you live only until Marcus has concluded his business. He is not a man to be insulted by anyone, least of all a slave.'

Was that so? He did not think it. 'That was not the impression I had; we did not part on bad terms. But Cassio, do take this knife. I have no use for it, and I do not want it owned by Gaius Marcius. Take it now as a token of our friendship.'

'If you insist, then I shall,' he replied. 'I was once proud to call it mine. And I shall find a present for you too. This belt – take it: I can get another from supply. You should have seen Marcus' face when he saw my native robes. I thought he would have apoplexy!'

He fitted the centurion's belt around Verluccus' tunic. 'Now take advantage of Marcus' generosity while you are here and come and exercise with us. We will show you the Roman skills of fighting. You will never have such an opportunity again. What do you say?'

Why not? he thought. *I do not have to spend my days with Gaius, and there is little else for me to do. Cunobarrus will not want me with him.* He said yes to the invitation and was relieved to see that all present welcomed the offer; none held back. He did not know they considered themselves privileged to have one of such a name come training with them.

'Sent you packing, has he?' was the greeting he received from Gaius when he finally returned to the tent he shared with his master, part of the suite designated as the praetorium. 'No longer has any use for you? I knew it! And now you think to come crawling back to me like a dog with its tail between its legs.'

Gaius was alone, if Titus had been allowed to come, he might have had a friend, but Titus was doing fatigues in Isca, the penalty for allowing his sword to be taken from him. Gaius had finished one skin of wine and was demanding another. 'Help me out of these stale clothes and find fresh ones.' The raucous sounds of men's laughter filtered into their tent. 'A party!' he cried. 'A party. I am going to a party. You can do as you please – Marcus Marcius' orders. "Verluccus is to do as he pleases,"' He mimicked and lurched already drunken from the tent.

Much later, Verluccus discovered him. He had not reached the party. He had staggered one uncertain step too many and slipped and then, too drunk to care, had lain in the mud and slept. His slave lifted him bodily and carried him back to his bed and sat with him until grey morning broke in the eastern sky.

'So you came crawling back last night?' Gaius nursed a painful head. 'Fetch me water. That is allowed, is it? You may bring me water?' He drank greedily from the pitcher and demanded more.

'Gaius,' he said, handing him a cup, 'do not do this. It was your own wish to be here. The remedy is patience, not wine.'

The cup was dashed from his hands. 'Do not "Gaius" me! Whatever Marcus Marcius may say, you are still my slave and I your master. He has no interest in you. You have performed a service for him, but that is done now. He has got his way and made a traitor of you to your kind. How proud you must be of yourself! Neither he nor that centurion will have further need of you, so why do you treat me like this? You owe me duty and obedience and should ignore the dictates of my uncle. I want you here to serve me, not have to fend for myself.'

'Master,' he responded carefully, 'I have no quarrel with you, and whatever Marcus Marcius may say, I know I am still your slave. When he hands me back to you, you may well punish me, but since I now may do so, I intend to enjoy this little freedom. I do not wish to bicker with you, and so I shall go in search of more agreeable company.'

He rose and walked out of the tent, leaving the boy screaming abuse at his back and raging with anger and promises of how he would reward such insolent ingratitude.

'Why did you not return to dine with me?' demanded Cassio. With his men he had been detailed to supervise the handing in of swords, shields, and spears. 'I suppose you too have discovered how pretty the girls around here are? When I am done here, I know of an icy pool where we can bathe if you have the stomach for it.'

'An icy pool? That sounds perfect. Lead us to it.' The voice was that of Marcus Marcius, who had overheard him. Clearly he and Vitellius intended to make the bathing facility their own. Cassio could have bitten off his tongue.

'Tell me,' said Marcus as they walked along, 'what is this story that is circulating that you saved Cassio's life? I do not doubt it might have been necessary, but I should like to hear the detail of it.'

His heart sank. So Cunobarrus had not thought fit to tell him. He looked at Cassio and saw the alarm he felt reflected in the centurion's eyes. Cassio too had supposed the truth to be out already and had spoken of it freely.

There was no escape from it. He tried to be brief, but it was as if the man must know the tale already, so quick was he to pick up on any glossing.

Marcus stopped in his tracks. Here was real anger. He had been tricked, misled, fooled, and he was furious. He brushed aside appeals for clemency both from Verluccus and from Cassio, ordering instead the centurion to assemble the cohort.

'Take me to this place!' he demanded of Dolbactan, a man cowering in fear of imminent death.

Dolbactan, Cunobarrus, and other lordlings including Deldon and Bodrogan were rounded up and bound with chains, and so was Verluccus. Gaius watched weeping in despair. He had said things to Verluccus he wished unsaid and wanted him to know it, but now he was beyond his reach, being marched out of the settlement and through the trees to the gods knew where. He followed fearfully behind with the rest of the community and the angry soldiers.

It was much as when they had last seen it, sodden and desolate, the stricken ash blackened from the flames of Jove's thunderbolt under a sky which now was brilliant and blue.

Each of them was bound by his wrists between the saplings – tree and man, tree and man. When those already seized proved insufficient in number, he seized more from the bystanders until every space in the ring of trees was filled. They waited in silence for what next he intended – in what manner death was to be delivered to them. The onlookers too were hushed and subdued, fearful that they would die next. The only sound was the mocking caws of rooks disturbed from their roosts above.

The executioners were to be spearmen. One for each prisoner, they stepped into the centre of the circle and now confronted them, their weapons poised for deadly release. Each would suffer one blow, and if the aim was less than certain, they would be left there to die where they were tied. Verluccus thought of Rignis and how he must have suffered, and he hoped the spear hurled at him would strike his heart. He stared into the face of the young lad whose duty it was to kill him and wondered if he had been among those he had bantered with only the evening before. That did not signify; the boy must obey his commander. How glad he was that Titus had not come. The young soldier's nervousness was showing, and he fidgeted with the pilum as he realized what he was about to do. Verluccus knew that he had been consigned to a very poor marksman.

Suddenly, above the drumming noise which was the thumping of his own heart, he heard speech – Cassio's voice. He could not see his face, but his voice rang loud and clear through the stillness in a desperate appeal for mercy. Foolish Cassio, to think he could turn Marcus from his design.

'Commander Marcus Marcius,' he heard, 'I beg you do not take this course. Exercise clemency here; be merciful. It is true that in this place I was condemned to die, but these are not the men who were to slaughter me. They, the priests, are gone, the man who would have been my executioner despatched by Jupiter himself when he launched a mighty thunderbolt from on high. Only two remain, and I name them Deldon and Bodrogan. They took part in this atrocity. Before your eyes is the proof of it: this blackened tree with its limb stricken from it. If it had been wish of Almighty Jove, then all of these men and more could have been killed by him that day, but he spared them. Jupiter, best and greatest of all the gods, does not ask for humans to be sacrificed to him. This is the province of the god he vanquished, Belenos. I know you are not a man who would scorn the will of Jupiter. When the great god spoke, these people listened, and because of his actions they have surrendered to you. It was Jupiter, best and greatest, who brought about their change of heart. The mission you sent Verluccus on was impossible. A mere mortal unaided had no hope of turning the hearts of these men to surrender, but with the help of mighty Jupiter, it was achieved. I beg you to extend now the mercy that the great god granted that day.'

There was a silence. Cassio had finished speaking. Verluccus waited for the order to loose the spears and for the pain of death to enter him. Then at Marcus' signal a command rang out. The men lowered their weapons but did not move from their posts.

The words which followed from Marcus he had repeated by an interpreter so that no one should be in doubt. 'Listen to what I say, you treacherous dogs and perfidious savages. I came to this place from Isca Silurum in good faith. I came to receive back that which was stolen from my control. I came to remove a renegade, a murderous butcher, from the seat of his crimes, not to put him to death or to imprison him but to return him to where he could live in peace and do no further harm. I came to bring you peace and prosperity. This brave centurion offered himself to be a hostage while Cunobarrus absented himself to attend me in Isca. You had no respect for that; at your hands he was condemned to die. Cunobarrus, you would not have come to me in Isca if Jupiter had not interceded. You, Dolbactan – your belief brought this evil thing here. And as for you, Verluccus, how kindly I have treated you, and yet you breathed not a word of it. I might have walked into an ambush. Thus I am rewarded for my generosity and kindliness to you.'

He addressed them more generally. 'This slave is probably the only one among you who knows the words brave Gnaeus Cassius has spoken on your behalf. This centurion, whom you tried to kill, has spoken up for you, you worthless scum. He asks that I spare your lives. I should kill you all, but he reminds me that Jupiter, best and greatest of all gods, chose to spare you; and because Jupiter showed mercy to you, I do also.' He then turned to Cassio and said, 'Pick out the two you named and spear them where they hang.'

They made no appeal for mercy but died by the spear, cursing the Romans as their lives ebbed away and their bleeding bodies, still chained, dragged the saplings downwards. Those who had anticipated a similar demise watched in horror, and cheers went up from the watching soldiers.

At Marcus' further command the chains were struck from the other captives, and they were herded into the centre of the glade, surrounded by the armed men. Marcus had more to say.

'I am persuaded that had Jupiter desired your deaths, he would have taken them. Here, instead of that filthy tree, you will erect an altar to the greatest of all gods in gratitude at his intercession. Cut down, uproot, and burn all these accursed trees and clear the ground. Seek out a suitable stone, and I will have it carved to dignify it. That is all. When it is done, we shall return and dedicate it with an appropriate sacrifice.'

It was Verluccus' end; he knew it must be. He would be put to hewing down the trees with the others, and then Marcus would restore him to Gaius and send him packing to Rome. He could not blame the man. He had seen this coming from the beginning. Surely Cunobarrus could have found a way to tell him the truth when they spoke in Isca? He turned and began to help throw chains around the first condemned sapling.

'Marcus wants you.' It was Cassio who had approached him.

'You spoke well, Cassio. I am grateful to you.'

He bowed to Marcus. Gaius was beside his uncle, looking terrified.

'I accept, Verluccus,' Marcus said, 'that you had no knowledge of what passed between Cunobarrus and myself. I did not invite your opinion or seek your advice, and though I am angry at the deception which has been practised on me, I find I do not hold a grudge towards you. My men even now are removing from Dolbactan's hiding places those weapons they did not surrender, and I shall see to it that they do not forget the lesson they learned today.' He broke off, suddenly noticing the belt Verluccus was wearing. 'I trust that is paid for? You and Centurion Gnaeus Cassius seem to be confused as to what is appropriate dress. Are you enrolled in the legion?'

The change in his tone was a huge relief. Verluccus sighed in relief at his levity.

'I have promised he may train with us!' protested Cassio.

'Enough of this.' He had not vetoed the idea. The two grinned at each other. 'I was promised a bath. Am I now to have it? Will you take us there?'

Cassio was right about the pool, but its chill was welcome relief.

Verluccus kept himself away from Marcus and Drusus Vitellius, supposing them to prefer that arrangement, and had been for some time lying on the bank with eyes closed dreaming thoughts of other pleasures when a voice in his ear said, 'Verluccus the Bloodspiller, get yourself onto your feet.'

It was Vitellius. He was standing over him holding a sword. He waited while Verluccus replaced his tunic and then thrust the weapon into his hand. 'It is time, I think, to give you a proper lesson. Remember, however, we are only sparring.'

'I hope you appreciate the great honour Vitellius pays to Verluccus,' Marcus told his nephew, who had trailed them to the water. 'Drusus Vitellius is not a man to consort with slaves. He is much too proud. To invite Verluccus to swordplay is a rare act and one I would never have expected from him.'

'Verluccus told me it was the tribune who opened his head,' said Cassio. 'When he said they had fought, I supposed his life to have been spared only until your business is concluded. I had no idea he was thought so highly of. I suppose now you will want him for a gladiator? What a crowd puller – Bloodspiller.' This last was directed at Gaius.

'That is the last thing he desires,' Marcus replied for him. 'He is afraid his property will be damaged by such dangerous play. He has little faith in his slave's ability – unlike Vitellius there. I lose patience with him. Now, Gnaeus Cassius, what if I took the lad into the legion? Could you make a man of my nephew?'

'I am not going to join your army! I would sooner go and fight the Dacians than serve under you! My plans now are to go to Rome, and Verluccus is coming with me, Uncle.'

'Rather fight the Dacians? That I most certainly can arrange for you,' a furious Marcus Marcius returned icily.

Marcus' mind was made up. He had his gold, he had Cunobarrus' oath of allegiance to Rome, he had the weapons surrendered and the young warriors all but emasculated and Dolbactan turned to civility and the Roman religion. There was no need to detain Cunobarrus longer. In fact, the sooner he was gone the better. He advised the man to prepare for departure.

Verluccus came to the principium tent and was admitted immediately. It never ceased to amaze him that Marcus Marcius should allow him so readily into his presence. He wanted to ask a favour of him and hoped it would not seem too cheeky.

'I think you should know', he said honestly, 'your brother Lucius Marcius has denied me this. He is embarrassed by the scar I bear. I swear that is the only reason. But before I depart for Rome, if I could visit my family, if only fleetingly – if I might return with Cunobarrus when he goes to Daruentum and see them for one last time – I would ask for nothing else.'

'Of course you shall go,' Marcus agreed instantly. 'I should have thought of it myself. And stay for as long as you wish – months, if necessary. I shall keep my nephew with me, and then, if you are not ready to leave before I go north, I shall put him under a duty to respect your licence. It cannot be forever; you must return before the winter storms put paid to sailings from the coast.'

'That will not be necessary. I only need a little time to assure them I am well and tell them of my adventures. I shall never forget your kindness to me, kindness and tolerance in the face of the abuse you have endured from my tongue. All of my hatred, all of my crimes, were achieved by the lies of my brothers Cunobarrus and Cadrus. I admit I have done many evil things and know that my punishment for them is slight, though not so slight as your punishment of Cunobarrus. My brother is a fortunate man; I hope he appreciates it. I truly and sincerely thank you for your kindnesses to me.' At an impulse he knelt and would have kissed the man's feet, but he was stopped and told his thanks were more than enough.

'The departure of Cunobarrus is to have no ceremony. You and he shall depart at dawn, and a small detachment will escort you to Isca. I shall prepare a letter tonight which you may deliver to my wife. I doubt that I shall see you again, but if you ever need to appeal for assistance to a higher authority than that of my brother, do not be afraid to think of me. I would be honoured to speak or act on your behalf. Needless to say, Neratius Marcellus and I, though we had to coerce you, are much indebted to you. You and Jupiter both – we must not forget the part Jupiter, best and greatest, played in this. You both have saved many men and much time.'

In the morning he was surprised to find Cunobarrus ready and eager to be gone. And shocked too.

'Does Marcus know you are wearing that?' His body was laden with golden ornaments.

'He has allowed me to keep those pieces which are jewellery, since he cannot prove they were stolen from him. He has robbed Dolbactan of all the ingots which he foolishly sat on. I, however, have enough to provide for a few necessities,' Cunobarrus assured him.

One of the soldiers handed Verluccus sealed tablets. He was to deliver them to the praetorium at Isca and await reply. It was a small enough request, and he thought no more of it.

At Isca they met Titus again and briefly told him how things were. Titus led them to the praetorium.

'I hear tell that Marcus' wife is a real beauty.' Cunobarrus leered. 'What a game that would be – to seduce her while he is away! She will see you if you claim it is his will.'

He brushed aside his brother's persistence and received the bundle which a girl brought to them. There was another letter also to be delivered to Gaia; the mistress hoped it would not be an inconvenience to him. They did not see Melissa; Marcus had cautioned her again about the danger of allowing her beauty to be seen by lustful Celts. She had smiled as she read his letter, kissed it, and slipped it between her bed covers because he had handled it.

'But these are mine!' Verluccus was amazed by what he had been given. 'Marcus gave them to Aelia, and yet they are here. How can this be?'

'Do not ask such questions! You are not such a poor man now that you have those returned. Let us be gone before she changes her mind.' Cunobarrus was all for Verluccus wearing them also, but he would not. He added the weight to his pack and asked Titus to tell whoever needed to know that they were ready to depart.

They were provided with a further escort to Glevum – just to ensure he got there, Cunobarrus rightly asserted. At the principia their arrival was reported and Marcus' letter of authority handed in.

'Have him wait; I wish to look upon this scourge for myself.' Neratius took himself to a vantage point to satisfy his curiosity. 'Marcus is generous to that slave, I see.' He read the legate's letter again. 'Bring them before me. I wish Cunobarrus to know he is a spent force.'

At Verluccus' urging Cunobarrus had concealed his jewellery beneath his garments, and so no demands were made that he surrender it. They were taken before Neratius and suffered his silent scrutiny of them. He did not speak directly to them, but Verluccus could understand perfectly the words he said to Glaucus.

'I want no proclamation of his return; he is not to be made anything of. Have them conducted to the gate and sent on their way. Our man in Daruentum can keep us informed if he steps out of line.'

They were to go. He remembered the letter Melissa had given him and turned to speak to Glaucus.

'Out!' said Neratius. 'You and your troublesome brother are not wanted here. Depart until your master reclaims you.' He spoke again to Glaucus. 'I see no further need for Marcus to delay. He should report to me in person very soon and we can move forwards. Again his somewhat unorthodox methods have achieved a satisfactory end.'

There was no hope of delivering the letter to Gaia. If there had been no escort, he might have deviated from the route to visit her house, but now there was no chance of that. He strode beside his brother, their strangeness attracting a little attention despite Neratius' wish, and then they were at the city gate, turned out of it, and abandoned onto the track to Daruentum.

BOOK VI

SERVING GAIA

1

It was all so very different – smaller, much smaller, than he remembered. Yet it was certainly the right place. They had passed the Roman house, its red tiles and pale walls concealed by the deep screen of trees, but Cunobarrus had paused at the fork and, with a degree of control which was a credit to him, had cursed it and those who dwelt within it. Verluccus wondered if Agricola was still in charge and what changes might have taken place there.

But now they paused again, hesitating and wondering. Had their old home too changed hands? There was an air of order and prosperity around the place which caused a sense not of unease but of strangeness, as if they had no connection with its present occupiers. What if Tanodonus no longer lived there? Verluccus remembered Lucius' words and Neratius' and Marcus' threats and told himself that it must be so.

Together they trod the path to the open doorway and made their presence known.

The young woman who came in answer to their voices was a complete stranger. A boy of about three hung around her skirt, and a tiny, yelling baby was cradled in her arms. She stared at them both with startled eyes and shock upon her face. But it was apparent that their faces were not as strange to her as hers was to them.

'Who are you?' she breathed when a long moment had passed with neither speaking. 'I do not know you … and yet …?'

'Is this the house of Cunobarrus?' asked the man of that name.

'It is the house of his son, Tanodonus. My husband is in the field

443

over there if you want him.' She pointed to indicate land hidden by storage huts.

'We will wait inside,' said Cunobarrus. 'Send to fetch him. Tell him – tell him that his brothers are come home.'

'Cunobarrus? Cadrus?' There was fear in her eyes. She shrank from them. Obviously Tanodonus had told her of their departure long ago. 'We thought you were passed over.'

She stood back to allow them to enter into the dimness. She lay down the screaming child in a snug cradle and took them by the hands and led them deep within, where a corner had been made with hangings. A huddle shifted in the dimness, and they found an enfeebled, aged woman clad as darkly as the corner she inhabited. The girl spoke softly, stroking the old woman's cheek with a gentle finger.

'Carantua, see – see who is come. Your sons are come home.'

It was as if a living corpse gazed at him, and a scrawny hand reached out. Both sons knelt and took a hand apiece to kiss and weep upon.

'I am not Cadrus, Mother. I am Verluccus, your own Verluccus returned to you. Do you remember me?'

Her face was streaming with tears, and so was his. To find her still alive was more than he had dared to hope. Her fingers grasped his in a vice-like grip and would not release him. He remained sitting on the floor beside her while her senses absorbed the truth of his presence.

Eventually Cunobarrus gently detached himself and moved away. He went outside in search of Tanodonus and to explain his presence. Verluccus was still there when the two returned with the little messenger who had run at his mother's bidding and arrived with a garbled story which the man could not fathom. Now Tanodonus entered, marvelling at the wonder of it, and the girl ran and clung to him, not knowing whether to laugh or cry. Cunobarrus filled the doorway, large and awkward, alien to them.

Carantua had not spoken a word. Nor would she loose his hand. It seemed he must remain there forever. He heard Tanodonus speak, felt his brother's hand fall upon his shoulder and a warm embrace surround him.

'I cannot let go. Wait until she sleeps. Cunobarrus can explain much, and then I shall tell you my story. Is this your wife? I had not thought – of course you will be married. And Colymmon? Is Colymmon still living here?'

'Of course he is!' Tanodonus was beaming. 'He is on the hill with his beloved sheep as usual. Belrutha, come. You thought this was Cadrus, but it is Verluccus. My dearest brother Verluccus has come back to us.'

The girl knelt and kissed him in greeting. Tanodonus spoke again. 'Get my brothers food. We will all dine well tonight. Wait – I shall get a beast killed and dressed.' He disappeared and shouted his orders.

'You are prosperous, Brother,' said Cunobarrus. 'You have hands to do your bidding.'

'We do not starve, but I work as hard as any,' Tanodonus answered tersely, uncomfortable in the presence of one brother and longing to have a closer knowledge of the other. 'Tell me, what has become of Cadrus? Why is he not with you? How is it that Verluccus is with you? You know what happened to him?'

There was so much to be said and all of it while Verluccus remained fastened by his mother's hand. She did not sleep, and her face glistened from her tears; but suddenly he became aware that the grip had altered – that her touch was different. He looked into her face and bid a flame be brought so that he might clearly see her eyes and saw that they were still and lifeless.

She had left them silently and without a word to him, but her unyielding grip and her tears had spoken volumes. He gently freed his hand and laid her down upon her bed.

'I am glad she was spared to see her Verluccus again,' said Tanodonus. 'She has been moribund for long enough, but something inside her seemed to hold on and now I know what it was. The old have special knowledge of what is to come.'

'I shall go to fetch my mother, and we shall prepare her for her burial,' said Belrutha. 'Come with me, Verluccus, so that they may see you again.'

He went gladly with her down to the house he remembered well, still overfilled with family but now with little ones also. Belanius and Brutha were still strong as ever. She explained her errand and who he was, and they crowded round him in amazement, as pleased to see him as if he were one of their own.

'No,' he had to admit, 'I am not free. I remain a slave and have to return to my master. This respite was a privilege granted for a service I have done. I must go to Rome with my master.'

Before he had finished speaking he sensed their withdrawal from him. As a free man he would have been made most welcome, a good prospect as a son-in-law, perhaps; but as a slave they did not know how to treat him and opted for caution. Even Belrutha was embarrassed to have brought him to them. He followed her and Brutha back to his brother's house.

They took it in turns throughout the night to sit beside Carantua, and in the morning they buried her beside her husband so that she might find him on the other side more easily, placing beside her sustenance for her journey in the manner she would have wished. They cried together for her, but Verluccus wept more than the others, for he knew she had lived only for his return and that wish had been granted her.

Tanodonus was shocked that Verluccus remained a slave. At his coming home, he had supposed him to be free. He said he would keep him there, defy the Romans to take him again, but he was warned he must not. Cunobarrus' freedom depended on his good conduct, and if there was any trouble brewing in the locality it would surely be laid at his door.

They ate well that night, but no neighbours came to join them. They began to tell their stories. Cunobarrus was first as was his right of seniority. Their eyes opened in amazement as he brought forth his gold and told them how he had come by it. He would pay his way, he told them; they would not find his presence a burden to them.

When two nights had passed, he yielded the floor to Verluccus.

'We have not heard a thing since you ran away. I was taken and questioned. They searched everywhere, and we feared you had been killed or found and sold off as troublesome. To think you have been so close for all these months,' Tanodonus complained. 'Surely you could have got word to us that you were safe and well?'

'I was forbidden. But I learned of you. Agricola has kept Lucius Marcius well informed, and he has seen to it that you have not suffered from my absence.'

It was the wrong thing to say.

'What can that slave maker know of my suffering? Do you think I count you in cash terms? That farmer! Spying on us? I have worked for all that I own and worked hard too. I owe Lucius Marcius nothing. Nothing – do you hear?' His response was furious.

Verluccus hastily assured his brother that was not what he meant, and wisely they decided that he had said enough.

Cunobarrus was gladly accepted in the community and rapidly acquired a following of young lads who hung on his every word. But he made no move to establish a house of his own and seemed unconcerned that his presence intruded into his brother's privacy. With Verluccus Tanodonus found no fault other than that he must lose him shortly. His days were spent in contentment working alongside Tanodonus in the fields as he had so often dreamed of doing, Gaius put firmly out of his mind and Gaia more firmly refused admission to it.

He shared a bed with Cunobarrus and was often woken in the middle of the night when his brother chose to return. One night, lying awake and awaiting the inevitable drunken disruption, he found himself listening to words exchanged between Tanodonus and Belrutha.

'He wants our home. He thinks the farm is his birthright,' she said to her husband. 'And you have done so much and worked so hard. You must speak up, Tanodonus. Tell him he has no right to it. Tell him before we are thrown out, homeless and destitute.'

'I don't believe even Cunobarrus would turn me out now,' Tanodonus tried to reassure her. 'He has never been one for working the land – never had any interest in farming and never wanted any. What need has he of our house when he has wealth enough upon him to purchase even the fine stone house that Bodellus has erected for himself? Perhaps he has it in mind to buy the Roman house and farm but is waiting until Verluccus has gone to spare his feelings.'

It was an absurd suggestion. Cunobarrus spared nobody's feelings. He continued, trying to soothe her.

'Let us be patient and not cause unhappiness for Verluccus while he is allowed to stay with us. It is shameful how our neighbours, even your family, treat Verluccus while Cunobarrus is welcomed and feasted wherever he goes. I know he ignores Colymmon too and acts as though he does not exist, but Colymmon does not mind that; he has no idea who our visitors are. He certainly does not connect Verluccus as he is today with his memory of the child he knew.'

She murmured something else which he could not catch. Then the children were calling out, awoken by the sound of their uncle's return.

He had tried to give his brother the gold pieces which Marcus and Melissa had returned to him, but Tanodonus would not take them. There was distaste in his eyes at such a suggestion now that he knew how Verluccus had come by them. Stealing gold bullion from the Romans – that he could now find acceptable. To sport jewellery plundered from butchered innocents was quite another thing. Nor would he allow them to be gifted to the little boy who also was named Verluccus and who followed his uncle's every footstep.

There were days though when it seemed that even Cunobarrus was making an effort to conform and would work beside his brothers, hoeing in the fields. That was what they were doing, the three brothers working in harmony, when they were startled by a shout from Belrutha. Soldiers were coming. They were asking for Verluccus.

'I thought I might stay longer than this.' He handed Tanodonus his hoe. 'I imagine that Marcus has arrived in Glevum and Gaius is with him. He will have persuaded Neratius Marcellus that Marcus is in the wrong to allow me this.' He resigned himself to his return to Gaius and stepped forward.

'Cassio!' He ran and embraced the centurion, shocking his family by the warmth of his welcome. 'Cassio! What are you doing here? Why have you come to do Gaius' dirty work? I would have thought you the last person –.'

Cassio laughed. 'This is not from Gaius Marcius.'

He indicated an oxen cart laden with vessels, jars, and crates.

'This is a gift from Marcus. He seems to think you might be starving.'

He guided them around it as they gaped in amazement. 'It is his gift – cattle, cart and all. I am not to take anything back. But I may help you to get rid of it, if invited.' He beamed hopefully at the family.

Verluccus turned to his brother. 'Tanodonus, I know how you feel towards the Romans, but Cassio is a good friend of mine. If you will not admit him to your home, you will cause me deep offence.' He had seen the stubborn set of his brother's chin.

'How can you accept a gift like this from a man who has done you such wrong?'

'No, Tann, this is from Marcus Marcius, the legate, not from Lucius Marcius. He is long gone now – gone back to Rome. Do not cause offence to a man I admire and respect like no other. And do not refuse admission to Cassio. I beg you – allow him to enter your home.'

'I think your brother does not like me,' observed Cassio. He spoke in Latin, and only Verluccus could understand him. 'Is it because Marcus threatened to crucify him?'

'No.' He hushed him. 'No, he does not know that – and he must not. Both he and Cunobarrus must never know of it. Cunobarrus believes that I did what I did for his own good – not that he thinks I actually did him any good,' he added ruefully. 'If he came to know it was for Tanodonus' sake, I dread to think what might come of it. No, Cassio, Tanodonus cannot forgive the Romans for the actions of Lucius Marcius. But he will accept this and you because I ask it of him. Today we shall have a feast, and the whole community may come if they wish.'

They came, all of them, some eagerly, some doubtfully, but they came. Tables were laden to groaning with cured meats, hams, fowl, stuffed dormice, jellied birds' tongues, cakes, and amphorae of oil and wine – the latter not Marcus' most thoughtful gift, as beer would have been preferred as some ungraciously pointed out. There was salt fish too and preserved fruits the like of which had before only graced the table of rich Bodellus. He was there, of course, with his family, eager to be in the centurion's company.

Cassio, when he judged the moment right, called for silence. He banged the table and stood a little unsteadily, for he had been sampling beer, as strange a drink to him as wine was to them.

'I am commanded to bring to your attention your host at this table, Verluccus.' He pulled Verluccus to his unwilling feet and made him stand while he continued. 'This table is provided by Marcus Marcius, and he wishes it to be known how very highly he esteems this man and that if he ever is in need of a friend – and that applies to his family also – he need look no further than to the commander of the Second Legion Augusta.'

Someone said, 'Then why keep him in slavery?' but was quickly hushed.

They did not understand it, and neither did he. But it seemed to be the law, and that law Marcus would not break.

Cassio tried to explain. 'Look how all owners of slaves would be placed if men other than they could grant freedom to their slaves. Marcus does his best on his behalf, but believe me, that nephew of his is a stubborn sod.'

The gift and announcement achieved much, however. Attitudes changed towards him, and he was made from then on as welcome in his neighbours' homes as Cunobarrus. More so, in truth, for Cunobarrus' personality was beginning to wear down his audience, and parents were growing concerned about the influence he was already having on their sons with his stories of raiding and bloodshed and the jewellery he shamelessly flaunted.

From Cassio Verluccus learned that Marcus was himself in Glevum with Neratius Marcellus, but the auxiliaries had already been sent to the north along with Vitellius and a detachment of legionaries. He took his leave and departed for Glevum and the land

450

he had been granted as a veteran, and Verluccus knew he must not delay his surrender for much longer.

'Before I depart I want to go to the farm,' he told Tanodonus. 'I know you have no time for Agricola and that you regard him as a spy, but he is a good man and he treated me well. I shall walk down to the stream in the morning and then up to the farm. Do not look for me. I may eat with him if asked.'

'I will not stop you from doing anything you wish since your time with us is so brief,' was his brother's reply. 'I would prefer to have you here beside me – you know that – but go visit your friend if you must. The Roman soldier I endured in my house for your sake; do not expect to bring the farmer back with you. He will not be welcome.'

2

The stream was little different from when he had left it. Even the timber remained untouched. Victor's aggression had driven his neighbours to find fuel elsewhere.

He thought about that time when Gaia had come there and he had lifted her onto the log and what had followed … And then later, when she had spoken so cruelly of him to Glaucus.

He refused to allow the memory of her kiss to touch him and hastily strode on along the path and up to the farm.

He was challenged by a stranger, a new overseer. The man took him to where Agricola was working in the smithy and established his credentials.

'I am so pleased to see you, Verluccus.' Agricola's welcome was warm and sincere. 'I can guess why you have kept away for so long since your return here. That brother of yours is a hard man. I can get nowhere with him, and yet the mistress bids me do all possible to help him. Advise me. What should I do? Try to persuade him to see me?'

'My brother is resentful towards this family. I cannot change him, though I think he may be softening a little.'

He was thinking that "the mistress" could only mean Gaia. He said casually, 'Your mistress keeps a close eye then? On the farm?'

Agricola was grinning slyly. 'Oh, very much so! She has persuaded the master that her knowledge is superior to his – on the subject of farming at least. He lets her deal with me exclusively. She has achieved my manumission, and it was she who obtained the new overseer for me. Her husband could not see the necessity of it.' His voice rang with approval for Gaia.

'So you see much of her? She comes here?'

He needed to know how she was, if she was happy, whether she was to become a mother. So many questions could not be asked, so many questions he needed answers to.

Now Agricola was grinning like a fool.

'She comes here very often, especially of late. Even now, if you were to go up to the house, you would find her. I don't know what she finds to do there, but she and Delia busy themselves. It is her intention to lease the whole property as soon as she finds a suitable tenant. Her husband's business will take them far away. But hasten – she will return to Glevum shortly, and I do believe she would be sorry if you came to the farm and did not call upon her.'

He thanked Agricola and carefully controlled his legs so that they did not yield to his urge to run. He passed the kennel he had shared with Polyphemus and passed through the gate. He strode under the covered walkway and approached the house.

The door was ajar, and he could hear the sounds of women's voices. He thought how stupid he had been to suppose only Delia would be with her. Any number of her friends might have come.

He drew away, but his step must have been heard, or his shadow had crossed the window; something had betrayed his presence.

Disappointingly, it was Delia who came to the door.

'Verluccus?'

Her face told him he was not welcome. He began to retreat. 'I shall go. I came just to see. I meant no harm. I shall go down and see Agricola.'

Another voice spoke. 'No, stay.' It was Gaia.

Suddenly she was there, standing before him. He could not speak.

'No, Delia,' she said. 'Leave us. I want to speak to Verluccus privately.'

The freedwoman passed him, but he did not notice. Gaia was all that he could see. She was so beautiful to him, though another would have said her face was doubtful, her eyes sad.

She motioned for him to enter, and they went into the triclinium, where the original couches still remained. She sat quickly; if he had been in a more rational mood, he might have noticed it was because her legs gave way.

Her mouth moved, but words did not come out and tears welled in her eyes. He stood towering above, as helpless as she to speak.

'Oh, Verluccus.' She began to cry and spoke between her sobs. 'I am so sorry. I cannot forgive myself for those things I said. Please, please forgive me. I have thought of nothing else for so long. I did not want Glaucus to know it was you who killed Virens. I was so frightened he would find out if he took an interest in you, so I said you were stupid and useless. I cannot forgive myself for the hurt it gave you. And it did hurt you so; I saw that at once.' She gathered up her gown and sobbed without restraint.

He knelt, gently took the fabric, and wiped her eyes, melting inside as he looked into them. She raised her mouth, and his descended, and they met in a kiss.

It was a long time before either of them moved other than to embrace more tightly. He felt her eagerness for him as much as his for her and saw no reason to hesitate.

'Not here.' She stopped him and took his hand. 'My bedroom. I want you to love me properly, not here but in my bed, where I would have you always.'

She drew him onto the bed, fearful that diffidence would inhibit him, and began to undo her gown. He took over the task and discovered that the breasts beneath which he once had so yearned for were as delicious as he had dreamed. She held him close and opened herself to him, now not the girl he had known but a woman, encouraging, arousing, knowing.

He needed no arousal. He embraced her so that her rapture was such as she had never known, and her passion was as wild as his.

'Will Delia betray you?' he wondered when both of them were satisfied that they loved each other equally, having run out of comparatives and superlatives.

'No.' She kissed him again. 'She will not. She may not approve of what I do, but she serves me and not Glaucus.'

'Is he kind to you?' He did not know whether he wished to hear her answer.

She kissed him again and again before she spoke. 'Glaucus is not a bad man, not bad to me. You must not think him unkind. To him I play the dutiful wife, but he is not you, and so I cannot be content.'

He pondered the thought that surely duty implied faithfulness, and it was as if she read his mind.

'Dutiful but unfaithful to him – yes, I know. But faithful always to you.' She sighed. 'I must go. Can you return tomorrow? I shall stay all night. I shall bring things and stay for the whole night with you. I would stay forever, but I think Glaucus might notice. Gaius certainly would if you do not return to him. He has behaved very badly. Marcus is furious with him and says he ought to be made to go into the army now and learn to be a man. It is only because he loves you like I do.' She meant her brother.

'No! Not like you do. Not this way. Never let anyone tell you so – or if they do, do not believe them. It is thought. I know it is thought. I cannot prevent men thinking as they do when Gaius behaves as he does, but it is you I love and I will have no other, man or woman. Never believe differently, for it will not be true.'

He demonstrated again how it was.

Reluctantly he helped her into her gown and summoned Delia to try to replace her hair as it ought to be. The freedwoman scolded her and him and ordered him to go. He kissed Gaia's neck and whispered that he would return tomorrow and hope to find her there. And she turned her lips again to say goodbye.

He tried to disguise the stupid grin which he knew must be inscribed across his face when he returned to the farm and took his meal with Agricola. He tried to respond sensibly to the words the man was uttering, and he hoped and prayed that the bailiff could not guess what most occupied his mind for the remainder of the day. He left when the sun had descended, promising to pass on to Tanodonus the offer of the use of the bull but knowing it would be rejected out of hand.

He would return to the farm on the following day, he told Agricola. The mistress was coming down again and wanted him to attend her; there was some work for a man to do within the house. He felt a traitor to her for saying even so much, but the visit could not be concealed from the bailiff. He just prayed that the man was more loyal to Gaia than to her husband.

On the way home he was waylaid. Cunobarrus was lying in ambush and complained bitterly at the delay in his brother's return. He had spent the evening drinking in Bodellus' house, but he was of a fairly sober mind.

'Before we go on, Verluccus …' He hesitated for once, and unusually, he was diffident. 'I know I have been less gentle than I might have been where you are concerned, and I expect you think you owe me no favours for the way I have been. But it was you who brought me to this, and I can tolerate it no longer. Today Tanodonus and I almost came to blows because you were not there to keep the peace. What will happen when you have gone? He thinks that I want to take his home from him. I know it is my birthright – I am the eldest – but I don't want to rob him of all that he has worked for. I just want him to make some improvements. Every time I make a suggestion about doing something a different way, I sense his resentment of me, and I am only trying to take an interest in it. I would build a house for us all in the manner of Bodellus' home, straight walls with stone and plaster, but he will not have it. You must speak up for me. The Romans will listen to you. What was it Marcus Marcius said? If we want a favour, we can go to him.'

'That was not what he said. And Tanodonus certainly won't do anything he suggests.' It was depressing to learn that in such a brief absence his brothers could quarrel.

Cunobarrus looked at him as if he were a simpleton. 'No, you have it wrong. Now don't laugh at this.' He refused to say more until a promise was secured. 'I am no good here, brother. I cannot live like this. I am only a man when a sword is in my hand.'

'You want to be a gladiator?' It was not a matter for laughter.

'No! No! Don't be stupid. I want to be a soldier. I want to enlist as an auxiliary soldier.'

He saw the incredulity in Verluccus' eyes. 'I knew you would laugh. You could talk them into it. Marcus would accept me if you spoke for me. Deny you owe me that much.'

'You want to enlist and serve as an auxiliary? Bloody Cunobarrus wants to fight for the Romans? Wants to enforce their laws? Wants to protect the empire? I am not laughing, Cunobarrus, but they will.'

'You have influence with Marcus. You ask him. Go to Glevum and ask him for me. He will not be there for long. Soon he will be joining his army again. I've heard it said they are to go to the north.' He kicked a stone, and it fell noisily away into the woods. 'I must get out of here, Verluccus; and he, through your appeal, is my only hope. I urge you to approach him and quickly.'

This was not at all what the other wished to do.

'As soon as I show myself in Glevum, I shall have to surrender to Gaius. He will be sure to know I am there and presume that is the reason for my return. I am not yet ready for that. How can you ask this of me when you are free and I am not?' He shook Cunobarrus' hand from his arm, resenting his brother's interference with his plans. 'I will think about it. I make no more promise than that. I think you and Tanodonus ought to settle your differences and learn to live, if not together, then as neighbours. I might be able to get something for you. Agricola would help with that. But as for your idea of becoming an auxiliary? Forget it. There is no chance of that. Yes, when I return to Glevum I shall speak on your behalf. That is the most I can promise.'

Cunobarrus arrested him in the track and took him by the shoulders, his face full on, glowering. 'But you have influence only with Marcus Marcius! If he is no longer there, you can achieve nothing. Do not forget it was you who brought me down to this – your betrayal, your treachery! And what of your regard for Tanodonus? What if, in a quarrel, I struck Tanodonus such a blow as killed him? How would you feel about that, knowing that you could have prevented it but did nothing?' The sobriety had disappeared and was replaced by a more familiar tone.

3

—— ❧ ——

Belrutha was pale and anxious when they entered the roundhouse. Her nervousness told him that the quarrel between his brothers had been really serious, though Tanodonus would say nothing. He, unlike Cunobarrus, was not eager for Verluccus to return to Glevum.

Quietly he announced his intention to spend the whole of the following day at the farm and probably the night also.

'I do not blame you, Verluccus', said Tanodonus, 'for wanting to keep out of our way. This is not the way I want it for the short time you are with us. I suppose he has told you? It is a strain on us, his being here. If only he would make a home for himself elsewhere. It vexes me sorely that he chooses Bodellus and his family as his friends, knowing how quickly they turned against us when you were taken.'

'Tann, Brother, ten years have passed since then. You must let go of your bitterness. I expect Bodellus said some things then which displeased you and you have made him pay for it ever since. But it has affected you badly. Agricola would befriend you if you would let him. He wants to help you. He has a bull which he is willing to bring across to your beasts. Why not accept him as a neighbour? He is a good man and a good friend to me though now freed. If he spies on you as you claim, it is no more than is demanded of him by one who has your welfare at heart. When I am gone away, let Agricola be your friend and you may hear news of me.'

—— ❧ ——

He remembered Melissa's letter and carefully removed it from his pack and concealed it in the fold of his tunic. Today he would deliver it. He knew this would have to be his last full day in Daruentum and he ought to spend it with his family, but would anyone do so who might instead lie with Gaia? Unthinkable. Tomorrow, when he returned, he would tell them he was ready to depart.

He walked to the gates where once there had been porters, but now they were firmly closed and fastened with a chain. He could have climbed the wall but went instead to the farm entrance to see if she had come and felt utter dejection to find no chariot, no conveyance standing where it should.

The house was cold and uninviting, and he was sure she must have been discovered – betrayed, perhaps, by Delia.

'Don't be so impatient,' said a voice in his ear. 'Give her time. She has to come some miles and you just a step across the clearing.'

He wheeled around and found Agricola.

'Do you think I am so stupid?' asked the farmer. 'I saw how she looked at you when you were making firewood of that tree. And I had no doubt as to the reason for her frequent visits these past days. Don't worry. I think you are a lucky dog, and I won't betray you. But if you go around Glevum with a grin on your face like you wore at my table last night, the whole world will know. Take Agricola's advice and be careful.'

'She is so …' He waved his hands helplessly. 'I just adore her. I cannot believe she –'

'Say no more. I do not want a confession from you. Leave me with my suspicions and go and look for her on the road,' replied the other. 'Have you spoken with your brother? Or did that escape your mind?'

'I think if you approach him again after I am gone, he may be more reasonable. He is a good farmer, and he will know the value of your offer about the bull. Give me the chance to speak to him again.'

He loped away towards the track and followed it as far as Cordatus' tombstone. He sat there and waited.

It was some time since the sun had passed its peak. He had set a stick in the ground to mark the time. No one else had come by, but if they had, he would have hidden himself. Now there was the drumming of two horses fast approaching – the bigarum. How foolish of him to wait there. She would have her own charioteer, a man loyal to Glaucus. The wife of Decimus Aemilius Glaucus would not be allowed to drive herself through the countryside unprotected.

But it was her, and she did so, alone but for Delia. She held the reins and guided the pair of matched white ponies with consummate skill just as she had ridden Candidus.

Her delight on seeing him there was unconcealed, and though Delia was present she simply ignored her and opened her arms wide to greet him.

'Have you been waiting long?' she needed to know, and he lied to her and told her no, but he would have waited forever if he had any hope of having her for himself.

'Neratius Marcellus has gone to Corinium. He has duties to attend to there, and Glaucus goes with him of course. Marcus has gone too, but he will surely not be away for long, as he must go to the north – so he says. It is Neratius who detains him though. I wish he would go; he and Glaucus are not at all friendly to each other. I had to spend some time this morning with Neratius' wife, Julilla, but for the afternoon I said I must come down here, for there is much to be done in the house.'

'That is true,' he whispered into her ear.

She laughed. 'And so there is no obstacle to my spending the night here. Glaucus and the others will be away more than a night.' She handed the reins to him, but though he was more skilled than she at controlling horses, they repeatedly went off line as she persisted in kissing and distracting him.

He gave her Melissa's letter, and she was occupied in struggling to read it while the vehicle jiggled along the uneven track.

'She is well and very, very happy. I don't know how anyone can love my uncle Marcus, but if he makes Melissa happy then I am glad.' It was another reason to put her arms around him while his hands were busy with the reins.

She had brought a warm wrap for Delia so she might sit in the garden.

'Delia will bring us supper when we require it. This afternoon and night are ours. Nothing is to spoil it. I will hear nothing but words of love, and nor shall you.' She led him into her bedroom and invited his embraces.

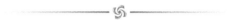

'If only this night could last forever,' he sighed much later.

She rolled over and looked into his eyes, her hair, freed from its braiding, brushing his chest.

'You once said that you would gladly lay down your life for me,' she said. 'I would for you. If you do not want this night to end, for us it need not. If that is what you want, it is what I want also.'

He was more shocked by this than he would have thought possible. 'That is not what I meant. You are too young and lovely to be a corpse. Death is not pretty; death is ugly. With death, secrets are not hidden but revealed. When I said those words I meant that if my dying would save your life, I would die happy. But I would not die happily if I was the cause of your death.'

She did not speak for a long time, and he rose and looked deeply into her eyes. 'Tell me the truth. Is Glaucus not kind to you? You should not speak of wanting to die.'

'Glaucus is not unkind to me. He has different views from my parents, but I can adapt to that. He is not cruel – not to me. Don't be fearful for me. I just know that I cannot bear to be parted from you. If we went to sleep in each other's arms and never awoke, I would die a happy woman.'

He sighed and held her close to him, stroking her skin and gently nibbling her while she lay in ecstatic bliss at his touch.

'I do not want to surrender to Gaius,' he admitted. 'I do not want to be his slave. If only he would free me and allow me to stay here, to be always near you. Can you not persuade him to give me up? Would he make a present of me to you? A parting gift from a loving brother

461

to his favourite sister? Ask him to sell me to you? Perhaps your pleading might grant me the freedom which Marcus says I deserve.'

'Verluccus, my darling love, I cannot. No one can turn Gaius. But even if I could, it would not help us. You would not be safe at my side, for I could not conceal my feelings for you. And if you lived here on the farm or with your brother, we would be forced to part, for Neratius Marcellus will move elsewhere, and Glaucus' business is in serving him. That is why I say let us die together, or else we must live apart.'

'No more of those ideas.' He closed her mouth with his.

'I know I have to return to Glevum,' he said sadly, 'perhaps tomorrow. My dreams of being with you again like this are hopeless. Hopeless and foolish. I shall have to surrender myself to Gaius and enter into your house and bow to you and be distant and correct. If you are unkind to me, you will break my heart. I know you fear his discovering that I killed his brother, his knowledge of us, but don't say hurtful things about me. I beg you not to say things which you know will hurt me. I shall think, *She means it. She really does despise me,* and I shall destroy myself.'

Her arms tightened around him. 'Verluccus, I shall never, never believe a bad thing of you. I may have to say something which hurts, never intending to cause you pain, only ever to protect you. But you must close your ears to any such injury, or you will destroy me. Know only this: I love you. I love you above everything, before everyone, in every way. Even before you laid a finger on me, I wanted to touch you, to feel you, to kiss you. I lured you onto that tree and put my hand onto your body that day because I could bear it no longer. I secretly wanted to caress you. I wanted my skin to touch your skin. I thought that to experience so little would content me; instead it lit a fire. The scars on your back allowed me to demand even more from you, but even when you confessed you adored me I did not know it was such a deep love that I felt for you. When I met Glaucus I was happy and proud to be his bride, and I thought that I would know that same passion for him as you stirred in me when we kissed. But that has not happened. It is you whom I love. I loved you even then, but

I did not know it. I know it now, and nobody – nobody – can make me feel differently. You must not think I say anything about you but for your own good. The way we are placed, you a slave and me the daughter of Lucius Marcius, the wife of Decimus Aemilius Glaucus, makes a gulf between us which we cannot openly cross. Do you think that I have not studied the ways we might escape? Not thought of how I might run away with you? Be reduced to your status, be a slave with you as is the law? Yes! I would do that! But Glaucus would find us. Marcus himself would hunt us down. For all his goodness to you, he would not tolerate such conduct, and we would have no happiness. I know we cannot be together, but if you go with Gaius at least I shall know always how you are, for he will not sell you. I know he will never part with you, and it would be impossible for him to write a letter to me without mentioning you. Please, my darling, for my sake, accept Gaius and stay with him.'

'It never occurred to me to have you run away with me! What a shocking woman you are!' he teased and kissed her, delighted with her words. 'Of course I should not do so. I would not have you a slave or a freedwoman should such a happy event be granted one day to me. The style of life I would be subject to would not be fitting for you.'

He rose, remembering something, and went to the room he had shared with Gaius, returning a few moments later.

'Now will you take this? It has been hidden since your last rejection of it. Wear it now? Marcus will account for it if Glaucus wonders where it has come from. Wear it for me?'

She allowed him to put the necklet around her throat. It was the only thing she was wearing, and she lay back and invited his embrace again.

In the morning he told her of Cunobarrus' idea of becoming an auxiliary soldier. She did not laugh but frowned.

'My understanding is his life is forfeit if he leaves Daruentum. Or perhaps it is your tribal area? I am not sure. Glaucus does not discuss such things with me. But if you need to speak to Marcus, time is short. When he returns from Corinium, there is no reason for him to delay his departure and rejoin his army. This must be our goodbye.

Oh, hold me, hold me. I do not want you to go from me yet. I do not need to go back to Glevum immediately.'

He held her fast. 'The last thing I want is to be parted from you. I wish I could take you across to my home, to my brother's home, and present you to my family and say, "This beautiful girl loves me," but that cannot be. Let me love you now one more time, and then I will sneak away like the thief I am and Delia can repair the damage as best she can.'

She cried when he had gone. She had wanted him to ride into Glevum beside her, taking the reins so that she might return him to Gaius, saying she had met him on the road. But he would not have it. He had to still his feelings, to bring them under control, so that when he stood at the door to her house and asked for his master and set eyes on her, nobody would know what he truly felt inside.

He told Tanodonus that he must go. His brother and sister-in-law and their children made this parting almost as painful as that from Gaia. He urged him again to make a friend of Agricola and obtained his reluctant agreement to at least speak to the man and not abuse him. Again he begged his brother to take the gold pieces, and again he was refused.

When he returned to the farm, Gaia had gone. He buried the jewellery carefully in the place where the necklet had been; when he had the chance, he would tell Gaia where it was and that if she ever had need, it was hers.

Cunobarrus was ready to go. He had determined that he too would come to Glevum and find lodgings in a tavern. It was not the best of his ideas, but it meant that he would know his fate more quickly, Verluccus conceded, and it would relieve the distress he caused to his family.

With a great deal of kissing from Belrutha and her brood and a tight hug from Tanodonus together with a firm assurance that he would contact Agricola, Verluccus and Cunobarrus raised their packs and marched away.

4

His master was in Corinium with the others still. He was offered admittance to the house but would not take it and instead went in a vain search for Cassio, discovering that he had now obtained his honourable retirement and had returned to Dolbactan's community in search of a wife. In the end he had to choose between calling on Justinius Severus and giving him news of his son Titus or spending a drunken afternoon and night with Cunobarrus. He chose the former.

Eventually he located Justinius at the baths, and his heart warmed to the veteran, who was proud of his son and pleased to receive news of him, to know that he was doing well despite a blow across his back and further punishment for having lost his sword. 'Good for him. A few blows never did a soldier any harm,' professed the father, obviously a devotee of the code of the centurion. Justinius Severus was a grateful audience, and he told him all that had taken place, returning with the man to his house to complete the tale and thankful to obtain quarters there for himself.

In the morning he went to the tavern, fearful that mayhem might have broken out. But there were no breakages for which Cunobarrus was held responsible; he was still in a state of deep unconsciousness, and there was no need for him to be woken. He left a message for his brother with the innkeeper and took up a position by the town gate where he could witness the return of Marcus.

The party returned late in the day and made for the home of Glaucus. They seemed to be in good spirits, and he followed them at a distance, debating whether first to approach Gaius or Marcus. It seemed the more diplomatic move to surrender himself to Gaius and

465

hope the opportunity to speak to Marcus would not be denied him. How soon might Gaius wish to be gone? With his return, it could be as soon as the morrow. It was in a gloomy mood that he sought his master. Gaius was dressing for dinner. Placidus was assisting him with his toga.

Gaius looked at Verluccus and set his face imperiously. His voice was laden with sarcasm. 'This is an unexpected honour! How gracious of you to attend our dinner! Are we to presume that you are now returned to us?'

'Yes, master. I am truly grateful to you for allowing my leave of absence. I was home in time to see my mother die and hold her hand while she departed this world.'

His words shocked Gaius as he had intended they should, and the young man's manner changed.

'Verluccus! Oh, Verluccus! I never thought about your people. I have heard so much from my uncle about my selfishness and lack of humanity, but … I would not have denied you that. You did not ask me to let you visit your people. Why didn't you give me the chance to grant you that? Am I such a monster that you will never ask any favour of me?'

It was tempting to say that he was, but he felt pity for the youth and denied it, saying instead, 'Your uncle offered me a reward for doing the service he demanded of me. And yes, to be honest, I would not have asked you that. Your father refused it, and I would not expect you to oppose his will.'

Gaius grinned. 'I should like my father to hear that! He thinks I do nothing but oppose his will. Forgive my rudeness and let me make amends by having you serve me at dinner tonight. There will be guests, and Neratius' wife Julilla will be present. Gaia too is to be there.'

Gaia too? Her brother had made it sound as if she did not normally eat in her own triclinium. He braced himself for their encounter. 'I hope I shall remember how,' he said in answer to Gaius in placatory tones and was immediately assured that he need have no fear; Glaucus' slaves were so competent that he need do very little.

The room had been redecorated since he last saw it, which was not since it had been sold by Calpurnius. He took station near to his master, knowing where Gaia must be reclining but refusing to look in that direction.

Marcus said, 'I see you have back your goods, Gaius,' and turned to speak closely with Neratius, who turned and looked at him with interest and nodded and laughed in a ribald way. They were scheming something which involved him, and he suspected it was to be at Gaius' expense.

Marcus waved a cup and looked him in the eye, determined that he should cross the room and replenish it, waving other attention away.

It was a wonderful opportunity. He poured the wine into the cup and quietly asked if Marcus would grant him the favour of allowing him to speak before he left.

'You may speak to me now, Verluccus. You do not need to make an appointment to speak to Marcus Marcius. I had not expected to see you quite this soon. You must have found it too hard to be parted from your master?'

He had a horrible feeling that he was forming part of the evening's entertainment.

'I returned earlier than I was ready in order to ask a favour of you.'

'What? Another favour? And the first barely spent. A little greedy, I think. And where are my thanks?'

'I hope, my lord, that Gnaeus Cassius conveyed my thanks for your gift. I would have thanked you for that in any case; it was more than generous of you and quite unexpected. My asking for another favour may well appear greedy, and it is not for me. You have been more kind to me than I had any right to hope for, and I owe you much, despite your terrorizing my mind about my brother Tanodonus.'

'And for allowing you to go down there,' he was reminded.

'Yes, my lord, my thanks for that too.'

'And as for your brother Tanodonus, I thought you understood. I had to do something to move you. So tell me. What more must I do to retain your good opinion of me?'

'If you will see me privately – I beg you?'

'If he is begging, have him on his knees,' recommended Neratius.

Glaucus was frowning. The entertainment he had engaged consisted of musicians and a comic reading. This was an unwelcome departure. He suggested that perhaps the favour could be delayed until the party broke up.

'Nonsense,' said Neratius. 'Marcus, have him beg properly. We will decide whether or not you may grant him his favour. Come, slave, this is a rare honour and a privilege for you to have the governor of Britain hear your petition.'

Verluccus was silent for so long that the man's patience was beginning to wear thin.

'Does your master know? Shall he tell us? I tell you what – shall we rack him to move his tongue?'

'I have no idea what it is,' Gaius admitted, wondering if he would really torture Verluccus just to make him beg the favour.

He was spared from that but thrown by what he did say. His intake of breath at the words was clearly audible.

'It is about becoming a soldier.'

It seemed safest not to mention Cunobarrus immediately. He had knelt before Neratius as demanded.

'Ah, that is easily answered. No. No slaves in the army – Roman citizens only.' It was Glaucus who spoke. He was glad to have the nonsense out of the way.

'Decimus Aemilius Glaucus has spoken correctly,' said Marcus drily. 'I would have you without a moment's hesitation, but I could not even make an auxiliary of the likes of you even if your master consented, and you know that he would not. So why don't you say what you really want? I have already estimated the price of this favour, and I should like to gain it.'

'It is not for me but for Cunobarrus. I beg on his behalf. He desires to enlist as an auxiliary soldier and serve the emperor.'

It was as he had said it would be. It was the funniest joke they had heard in a lifetime. They laughed long and hard, and when they had stopped, they began again. Julilla's shrill voice could be heard clearly among the deep, masculine guffaws but not Gaia's. For the first time he looked directly at her, and their eyes met. She smiled and held out her cup.

He poured the wine with a trembling hand, wanting to give her a secret sign but knowing that in that room, with so many eyes of slaves and owners, nothing could be secret except their thoughts.

'I am pleased to see you safely back with us,' she said. 'My brother has need of you. Take up your station now.'

Neratius was debating. 'The question we are asked is whether a criminal, one who ought rightly to have been executed or at least enslaved but who has most generously been pardoned and allowed to live among his own people on condition that he does not bear weapons or incite disaffection for us, enlist in our crack auxiliary army. Is this a matter we can decide now, or should I call a council to consider the matter tomorrow?' He turned to Marcus. 'What was the price you had in mind? Does it still apply if the beneficiary is Cunobarrus?'

'Indeed it does,' said Marcus, 'but to be extracted from this one, not the other.' He pointed towards Verluccus and whispered in Neratius' ear.

Whatever it was pleased Neratius immensely. 'Excellent, excellent. That is to be our decision. Gaius Marcius, put your slave before us.'

Verluccus was kneeling again at the governor's couch. 'Do you know where we have been?' he was asked, and he had to admit that he did.

'While we were there, my good friend Marcus Marcius made what was then a frivolous wager with me. It was frivolous because there was no prospect of it being called to account. Have you any idea what it may have been? You may speak.'

'No, my lord. I have no idea.'

'We watched some mediocre sport. There was but one among the sword fighters who had any ability, and Marcus said he knew of one who could beat even Leo – that was his name: Leo. I doubt if you have ever seen a lion, but that is what his name means, and take it from me, it is a very vicious beast.' He stood up and began to examine Verluccus' legs and arms, checking their muscularity as if he were making a purchase. 'Gaius, we have need to detain your man a little longer from you. Will you loan him again to your uncle?'

What could he say? Gaius wondered. Saying no to Marcus had proved impossible; to say no to both Neratius and to Marcus was doubly so. He shook his head in resignation and looked at Gaia. She seemed even less happy about the prospect than he.

'Verluccus is not trained,' he said carefully. 'He may be strong and he may have fought against your soldiers and against that tribune, but he was beaten on both occasions. And he has never been in a gladiatorial contest. It would not be a fair fight. I would have thought the prospect of having such as Cunobarrus fighting on our side would not need a price. Verluccus has done a great deal in your service already and given us much amusement at my brother-in-law's triclinium. Let that be enough.'

'Good, good, then that is settled.' Neratius rubbed his hands together and resumed his couch. 'Now, Marcus, you have your man, and you have heard what Gaius Marcius has to say. The boy requires training. Who should train him?'

'He does not require as much as Gaius suggests. Vitellius gave him a few pointers. I shall appoint a suitable trainer, and we will set a date for the contest. In about four days, perhaps?'

Verluccus whispered to Gaius. He was not at all daunted by the price he must pay. 'May I make a suggestion?'

'Do you really have to? Sparring with Vitellius is one thing, fighting for your life to entertain my uncle quite another. If we cannot train you, the contest may be called off. I don't care if they won't have your brother in the army. Let him stay where he is. I shall send word down that the petition is denied.'

'You do not have the authority.' Marcus had overheard the exchange. 'Will you never learn, boy? You have a suggestion, Verluccus? What is it?'

'Justinius Severus, the veteran centurion, my lord. I went to see him to take news of his son, Titus Justinius. I believe he might be the man you need.'

Gaius flushed as he realized he had not given the old soldier a second thought on his return but comforted himself that no doubt Titus had specially asked Verluccus to see his father if he could. But what Verluccus was suggesting was correct. If anyone in the town could do the job, it probably was the elder Justinius.

Verluccus returned to his master's room that night and told Gaius that Cunobarrus was in fact come to Glevum. He begged to be allowed to see him, to tell him to return to Daruentum and lie low until the fight was over. 'I will waste no time in returning to you,' he promised.

'You may go down in the morning. The tavern keeper will not thank you for arriving at this time. Your place is with me now, and I need help to remove my toga.' It occurred to Gaius that if Neratius learned that Cunobarrus had breached his parole, then he might have him put to death and the contest nullified.

It was shocking for Verluccus to find stripes laid into Gaius' back. 'Did your uncle do this? Why? For what?'

'For nothing – for anything. He says it is to make a man of me. Perhaps it will if that is what made a man of him and his brothers, Father included. My father never struck a blow on me, never, though he threatened it often. Marcus Marcius, the man you esteem so highly, flogged me with his own hands – me, a man of seventeen years!' He remembered the humiliation of it when after yet another argument and some cheap but true jibes about Melissa's origins, Marcus' patience had terminated abruptly and he had sent Tertius to produce his whip. There had been only six strokes across his back, fewer than Verluccus had suffered, but they were heavily struck and had broken his defiance. He had far more respect for his uncle now, though he loathed him intensely. 'There is some ointment there.' He winced as the cold cream was applied to his skin.

Anxious that Cunobarrus should return to Daruentum to await the outcome of the contest, Verluccus rose before dawn and would

471

have left immediately to warn him away, but Gaius forbade this, saying he needed his breakfast first and Verluccus must prepare it for him. While the young man was eating – it was only bread and fruit, but he was eating very slowly – Marcus and Glaucus joined him and so did Gaia.

Verluccus had thought about her during the night, imagining her lying in her husband's arms and being wife to him. He told himself she looked pale and strained and decided his presence was a burden to her and wished he might leave, and yet he wanted nothing more than to remain there and serve her.

Marcus was courteous and amiable to both her and her brother. If he felt any remorse for what he had done to Gaius, if he even knew how damaging his blows had been, he appeared to have completely forgotten it. His mind was set on sending out for Justinius Severus to be brought to them so that they might sound him out; Verluccus was eager and glad to be the one sent on the errand.

He had not reached the door, however, when a slave entered to announce that tribune Antonius was seeking admittance. The man was told not to be a fool but to send the tribune in. But any welcome they might have had for him was wiped out by the expression upon his face. It was Marcus he had come to see.

'Cunobarrus is in chains. He claims he was here on business to see you.'

Verluccus admitted that it was true. Cunobarrus had come with him to Glevum. He had been lodging in a tavern awaiting news. Was even visiting the city denied him? Verluccus decided to take the line of innocent mistake.

'I don't know what the term *visiting* means to the likes of your slave, Gaius Marcius,' said Antonius, not bothering to speak to Verluccus, 'but burning down three houses and causing a riot is not visiting in my book.'

'Three houses and a riot?' Marcus was delighted. 'How many dead?'

'None, thankfully. And to be honest, it was only one building completely burnt down, the drinking house itself. The building next door is not quite gutted, and the further one is slightly scorched. There was no building on the other side. The landlord is raging as you might well expect.'

'Do we know why? Why he burned the buildings and caused the riot, I mean?' asked Gaius.

'He is Cunobarrus,' said Glaucus, as if that were explanation enough, 'our would-be recruit. A subversive, I think.'

Eyes turned to Verluccus for explanation. 'It might have been an accident?' he suggested more in hope than belief.

'No.' Antonius lacked Marcus' sense of humour. 'From what I can make out, he was bragging about how his brother took on Drusus Vitellius and not only lived but drew blood from him. There were a few veterans present who took exception to such boasting.'

'And now he is confined?' It was Marcus who asked.

Antonius nodded grimly. 'Both for his penalty and his protection. The landlord is demanding compensation.'

Marcus turned to Glaucus. 'I will pay for the damage. Send that freedman of yours round to make an assessment for me. And now, Antonius, I shall accompany you to where you hold him. Verluccus, you come with us too.'

5

'He is to remain here.' Marcus told the guard when he had seen the miscreant for himself. 'Do not remove him to Corinium. And see that he is properly fed. After four days, I shall send word as to what's to be done with him.'

Verluccus had told Cunobarrus that but for his stupidity, he would have been granted his wish to become a soldier. Now he must await the outcome of the contest if he had any hope of joining the army.

'I will fight the gladiator instead of you,' Cunobarrus urged. 'Tell Marcus that. This is my doing.'

'Shut up, fool,' said his brother. 'Don't put such an idea into Marcus' head. I know him. He would see more sport in us fighting one another. Stay quiet and keep your temper. At least here you must remain sober.'

Justinius Severus was delighted with his assignment. But he laid down his necessities. If he was to train a fighter, then he must have him wholly to himself with no distraction. Verluccus must move into his house and suffer his regime. It would cost money. His food would have to be the best available, and he would need equipment, leathers, boots, sword, helmet, and shield, all made especially for him.

All of it was agreed.

'You are investing a lot of money in one event,' said Justinius Severus. 'It is for the one event?'

He had asked the question neither Gaius nor his sister dared voice.

'Sadly, it is. I must relinquish him to his master when this is done. And you are right. Taking into account my newly acquired property, which consists of the ashes of three buildings, of doubtful value; compensating the landlord for his lost trade; and providing my champion with the best that can be obtained, this bout is costing me a tidy sum.' He turned to Verluccus. 'The amount which Neratius Marcellus wagers on your being defeated comes nowhere near what I am laying out. I am looking to you to provide me with singular entertainment. I believe in your ability. Do not let me down.'

Gaius was forced to console himself with his sister's company. She urged him to go to the farm, to visit Agricola, to ride to Corinium, to visit Marcia but not, on any account, to go near to Verluccus while he was in training.

A visit to his other sister was the option which seemed the least unappealing, and he departed, making Cervus happy if not himself.

The training seemed to be going well. Sometimes Marcus sneaked into the gymnasium and saw his protégé being put through his paces. And sometimes he caught sight of him running across country or around the racing track while his taskmaster pursued him on horseback and berated him and ridiculed his efforts.

'You will have me doubting him,' he said to Justinius when the horse halted beside him, but the runner was sent away again with a pacesetter. 'Is he really so bad?'

'Physically he could hardly be in better shape. He tells me that he has been working on a farm which accounts for it,' Justinius responded with little enthusiasm.

'Yet I sense there is still a problem? He can handle a sword well enough; that I do know. So what is it? You had better tell me. What makes you doubt him?' He prepared himself for the negative speculation, failure he had not even considered a possibility.

'Well,' said Justinius, looking even more worried, 'in the first place, he is insisting on fighting native style – using weapons familiar to him. No, not a chariot, just a long British sword and a shield. But no proper protection. He wants his hair to be limed and dressed and his body painted with woad dye.'

'That is no bad thing,' responded Marcus. 'Seeing him so will chill his opponent to the core. You have seen Leo. He is not up to much – certainly not up to Verluccus' ability. Remember he survived long enough so clad. It will provide a greater spectacle. So that is your first concern put away. Name the next.'

'The other is a much more difficult problem. It lies within him. He goes into this fight intending to die. That I cannot train out of him.'

Marcus gaped and almost laughed. 'I think you have scared him by exaggerating his opponent's ability. Let me reassure him.' He raised his hand to wave for the runners to return to them.

'No, General, it is not that.' Severus waved his hand that they should continue. 'The problem is unfinished business. Native unfinished business,' he added enigmatically.

As Marcus could only look at him in bewilderment, he had to explain.

'I agreed to take him to the shrine of Mercury and Rosmerta. He said he needed to make prayers, and I, thinking that in order, some ritual he needed to complete his preparations, even gave him the money he needed to buy his prayers with. He purchased a few. I had best not divulge their content save to say there is a man named Cadrus who has preceded him into the other world, and he is determined to follow and wreak his revenge upon him. He believes that to go over in warrior garb with a sword in his hand will gain his admission to where the other is gone.'

Marcus saw now that the problem was real.

'By all the gods! I'll give him prayers! I thought that matter settled. The man Cadrus is or was another of his brothers, dead at Belconia. He did him a great wrong. Verluccus even tried to kill the tribune Drusus Vitellius because he believed he was responsible for the harm that Cadrus did.'

He thought for a few minutes in vain. Somehow he must find some reason why Verluccus should want to live, some way to vanquish his desire to pursue the dead.

Verluccus and his pacesetter were heading towards them, sweat freely running down their nearly naked bodies. Marcus followed them into the stable. He went on the offensive.

'Did I not receive from you your oath of peace with Cunobarrus? Now I am told you would even pursue the dead beyond the grave! What folly is this? I am paying for an honest fight and not a suicide.'

'You will have your fight,' responded Verluccus, glowering at the treachery of Justinius. 'I will scare Leo shitless before I accept his blade. No one will know it is my doing that he wins.'

'I shall know, for one,' responded Marcus. 'You arrogant bastard! You brag about your ability and then make up some feeble tale to cover up the fact that you lack it. I was wrong to boast that you could beat the Beast. You are nothing but a puny girl! What of Cunobarrus? I promised him his life, and with you he too shall die.'

'So be it,' Verluccus answered quietly, rubbing himself down with a towel. 'It will not be done by my hand. That is what I swore – not to raise my hand against Cunobarrus.' He turned his back on Marcus and pulled on his tunic.

'And what do you suppose this madness of yours will achieve? Over there, in this other world of yours? You cannot kill the dead! Souls gone to Hades are indestructible. You condemn yourself to some fruitless pursuit through the everlasting shades after a quarry upon which you will never, not for the whole of eternity, be able to lay a hand! The man is dead. Let it be. If he were alive, you could do no more than kill him, and another has already done that service for you. Better that you live, even in the service of my nephew, than for ever more and vainly pursue the maniacal laughter of a deranged shadow!'

He received no response, only the view of a squared back and an ominously rigid spine. He glowered and stalked away without another word.

Neratius was in a cheerful mood. Leo had arrived and was quartered at the Glevum arena, and there too Verluccus was installed. 'Let us visit our champions before we take our seats and so encourage them to their best efforts,' he decided.

Gaius declined, sulking. He had not come willingly to this but had been goaded by his uncle not to be absent at such a crucial time. He should show Verluccus that he had faith in him. Nor was Gaia allowed to be excused. Marcus would have none of that, despite her husband's objections. He took her firmly by the arm and walked her beside him.

'Your wife is somewhat pale today,' he said to Glaucus. 'Are we to presume a happy event in the offing? You are a fortunate man to have such a lovely young bride and the estate at Daruentum too.'

Glaucus glanced towards her. She shook her head, and he frowned. 'This is no place for my wife to be seen whether she is with child or not. She is young, yes, and pretty enough. But her sister has the larger property. I would buy more land at Daruentum and expand the farm, but Gaia assures me the locals will not sell their land.'

'How inconsiderate of them,' Marcus replied solemnly. 'You should have married her elsewhere. Her father has larger estates at Corinium and near Lindum, as I recall.' To Gaia he said, 'Of course, were it me, I would not wait upon them selling their farms. I would just evict them and seize their land. That is what you are thinking?'

'Not at all, Uncle Marcus. I know how strictly you adhere to the laws you enforce.'

'Hah! There speaks the mother's daughter! What a pity Aelia Paula is not here to appreciate you.' He glanced to where Gaius was loitering outside, refusing to enter. 'See your brother? How miserable he is. Gaius Marcius is certain that Verluccus will die today. Perhaps he will. Would that upset you as much as it would my nephew?'

'I thought you had him trained,' she whispered, near voiceless. Her face drained so that her complexion became like porcelain.

Justinius was putting some finishing touches to his fearsome-looking champion, a Verluccus she barely recognized, his hair whitened and stiffened despite its shortness and now a crest on his head, thick with liming. His arms and chest had been liberally daubed with blue designs, triskeles and figures of a warrior. For the sake of decency he was wearing a leather thong, and Justinius was fastening leather protectors onto his arms and legs. Both were clearly shocked to see the girl brought there. Verluccus could only stand speechless.

Justinius explained what he could of the significance of the markings, and Neratius and Marcus listened gravely, speaking of and not to Verluccus as if he were some animal unable to converse. Then, satisfied, Neratius moved away to where Leo was awaiting his inspection. Marcus drew Justinius aside for a few words, and Verluccus and Gaia seized upon a precious moment that could not be missed.

They broke their silences simultaneously. 'This is no place for you, this dark and filthy, stinking hole,' he began to say, and then deferred to her.

'Verluccus, you must win. Please tell me you can do this. I cannot bear it. Marcus is going to make me watch, and I do not want to see you die. Please, please, my darling, assure me that you can beat this fellow!'

'What has he said to you?' He was so close to her, and yet dared not touch. 'What has Marcus said to you?'

'Nothing. I am just so frightened for you. I shall follow you. If you are killed, I shall kill myself. I swear to you now if you leave this world I shall go too. I shall find you. If I have to search forever, I shall find you.'

Marcus had turned his head and was watching them sidelong.

'You must not talk like that,' Verluccus whispered. 'I will not allow you to die for my sake. Do not fear for me. I have more skill than any Leo.'

They could not kiss, dared not even touch, for he knew that if he did what he desired she would be instantly torn from his arms and he would have no means to help her. She stood before him still and silent with her eyes glittering until her uncle approached them again.

'Come and sit beside me, Gaia Marcia. You do not mind, Glaucus, that I borrow your wife for company?' Without waiting for a reply, Marcus took her by the hand and led her to where he intended to sit.

'I think I am unwell. I should leave now before they start.'

His grip tightened. 'You go nowhere. You sit down and enjoy what is to come. Or else let your husband know what I know.'

'What do you mean?' She struggled to free herself.

He touched the beads she wore around her neck. 'You know exactly what I mean. Who has hair of amber? Who has eyes as blue as lapis?' There was a sneer on his face as he looked across at Glaucus, a paler man.

How could he know? She froze, wondering what he might say or do next. Nothing which she and Verluccus had done or said in that fleeting moment could have led him to such a conclusion. Verluccus would not have told him; he could not. Gaius did not know. And she had been so careful, so circumspect.

She forced herself to say, 'Indeed, I do not know what you mean. I think you are too mysterious. These are the beads which you gave to me. Have you forgotten?' As she spoke she remembered, and sudden realization came to her. 'This is what you planned all along, isn't it? The day you returned Verluccus to us, you wanted him to be your gladiator, and now you have engineered it. I wish to go. Let me go! I prefer to sit beside my husband!'

His hand clamped her to her seat. 'No, you will not do that to him. In a few moments from now, he is going to enter this arena and fight for his life. And I want him to live. The sight of you may just inspire him to do that. Stay here and do him that kindness.'

She could not say more. The seats – there were no more than a hundred placed for the privileged – had now been filled, and to the sudden blare of trumpets, a silence fell as the combatants entered and came before Neratius to bow and pledge their lives as sport for him.

He looked up and saw her. He moved towards them, and she mouthed, 'I love you; do not die.'

'Pass me your sword,' said Marcus, and then he offered it to Gaia and asked her to kiss the hilt to bring its holder good fortune. She did so and passed it to him, and his hand fastened where her lips had been and he raised it in a salute to her. She looked into his eyes and thought she would die for love of him.

'Good girl,' Marcus whispered into her ear. 'I am not a man to stand in the way of true love. Has he had you yet? What reward should he have for winning today? Shall I give him some pretty little thing with beads on?'

'Please, please,' she moaned. She was not accepting his offer – just terrified of him and begging him to leave her be.

'I could not persuade him to wear a helmet,' said Justinius, sitting somewhere behind Marcus. 'That scar on his head could not be disguised, and Leo will go for it.'

'It is a cuirass he ought to have worn,' Marcus responded drily. 'And that some time ago; it is too late now.' The witticism was lost on Justinius.

The Beast of Corinium, otherwise known as Leo, was being paid a good sum for demeaning himself to fight an unknown barbarian upstart who had been announced as Verluccus the Bloodspiller. He shrugged. It was a fair purse, and when it was over, he would have the freedom of the local brothels. He raised his sword again to Neratius Marcellus. That man had made it clear where his money was wagered.

They had not met until now. The closest they had been to one another was within the stables when they had been within shouting distance of one another, and that time had not gone to waste. He had received reports from his spies, of course, and they were all favourable. The gods were on his side and skill and experience too. The newcomer was tall and might well be as strong as he looked, but he was untested. Leo circled him and taunted him to make the first wild lunge.

Justinius Severus had done as much as he could; so had Marcus. The man was right; it was folly to think of pursuing Cadrus. He should regret only that he had struck down the man who had killed him. That man, he had long since convinced himself, surely had been Virens.

He pulled his mind together to concentrate on the immediate, and his hands tightened on sword and shield. They felt good. He glanced again at the pallid face of Gaia, so terrified for him. She would have her wish, he promised the gods: Gaia would not see him die.

There was truth in what Marcus had asserted. In this environment he had purpose, he had power, and he drew a following instead of constantly being the follower. His chest had swelled as he preened before Leo and teased the crowd, raising the sword and shield above his head and shaking them threateningly and screaming his contempt for his Roman adversary. He heard men once his enemies calling for him, calling out, 'Verluccus the Bloodspiller!' It was a name he had never dreamed he would hear a Roman shout with approval.

He licked his lips and tightened his body. The grip on his sword and shield shifted so that he absorbed them and they became part of him. He faced his enemy with a determination matched only by that of Leo himself.

Leo too had his supporters, voices calling for the Beast to 'sort him out'. There was no chance of that. Not for one moment did Verluccus doubt his skill and stamina, though neither did he doubt Leo's ability. The man had not survived for as long as he reputedly had and become the best in Corinium without much killing. Leo had survived more contests than he was likely to know of.

But Verluccus the Bloodspiller had learned his trade in arenas where there was no referee to appeal to for clemency when the contest was over and you were begging for your life to be spared.

Leo was performing for the crowd too, closing his ears to the blood-curdling yells and the prancing war dance. He chose to mock the barbarian ritual and reduce the crowd to laughter. He knew that the man had trained only briefly, though hard, and was probably quite unfitted for the task before him.

He was right; the first jab was easily parried. It meant nothing. They were just feeling each other's weight and reach. He invited another. The so-called Bloodspiller kept his distance, expecting a return blow. Leo waited and circled him.

Now the crowd were not amused, and the approving cheers and laughter turned to hoots of derision. They obliged the audience by making noisy clashes of sword on sword. It sounded good, but both knew it merely helped to weary them.

The advantage suddenly came to Leo, and he took it. He went for the momentarily unguarded torso, the glistening blue skin, sweating and wanting to be pierced and made red.

But the shield was quicker than the blink of an eye, and he knew he had been fooled when his sword stuck in it and was pulled from his hands. The hilt vibrated mockingly in his face, its weight pulling down the shield on his opponent's arm. He stepped back, appalled at his stupidity, his bad judgement, and its inevitable outcome, wishing that he had a spear he could turn to.

'Take it out.'

Leo did not move. Disarmed as if he were a novice, he was at the other's mercy.

'Take it back. I am not going to continue if you have no sword. Take it out.'

They continued with the gladius restored to Leo's hand. He had not encountered the likes of this one before. If he had made such an error in Corinium, he would have been dead meat by now, dragged unceremoniously across the sand and into oblivion.

Gaia had closed her eyes long since and had no idea of what the sudden whoops and shouts and cheers signified. She could hear the ringing sound of metal smashing into metal, the scuffling of feet in the sand, and their breathing, panting as their strength was sapped. And she could feel the hot sun beating down onto her head. She wanted it to end but at the same time did not want it to for fear of what the end might be.

Suddenly the fight was stopped – stopped by an outside agency. She opened her eyes and saw that a steward had intervened on Neratius' order. Neratius had sent down a message; he had chosen Glaucus to be its bearer. 'The governor wants no more of this poncing about; he is getting hungry and wants his supper. Get the job finished quickly. There is a double reward for Leo if he is quick about it.'

Grateful for the breather, Leo launched himself towards the upstart with all the power and skill he could muster. Their swords met with real ferocity, and seizing another chance, Leo now went for the head wound. He struck only a glancing blow before his weapon was parried, but he sent Bloodspiller staggering backwards and knew the end was close. He moved in for the kill, urging his victim to raise his hand in appeal.

Gaia shut her eyes again. She thought she must surely faint. Her hands were clinging tightly to something. It was her uncle's arm, and her nails were drawing blood, though she did not know it.

Verluccus ducked and twisted away, and the lunge from Leo was wasted in air. He somersaulted and turned again, knowing that the damage to the head must have an effect and he must move quickly to keep the advantage.

'Beg for mercy,' Leo urged, remembering the chivalry of the other but foolishly ignoring the expression on the Bloodspiller's face which had told many men before him that their death was imminent. Verluccus shook his head. 'It is for you to beg,' he said.

'He just walked onto his sword.'

'No, he ran onto it.'

Opinions were divided for long afterwards, but they made no difference.

At the moment of his victory, or what he had perceived to be his victory, Leo had died. His body lay at Verluccus' feet, his face still bearing the surprise he felt at the moment when he thought he was wielding the fatal blow but found that it was instead within himself.

'I don't know how he did that.' Neratius was shaking his head in bafflement. 'Did you see how he did that, Glaucus? Gaius? I must ask Justinius exactly how it was done.'

He was walking to the exit still shaking his head in puzzlement and turned to Marcus, who was supporting a shaking, sobbing, but greatly relieved Gaia. 'Marcus, you were nearer at the end of it. Did you see how he did it?'

'No need; I just knew he would,' he chortled, making a fist. 'Get your purse ready, Marcellus. Here, Glaucus, take your wife. You were right – this was no place to bring a woman. They just don't appreciate the art of it.' He abandoned her and, taking Gaius by the arm, went to congratulate the winner.

'Justinius Severus, you must dine with us tonight. Neratius is feasting our party in the praetorium. But first go to the prison and get that fool Cunobarrus released. Will you take him to your home and have him kept out of harm's way? He shall come with me when I ride to the north, and we will find a suitable cohort to put him in.' He showered Verluccus with hearty congratulations and bade Gaius do likewise.

'You shall have a present, Verluccus. What would you most like in all the world? You have only to say, and if it is within my means, you shall have it. The equipment, perhaps? You may find further use for it.'

'May I now see Cunobarrus?' He was very tired and did not feel the elation he ought to.

'Go with Justinius Severus.' Marcus nodded. 'He is about to free him and take him into his home. Bid farewell to him. He now has his wish and shall pledge his life to Trajan. As for you? I think your master will lose no speed in removing you from Britain.'

Gaius confirmed his intention and refused the equipment, saying there would be no use for it in future. Marcus laughed; he had known what the answer would be. They were, he said, to leave the following day.

'Before you go,' said Marcus to the slave, ignoring his nephew, 'come to me. Tomorrow I shall have a letter ready for you to take to my brother Lucius. Hand it over to no one but him.' He patted his champion and left him to Gaius, going himself in pursuit of Neratius.

6

Gaius had to attend the dinner. Marcus insisted on it. He insisted too that Verluccus needed to rest. He had performed a Herculean feat, and for that night the young man could manage perfectly well without him. In fact, if he had any consideration at all, he would leave him be all night long. There was room enough to sleep in the praetorium and girls or boys available at his whim. Marcus himself intended to sleep there – just to make sure that Neratius paid his debts, he said.

'Marcus knows about us.'

Gaia and Verluccus were alone except for Delia, who had to remain for the sake of appearances. Verluccus was present to serve her dinner.

'How can he? We have given no sign. You must be mistaken.'

'I am not mistaken, Verluccus. He told me so. He told me quite specifically. I did not mistake his meaning. He made remarks about these beads and why I wear them, and he made me sit beside him and watch you because he knows I love you and because to cause pain is a thing which amuses him. Look at us now, here, ostensibly alone. He has engineered this. He has left you here with me and taken Glaucus and Gaius away for the evening, perhaps for the whole night.'

He was kneeling by her couch, ready to pass whatever dish she required, wanting to touch her but fearful to do so. Though they were alone in the triclinium, the house was full of Glaucus' slaves. 'Do you think he has set a trap for us? I have not seen Demetrius. Where is he?'

'I would not put it past him to set a trap but not with Demetrius – he has been sent to obtain a house suitable for me for when Neratius departs for Londinium.' She looked into his eyes and fed him a sweetmeat from her plate. 'Kiss me.'

He obliged happily.

There was ample room on the couch for both of them.

'It would disgrace his family if you were discovered consorting with a slave. Marcus would not sanction that,' he mused some little time later.

'My uncle has little regard for Glaucus. I have noticed the way he speaks to him. He does not suffer gladly those he thinks of as fools.'

'Your husband is no fool. He is a clever man.'

'But you are right,' she admitted. 'Marcus may do many dreadful things, but he would never disgrace his family or allow it to be disgraced.'

'So for that reason, why should he connive to have his niece disgrace it?'

She sighed and kissed his face. 'I expect you are right. Perhaps he does not truly know; perhaps he only suspects. But even so, if he suspects and he knows we are alone, what better moment for him to embarrass Glaucus?'

'Do you think he cares more to embarrass Glaucus than he does for the damage he would cause to you and his family name?' He did not want to hear her answer and prevented her from responding by covering her lips with his own. 'Let me love you now, here, just one more time. You then must go to his bed and sleep alone and I to mine. But first let Delia be silent and keep watch.'

When they ceased it was of their own volition. Nobody had burst in; not even a slave had tapped the door to clear away the dishes. Delia had firmly turned her back on them and closed her ears.

Gaia lay on the dining couch with her hair spread across it and her gown in pieces and gazed lovingly at him.

'My darling, I don't care if he does come in and discover us. Now I could die happy.' She stroked his cheek.

'No,' he moaned and kissed her breasts, 'no, not for me. For me you must live. Let Delia put you together again, and go to your bed. I shall deal with the room and go to mine. Yes,' – he put his hand on her protesting lips – 'it has to be so.' He told her then where he had hidden his jewels and that they were hers should she ever have need of them.

He left her, knowing that the menials would soon be stirring. The first hint of dawn had come. Shortly afterwards he heard the blundering of Gaius and Glaucus making a clumsy return.

'Go back to sleep; you must be exhausted,' said Gaius as Verluccus made as if to rise. 'I can manage for myself.'

Later that morning he was packing for their journey.

'What is that?' Gaius' sharp eyes had spotted the scroll holder which he was sliding among his own things.

'Your uncle gave it to me. It is a letter he orders me to hand to your father.'

'Then put it with my things. I shall deliver it.'

'He was most specific. I have to hand it over to no one else, not even your mother.'

'You know what it is, don't you? It condemns me. It is his letter of criticism about me. How dare he employ my own slave to do such work? Hand it over now.' He glowered and held out a demanding hand.

'Please don't ask this of me. Your uncle has been good to me, and I don't know what the letter contains. He could easily send another messenger to your father if he wrote only to censure you.'

'Hand it over now.' Gaius was angry. 'As you have sworn to obey me, your master, hand it over. I will have it, Verluccus, even if I have to get the whole household to take it from you.'

'It is in my pack. I cannot give it up. You must take it if it is so important to you.'

Gaius seized the pack and pulled the tube from it, breaking the seal and unravelling its contents. He read rapidly, his face growing more thunderous as he did so. A flame burned on a nearby table. He returned the scroll to Verluccus. 'It is as well you cannot read. You should not know the contents of this. Burn it. Burn it now.'

For several moments he defied him. The two stared angrily at each other, and then finally Verluccus pushed the scroll onto the flame and saw it turn to ash. He had hoped it might be an appeal to Lucius to make Gaius free him. But suppose it was not – what if Marcus had written to tell Lucius of his daughter's infidelity? Was that what had made Gaius so angry?

He waited for confirmation of his doubts, but it did not come.

Gaius sighed. 'I must say goodbye to my sister. It is too bad of her to lie in bed this morning. She might at least have risen to bid me farewell. Go and take our stuff and wait by the horses.'

He took a risk. 'Your sister has always treated me with kindness. May I not say goodbye to her also?'

'I shall tell her for you. Go outside. I intend to delay our departure no longer.' Gaius was still annoyed but not, it seemed, aware of what he feared.

By the time his master came to him, a puzzled expression on his face, Verluccus had explored and rejected as too dangerous every conceivable excuse he could think of for entering her bedchamber.

'I cannot reason with her,' he complained. 'She won't get out of her bed and sobs distractedly. Yet she knew I must go. We would have gone long ago if it had not been for Glaucus discovering that you and Cunobarrus are brothers. I really do regret that you killed Virens; things would have been quite different if he were her husband. I told Gaia that if she carries on weeping as she is doing Glaucus will suspect her of a relationship with me which is quite improper – he already believes that of you.'

Verluccus found a voice. It did not sound like his own. 'What do you mean?'

'Oh,' said Gaius loftily, 'Glaucus is not alone. Marcus and Neratius both supposed that you and I were lovers! Quite ridiculous!'

He drove his heels into Cervus' flanks and set off in pursuit of his parents and Rome.

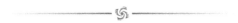

He found her as Gaius had indicated. She was alone except for Delia and was sobbing distractedly. He knelt beside her and took her hand in his and then threw caution to the winds and cradled her head in his arms and held her tightly.

'I cannot go from here and leave you weeping. Have I not promised you that I shall always be with Gaius? That I shall stay with him always and take care of him and so you will hear of me and I of you? It is hard enough for me to leave you, but I do so because you asked it of me; and whatever you require of me, that I shall do. Now I have to go far away from you, across the ocean even, and that terrifies me. But I go – not willingly but dutifully for you. But it is too cruel of you to make me go away and leave you in tears. Smile for me so that I shall remember how beautiful you are and not how much misery I have brought into your life. Oh, if only I had not killed Virens! I am sure he would have made a fine husband for you and taken you away quickly so you and I could not have glanced at one another. Think now, if you can, of some moment when I made you smile, and be glad and hold on to that. I shall be with your brother, shortly with your parents. Think of me when you speak of Gaius; think of me when you speak of your father and your mother and Quintus and the rest of the household. And when you can do so without endangering yourself, speak my name also. Remember me and that I worship you. With that we must be content. One last kiss … and a smile … and then I go.' He put his mouth upon hers, and her tears were soft upon his cheek.

'Where is Gaius?' she whispered, fearful for him.

'In Corinium by now, I should think,' he said wryly, remembering the pace at which Cervus had taken off.

She smiled then. It was a weak and thin smile, but she had stopped crying.

'He will ride all the way back too if he thinks he has mislaid you. I shall be all right. Don't fear for me, my darling. I wept because I was foolish and selfish. I shall not weep again. You must go. I know you will be safe and greatly loved by Gaius and that you will stay with him and take care of him, and so I am happy for you. There have been many times when you made me smile, made me laugh aloud.

490

Of some of them you did not even know, but I shall always remember those moments when I am thinking of you, not of unhappiness. And I shall remember that you love me.'

She lit her face with a brief, dazzling smile. 'Dearest Verluccus, please, please go now, please. It is no use our hoping or wishing that things might be otherwise, for they cannot. Go from me, and I shall be at peace in my mind. I know you are unafraid of anything except my safety, but even as you are uncaring of your own safety I beg you to go and so know that mine is the more secure.'

She handed to him tablets, letters to her family. 'I asked Gaius to take these, but he left them behind. This is the letter from Melissa. Will you show it to Marcia for me and then take it on to Mother? And here is a letter I have written to Marcia, and his one is for Father and Mother.' She guided him to the door and kissed his cheek. It was with the greatest reluctance that he finally released her hands.

Florus was working, cleaning in the atrium. He acknowledged his passage through it with a friendly grin and a raised hand, noting the tablets. Verluccus was thankful to have them.

Behind him someone closed the bedroom door with a gentle but firm thud. He stepped into the street and the bustle of the hot June day, ignored by the uncaring mass of humanity intent on business of its own. A slave had been deputed to hold his abandoned mount.

He did not thank him; his mouth was too firmly closed for words. He turned his horse and his face towards the city gate and began his most reluctant journey.

People and Places Named In the Text.

<u>At Glevum Nervensis</u>

Military Tribune Decimus Aemilius Lepidus Virens (to Isca Silurum)

Military Tribune Publius Antonius Secundus

Retired Centurion Justinius Severus

His son, Titus Justinius, friend of Gaius (to Isca Silurum)

Citizen Cloelius Draco his wife Lydia, his daughter Cloelia

Citizen Calpurnius

His son, Calpurnius Drusus, friend of Gaius

Gnaeus Petronius, friend of Gaius

Citizen Anicetus, Schoolteacher

Mango, a slave dealer

Bonus, slave of Titus Justinius

Agasus, slave of Calpurnius Drusus

Military Tribune Decimus Aemilius Lepidus Glaucus

Neratius Marcellus, Governor of Britain, his wife, Julilla

<u>At Isca Silurum fortress</u>

Marcus Marcius Phillipianus, military commander (brother of Lucius) in Britain, married to Claudia (in Rome) has mistress Melissa in Isca Silurum

Military Tribune Gnaeus Vitellius Drusus

Military Tribune Annius Festus

Military Tribune Sestus Gallus

Military Tribune Decius Rufus

Military Tribune Assinius

Military Tribune Servius

Centurion Gnaeus Cassius (known as Cassio)

Tertius, slave of Marcus Marcius

Peritus, a medic

<u>Natives at Daruentum</u>

Carantua, widow of Cunobarrus and mother of:

Cunobarrus, left home to fight Romans.

Cadrus left home with Cunobarrus
Tanodonus, farmer, later married to Belrutha
Colymmon, a simple-minded man, shepherd
Verluccus – enslaved by Lucius Marcius

Belanius – farmer neighbour
Brutha, his wife
Belrutha his daughter
Bodellus - farmer neighbour

Native Britons in the western mountains
Merriol, an old woman owner of Verluccus
Bodlan, married to Elen.
His sons young Bodlan and Bodecus, Bodyn, his daughter, betrothed to Verluccus.
Caella, cousin and betrothed to Bodecus.
Rignis, local head man,
Trenn, his son
Enemno, shepherd, Mona, his daughter
Engor, a smith

Others
Macrinius, a builder
Bodenius, itinerant trader
Mango, slave dealer
Coridumnus, a healer

Rebel Britons in the western mountains
Cunobarrus
Cadrus, the laughing man
Calla, his woman
Belcon, a tribal chieftain. His sons Belacon and Belcadon
Rosa, a slave owned by Verluccus.
Rogan
His son, Bodrogan

Lurgis
Deldon
Dolbactan, a tribal chieftain
Bodrogan

Places
Daruentum – a fictitious community
Glevum - now Gloucester
Corinium – now Cirencester
Isca Silurum – now Caerleon
Venta Silurum – now Caerwent
Belconia – fictitious community
Londinium – now London
Eboracum – now York

ABOUT THE AUTHOR

M.E. Taylor is a native of Gloucestershire and so grew up in a county in England in which the remains of many Roman buildings, military and domestic, may be seen today. This generated a lifetime of fascination with our Roman ancestors and their lifestyles. She is a member of several historical and archaeological societies and a volunteer at a local Roman museum. Her favourite pastime is visiting Roman sites in Britain and Europe in the company of like-minded friends. Her interest extends to an interest in Roman cookery and in a garden containing only plants from the Roman Empire (subsequently many native plants which sensible gardeners call 'weeds').

Lightning Source UK Ltd.
Milton Keynes UK
UKHW010731230321
380832UK00001B/2